Professor Bernard Knight, CBE, became a Home Office pathologist in 1965 and was appointed Professor of Forensic Pathology, University of Wales College of Medicine, in 1980. During his forty-year career with the Home Office, he performed over 25,000 autopsies and was involved in many high profile cases.

Bernard Knight is the author of nineteen novels, a biography and numerous popular and academic non-fiction books. *Figure of Hate* is the ninth novel in the Crowner John series, following *The Witch Hunter, Fear in the Forest, The Grim Reaper, The Tinner's Corpse, The Awful Secret, The Poisoned Chalice, Crowner's Quest* and *The Sanctuary Seeker*.

Also by Bernard Knight

The Sanctuary Seeker
The Poisoned Chalice
Crowner's Quest
The Awful Secret
The Tinner's Corpse
The Grim Reaper
Fear in the Forest
The Witch Hunter

FIGURE OF HATE

Bernard Knight

POCKET
BOOKS

LONDON · SYDNEY · NEW YORK · TOKYO · SINGAPORE · TORONTO

First published in Great Britain by Simon & Schuster UK Ltd, 2005
This edition published by Pocket Books, 2005
An imprint of Simon & Schuster UK Ltd
A Viacom company

3 5 7 9 10 8 6 4 2

Simon & Schuster UK Ltd
Africa House
64-78 Kingsway
London WC2B 6AH

www.simonsays.co.uk

Simon & Schuster Australia
Sydney

A CIP catalogue record for this book is available from the British Library

ISBN 0-7434-9214 5

Typeset in New Baskerville by Palimpsest Book Production Limited,
Polmont Stirlingshire
Printed and bound in Great Britain by
Bookmarque Ltd, Croydon, Surrey

'Comfort me by a solemn assurance, that when the little parlour in which I sit at this instant, shall be reduced to a worse-furnished box, I shall be read with honour by those who never knew nor saw me and whom I shall neither know or see.'

History of Tom Jones,
Henry Fielding, 1749

bISTORICAL NOTE

In the Middle Ages, especially from the thirteenth century onward, the tournament was an important aspect of medieval life. Although actual participation was confined to the knightly classes, it was also a popular spectator sport, giving rise to the medieval equivalent of today's football mania, even to serious hooliganism and rioting. The 'fans' were forbidden to bring any weapons to the tourney grounds, for fear of provoking mayhem!

At the period of this story, the 'tourney' had not developed the flamboyant complexity of later centuries, with no heavy plate armour or enclosed helmets, nor the use of the 'list', a long barrier separating the charging combatants. Norman knights wore their usual chain-mail tunics and round helmets, fighting on their destriers, huge warhorses whose descendants became the carthorses of more recent centuries, replacing the oxen that were previously used as draught animals.

Originating in France in the eleventh century, the tournaments were 'war games' meant to keep knights in practice for battle and for them to show off their prowess. The earlier tournaments were large-scale mock battles, called mêlées, in which scores of mounted warriors fought in teams across wide tracts of countryside, often with fatal casualties and extensive damage to local property. Both the Church and kings frowned on these activities, as they caused the unnecessary death and injury of valuable fighting men – and posed a potential threat by training baronial armies that might challenge the monarchy. Papal decrees condemned them and Henry II forbade tournaments in England, which drove many enthusiasts to the Continent. In 1194 Richard the Lionheart relaxed his father's prohibition and licensed five tournament grounds in England, mainly to raise money from the high fees he charged. One of these was at Wilton, near Salisbury. There were still many illegal tournaments, however, and knights would travel all over the kingdom and often go abroad to compete, some making or losing their fortunes in the process. The object was to defeat an opponent, whereby his horse, armour and weapons would be forfeited, and, if rich, the loser could be held to ransom. There were also large wagers placed on the combatants both by the knights and by gambling spectators.

The mêlée was so dangerous and destructive that by the end of the twelfth century the joust, in which a pair of knights fought each other with lance, shield and sword under the scrutiny of judges, had become more popular. Subsequently, the more colourful and romantic concept of tournaments developed – they became lavish and ornate festivals with ladies bestowing favours and their champions claiming amorous rewards from them. In the early years there were virtually no rules, but in later times a highly complex code of chivalrous behaviour developed, which persisted up to the sixteenth century.

In Devon in the late twelfth century, the most common language spoken would have been early Middle English, unintelligible to us today. The Norman ruling class would have spoken Norman French and the language of the clergy in which almost all documents were written would have been Latin. In addition, many in Devon would still have spoken 'western Welsh', the pre-Saxon Celtic language that persisted as Cornish and still flourishes in Wales.

The vast majority of the population were illiterate, and the ability to read and write was confined to about one person in a hundred, mainly the 'clerks', those in religious orders. Most of these were not ordained priests, being in 'minor orders' as lectors, acolytes and subdeacons, as opposed to deacons, priests and bishops, who were the only ones able to celebrate the Mass and absolve penitents.

The only coin in circulation, apart from a few foreign gold coins, was the silver penny. The terms 'pound' and 'mark' were notional accounting values, not actual currency. The pound was 240 pence or twenty 'shillings', the mark being 160 pennies or 13 shillings and fourpence. Pennies were cut into halves and quarters for convenience, as a penny was about half a day's pay for most workers.

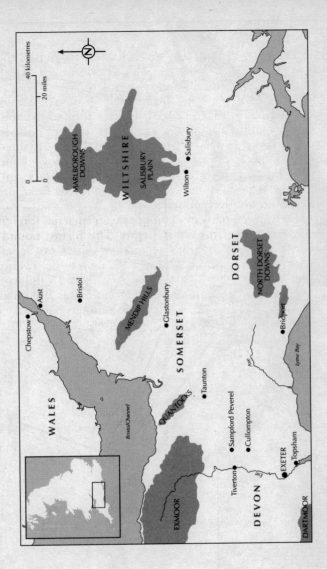

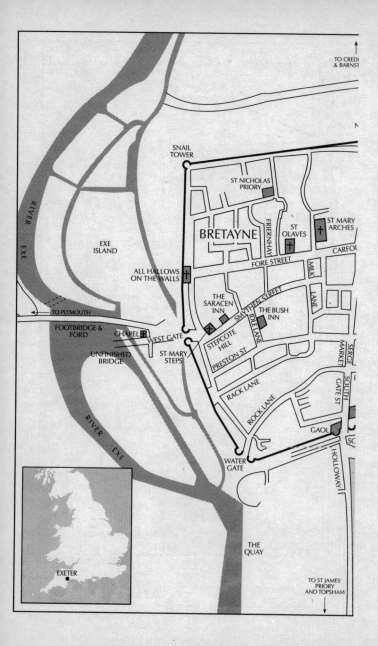

TO CREDI
& BARNST

SNAIL
TOWER

ST NICHOLAS
PRIORY

BRETAYNE

FRIERNHAY

ST
OLAVES

ST MARY
ARCHES

CARFO

FORE STREET

MILK
LANE

ALL HALLOWS
ON THE WALLS

RIVER
EXE

EXE
ISLAND

THE
SARACEN
INN

SMYTHEN STREET

THE BUSH
INN

IDLE LANE

WEST GATE

STEPCOTE
HILL

CHAPEL

FOOTBRIDGE &
FORD

ST MARY
STEPS

PRESTON ST

TO PLYMOUTH

UNFINISHED
BRIDGE

SERGE
MARKET

RACK LANE

SOUTH
GATE ST

ROCK LANE

RIVER
EXE

GAOL

SO

WATER
GATE

HOLLOWAY

EXETER

THE
QUAY

TO ST JAMES'
PRIORY
AND TOPSHAM

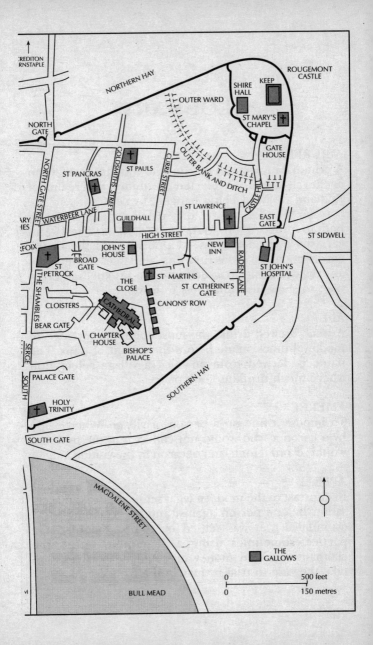

CREDITON
BARNSTAPLE

NORTHERN HAY

ROUGEMONT CASTLE

SHIRE HALL

KEEP

OUTER WARD

NORTH GATE

ST MARY'S CHAPEL

ST PANCRAS

ST PAULS

GOLDSMITHS STREET

CURRE STREET

OUTER BANK AND DITCH

GATE HOUSE

CASTLE HILL

ST LAWRENCE

EAST GATE

ST SIDWELL

MARY
HES

NORTH GATE STREET

WATERBEER LANE

GUILDHALL

HIGH STREET

NEW INN

ST JOHN'S HOSPITAL

FOIX

ST PETROCK

JOHN'S HOUSE

BROAD GATE

ST MARTINS

ST CATHERINE'S GATE

RADEN LANE

THE SHAMBLES

THE CLOSE

CANONS' ROW

CLOISTERS

CATHEDRAL

BEAR GATE

SERGE

CHAPTER HOUSE

BISHOP'S PALACE

SOUTH

PALACE GATE

SOUTHERN HAY

HOLY TRINITY

SOUTH GATE

MAGDALENE STREET

THE GALLOWS

0   500 feet
0   150 metres

BULL MEAD

GLOSSARY

ABJURER
A criminal or accused person who sought sanctuary in a church and then elected to abjure the realm of England to avoid being hanged, by confessing to the coroner. He had up to forty days in sanctuary, then had to proceed on foot, dressed in sackcloth and carrying a wooden cross, to a port nominated by the coroner and take the first ship available. If there was any delay, he had to wade out up to his knees in every tide, to show his willingness to leave.

ALE
A weak brewed drink, the most common beverage of medieval times, made before the advent of hops. The name is derived from an 'ale', a village celebration where much drinking took place.

AMERCE
To impose a fine on a person or village. When made by a coroner who would not collect it at the time but would record it for a later decision by the visiting judges.

APPEAL
In contrast to the modern legal sense, this was an accusation by one person against another, claiming some criminal act. It was settled by combat between the parties, sometimes using a champion, unless the claimant accepted money or could be persuaded to take the case to trial by jury in the royal courts.

ATTACHMENT
A summons to appear at a court, usually enforced by imposing a bail payment, which would be forfeit by the person or his family if he failed to appear.

AVENTAIL
A flap of chain mail attached to the front neckline of the hauberk, which could be pulled up to protect the chin and mouth.

BAILEY
Originally the defended area around a castle keep ('motte and bailey') but later also applied to the yard around a dwelling. A similar word is 'ward', applied to the inner and outer defensive areas of a castle or fortified manor house.

BAILIFF
An overseer of a manor or estate. He would have manor-reeves under him and would report to the steward or seneschal.

BOTTLER
The servant responsible for providing drink in a household – the origin of 'butler'.

BURGESS
A freeman of substance, usually a merchant, in a town or borough, his dwelling being a 'burgage'. A group of burgesses ran the town administration and in Exeter they elected two portreeves (later a mayor) to lead them.

BYRNIE
A Saxon word for the hauberk or chain-mail shirt.

CARUCATE
A measure of land, originally that which could be ploughed by a team of oxen each year. It varied greatly in size in different parts of England, but was often taken as about a hundred acres (three 'virgates').

COB
A mixture of clay and straw used for forming the walls of wattle-and-daub buildings.

COG
A small merchant ship with one mast and sail.

COIF
A close-fitting cap or helmet of felt or other cloth, tied under the chin. Worn by both men and women.

COMPLINE
The last of the nine religious services of the day, usually in the late afternoon or early evening.

CONEY
A rabbit, introduced into England by the Normans.

CONSTABLE
Has several meanings – either a senior military commander, usually the custodian of a royal castle such as Exeter, or a watchman, who patrolled the streets to keep order.

CORONER
A senior law officer in each county, second only to the sheriff. The office was instituted in September 1194, though there was a brief mention of a coroner in Saxon times. Three knights and one clerk were recruited in

each county to perform a wide range of legal duties, mainly recording cases so that no money would be lost to the King's courts. The name comes from the Latin phrase *custos placitorum coronas*, 'keeper of the pleas of the Crown'.

COTTAR
A low-grade villein, an unfree man in the feudal system. He had no field strips to work, but had a croft and toft. He worked at various tasks, such as hedging, thatching and labouring, for his manor-lord and others.

COVER-CHIEF
More correctly *couvre-chef*, a linen head-cover worn by women, held in place by a band around the head and flowing down over the back and front of the chest. Known as a 'head-rail' in Saxon times.

CRESPINE
A hairnet, often gilded, holding two plaited coils of hair over each of a lady's ears.

CROFT
A plot of ground in a village belonging to a freeman or villein, upon which a 'toft' or cottage was built.

CURFEW
Derived from *couvre-feu*, the covering or banking down of fires. Open fires were prohibited in towns after dark, owing to the fear of starting a conflagration. During the curfew, which lasted from dusk to dawn, the town gates were closed – one thirteenth-century mayor of Exeter was hanged for failing to ensure this.

CURIA REGIS
The royal court, consisting of the major barons and senior bishops who supported and advised the King and provided the judges for the courts.

DAGGED
The lower edge of a man's tunic or cape, when cut in steps like battlements.

DEODAND
Literally 'a gift from God', applied to the forfeiture of any object that caused a death. Anything from a knife to a mill-wheel could be confiscated by the coroner and sold for the Treasury; occasionally the proceeds were given to the family of the deceased.

DESTRIER
A large warhorse capable of carrying an armoured knight. When firearms made them redundant, destriers became shire horses, replacing oxen as draught animals.

EXIGENT
To declare someone exigent was the legal mechanism for making a person an outlaw (q.v.).

EYRE
A sitting of the King's justices, introduced by Henry II in 1166, which moved around from county to county. There were two types, the 'General Eyre', held at very infrequent intervals, which scrutinised the administration of each county, and the 'Eyre of Assize', which was the forerunner of the assizes and the more recent Crown Courts. As the eyres also occurred infrequently, there were additional sittings by Commissioners of Gaol Delivery, to clear the jails of prisoners awaiting trial.

FARM
The taxation from a county, collected in coin by the sheriff and taken personally by him twice a year to the Exchequer at Winchester or London. The farm was fixed each year by the Curia Regis, but if the sheriff could collect more, he could keep the difference.

FIRST FINDER
The first person to come across an unattended dead body. He had a duty to knock up the four nearest households immediately and 'raise the hue and cry' to try to apprehend any killer, then report the death to a bailiff or constable, for notification to the coroner. Failure to do so would result in amercement (a fine).

FRANKPLEDGE
A system for self-regulation of both freemen and serfs, where all men had to form groups of ten (later twelve) who were mutually responsible for each other's behaviour. If one failed in some legal obligation, the rest were fined.

GAMBESON
A padded, quilted garment worn under chain mail, to diffuse the force of blows.

HAUBERK
A long armoured tunic of chain mail, the lower part slit for riding a horse.

JUSTICIAR
The chief minister in Norman times, a great noble or churchman appointed by the King. At the time of this story it was Hubert Walter, Archbishop of Canterbury, who had also been Richard the Lionheart's second-in-command at the Crusades and who was virtually regent,

as the king never returned to England during the last five years of his reign.

KIRTLE
A woman's dress, usually reaching her feet. The style, especially of the sleeves, varied considerably at different times. It was worn over a thin chemise, the only under-garment.

LEMAN
A mistress or concubine.

MANOR-REEVE
A foreman elected by his fellows in each village to organise the daily farm work. He was usually a villein, not a freeman.

MURDRUM FINE
This was applied to any unnatural death where the community could not prove 'presentment of Englishry' (q.v.). It was assumed that a Saxon had murdered a Norman and was the origin of the term 'murder'.

ORDEAL
Though sometimes used to extract confessions, the Ordeal was an ancient ritual, abolished by the Vatican in 1215, in which suspects were subject to painful and often fatal procedures, such as licking red-hot iron, picking a stone from a vat of boiling water or walking barefoot over nine red-hot ploughshares. If they suffered no significant burns they were judged inno-cent, otherwise they were hanged. Women were bound hand and foot and thrown into deep water – if they sank they were innocent!

OSTLER
A servant in a stable or inn who took charge of horses.

OUTLAW
A man 'outside the law' who had no legal existence. Usually escaped prisoners or sanctuary-seekers, they were declared 'exigent' by a coroner if they failed to answer four calls to appear before the county court, either as a defendant or witness. An outlaw could be legitimately killed on sight by anyone, who could then claim a bounty of five shillings if he took the head to the sheriff.

OUTREMER
The four Christian kingdoms in the Levant at the time of the Crusades, of which one was Jerusalem.

PALFREY
A small, docile horse suitable for a woman to ride.

PEINE FORTE ET DURE
Literally 'severe and hard punishment', whereby prisoners who refused to confess were tortured by having progressively heavy weights placed on their chest until they submitted or died.

POMMEL
The raised front of a saddle, across which the jousting lance was rested. The medieval saddle, of wood and leather, was like a deep chair, with the pommel in front and the cantle behind, to give the rider maximum stability when fighting.

POSSE
The '*posse comitatus*' was established by Henry II and was a group of armed men which could be called out

by a sheriff in order to hunt criminals or defend the realm.

PRESENTMENT OF ENGLISHRY
After the Conquest of 1066, many Normans were killed by aggrieved Saxons, so anyone found dead was assumed to be Norman and the locals were heavily punished with a 'murdrum fine' (q.v.) unless they could prove at the coroner's inquest that the deceased was English (or Welsh or Scots). This presentment continued for several hundred years, though it became merely a cynical device for extorting money.

RECET
An area of sanctuary set aside at mêlées and tournaments for resting men and horses and treating the wounded.

SACKBUT
A medieval musical instrument resembling a trombone.

SANCTUARY
See 'Abjurer'.

SECONDARY
A young man training to be a priest, under twenty-four years of age. They assisted vicars and canons in their cathedral duties.

SHALMES
A medieval stringed instrument.

SHERIFF
The 'shire-reeve', the King's representative in each county, responsible for collecting the 'farm' (the

county taxes) and for keeping law and order. The post was much sought after because of the opportunities for extorting money. Corruption was so rife that in 1170 Henry II sacked all his sheriffs.

SQUIRE
A supporter and servant of a knight, usually a young man aspiring to eventual knighthood himself.

TILT
A device for training men for both battle and jousting. A horizontal bar was pivoted on a post with a target hanging down from one end and a sack of sand on the other. The horseman had to gallop past and strike the target with his lance, but avoid the weighted sack that would swing round at him.

TRENCHER
A thick slice of the previous day's loaf, used instead of a plate to hold cooked food. Soaked in the juices, it was often given to the poor after use.

UNDERCROFT
The lowest floor of a fortified building, often partly below ground level. The entrance to the rest of the building was on the floor above, which had no communication with the undercroft. In times of siege, the removable wooden steps could be thrown down to prevent attackers from being able to reach the main door.

VARLET
A young man learning to be a page, who in turn often aspired to become a squire to a knight.

VICAR
A priest employed by a more senior cleric, such as a

canon, to carry out some of his religious duties, especially at the many daily services in a cathedral. Often called a 'vicar-choral' from his participation in chanted services.

VILLEIN
The upper grade of unfree men in the feudal system. A villein was granted a toft and croft and his own strips in the village field system, but had to work for the lord on certain days. He might be more wealthy than some freemen.

VIRGATE
A measure of land, which varied in size from place to place, often being thirty acres.

WIMPLE
Linen or silk cloth framing a woman's face and covering the throat.

PROLOGUE

Spring 1195

The tournament was in its second day when tragedy first struck.

It was not that such accidents were all that uncommon. The war-games that were so beloved of Norman knights were intentionally dangerous affairs – if it had been otherwise, they would soon have lost their appeal. The previous day, a blustery Monday in early April, a Warwickshire baron had been unhorsed and had fractured his thigh. With the broken bone protruding through the skin, everyone knew that he was sure to die once it became purulent. Another combatant was in his tent, anxiously tended by his squire as he vomited dark blood, after a blunted lance had caught him in the stomach. Otherwise the day had been fairly benign, apart from the numerous bruises and gashes that were too common to be noticed by the jousting fraternity.

It was the next day of this three-day mêlée that claimed the first life.

Sir William Peverel, manor-lord of Sampford Peverel in east Devon, was one of the hundred and twenty knights taking part in this escapade – and he was the first to perish. Some would say that at fifty-five, older than most of the participants, he should have been wise enough to stay at home, rather than rampaging about

1

the countryside like someone thirty years his junior. But William had been competing in tournaments for most of his adult life and owed some of his fortune to the spoils he had won in this dangerous pastime. He saw no reason to give up now, having a wealth of experience to add to his still-brawny arms and his excellent eyesight.

Soon after dawn that morning, the two armies had assembled on the tournament ground between Salisbury and Wilton. It was a stretch of undulating countryside two miles long and half a mile wide, mostly open common with some thickets and copses of trees scattered within it. This Wiltshire site was one of the five that had been officially sanctioned by King Richard as the only places in England where tournaments were allowed – though this rule was flouted more often than it was observed. The Lionheart, however, with his usual dedication to collecting money to finance his endless French wars, charged a stiff fee for participation, ranging from twenty marks for an earl to two for a landless knight. The common folk were strictly excluded, as tourneying was only for the aristocracy and the mounted soldier – though the peasants turned up to watch and to wager on the winners.

On this Tuesday, William Peverel was part of the Red team – in fact, he was one of the leaders, if such a term could be applied to a disorderly mob for whom team spirit came a poor second to personal gain. His sixty combatants massed their great warhorses at the top of a gentle rise, each wearing something scarlet to distinguish them from the Blues, who were waiting on the next hillock a quarter of a mile away. Some wore a red tabard or a surcoat over their armour, others just a crimson scarf or a length of red cloth tied around their shoulders. Though these distinguishing markers were many and varied, they all wore similar armour consisting of chain-link hauberks. Some were ankle length and others only came to the knee – and a few had mailed leggings. Only a handful of the poorest knights wore cuirasses of thick boiled leather instead of mail, but everyone had a round iron helmet with a prominent nose-guard, and most protected their necks with a hood of steel links and an aventail that could be pulled up over the chin. Everyone had a long blunted lance, a broadsword and an oval or heart-shaped shield, many of these having a crude heraldic device painted on the toughened wood. The two groups readied themselves, the men now silent, though some of the destriers snorted, tossed their heads or pawed the damp ground, excited at the prospect of a gallop and the clash of arms.

Away to Peverel's left, midway between the armies, was a small group of mounted men, wearing chain mail but carrying no lances or swords. These were the marshals and the judges, all prominently wearing white surcoats over their hauberks and some holding tall staffs from which fluttered white flags.

Behind them was the recet, a half-acre marked off by posts and ropes, in which were a few tents and troughs of water. This was the 'safe area' to which injured or exhausted men and horses could retreat for a respite from the battle – and to which the badly wounded and dead could be brought to be tended by their squires, scores of whom now stood there waiting anxiously, wondering whether the end of the day would see them sharing their master's good fortune or his destitution.

All eyes were on the marshals, who would give the signal for the mêlée to begin – it might well last for up to ten hours that day.

In the tense silence, a man coughed and a stallion neighed.

3

Then they saw the white flags wave as a warning to be ready. A moment later, a trumpet shrilled a discordant blast and the umpires retreated nearer the recet, to avoid being trampled by the combatants. The previous quiet was suddenly shattered by roars and screams as the teams spurred their ponderous horses into action. The two massed groups gradually accelerated towards each other, aided by the slight slope down into the small plain between the two hillocks. The Reds and the Blues chanted their rehearsed war-cries, partly to work themselves up into an aggressive hysteria, but also to intimidate their opponents. The thunder of over a hundred huge steeds, each weighing almost half a ton, shook the ground, and when the front ranks smashed into each other, it was as if giant cymbals had been clashed.

William Peverel was in the centre of the front rank, and as he approached the Blues he picked out his first opponent, a tall, erect man on a black horse who came at him with similar intent. Lowering his lance, Peverel tucked the butt into his waist and aimed for the rivets in the centre of the man's shield, where the handle was attached. In the split second before impact, he saw that the shield had three white birds painted on a green background. With an ear-splitting crash, they made contact simultaneously, and the lance of each man hit the opposing shield with the momentum of a ton of horseflesh travelling at a combined speed of thirty miles an hour. The butt of his own lance slammed into his side with a force that made William grunt, and his lower back was whacked painfully against the high cantle of his chair-like saddle.

His shield jerked on his left arm, but he had angled it away so that the other knight's lance slid off, losing much of its impact. With his feet jammed in the stirrups and his knees locked against the front of his saddle, he had no difficulty in staying on his destrier's broad back.

William's own strike had been dead centre on the white bird, and the owner of the shield took the full force of the twelve-foot lance, jerking back and almost falling from his horse. But like Peverel he was a seasoned fighter and managed to keep his balance. A fraction of a second later they had passed each other, and though the mêlée had widened out, there were other horsemen all around. Before he could draw breath, another knight charged at him, and though William managed to nick the edge of the other's unemblazoned shield he was more concerned with turning away the poorly aimed blow of the fresh-faced young man. Another few seconds and he found himself through the ranks of the Blues. It took a good many yards to slow the big horse and haul it around again to face the fighting, and as he did so another Red fighter cantered up to him. It was his second son, Hugo Peverel, his ruddy face sweating from excitement and exertion.

'We're too evenly matched today, Father,' he yelled, as he turned alongside. 'We need a couple who are still wet behind their ears to get us warmed up!'

As they started to wheel their horses back into the crush, William shouted back. 'I've just had one boy trying to poke me, but I didn't have time to settle with him. He didn't look worth much of a ransom, anyway.'

Another Blue knight cut short their conversation by attacking Sir William from the right, just as another man on a white mare came at his son from the other side. For five minutes there was a confused thrashing of men and horses, without much result as far as the Peverels were concerned, as neither managed to unseat any of their opponents.

The prime object of the tournament was to defeat

individuals from the other army, either by knocking them from their saddles or by striking them on trunk or limb with a broadsword. Though there were almost no rules of combat, it was accepted as a matter of honour that neither a man's head nor his horse should be attacked, nor swords used by mounted men. If a knight was unhorsed, he would have to submit if his opponent hovered over him with his lance pointed at his vitals. If he could scramble to his feet and draw his sword, then the other man should dismount and fight it out with a similar weapon. A clean strike against arm, leg, belly or chest constituted a win, and the vanquished fighter lost his horse, armour and arms to the victor, as well as facing the possibility of being captured and ransomed for a sum of money.

After a third indecisive bout, the momentum of William's stallion again took him out of the main mêlée, and when he hauled himself around he saw that the previously tightly packed mass of combatants had spread out into a large sunburst of hoarsely shouting men and prancing beasts. A number of fights on foot had begun, and other pairs of horsemen were wheeling and circling around each other, lances clashing on shields.

Already several defeated knights were dejectedly walking back to the judges and the safe area, where they faced the loss of their property and perhaps even their liberty until they came up with a ransom. William saw another mounted man also making for the recet, one arm dangling helplessly, blood pouring off his fingers on to the ground.

Annoyed that he had not yet scored a win, the lord of Peverel manor spurred his destrier forward, aiming again for the centre of the thinning battle. There was more room for manoeuvre now – rather than just crashing into a mass of men and horses, he was able to single out his target. It was the same tall knight on the black stallion who he had encountered before, and he lowered his lance and jammed it tightly against his side with his elbow. With a roar of exhilaration he struck the white birds on the shield, again catching it dead centre, as he fended off the tip of his adversary's weapon. This time there was no mistake, as the impact threw the man back over the cantle of his saddle. As they thundered past each other, out of the corner of his eye William saw the fellow tumble to the ground and he let out a yell of exultation at his first 'kill' of the day.

His triumph was short lived as at that very moment a faulty saddle-girth gave way under the force of the encounter and the heavy wooden saddle slid from the horse's back. Helplessly, Peverel rolled over sideways, his arms so encumbered with lance and shield that he had no time to grab his horse's neck. In itself, this was not an inevitable disaster, as he had survived many a worse tumble. He slithered rather than fell overboard, letting go of the reins to avoid being dragged along by the still-lumbering destrier.

As he hit the ground, cursing and blaspheming at his bad luck, a great shadow enveloped him and four large hairy hoofs trampled him into the mud, crushing his chest and splitting his skull. The yelling and clashing of arms all around did not miss a beat – the combatants were too concerned with their own situations to worry about someone suffering the accepted perils of the tournament. Only two men hurried back to the stricken knight. One was on foot, the tall, dark man whom William had vanquished – and the other was the horseman who had ridden over him.

It was his own son, Hugo Peverel.

CHAPTER ONE

In which Crowner John goes to a celebration

'Cheer up, Crowner, at least there's plenty to drink, even if the food's lousy!'

The fat priest, who was the garrison chaplain, winked and moved away, stuffing another meat pasty into his mouth. Sir John de Wolfe, the King's Coroner for the county of Devon, looked sourly about him, unimpressed by Brother Rufus's optimism. The bare hall of Rougemont, the name by which Exeter's castle was generally known, was a dour place for a midday party. A high oblong chamber with the entrance door at one end occupied most of the first floor of the keep. Below it, partly subterranean, was the undercroft which housed the prison – and above was a warren of rooms for clerks, servants and stores. There were slit windows along two of the walls, their shutters wide open on this mild October morning. On the other long wall several doors opened into the quarters of the sheriff and the castle constable. Apart from a few battered shields and crossed lances, the grey stone walls were bare, and de Wolfe was not surprised that the previous sheriff had failed to persuade his wife to live here with him, rather than at one of their more comfortable manors.

The thought of his wife's brother, the former sheriff Richard de Revelle, jerked him from his reverie, as the reason for today's gathering was to celebrate the official installation of Richard's successor. The new sheriff, Henry de Furnellis, had been sworn in several hours ago by one of the King's Council at a brief ceremony in the Shire Court, an even more dismal building a few yards away in the inner ward of the castle. Before that, there had been a special service in the cathedral, from which Bishop Henry Marshal had been diplomatically absent, the Mass being conducted by John de Alençon, the Archdeacon of Exeter and a close friend of de Wolfe.

Now the great and good of the county, together with many lesser hangers-on, had adjourned to the hall for refreshment. The trestle tables and benches, which usually served ale and food to a motley collection of men-at-arms, clerks, merchants and suppliants seeking justice, were today filled with a cross-section of Devon society, from manor-lords to parish priests, from burgesses to bailiffs and constables to canons.

There were many wives among them, and John experienced a stab of conscience when he looked down at his own wife sitting at a nearby table, nibbling listlessly at a capon's leg. Matilda normally relished any public celebration where she could rub shoulders with the county aristocracy, show off her latest gown and gossip to her snobbish friends. But this gathering was almost a badge of shame to her, and he had had to persuade her to come with him, such was her reluctance. Though by no means a sensitive soul, de Wolfe realised that she must feel that people were casting meaningful glances at her and murmuring to each other under their breath. For was she not the sister of the man who had been ejected from the highest office in the county for corruption, theft and suspected treason? Some of them wondered why Sir

Richard de Revelle still had a head on his shoulders, let alone being free to live peaceably on his manors near Plymouth and Tiverton.

De Wolfe sighed and turned his attention to the throng in the hall. Though many, especially the ladies, were sitting at the tables, there was a large contingent who preferred to stand or wander around with a pot of ale or cup of wine in their hand, meeting acquaintances and exchanging news and gossip. The new sheriff – though in fact he had already briefly held the same office the previous year – was talking to Ralph Morin, the constable of Rougemont. As John watched, they were joined by Sir Walter Ralegh, the member of the Curia Regis who had that morning administered the oath of fealty to the new incumbent, for as usual Richard the Lionheart was in France and was probably still unaware of the recent crisis in Devon. Then the archdeacon drifted towards the group and de Wolfe moved over to stand with them, as all four were friends of his, not least because they were all staunch supporters of King Richard. In these days of whispered intrigues about a renewal of Prince John's ambition to unseat his elder brother from the throne of England, loyalty could never be taken for granted.

'Once again, congratulations, Henry,' he said to the new sheriff. 'Let's hope you stay in office much longer this time!'

Henry de Furnellis grunted his bluff thanks. He was not an articulate man and spoke only when he had something to say, unlike some of the babblers here who paraded their tongues along with their stylish new clothes. In fact, Henry was a very dull man, elderly and reluctant to exert himself in his duties as sheriff. He had been chosen by Hubert Walter, the Chief Justiciar and virtual regent of England during the King's absence, for being a safe, if unenthusiastic, pair of hands, unlikely to indulge in the corruption and treachery that had caused de Revelle's recent downfall.

De Furnellis was a large, lumpy man, with a clean-shaven red face, watery blue eyes and a big nose. His sparse grey hair was cut short and his downturned mouth and the loose folds of skin under his chin gave him the appearance of a sad hunting hound.

'I doubt if I'll be here for much longer this time,' he added phlegmatically. 'I'm well aware that Winchester only put me here to tide things over following the sudden departure of de Revelle. I want to get back to my manor as soon as possible, de Wolfe – so I hope you'll not burden me with too many problems in the coming months.'

The mention of the former sheriff made them all uneasy, and the coroner noticed Ralph Morin look rather furtively over his shoulder.

'Has anyone seen him lately?' asked the constable, a tall, muscular man with a forked brown beard and the look of a Viking chieftain.

John de Alençon shook his tonsured head. 'I suspect he's lying low at either Revelstoke or Tiverton. In spite of his misdeeds, I feel some compassion for him, being ejected in disgrace from such a high position.' The archdeacon was thin almost to the point of emaciation, his ascetic mode of life relieved only by a dry sense of humour and a taste for fine French wines. He was dressed in a long black cassock with a plain silver cross hanging around his neck, above which a pair of lively blue eyes sparkled in his lined face.

'He was damned lucky to escape a hanging!' snapped Walter Ralegh, who was a Devonshire baron, though much of his time was spent either at the royal court or touring around the southern counties as an itinerant justice. A large, grizzled man with a bluff, impatient manner, he was an old comrade of de Wolfe's, having campaigned with him both in Ireland and the Holy Land.

This talk of Richard de Revelle's fall from grace again caused John to look across at Matilda, sitting alone and dejected at the table. Though she did not openly accuse him of being the instrument of her brother's downfall, the implication was always there. Relations between them had been strained for most of the seventeen years of their marriage, and this latest fiasco had done nothing to heal the wounds.

He was just about to move back to her, to keep her company and try to make some conversation, when thankfully he saw a dandified figure slip on to the bench alongside her. It was Hugh de Relaga, one of Exeter's two portreeves, the provosts chosen by the other burgesses to lead the city council. De Relaga, a prominent merchant, was de Wolfe's business partner and another good friend. The loot that the coroner had brought home from numerous campaigns across Europe and the Levant had been wisely invested with Hugh in a joint wool-exporting business. Second only to Dartmoor tin in the economy of south-west England, wool provided a steady income for de Wolfe – in fact, it was a prerequisite for appointment as a coroner that the incumbent had an income of at least twenty pounds a year. The reasoning was that those with such riches had no need to embezzle from the funds in their keeping – a rather naive hope in many cases, though John de Wolfe happened to be scrupulously honest.

As he watched his short, portly friend exert himself to be pleasant to Matilda, a voice in his ear jerked him back to the group of men he was neglecting.

'I said, John, d'you think there'll be any trouble at this damned October fair this week?' Walter Ralegh nudged his arm to emphasise his point.

'Fair? There's always trouble at fairs, it's the nature of the beast,' replied John. 'But it's the tournament on Wednesday that's likely to cause the most problems. High-spirited young knights, drunken squires and the usual run of cut-purses and pickpockets – probably even a few horse thieves.'

'But this is not going to be one of those terrible mêlées, surely?' objected the archdeacon, who strongly supported the ecclesiastical disapproval of tourneying. 'Men end up dead at those, a sacrilegious waste of human life, to say nothing of the damage they cause to property and the poor people in the vicinity!'

Walter guffawed at the canon's severe view of a true Norman's favourite pastime. 'They stop a good warrior from going rusty, Archdeacon! You'd be among the first to complain if England was overrun by Philip of France because our knights were out of practice!'

The coroner hastened to reassure his friend. 'Don't concern yourself, John, this will be a small-scale affair, just a one-day event tagged on to the fair. There will be only individual jousts down on Bull Mead – there's no room for rampaging there.'

'But there'll be even more high-spirited men in the city than if it was just a fair,' grumbled the castle constable, whose men-at-arms would have to patrol Exeter to try to keep the peace. 'These events attract too many thieves, rogues and vagabonds as it is, without adding to the trouble with a tourney!'

The four men continued arguing the matter as they stood between the tables. From his position leaning against a nearby wall, an unusually large fellow regarded them with a grin on his face. He was huge, being both tall and broad, but he was even more noticeable for his tangled mop of bright red hair and a huge drooping moustache of the same colour which overhung his lantern jaw. A large nose and a ruddy face were relieved by a pair of eyes as blue as the archdeacon's.

'What are you leering at, you great oaf?' snapped the man standing alongside him, one who was as great a contrast to the ginger giant as it was possible to imagine. He barely came up to Gwyn of Polruan's shoulder and was as skinny as the Cornishman was muscular. In contrast to the scuffed leather jerkin and serge breeches of the big man, a long, patched tunic of faded black hung from Thomas de Peyne's thin, stooped shoulders, giving him a clerical appearance. This was the impression he always strove for, as he had in fact been a priest at Winchester until unfrocked three years earlier for an alleged indecent act with one of his girl pupils in the cathedral school. Recently his name had been cleared, but the Church had still not got around to publicly restoring his reputation, which partly accounted for the habitually dismal expression on his narrow pinched face. He had a high, intelligent fore-head, but a long thin nose and a receding chin added to his unattractiveness, made worse by a slight crook back and a limp, caused by disease in childhood.

'Why are you staring at our master over there?' he insisted in his reedy voice.

Gwyn, de Wolfe's squire and bodyguard, lifted a quart pot of ale and swallowed almost half the contents before replying to the little man, who was the coroner's clerk.

'I'm watching our crowner trying to be friendly to the new sheriff, though I know full well he thinks he's an old fool,' rumbled Gwyn.

'At least he's said to be honest and not ambitious for his own advancement, as was the last one,' objected Thomas, who almost on principle disagreed with everything the coroner's officer said. Though the two bickered incessantly, they were good friends, and Gwyn displayed an almost paternal attitude to the little man, born of the troubles that had afflicted him for much of his life.

Gwyn sank the rest of his ale and wiped his huge moustache with the back of his hand. 'True enough, but I suspect John de Wolfe will have even more work to do in future, as this new fellow is unlikely to move himself to do more than necessary.'

They watched the shifting patterns of men and women in the hall, as people moved around gossiping, taking more food and drink from the tables and from the trays and jugs held by servants. The costumes were many and varied, especially among the merchants and burgesses of the county, who tended to be more colourful in their garb than the soldiers and officials. Although most of the men wore belted tunics, some had long ones to their calves, slit at the front for riding a horse, whilst others sported thigh-length robes over breeches, many with cross-gartered hose above shoes or boots. The more dandified had footwear with long pointed toes, some curled back almost to their ankles. There were men like strutting peacocks, whose tunics and surcoats were bright red and blue, unlike some more sober knights and clerks, whose clothing tended to be of brown or dull yellow, with more practical boots designed for riding.

Thomas de Peyne nibbled at a mutton pasty – being poorer than a church mouse, to him any free food was manna from heaven. As he chewed, his sharp little eyes flitted around the chamber and settled on Matilda de Wolfe. He was a compassionate young man and felt sorry for her at a time when she must feel shame for her only brother's disgrace. He knew that Richard de Revelle had been almost idolised by his younger sister, which made his fall from grace all the harder for her to bear. For it to be her own husband who had brought about his downfall must be an even more bitter pill for her to swallow. The clerk said as much to his big companion, but Gwyn merely shrugged.

'The swine had it coming. Our crowner was too lenient as it was, I reckon. He should have denounced him long before, as de Revelle had been up to his treacherous tricks for months.'

Unlike the clerk, Gwyn was not a sensitive soul but a bluff soldier who saw everything in black and white, rather than shades of grey.

De Peyne went back to staring at the coroner's wife as she sat at the table, listening to the prattle of Hugh de Relaga. The portreeve was one of those who delighted in gaudy raiment and he wore a long surcoat of plum-coloured velvet over a tunic of bright green silk, girdled over his protruberant belly with a belt of gilded soft leather, the free end dangling to his knees. His head was covered by a tight helmet of saffron linen, laced under his double chins. As he chattered away to Matilda, obviously trying to divert her and raise her despondent mood, his beringed fingers rested on her sleeve.

Thomas had an insatiable curiosity about almost everything, especially people, and his gaze now returned to his master's wife. He knew that she must now be forty-five, as she was four years older than her husband. Matilda was a solid woman, not obese, but heavily built with a short neck and a square face. Small dark eyes were not enhanced by the folds of loose skin that hung below them, and her features always

17

seemed set in a rather pugnacious, sour expression. The clerk felt that she had plenty to be sour about, with a husband like John and Richard for a brother! Even though Matilda despised him for being a failed priest, Thomas admired her for her devotion to the Church, as he knew she spent much of her time either at services in St Olave's in Fore Street or in the cathedral. He also knew that she had a leaning towards taking the veil, and not long ago had entered Polsloe Priory as a novice, after what she considered to be one of her husband's more outrageous lapses of morals. Though the outside attractions of good food and fine clothes had finally dissuaded her from taking her vows, Thomas still gave her great credit for her piety and devotion to God.

The Cornishman began to get restive, as he had little of the clerk's interest in people. Now that he had eaten and drunk his fill, he was anxious to be off to find a game of dice in the guardroom of the castle gatehouse, below the coroner's bleak office on the upper floor.

With a grunted farewell to Thomas, he lumbered across to the door of the hall and clumped down the wooden staircase outside, a defensive device that could be thrown down in times of seige so that there was no access to the entrance twelve feet above ground.

Rougemont was built into the north-east corner of the city walls, which had first been erected by the Romans and later strengthened by both Saxons and Normans. The castle was at the highest point of Exeter, the city sloping away westward to the river, half a mile away. The inner ward was formed by a curving rampart of red Devon sandstone, which gave the castle its name. It was built with a gatehouse in the southern part, the first part of the fortress to be built by William the Bastard after he had broken the resistance of the Saxons three years after the battle at Hastings. A drawbridge stretched across a deep dry ditch and a steep slope separated the inner ward from a much larger area outside, which itself was protected by an earthen bank topped by a timber palisade. In this outer ward were huts and sheds where the soldiers and their families lived, as well as stables, stores and workshops. As Rougemont had not been attacked since the civil war between King Stephen and Empress Matilda almost fifty years earlier, security was lax. Washing dried on bushes, wives and strumpets ambled about and urchins played between the jumbled mass of wooden buildings that turned the place into a small village rather than a military camp.

Gwyn ambled across the rubbish-strewn inner ward, where the ground had been beaten into sticky mire by the feet of horses, oxen and people. It had not rained today, but this had been one of the wettest seasons for years, and there were fears of a lean winter ahead for much of the population after such a poor harvest. He reached the gatehouse, a tall, narrow tower straddling an arched tunnel. On the ground floor, next to the raised portcullis that protected the entrance passage, was the small guardroom, with a cramped stone stairway at the back which led up to the coroner's chamber two floors above. Inside, three men squatted on a horse blanket spread on the earthen floor, intent on a game of 'eighteens', using three dice cut from bone. Though, like most folk, none of them could read or write, they had not the slightest problem in counting the spots on the dice with lightning rapidity, especially when there was money riding on the game.

Two of them were fairly young men-at-arms, the other

their sergeant, a grizzled veteran called Gabriel, who had a face like a dried apricot, but an amiable expression when his toothless mouth broke into a smile.

'Sit you down, Gwyn, we've been waiting patiently to take some pennies off you. Where the hell have you been?'

The coroner's officer grunted as he lowered himself to the blanket and reached for the dice. 'Seizing a mouthful of the new sheriff's free food. But they're all gabbing too much for me over there, the place is full of the high and mighty, not common folk like us.'

Gabriel cleared his throat noisily and spat on the floor. 'It'll not be the same somehow, without the old sheriff! How will Crowner John manage, without someone to hate?'

'He'll not have time to hate anyone, from what I gather. Furnellis was a lazy old bugger last time he was sheriff and I doubt he's changed much.'

They played on in silence for a while, the chink of quartered and halved pennies the only sound, until Gabriel sent one of the soldiers to a shelf for some chipped pottery mugs and a pitcher of rough cider. Outside, on the top of the drawbridge, another youthful soldier stood sentinel, grasping his pike and staring glumly down Castle Hill. He was thinking of the plump bottom of the girl he had had last evening behind the White Hart tavern, and the fact that thanks to Gabriel and his dice he had no money to see her again that night. With the three-day October fair starting the next day, being penniless was a miserable prospect for any virile young fellow.

He listened enviously to the chink of the pottery jugs and the rattle of the dice until his attention was drawn to a thin figure hurrying up the steep slope towards him from the gate in the palisade of the outer ward.

As he came on to the drawbridge, the sentry saw there was no need to challenge him, as it was Osric, one of the city's constables, employed by the council of burgesses to keep order on the streets – an ambitious task for only two men in a town of over four thousand.

The skinny Saxon paused under the archway to get his breath back, leaning on the long staff that, apart from a dagger, was his only weapon.

'Is the crowner up in his chamber?' he panted. 'We've got a body already and the damned fair hasn't even started yet!'

The man-at-arms shook his head. 'I think he's in the hall celebrating with the new sheriff. But his officer's in there.' He pointed towards the guardroom and Osric scurried inside, bending his head to clear the low lintel.

Gwyn of Polruan looked up from his game and groaned when he saw who it was. 'Here comes trouble! What have you got for us this time?'

Four faces looked up at him expectantly, the dice forgotten for the moment.

'The flood tide has just washed up a corpse near the quay-side. One of the wharf porters saw it and fished it out not half an hour ago.'

The red-haired Cornishman seemed unimpressed. 'God knows how many drownings we've had this year, with all this rain. The river's been continually in spate since midsummer.'

Osric shook his head, a large Adam's apple bobbing in his long neck as he disagreed.

'No drowner this one, Gwyn! He was stark naked and his face beaten in so much his own mother wouldn't recognise him!'

The officer lumbered to his feet, a stubborn look on his face.

21

'A few days or even weeks rolling in the river can tear off their garments, man! And their faces get smashed against rocks and dragged along the stony bottom.'

Equally obdurate, the constable shook his head again. 'Not this one! He's fresh, limbs still stiff and not a hint of corruption on his belly. Not been in the water more than a day, I'll wager.'

Gwyn sighed and bent to pick up the three half-pence he had already won.

'I'll have to come back later to take the rest from you losers!' he said gruffly to the men on the floor. 'Stay here, Osric, I'll go and get Sir John.'

The crowd had thinned out since Gwyn had left the hall, but there were still many people left, reluctant to leave while there was still food and drink remaining. He stood inside the door and saw that his master had now moved to stand over his wife and his friend the portreeve, who was still chattering away like a gaudy tomtit.

Gwyn wondered how often over the past year he had brought his master messages similar to the one he now had to deliver. It had been late the previous September that John de Wolfe had been appointed as the first coroner in Devon on the direct recommendation of the King, through Hubert Walter, his Chief Justiciar and Archbishop of Canterbury. Since then, they had dealt with scores of dead bodies, rapes and assaults, as well as a few fires, wrecks, troves of treasure and even catches of the royal fish, the whale and the sturgeon. During this eventful year, the twenty-year bond between the Cornishman and his master had strengthened, as each had saved the life of the other yet again. This time, the rescues had been within the county boundary, rather than in campaigns across the known world from Ireland to Outremer.

Gwyn looked across the hall at the man whose life was inextricably bound with his own. He saw a tall, slightly hunched figure, jet-black hair swept back from his forehead, long enough to fall to his collar, unlike the usual severe cropping of the neck and sides effected by most Normans. His face was long and hollow cheeked, with a large hooked nose surmounted by bushy eyebrows. Though de Wolfe shaved once a week, there was usually dark stubble on his face, and this, together with his habit of invariably dressing in black or grey, had long earned him the nickname of 'Black John' among the soldiery with whom they had spent much of their lives until three years ago.

Gwyn had been his companion, bodyguard and friend for almost two decades, since he had given up being a fisherman in Polruan to become John's servant in one of the early Irish wars. Their final campaign had been as part of the small band that accompanied the Lionheart on his ill-fated journey home from the Crusade, when a shipwreck in the Adriatic drove him overland to be captured in Vienna and held prisoner in Austria and Germany for well over a year. Both Gwyn and de Wolfe still blamed themselves for not being able to prevent the ambush, especially as they had managed to escape.

Now he stood in the hall and looked across with dogged affection at his master, as he hunched like a great crow over his wife and friend. He knew that de Wolfe's relations with his wife were stressful, there being faults on both sides. The marriage had been arranged by their respective fathers and both were reluctant partners. De Wolfe had solved much of the problem by managing to be away for most of the seventeen years of his married life, finding wars, campaigns and crusades to keep him far from Exeter. In all that time, Gwyn doubted that they had spent more than a month in any one year at home. It was only when they returned from Austria that they found that they had run out of wars to fight, as well as becoming too old at forty to have the stamina for prolonged campaigning.

Gwyn shrugged off this rare moment of reverie; he was like his master in that contemplation and emotion were foreign to his nature. Pushing past a couple of kitchen servants who were collecting empty mugs and tankards, he walked between the trestles and benches to within a few yards of the coroner and made a discreet signal to him.

With an alacrity that showed that he was relieved to get away from Hugh de Relaga's prattling, de Wolfe moved across to his officer, a questioning look on his long face.

'Well?' he snapped, the severity of his tone being his normal method of address.

'We've got a corpse from the river, Crowner,' drawled Gwyn easily. 'Osric reckons it's fresh. Naked and beaten up, so he's unrecognisable.'

John rubbed his hands together. He was not delighted at the thought of another man's death, but pleased to have an excuse to get away from this gathering, as the effort to be sociable was becoming a strain.

'I'll arrange to have my wife taken home, then I'll come. Where's the body?'

'Still down on the quay-side. They're learning at last that no one is to interfere with corpses until you view them.'

John turned on his heel and stalked back to the nearby table, where Gwyn saw him making some excuse to Matilda and a request to the corpulent portreeve. Then he was back at his officer's side.

'I see our brave clerk is still here. Get him to come down with us.'

Gwyn signalled to Thomas, who was talking to a vicar-choral of his acquaintance, and a few moments later the three of them collected Osric from the guard-room. They began striding down Castle Hill towards High Street, which ran from the East Gate to the centre of the city. Thomas de Peyne limped behind on his short legs, as the constable repeated the meagre information to de Wolfe.

'Close in to the bank he was, according to the fellow who hauled him out. Could well have gone in on the Exeter side of the river, anywhere between here and Topsham.'

This was the port a few miles downriver, where the Exe widened out into its estuary, six miles from the open sea.

'And there's nothing at all to show who he might be?' demanded de Wolfe.

The Saxon shook his head as they hurried through the crowded main street. 'Doesn't look a rough fellow, Crowner. He's shaved and has a decent haircut. Hard to tell how old he is, but he's not a young man. There's a belly on him and his hair has a bit of grey at the temples.'

The town was already filling up ready for the fair the next day, and the press of people, barrows, hand-carts and heavily laden porters slowed their progress until they got past Carfoix, the central crossing of the four main streets. Then they turned into side alleys and began going down the steeper lanes towards the quay-side. At the bottom of Priest Street, they turned left to reach the Watergate, driven through the south-west corner of the city walls in recent years to give better access to the busy wharf and warehouses that Exeter's rapidly growing commerce demanded.

'He's just past that last cog, Crowner,' said Osric, pointing to the most distant of three vessels that were tied up at the stone quay. As the tide was well in, they were floating upright and would stay like that until the ebb dropped them down on the thick mud to lean over against the wharf. The whole place was busy with men jogging up and down gangplanks with sacks and bales on their shoulders. Shipwrights and sailors yelled garbled orders at the tops of their voices and merchants and their clerks were standing around heaps of cargo on the wharf, checking items by means of notched tally-sticks or knotted cords, as well as from a few parchment manifests.

Ignoring the noisy activity, John de Wolfe led his party onward, threading through the merchandise and shoving the odd labourer out of his path until he reached the last cog, which looked like a fat, blunt-ended Norse longboat, its single sail now tightly lashed to the yard that crossed its stubby mast. Just beyond it were two figures, standing guard over something covered with a piece of canvas. They were rough-looking men, one dressed in a ragged tunic, the skirt of which was pulled up between his legs and tucked into his belt. The other had a leather jerkin over breeches of coarse cloth, and both were barefooted, the lower part of their legs being caked in brown river mud.

'These men found the corpse, Crowner,' declared Osric. 'And this is him,' he added unnecessarily, jerking a thumb down at the canvas-covered mound.

The two men mumbled something and shifted uneasily, as any contact with officers of the law was something to be avoided, however innocent a man might be. The coroner's trio stood around the body, Thomas as reluctant as ever, for even a year's famil-iarity with his job had not inured his sensitive soul to the sights and smells of sudden death.

De Wolfe nodded at Gwyn, who, well used to the routine, bent and whipped off the piece of sailcloth to expose the corpse.

As Osric had promised, the deceased was stark naked, lying on his back, and against the dark muddy ground his pallor was almost obscene, like that of a plucked goose on a butcher's slab. The belly protruded, and Gwyn gave it a firm prod with his forefinger.

'That's fat, not gassy corruption!' he observed with satisfaction.

'I told you he was fresh,' said the constable, indignantly. 'Look at his hands, they're hardly wrinkled, so he's not been in the water long.'

De Wolfe, who considered himself an expert on injury and death, was not going to let a town constable lecture him on the subject, and he dropped to a crouch to examine the body more closely.

'Still stiff in the arms and legs,' he barked, as he cranked the elbows and knees of the dead man. 'And eyes not clouded yet!' He prodded the eyelids with a long finger as he spoke.

'The face is a proper mess, looks as if he's had a kicking,' said Gwyn judicially. From eyebrows down to jawline, the face was a welter of lacerations and bruises, the skin ripped, the lips puffed and torn and the nose smashed out of all recognition.

Thomas plucked up enough courage to venture a comment, similar to the one Gwyn had made earlier to the constable. 'We've had corpses from the water before, where you've said the injuries were due to being knocked around against stones and rocks after death. Could this not be the same?'

The coroner shook his dark head. 'The cuts and wounds are only on his face and neck. The rest of him is intact. When a corpse drags along the bottom, the knees and backs of the hands get ripped as well.'

Gwyn hoisted up one of the stiff arms. 'And look at these, Crowner! Bruises on both his forearms and hands.'

Thomas was uncharacteristically stubborn today. 'Isn't that what the crowner just described?'

De Wolfe, content to expound further, prodded the blue marks with his forefinger. 'You can't bruise a corpse, Thomas! These were inflicted during life, though they're very recent, still being blue in colour.'

His officer nodded sagely. 'Men get them from holding up their arms to defend themselves against a beating. This poor fellow's had a good old hammering.'

They stood in a silent ring around the body for a moment, looking down at what had been a living person not long before. Thomas crossed himself several times and murmured some verses of a Latin requiem under his breath.

'We know how he died, but who the hell is he?' grunted Gwyn.

De Wolfe questioned the two labourers and the constable, but none of them could offer any suggestions, which was hardly surprising given the state of the man's face. Crouching again alongside the body, John picked up the hands and studied them, turning them over to see both the backs and the palms.

'He's no rough peasant or manual worker. His hands are free from calluses – though he seems to have a number of small scars and old burns on the inside of his fingers. Maybe he was some kind of craftsman.'

After Gwyn had rolled the corpse on to its face to allow them to examine the back, de Wolfe motioned him to pull the makeshift canvas shroud over it again.

'Nothing more we can do here. We'll have to wait for someone to report their husband or father missing

– though he may have come up on the flood tide from Topsham. I doubt it would be as far away as Exmouth, the corpse is too fresh.'

'Where shall we lodge him, Crowner?' asked Osric. 'It's a long way to carry him up to Rougemont.'

Corpses from the central part of the city were usually housed in a cart shed in the castle, but on standing up and looking around, de Wolfe decided on an easier option.

'We can put him in one of the lower chambers of the Watergate – no one is likely to steal him!'

The two wharf workers found a wooden device that porters used for carrying heavy crates or bales from the ships, a stretcher with short legs that looked remarkably like a bier. On this they carried the unknown victim, decorously covered with the sailcloth, to the nearby gate in the city wall. This had a narrow tower on each side, in one of which lived the watchmen who had the strict duty of closing the large gates when curfew was rung at dusk. In the base of the other bastion was a dank chamber half filled with junk and rubbish, but with enough space to leave the corpse on its trestle.

Gwyn pulled some lengths of timber across the small arched entrance to discourage intruders and Osric went across to the gatekeeper to order him to keep an eye on the place until further notice.

'Not much point in holding an inquest until we get some news as to who he might be,' said the coroner, as they started back up the hill towards High Street.

'With the fair starting tomorrow, there'll be hundreds of strangers in Exeter – maybe a thousand or more, given that the tournament is here as well,' growled Gwyn. 'Maybe he's one of those and we'll never get to know who he was.'

John made one of his throat-clearing rumbles, which could mean almost anything. 'I've got a feeling in my water that he's a man of substance, rather than some nonentity. If that's so, then he's more likely to be missed.'

A few minutes later, he somewhat reluctantly turned into Martin's Lane to reach his front door, all too aware that he would get black looks and sullen recriminations from Matilda for leaving her in the lurch so abruptly at Rougemont.

CHAPTER TWO

In which Crowner John goes to the fair

When John entered his tall, narrow house, one of only two in the narrow lane that joined High Street to the cathedral Close, he found that he had a reprieve from his wife's acidulous tongue, for she had taken herself off to her favourite church, tiny St Olave's at the upper end of Fore Street. Whether she was praying for her own soul or that of her brother, he knew not, but doubted that his own welfare was on her devotional agenda.

He put his head around the door which led from the small outer vestibule into the hall, a high, gloomy room that reached right up to the bare rafters of the house. A glance showed him that it was empty, so he went to the other end of the vestibule and walked along the narrow covered passage that ran down the side of the house to the back yard.

The plot of muddy earth that was his demesne contained the kitchen shed, the wash house, the privy and a pigsty, all built of a mixture of wattle panels and 'cob' – a plaster made from clay, straw, dried ferns and horse manure. The house itself was of timber, with a roof of wooden shingles. At the back, a solar projected from the upper part, reached by an outside wooden staircase, under which was a hut that housed Lucille, Matilda's rabbit-toothed French maid. The solar was his wife's retreat, but also served as their bedroom, being the only other room in the house other than the hall and its vestibule.

There was a well in the middle of the yard, and bent over this was the rounded backside of a woman, hoisting up a leather bucket. John loped across and gave it a slap, grinning as his cook-maid swung around to glare at him in mock outrage. Mary was a handsome wench, her dark hair a legacy from an unknown father, who had probably been a soldier passing through the city some twenty-five years earlier.

'Stop taking advantage of a poor servant, Sir Crowner, else I'll tell your wife – or even worse, your mistress!' she chided, but let him slip an arm around her and give her a smacking kiss on the lips. There had been a time when they did far more than kiss, but since the nosy Lucille had been in residence, Mary had resisted his advances, afraid that she would carry tales to John's wife.

Pushing him away with one hand, she carried her leather pail of water into the kitchen, where she not only cooked for the household but lived and slept as well. John dropped on to a stool and fondled the head of his old hound Brutus, who was dozing by the fire-pit in the centre. He looked at a ring of griddle cakes cooking on a bakestone over the fire.

'The food at the new sheriff's installation was miserable,' he said pointedly, and with a sigh Mary lifted off a couple of hot cakes with a wooden spatula and offered them to her master.

'The honey's in that pot by your elbow,' she said, as she ladled some water from her bucket into a small cauldron of stew that was simmering at the edge of the fire. Then she sat on the hay-bag on the floor which served as her bed and looked at him expectantly. They were good friends, the coroner and his house servant, and she looked after him as well as any wife – and much better than the one he actually had. He always regaled her with news of his day's exploits, and she often fed him titbits of gossip picked up at the baker's shop or the butcher's stall, which were sometimes of use in his investigations.

He described the ceremony at the castle, then told her of the discovery of the body in the River Exe. 'I suppose you've heard no tittle-tattle in the town about anyone gone missing?' he asked hopefully.

Mary shook her head as she poured him a mug of ale from a pitcher on the earth floor. 'The place is heaving with people for the fair – strangers everywhere, it's hard to get near the stalls to buy our food!'

'At least they'll be staying open, not like some places,' he remarked.

In a number of other towns, the local shops had to close down during fairs in order not to compete with the visiting stall-holders, who paid stiff fees for the privilege of trading there for three days. Exeter allowed its own traders to carry on, however, though many of these also took booths on the fairground outside the city walls to make sure that they got their share of the extra business.

The pair chatted for a while until John had eaten his cakes and drunk his ale, by which time the late afternoon bells were ringing from the nearby cathedral to summon the clergy to vespers, the last service of the day.

'There's a duck for supper, with turnips, onions and cabbage,' advised Mary. 'So don't go feeding too much down at the Bush!' she warned, knowing full well that the coroner would take advantage of Matilda's absence to take the dog for a walk, his excuse to slip down to the tavern in Idle Lane to see his mistress.

He gave another of his lopsided grins and planted

another quick kiss on her forehead. Whistling to Brutus to follow, he strode away towards the front door of the house, his alibi loping after him. In Martin's Lane, he turned right into the Close, the large open area surrounding the great cathedral church of St Mary and St Peter. Completed only a few years earlier, the great twin towers rose majestically into the sky, but at ground level the appearance of the Close was anything but elegant. It was a confused tangle of muddy paths between open grave pits, old grave mounds, piles of refuse and dumped offal. Populated by beggars, drunks and urchins playing tag and football, it was also infested by cut-purses eager to fleece unwary visitors. At this time of the October fair, there was an even greater number of loafers in the Close, some come to gape at the great church, others adding to the number of passers-by being importuned by pedlars with their trays of sweetmeats, pasties and trinkets.

John de Wolfe strode past, almost unaware of the hubbub, as the scene was so familiar to him. With his lean hound criss-crossing in front of him to seek out each new stink and odour, the coroner made for the Bear Gate, one of the many entrances to the Close, which lay on the opposite side to Martin's Lane. From there he crossed Southgate Street and continued downhill into the small lanes leading to the river, following much the same route as he had used earlier when he went to see the corpse on the quay-side. Halfway down Priest Street, however, where many of the clergy had lodgings, he turned left into a short cut across a patch of waste ground, where a fire had destroyed some houses several years before. They had not been rebuilt and the street had become known as Idle Lane. The only building was the Bush Inn, which itself had just been rebuilt after a recent fire had destroyed its upper floor. It was a square stone structure with a high roof, thatched with new straw which came down almost low enough for a tall man like de Wolfe to touch the eaves. In the middle of the front wall was a low door, with shuttered window openings on each side and a dried bush hanging from a bracket above. This was the inn's sign, an indicator of a tavern since Roman times. At the back of the alehouse was a large fenced yard, containing a kitchen hut and the usual outbuildings, including a brewing shed from which came the best ale in Exeter.

John ducked under the lintel and went into the taproom, which occupied all the ground floor. The first fire of the autumn was glowing in a clay pit in the centre of the room and its smoke added to the fug, an eye-smarting mixture of cooking, sweat and spilt ale. A number of rough tables, benches and stools were scattered about, and at the back, where a door went out into the yard, a row of casks sat on the rush-strewn floor, holding the supply of ale and cider. Near by was a wide ladder to the loft above, where travellers could rent a straw mattress for a penny a night, which included a meal and drink.

De Wolfe made for his favourite table next to the fire, and a pair of young apprentices hastily moved away, as all the patrons knew that this was the coroner's place, sheltered on one side by a wattle hurdle that kept off some of the draught from the doorway. His bottom had hardly touched the bench when a pottery jar containing a quart of ale was set in front of him. This time the drink was brought not by the usual potman, the one-eyed old soldier Edwin, but by the landlady herself, the delectable Nesta. She stood over him, her round Welsh face wreathed in a welcoming smile.

'John, you look very comely today, in your best tunic and Moorish belt!'

His usually stern features lit up with a returning smile of pure pleasure, partly at seeing her look so well, after the stress she had suffered a month past, when she had been pulled out of the burning tavern just before the roof collapsed. This was the first time he had noticed that she seemed fully recovered, with a pink bloom on the cheeks that had been so pale for many weeks. Today she had left off her usual linen cap and her rich red hair was plaited into two ropes that hung over her shapely bosom. De Wolfe had had many women over the years, but none plucked at his heartstrings like Nesta of Gwent. He held up his hand to take her fingers in his own.

'I'm in my best finery today because of the installation of this new sheriff. Come and sit with me, dear Nesta!'

She slid on to the bench and he put an arm around her waist and hugged her to him, ignoring the covert glances of other patrons.

'A couple of minutes only, John. There's cooking to be seen to – we're run off our feet with all these people coming into town.'

Nesta ran the tavern with bustling efficiency, helped by Edwin and two maids. It was now a thriving business, renowned for good food and the city's best ale. The rushes on the floor and the mattresses upstairs were the cleanest in Exeter, so there was never any lack of custom. Nesta's husband Meredydd, a Gwent archer who had campaigned with John de Wolfe, had bought the inn several years ago, but later died of a fever, leaving his widow deeply in debt. John had come to her rescue for the sake of his friendship with her husband, and gradually, by dint of his money and her hard work, they had turned disaster into success. In the process they had become lovers, and John's miserable marriage had become all the more irksome because of the contentment he felt when he was with Nesta.

'Shall I get the girls to cook something for you, John?' she said, her concern for his appetite coming to the surface as usual. He squeezed her more tightly as he shook his head. 'I had some small stuff at Rougemont – and Mary has threatened me with hideous torment if I fail to eat the duck she's cooking for supper.'

They sat for a few moments, she listening contentedly while he gently kneaded her breast with his free hand as he told her of the day's events.

'So you've no idea who this poor dead man might be?' she asked, after he had recounted the tale of the washed-up body. Nesta was always full of sympathy for the afflicted, be they paupers, lame dogs or the nameless dead.

'No, he's a mystery man as yet. You've heard nothing of any fights or assaults in the last day or two?'

Like Mary, the innkeeper often heard gossip about happenings in the city, indeed the whole county, especially as the Bush was a favourite inn for carters and travellers. But this time, Nesta had nothing to suggest.

'If no one recognises him, he must surely be one of the many who have come for the fair,' she reasoned.

John didn't press the point that with a face as battered as his, the corpse was totally unrecognisable. He changed the subject by pointing to the new beams and boards above their head, which formed the floor of the roomy loft.

'They did a good job in such a short time, Nesta. Apart from the look of such new timber, it's hard to know what ruin there was before.'

In August, the tavern had been deliberately set on fire and the place had been gutted, only the stone walls remaining. But thanks to willing workers and timber from John's manors at the coast, it was now back to its former glory – even Nesta's small room on the floor above had been rebuilt. This was where they had spent many a pleasant hour together, though the fire had destroyed her pride and joy – the large French bed that John had imported from St Malo, probably the only one in Exeter. Until he could get a replacement, they would have to make do with a mattress on the floor, like most other people. The thought of the little chamber in the corner of the loft caused him to give her another squeeze.

'Are you too busy this evening to climb the ladder, my love?' he whispered in her ear. She jabbed him playfully with her elbow, then pulled herself free from his encircling arm.

'I must go and see to the girls in the kitchen now,' she said, rising to her feet and smoothing down the green kirtle that flowed over her shapely figure. 'But if you can find the strength to walk down again after glutting yourself on Mary's duck, then maybe I can find a few spare moments later on this evening!'

She made her way to the back of the room, laughing and making small talk with her patrons along the way. A popular woman, she had the gift of being unfailingly pleasant to everyone, yet firm enough with drunks or the few who tried to take advantage of her, as a woman innkeeper was a vulnerable rarity in the many alehouses of the city.

The coroner sat with his pot and also exchanged salutations with some of the regulars in the taproom. They all knew of his long-standing affair with the landlady and most heartily approved and wished them well. Though there was many a nudge and wink, none ever made any audible jest or comment, as Black John's short temper and strong arm were too well known for any liberties to be taken with him.

De Wolfe was chatting to a carpenter on the next table

about the good quality of the repairs to the building, as the man was one of those who had worked on it, at John's expense. Under the table, Brutus was contentedly gnawing on a mutton knuckle that another patron had thrown to him. The scene was one of peaceful serenity, too good to last. The early evening sunlight coming through the open door was momentarily blocked by a large figure as Gwyn of Polruan came in and crossed to de Wolfe's table. The coroner groaned as he saw the familiar look on the big man's whiskered face.

'Tell me the worst, then! I was just getting comfortable,' he grunted.

Gwyn dropped on to the opposite bench, which creaked ominously under his weight. He ran thick fingers through his dishevelled red hair, then waved them at Edwin to summon a jug of ale.

'There's been something found, Crowner. Something that might have a bearing on our corpse.'

The Cornishman had a habit, infuriating to his master, of spinning out any story in instalments that delayed the actual facts.

'What "something", damn you? Spit it out, for God's sake!'

Edwin limped up with Gwyn's ale and the officer took a deep draught and gave a sigh of satisfaction before answering the exasperated coroner.

'Garments, that's what. Bloodstained and hidden in a hole.'

Between gulps of Nesta's best brew, the story came out. Two young boys had been playing on the river bank about a quarter of a mile downstream of the wharf, where the Shitebrook disgorged its filth into the Exe. This was a foul stream that acted as the main sewer for Exeter, most of the ordure draining through culverts in the city walls to find its way into the aptly named brook which trickled sluggishly down a small valley to the river.

'They had a mangy dog with them and they were throwing sticks into the river for it to fetch,' explained Gwyn. 'Then it suddenly lost interest in the game and started digging into the bank, in what seemed like an otter run.'

John waited impatiently for his old friend to get to the nub of the matter.

'The upshot was that the cur dragged out a bundle of what the lads thought were rags, but which turned out to be a tunic and surcoat. The upper part of both of these was stiff with blood.'

He went on to explain that when the boys ran back up to the wharf, some of the men there challenged them, thinking they had stolen something. One happened to be the fellow who had found the body earlier in the day. He called Osric, who in turn asked Gwyn to notify the coroner.

'Where's the stuff now?' demanded de Wolfe.

'Osric has it in that shack behind the Guildhall that the constables use for their shelter.'

The two men downed the remainder of their drink and John told Edwin to tell his mistress that he would see her later that evening. They stepped out into Idle Lane, feeling one of the first chill breezes of the autumn as they strode back towards the city.

The Guildhall was in High Street, not many yards from the turning into Martin's Lane. It was newly built in stone, one of the grandest buildings in the city, as befitted the home of the many merchant guilds and the place where the burgesses held their council. In a lane behind it was a small thatched hut left by the stonemasons, which had been appropriated as their shelter by Osric and his fatter colleague, Theobald. John thrust open the rickety door and went into the shed, almost bare but for two old stools and a bench on which were some cups and pots. Neither of the constables was there, but Gwyn pointed to a jumble of cloth on a shelf nailed to the wall.

'That's the stuff, Crowner. Have a look at this.' He unrolled the clothing on the bench and John saw a long yellow tunic of good-quality cloth, together with a surcoat of blue serge. They were both muddy, but more significantly the areas around the neck and upper chest were stiff with dark dried blood.

De Wolfe felt the material between his finger and thumb. 'Good stuff, though not showy. If this did belong to our corpse, then he was no common labourer, as I thought from the state of his hands.'

Gwyn nodded sagely. 'But neither does he seem some foppish fellow with more money than sense. There's no fancy embroidery on the tunic and the surcoat has no brocade or velvet frippery.'

The coroner stood staring down at the soiled garments. 'But no belt, dagger, hose or shoes – nor a pouch or purse.'

'Smells like a robbery to me,' grunted his officer. 'But why take his clothes off and hide them?'

'To confound or certainly delay us putting a name to him,' snapped de Wolfe. 'It's the merest chance that those urchins and their dog found this stuff.'

Gwyn remained unimpressed by their luck. 'Doesn't help much unless we find someone who knows him and knows what he was wearing!'

His master shrugged and turned to the door. 'Let's see what tomorrow brings. You can tell Osric to take that stuff down to the Watergate. It may as well stay with the body, in case we find someone who can have a look at them both.'

With that, he strode off towards his house, ready to face both Mary's duck and his wife's dour company.

*   *   *

Everyone in the city seemed to be up and about even earlier than usual the next morning. Even before dawn broke, there were people milling around the five gates, impatiently waiting for them to open. As soon as the porters pulled back the massive oaken doors, there was a scramble in both directions, though most were waiting to spill out, especially at South Gate, as the fair was centred on Southernhay, the expanse of meadows and gardens beyond the south-east wall of Exeter. Those coming in were the usual crowd who daily brought provisions to the shops and stalls, pushing barrows of vegetables, wicker crates of fowls and ducks, carrying baskets of eggs and freshly caught fish. Others were adding to the confusion by driving pigs, sheep and cattle to the slaughterers in the Shambles at the top of Southgate Street.

Today, however, many merchants were going out to the booths they had erected in Southernhay, to draw in as much profit as they could from the fair. Some were Exeter burgesses and craftsmen, but there were also many strangers who had arrived early and stayed in the city overnight. Some had come from as far afield as London, Lincoln and Chester – and there were even a few who had taken ship from Cologne and Flanders, drawn by the reputation of the October fair. This year, it was an even greater attraction, as the one-day jousting tournament meant that even more people would be attending, some of them wealthy knights and squires who might be persuaded to part with their money more liberally than the cautious townsfolk and peasantry.

John de Wolfe was also up early, determined as a senior law officer to play his part in keeping the peace, especially as he knew that the new sheriff was unlikely to be exerting himself in this direction. The coroner also wanted to see what could be discovered about the previous day's murder – even if there was little hope of catching the culprits, it was essential to try to put a name to the victim, for the sake of his family.

John threw aside the sheepskin coverlets and climbed naked from his feather-filled mattress, set on a low plinth of the floor of the solar, leaving Matilda snoring on the other side. The previous evening she had been subdued and uncommunicative after returning from her devotions, which John rightly attributed to the induction of a new sheriff, reminding her again of her brother's fall from grace. After a silent meal, Matilda had retired upstairs for Lucille's ministrations to her hair, then gone to bed. John had slipped out to the Bush and had a satisfactory hour in the new loft, coming home before the cathedral bells rang for midnight matins.

Now he was ready for the new day, and in honour of the fair he pulled out his second-best grey tunic from the heavy chest that held his few clothes. He pulled on his long hose and tied the laces to the under-belt around his waist before shaking down the skirt of his long tunic and buckling on his wide leather belt, complete with scrip pouch at the front and sheathed dagger at the back.

Slipping into house shoes, he opened the solar door and shivered slightly at the chill morning breeze that was chasing dark clouds across the sky. Once down the wooden steps, he made for the cook house and soon was tucking into oatmeal gruel with milk and honey. By the time he had spooned this down, Mary had a manchet of yesterday's bread for him, piled with three eggs and a thick slab of bacon fried in butter. Half a small loaf and a pint of her own ale completed his breakfast, and soon he was squatting in the odorous privy at the end of the yard, before making for the vestibule to pull on his boots.

As he reached for his mottled wolfskin cape to throw

over his shoulders, Brutus came loping around the corner from the yard. The big brown dog looked beseechingly at his master.

'Come on, then, but behave yourself,' he grunted. 'There'll be a lot of horses down there, so keep from under their hoofs!'

John's first destination was the tourney ground at Bull Mead, just beyond Southernhay. As an older and very experienced warrior, he had been asked to act as one of the judges for the contests the following day and, having agreed, wanted to have a look at the arrangements beforehand.

As he walked through the early morning bustle in the streets and lanes, he thought about the amount of organisation that these fairs entailed. The financial returns to the city and its burgesses must be well worth the effort, he mused, as weeks of work preceded each of the four major fairs every year. Because Exeter was a free chartered city, there was no lord to monopolise them, so the fairs were controlled by the two portreeves – his friend Hugh de Relaga and Henry Rifford, a wealthy leather merchant. Together with leading burgesses and guildmasters, they set up a committee, and this delegated all the hard work to others. Clerks dispensed permits to trade at the fair and collected the substantial fees, some of which had to be paid to the King's treasury under the terms of their charter. Builders and carpenters erected all the booths and the fencing for the tourney ground. Arrangements had to be made with the sheriff and the castle constable for men-at-arms to patrol the fairground and attempt to keep some order. Though the substantial ecclesiastical community had no direct part to play – and officially the Church disapproved of jousting activities – they were not reluctant to accept the extra donations and alms from the many visitors who came to gape at their grand new cathedral and leave offerings at the many altars and shrines, as well as paying for Masses to be said for the souls of their relatives.

As the coroner pushed his way through the throng at the South Gate, he appreciated anew the massive increase in population that this week had brought. He hoped that there would not be a similar increase in crime during the next three days. Drunkenness, fights, brawls and assaults were inevitable, but he prayed that there would not be too many deaths for him to deal with, though yesterday's corpse was a poor beginning.

Outside the gate was a straggle of timber houses, where the thriving city overflowed its old boundaries. To the right, the ground dropped away steeply towards the quay-side, and to the left gardens and meadows stretched around the city wall, forming the acres known as Southernhay.

Just beyond the gate the road forked, one branch going straight on, marching above the river towards Topsham and the sea. The left branch struck off at an angle to form Magdalen Street, a country road that headed out past the gallows to become the main highway east to Honiton, Yeovil and eventually Winchester and London, though these places were too remote for most people even to contemplate. In the angle between the two roads was Bull Mead, common land that was the venue for tomorrow's tournament.

As de Wolfe stepped out towards the mead, he looked to his left and saw that almost the whole of Southernhay was now covered by stalls and booths, mostly flimsy structures under gaily coloured awnings. The majority were little more than a trestle table with four poles supporting a sagging roof of striped cloth, though a few were more substantial with wattle or planked walls. The stalls were arranged in lines parallel to the city wall behind them, and stretched outwards for a hundred paces, the rows running for most of the distance between Exeter's south and east gates. As John looked at them, he was reminded of an ant-hill or a hive of bees, for although it was early in the morning the fair was already crowded with people. Many were the traders and their families, but visitors, both local and from far afield, were ambling up and down the rows, hoping for an early bargain. He stopped to watch for a moment, and saw that in the centre of the fairground the rows of stalls had been interrupted to leave a wide space around a raised platform, which had high screens at the back. At the moment it was empty, but he knew that this was where various entertainments would be staged, from jugglers and tumblers to musicians and the miracle plays, which the Church insisted on as an antidote to the otherwise totally mercenary nature of the fair.

De Wolfe was brought back to earth from his contemplation by a sudden snarling and had to yell at Brutus, who was involved in a nose-to-nose confrontation with a skinny cur that was helping a shepherd to drive a score of sheep along the road towards Southgate and the slaughtermen beyond. Reluctantly, his own hound lowered the bristling fur on the back of its neck and slunk after him, as he strode on to get Brutus away from further temptation. Another few hundred yards along the crowded road brought him to the gap in the rough fence of hazel palings that fronted the twenty acres of Bull Mead. Turning in, he entered the undulating common land and made for the centre, where a scattering of workmen were hammering in posts and rigging up a rope barrier to mark out a large square where the actual contests would take place. At one end was a crude stand for privileged spectators, little more than three levels of planking nailed to some stout posts. At each side were some small circular tents that did service as pavilions for the contestants, and at the other end of the enclosure were a few more, together with some open-sided booths, similar to the stalls in the fairground. Though the whole set-up was flimsy and obviously designed to survive for no more than a day or two, a brave effort had been made to brighten it up, with flags flying from poles and coloured pennants streaming above the tents.

The coroner walked towards the front of the stand, where a small group of men were huddled in discussion. He could see at a distance from the bright colours of his clothing and the gaudy floppy hat that one was Hugh de Relaga. Next to him was a much more sombre man, fellow portreeve Henry Rifford, older, heavily built and almost totally bald. When John joined the group, he found that two of the other men were burgesses' clerks, together with the master of works, who clutched a parchment roll bearing details of the tourney field.

After greetings all round, Henry Rifford asked de Wolfe about the organisation of the jousting the next day.

'I know that de Courcy has taken charge of the arrangements for us,' he said in his mournful voice. 'But is everything going smoothly, de Wolfe?'

John shrugged. 'I've only been foolish enough to agree to be a referee, so I know little of the organisation. But from what I know of Reginald de Courcy, he'll have everything under control.'

De Courcy was a wealthy knight and landowner in the county and a staunch King's man, like Guy Ferrars, a greater baron who was also a patron of the tournament. In fact, it was these two who had suggested its addition to the fair, and Ferrar's prominence in the affairs of state would deflect any official disapproval of the tourney, which strictly speaking was illegal, because it was not being held at one of the King's authorised sites and no licence had been obtained from Winchester to hold it. It was well known that there were many such small events across England, however, and as long as they did not degenerate into uproarious mêlées, a blind eye was turned, especially if the palms of senior Treasury clerks were crossed with sufficient silver. The influx of so many contestants and visitors was a major financial boost for Exeter, as well as satisfying the growing enthusiasm – indeed obsession – of so many knights for the jousting field.

After a few moments' conversation, John made off to walk around the enclosure, looking at the tents that the contestants could use to don their armour and take a rest – and, if needs be, be treated by their squires for injuries. He inspected the wooden troughs for watering the horses, the hitching rails and the ox-cart filled with hay and another with sacks of oats for the sustenance of the large destriers that would throng the place the following day.

A few knights and their servants were already on the scene, doing exactly the same as the coroner, making sure that the venue for their bouts was in good condition. De Wolfe spoke to several and sensed their eagerness and impatience to get on with the clash of arms the next day. One of them, a young man with a wispy blond beard, recognised the coroner and was enthusiastic about his chances of winning.

'This means much to me, Sir John,' he declared. 'I am but the third son of the lord of a small manor near Okehampton. I have little chance of support from my father and even less of inheriting anything from him. If I can vanquish one or two men tomorrow, the value of their horses and armour will provide me with funds enough to travel to France and join the King's campaigns, with the glorious prospect of loot and ransom before me!'

De Wolfe smiled at the lad's fervent hopes – he recognised himself in the young man, exactly as he had been twenty years earlier when he rode off to Ireland with Gwyn at his side, determined to make his fortune. It had worked for him and he wished the youngster the same luck – though luck was not enough, as he would need much skill with lance and sword, as well as the fortitude to bear rough living, discomfort, hunger and pain.

Satisfied with his survey of the tourney field, John walked across it to Magdalen Street, here a well-worn strip of stony earth, rutted by the iron-girt wheels of generations of ox-carts. It now formed the boundary of the fairground and, whistling again to Brutus to come to heel, he went straight across and strode between the stalls, their canopies flapping in the cold breeze. He shouldered his way through the ambling throng, a head taller than most of them, his distinctive black-clad figure drawing glances from many eyes, both curious and covertly wary. As he ploughed along, he was deaf to the cries of the tradesmen vainly trying to sell him bolts of brown serge, oranges from France, knives from the Rhine and medicines claiming to cure every ailment from earache to cow-pox. There were booths festooned with cat-skins, the fur being known as 'poor man's ermine', men with pincers offering to pull aching teeth and others tempting customers with the aroma of roasting chestnuts. Pedlars paraded up and down with trays slung from their necks, offering ribbons, needles, thread and sweetmeats. When they saw stewards approaching, they melted away between the booths to reappear in the next lane, as few had hawkers' licences. These stewards were mostly clerks, each with a more lowly servant to accompany them.

They wore a red cloth tied around their right arm as their badge of office and were mainly responsible for checking the permits of the traders, to make sure that they had paid their dues. As few of the stall-holders could read, when they handed over their fees each was issued with a wooden tally with a number carved into it. This was displayed to the steward, who checked the number against a parchment list. Because literacy was at a premium, these stewards had to be drawn mainly from the clerks to the courts and from the burgesses' assistants. Though by far the largest group of literates were the clerics of the Church, all but the lesser orders of secular clerks were forbidden to become involved in this work of Mammon.

All the blandishments of the traders were wasted on John de Wolfe, as there was nothing he wanted to buy. He left all the purchasing for his household to Mary, as Matilda was indifferent to shopping for anything but her own finery. He loped along the middle lane until, just as the cathedral bells rang out the summons to Prime, he reached the centre of the fair, where the stage was set up. Two familiar figures were waiting at the foot of the steps that led up to the platform, one large, the other small. Gwyn and Thomas were here by prior arrangement and had already carried out part of the task he had set them the previous day.

'Any luck so far?' demanded their master, after a brusque greeting.

Thomas shook his head, the cold morning air causing a dewdrop to fly from the tip of his sharp nose. 'We've been along both sides of the row nearest the city wall and questioned every stall-holder, but they know nothing of any of their fellows who might have gone missing.'

Gwyn, hunched in his worn jerkin with the pointed

hood pulled up over his tangled hair against the morning chill, nodded his assent.

'But there's plenty more booths to tackle yet, we've twice as many to visit before we give up.' He beat his arms across his chest and looked longingly at a nearby cook-stall. 'Bloody cold standing here, Crowner! I could do with something hot to warm my guts.'

John sighed at his officer's insatiable appetite, though presumably his giant frame needed twice as much sustenance as normal folk.

'I'll treat you both to a pastry, then we must get on with it. Have you got that clothing from the Watergate?'

Thomas held up a shapeless bundle tied in a cloth. 'We've found no one yet to show them to, as everyone denies any knowledge of a missing man.'

Their fortune in this respect was soon to improve, however. As they stood near the baker's booth, where for a quarter-segment of a penny the fat cook provided them each with a folded pastry filled with chopped meat and onions, two men hurried down towards them from the direction of the East Gate, at the farther end of the fairground.

From the red kerchief around his upper arm, John could see that one was a steward; the other carried the staff of a city constable.

'Here's Theobald, rushing as if he's desperate to get to the privy!' observed Gwyn, sarcastically, as the fat constable was not one of his favourite people. He found Osric, the thin Saxon, amiable enough, but thought his colleague pompous and self-important.

Theobald puffed up to the stall, out of breath but able to jerk a thumb at the steward, a lean middle-aged man with a set of rotten black stumps for teeth. Away from the fair, he was the senior clerk at a fulling mill on Exe Island, keeping the accounts and tallying the stock.

'I've found Robin here, who has some information which may well have a bearing on that corpse from the river, Sir John,' wheezed the constable.

De Wolfe's beaked nose turned to the fellow with the red armband, hoping that his news might save them much labour around the fair.

'What can you tell us, Robin?' he growled.

'Not so much me, Crowner, but two men at a silversmith's booth up at the end of that row.' He pointed a bony finger back in the direction from which he had come. 'They sought me out as soon as the fair opened this morning, for their master didn't turn up – nor did his servant.'

'Who was he?' demanded de Wolfe.

'A silversmith from Totnes, sir. I didn't ask his name, I thought it best to report it as soon as I could. Theobald here was the first to know and he said I should tell you in person. All I know is that the missing man is about forty years old.'

Within minutes, the entourage had marched up almost to the end of the middle lane of the fair and assembled in front of a larger stall, the back and sides of which were wattle panels made of woven hazel withies, under a red striped canvas roof.

A trestle table stretched across the front, on which were a wide selection of silver objects. There were shoe buckles, belt buckles, brooches, rings, bracelets, earrings and several silver platters, and even a three-branched candlestick. Though John was no expert, he saw that the workmanship was fine and that the display was worth a considerable amount of money. A ring of curious onlookers began to gather behind them, sensing that something out of the ordinary was going on, but de Wolfe set Theobald and the steward to clearing them away.

Behind the trestle were two men, both dressed in

the sober tunics of craftsmen, one with a leather apron covering his chest and belly. The other was hunched over the end of the table, working on some intricate design with a small hammer and punch. John noticed that a pair of heavy cudgels and a stout staff leaned against the back of the booth, no doubt to deal with any attempt at robbery of the valuable stock.

As the imposing figure of the coroner and that of his massive officer appeared in front of their stall, the two men straightened up and touched their fingers respectfully to their foreheads. There was no need for them to be told who he was, and they went straight into their story.

'Our master is missing, sir,' said the one in the apron, a short fellow with a bulbous nose and a thick neck. 'We've not seen him since Sunday evening.'

De Wolfe held up a hand. 'Wait, start at the beginning. What's his name and where's he from?'

'He's August Scrope, Crowner. A master silversmith from Totnes – in fact, he's warden of our guild in that part of Devon. We are two craftsmen from his shop there.'

'What age was he?'

John used the past tense, but they seemed not to notice.

'Not quite sure, Crowner – but he looked about forty.' He glanced at the other man for support; the latter nodded his agreement. 'He was a widower, though he now lives tally with a younger woman, who warms his bed and makes his food.'

'Why d'you think he's gone missing, and not just decided to go on a drinking spree or bed a wench?' growled Gwyn.

The spokesman of the pair shook his head firmly. 'Against his nature, sir, he's not much of a drinker and

53

he seems content with his own woman. Anyway, his man has vanished with him!'

The story soon came out in detail, related alternately by the two metal-workers from Totnes, a substantial town in the south of the county. August Scrope, who was proud of his widespread reputation for fine work-manship, had a previous commission from a wealthy shipowner in Topsham to make a matching set of heavy bracelets and a necklace for his wife. They were made ready by the time of the fair and Scrope arrived in Exeter a day early so that he could make a side trip to the nearby port and deliver them personally and collect the payment. Staying at the New Inn in the city's High Street on Sunday night, he was to leave early the next morning for Topsham, taking with him his body servant Terrus as protection while carrying the valuable silver. The two craftsmen had been left behind in their more modest lodgings to guard the rest of the stock for display at the fair until their master returned on Monday afternoon – but neither he nor his henchman had shown up.

'Is this man Terrus reliable?' demanded de Wolfe. 'Might he not have robbed his master and made off?'

The elder silversmith shook his head emphatically. 'Never, sir! He's been with us a dozen years and accompanied the master many times with far more valuable pieces than those. I fear they've been waylaid somewhere.'

The coroner sombrely told them of the finding of a body in the river and motioned to Thomas to unwrap the bundle of clothing and show it to the two men. Their distress was only too evident when they imme-diately confirmed that the garments belonged to August Scrope, especially when the extensive blood-soiling spoke mutely of the wounds he must have suffered.

Rather than launch into a description of the body from the river, de Wolfe took the two men to the dismal chamber in the tower of the Watergate, leaving Theobald and the steward to guard the silver-strewn stall while they were absent. Though the face was ravaged beyond recognition, they unhesitatingly confirmed that the body was that of their master. The younger smith was devastated, falling to his knees among the clutter around the body and sobbing out some prayers. Thomas, ever sympathetic to another's distress, laid a hand on his shoulder and murmured some consoling words.

'How can you be so sure, with his features so ill used?' John asked the older man, who, though pale and drawn, seemed less affected than his workmate.

'Everything about him cries out August Scrope,' he replied bitterly. 'His size, his hair, even the rough skin of his neck which I have stared at in the workshop these many years.' Then he pointed at the head of the corpse. 'And those ears, sir! One sticks out, the other is flat and has that pointed lobe. It's him right enough – now what's to become of us, with no one to serve?'

Though undoubtedly regretting the violent demise of his master, looming unemployment seemed his main concern.

John, though not lacking in sympathy, had more urgent matters in mind. 'Who was this customer he was to visit in Topsham?'

The smith gave him a name, but had no address, though this was of little consequence in such a small town as Exeter's seaport.

Within the hour, the coroner and his two henchmen had gone back to the city to fetch their horses and were on their way down the river road to seek news from the purchaser of Scrope's silverware. Even slowed

55

down by their clerk's awkward riding – for Thomas had reverted to his side saddle in spite of Gwyn's efforts to get him to sit on his steed like a man – they covered the six miles well before mid-morning. The busy quay-side was at the end of the single street that straggled past the new church, and here John reined in to sit on his horse Odin, looking at the boats while Gwyn went off to seek William le Bas, the shipman.

The tide was now out, and he looked across an expanse of mud to the flat marshes on the other side of the river, which widened out into the estuary on his left. In the distance, low hills marched down towards Dawlish on the coast, and for a moment his mind strayed to the woman who lived there, the delectable Hilda, the passion of his younger years and, until recently, still his occasional lover. He wondered idly whether her much older husband, Thorgils the Boatman, was away on a voyage at the moment. Then the image of Nesta floated into his head, and with an almost guilty sigh for days gone by he pulled Odin's great head around and waited for Gwyn to come lumbering back to where Thomas was holding the reins of both their horses.

'We've had a wasted journey, Crowner,' called the Cornishman, as he came up to his mare. 'I chanced upon the man himself, outside his dwelling. He says he's seen neither hide nor hair of the silversmith and is wondering what's happened to his wife's gift.'

De Wolfe cursed under his breath as Gwyn and Thomas hoisted themselves back up on to their steeds. It now seemed obvious that August Scrope had been waylaid on his way down from Exeter and had never reached Topsham. There was nothing to do but return to the city, so he walked Odin across to join the others.

'What about this servant of his, what can have

happened to him?' asked Gwyn, as they weaved between carts and heavily laden porters in the busy main street.

'God knows! Probably his body lies rotting in the woods alongside the road – unless they threw him into the river along with his master,' replied de Wolfe angrily. He was frustrated by the lack of progress concerning this death, as well as the time wasted in a futile ride to Topsham.

After a couple of miles, Gwyn's habitual need for food and drink began to plague him and he bemoaned the lack of an alehouse on this stretch of road. John also felt that he could do with a jug of ale.

'The priory will oblige us, I'm sure,' squeaked Thomas, always eager for the chance to visit any religious establishment. They were just coming up to a side lane which led down to the river where St James' Priory was situated. It was a small Cluniac house, a cell of the Abbey of St Martin in Paris, with only four brothers under a prior. John had had dealings with them before, on one occasion when a sturgeon had been caught near by. As a 'royal fish', along with beached whales, it belonged to the Crown, and as such became the subject of a coroner's inquest to determine its value.

There were no fish today, but as a mild excuse to seek refreshment, de Wolfe thought they might ask the brothers there whether they had heard of any robbery or assault on the Topsham road. As they turned down the lane that dropped off the low escarpment down to the riverside, he sent Thomas ahead, knowing that he would relish the chance to bob his knee and cross himself in the little chapel.

For once, the little man scurried away at high speed, with the coroner and Gwyn jogging well behind. It was a surprise, then, to see their clerk pop out of the priory gateway as they approached, apparently in a state of agitation. Behind him appeared a black-robed monk who John recognised as Brother Francis, the infirmarian.

'Crowner, I think he's here!' babbled Thomas excitedly. 'It sounds like the servant of the silversmith, badly beaten.'

As de Wolfe and his officer slid from their horses, the infirmarian, a thin old man with a bad squint, came up to explain.

'He was found just before noon yesterday by local men attending their fish traps at the edge of the river. When they brought him here, the poor fellow was almost dead – he must have crawled out of the water and collapsed. He has a problem breathing, from taking in so much dirty water, I suspect.'

As they hitched their horses to the rail outside the gate in the wall around the priory, John probed further.

'Can he speak? Has he said who he is?'

Brother Francis shrugged. 'Just managed to gasp his name, which is Terrus, but otherwise he merely wheezes and mumbles, as he has a fever. He was dressed like a serving man and he has wounds upon him, mainly about the head and arms.'

John was about to upbraid the monk for not reporting a serious assault to him as the law demanded, but then closed his mouth again, thinking it was pointless to antagonise a religious house to no purpose.

'Let's see him, quickly,' he demanded instead.

Inside the wall was an area of garden, rows of vegetables being tended by a pair of monks with their habits girt up around their thighs. They stopped hoeing to watch the visitors hurry into the modest buildings, a chapel and a small block containing a refectory, dormitory and workshops. On the ground floor at the back were two cells used as sick quarters, and the infirmarian showed them into one, furnished only with a mattress on the floor, a stool and a wooden cross hanging on the whitewashed wall. In the light from a narrow window opening, they saw a man lying on the pallet, restlessly squirming and muttering to himself between coughs and gasps.

'You'll get little sense from him, Crowner,' warned the monk. 'But see his face and limbs, he's been badly used.'

The coroner's team saw that the man, who appeared to be about thirty years of age, had a long, shallow gash across his forehead, still caked with dried blood. Much of the rest of his face was red and purple from over-lapping bruises, and his right eyelid was black and swollen, closing the eye completely. Both his arms, which were outside the coarse blanket that covered him, were similarly bruised and scratched.

'The sides of his chest and loins are also bruised,' commented Francis. 'I think he's had a kicking as well.'

John bent over the bed and in a loud clear voice tried to get some answers from the victim, but though the one good eye seemed to focus upon him, no recog-nisable words came between the wheezing and splut-tering from the man's throat.

'He's got a phlegmatous affliction of his lungs, Sir John,' said the infirmarian. 'He must have been thrown into the river and sucked a fair amount of water down into his vitals, so he's contracted a fever. It may yet carry him off.'

Undaunted, de Wolfe again crouched by the mattress and this time tried to get a response to simple questions.

'Your name is Terrus?' The eye swivelled and the rapid wheezing seemed to take on a different note. Encouraged, de Wolfe tried again.

'Was August Scrope your master?' This time Terrus managed a slight nod as well as a variation in his gasping.

By means of half a dozen leading questions that required only an affirmative answer or an apparent denial, John managed to learn that the man and his employer had been attacked by two mounted men who had followed them down the Topsham road until they reached a place between the trees where no one else was in sight. It seemed that Terrus must have lost conciousness then, as he had no further recollection of anything.

By the time John had got this far, the victim had collapsed sideways on to his palliasse and was gasping for breath, his one good eye no longer visible. The infirmarian declared that he must be left alone, to either recover or die, and reluctantly the coroner left the cell. They sat in the small deserted refectory, where the cellarer brought them some ale and bread, and discussed the latest turn of events.

'If they were followed down the road by men on horseback, then it was not forest outlaws who robbed them,' declared Gwyn, wiping ale from his moustache with the back of his hand.

'Sounds as if their assailants knew that they had something valuable with them,' observed Thomas reasonably. 'But how could they know that?'

'From the fair, I suppose,' replied Gwyn. 'A silversmith is always fair game for robbery.'

De Wolfe shook his head. 'The fair wasn't open on Monday, when they were attacked. The silver goods were not on display until this morning. So it must have been at the New Inn – perhaps someone in the tavern overheard Scrope telling of his trip to Topsham.'

They finished off their refreshments and made for the door, to thank the monks for their hospitality.

'We'll get no more sense out of this Terrus until he recovers – if he recovers!' grunted Gwyn. 'We need some description of these miscreants.'

John turned to Thomas and said something that gladdened his heart.

'Our good clerk here is the best link to any religious house. He can keep in touch with this place and discover if and when the man gets his wits back. Meanwhile, there's plenty for us to do back in the city.'

ChAPTER ThREE

In which Crowner John acts as an umpire

When John arrived at his house in Martin's Lane, he again found his wife missing. He was too late for their noontide dinner, the main meal of the day, and obviously Matilda had not waited for him.

'She's gone to her cousin in Fore Street,' announced Mary briskly, as she hurried in with a tray of bread, cheese and cold meat for him. He sat in the cheerless hall, perched on a stool at the end of the long oaken table, glaring at the faded tapestries that tried to conceal the bleakness of the timber walls. His maid-of-all-work banged a quart pot of ale in front of him. 'But she said she'll be back in time for supper – and that her brother will be coming to join you at the meal!'

De Wolfe swore out loud. 'What in hell is that scoundrel coming for? That's spoiled my appetite already!' he exclaimed, immediately giving the lie to his words by energetically attacking a slice of mutton with his dagger, as if it were Richard de Revelle's gizzard. As the thought of his brother-in-law invading his house and his privacy spread deeper into his mind, he threw down the knife and grabbed his tankard angrily.

'To hell with him, I'll not sit down at table with that traitor and thief!' He sucked down some ale and banged the pot down again. 'I'll be eating supper at the Bush tonight, Mary. At least there I can choose what company I keep!'

His cook-maid shrugged as she picked up his cloak from the floor where he had thrown it on coming in. 'It's your house, Crowner – but the mistress will give you a hard time if you don't turn up.'

'Ha! What's new about that, girl? She hardly speaks to me as it is.'

Mary made for the door, muttering something under her breath as she went. Usually she supported John against his wife, as far as it was possible without jeopardising her job, but sometimes he felt that she had joined the legion of women who conspired to make his life miserable. Even the usually amiable Nesta had her moments of provoking annoyance and aggravation, though admittedly, since taking up with John, she had suffered enough distressing events to give her good cause.

He sat alone, champing his way through the food that had been set before him, pouring more ale from the pitcher Mary had left on the table. Now that it was October, a pile of logs glowed in the hearth, below the conical chimney that was his pride and joy. The only part of the house that was built of stone, it took the smoke up through the roof, a fairly novel idea for Exeter and one that he had had copied after seeing a similar device in Brittany.

John took his last pot of ale to sit in one the cowled monk's chairs near the fire, where Brutus was already stretched out to enjoy the warmth. As he slowly savoured the last of his drink, he thought about what he had to do for the rest of the day. He should tell the portreeves about the murder of one of the stall-holders, as they were the main sponsors of the fair that had brought August Scrope to Exeter. They were also both senior men in the city's merchant guilds, and given that one of the prime purposes of these organisations was the well-being of members and their families, no doubt they would help in getting the silversmith's body back to Totnes and seeing that the local guild attended to his affairs, though as he was said to be a widower with a new mistress, perhaps that was not such an urgent issue. De Wolfe decided that he would have to keep the new sheriff informed of what was going on – not only telling him about the killing, but reassuring him that all seemed in order at the tourney field. It was a sensitive topic for all towns that had scores of high-spirited knights and squires assembling for what was essentially a battle. Even if the sport was not meant to be lethal, the combination of pent-up excitement and aggression, fuelled by excessive drinking among volatile young men, was an inflammable situation which could easily be ignited by a spark from some personal quarrel.

John decided that he would also have a word with his good friend Ralph Morin, the castle constable, to ensure that as many men-at-arms as could be spared were sent to Bull Mead the next day. The fair itself could be left to the constables and the stewards, though after dark the main trouble would be in the city streets, where thieves and cut-purses would have been attracted by the crowds, and where the taverns would be bursting at the seams with rowdy drinkers looking for a fight.

With a sigh, he hauled himself from his chair and, forsaking the warmth of the fire, went around to the back yard to see Mary. He found her sitting in her cook house, talking to Lucille, his wife's maid. Mary was wary of the skinny girl, as she knew she carried every bit of tittle-tattle back to her mistress, but she felt sorry for her. Lucille was a refugee from the Vexin, a part of Normandy north of the Seine which was fought over endlessly by Richard and Philip of France. Her parents were dead and she had been palmed off on Matilda by the latter's Norman cousins, of whom Matilda was inordinately proud, as they validated her own ancestry. Though she had been born in Devon and had spent barely a couple of months visiting across the Channel, she acted to her friends in the town almost as if she were a direct descendant of William the Bastard himself. John hardly ever said a word to Lucille and she was obviously in awe of him, bobbing her knee and running off to her box under the solar steps as soon as he came into view.

'Anyone would think that I was going to eat that bloody girl,' he growled to Mary. 'I'm off to Rougemont and then I'll be going down to the Bush, so you can tell my dear wife that I'll not be sitting at table with her and her damned brother!'

He stalked away and minutes later was in the Guildhall, just around the corner from his house. Here he found his friend Hugh de Relaga fussing with final details of the finances of the fair and of the arrangements for the guild pageants that would help to entertain the crowds over the next three days. With clerks scurrying around him with parchments, John had difficulty in catching his attention and when he managed to tell him that he had lost one of his stall-holders, the Portreeve was too distracted to take much notice, apart from clucking in sympathy and putting a line through August Scrope's rental payment on a document.

De Wolfe abandoned him to his duties and went back up High Street and turned left before the East Gate, climbing the steep lane to cross the drawbridge into the castle at the top end of the city. The weather was overcast but dry and the mud in the inner ward was setting into a hard red crust, crunching under his feet as he walked across to the squat keep on the other side. There was the usual bustle in the hall, which served as a meeting place, refectory and business office for the mixture of soldiers, clerks, merchants and supplicants to the sheriff that normally milled around inside its sombre walls.

The first door on the left led to the sheriff's chambers and he nodded curtly to the man-at-arms who stood guard upon it. As he opened the door, he thought how strange it was that he was not going in for his usual confrontation and shouting-match with Richard de Revelle, who had occupied these rooms ever since John had been coroner. He gave a rare grin as he decided he would be unlikely to surprise the new man in his shirt or dressing robe, with a whore in the bedchamber beyond, as he had with his brother-in-law on two previous occasions.

Inside the room, he found that he was right, as Henry de Furnellis was sitting behind a table with his exasperated chief clerk, Elias Pulein, who was trying to explain the contents of a parchment roll spread out before them. Like John, the new sheriff was virtually illiterate, barely able to write his name, whereas de Revelle, for all his many faults, had been an educated man. Now de Furnellis, once more sitting in this chamber as sheriff, was again dependent upon his clerks and scribes to guide him through the intricate task of running the county of Devon, especially overseeing the collection and delivery of 'the farm', the twice-yearly submission of taxes to the treasury in Winchester. Though getting old and weary, Henry was no fool, and had sufficient wealth and lack of ambition to disdain corruption and embezzlement.

He looked up as John entered and, with a sigh of relief, used his arrival as an excuse to dismiss his irritating clerk and reach for a jug of wine and two cups. His somewhat haggard face creased into a weak smile as he motioned to John to sit down on a stool on the opposite side of the table.

'I've managed to survive the first day without clouting that damned Elias across the head, in spite of his sneering at my lack of understanding of these blasted accounts!' he said, raising a fist that could have laid a larger man than the clerk flat on the floor. John knew that the older man had been a doughty fighter in his day – he had been with Strongbow, Earl of Pembroke, on the first invasion of Ireland a quarter of a century earlier, and even some years later, when de Wolfe and Gwyn had been fighting there, Henry de Furnellis was still a well-known figure in that bloody campaign.

The coroner took a sip of wine and found it to be a good Bordeaux red – the new sheriff was not one to drink common gut-rot and he could well afford to have the superior stuff brought from his town house near the East Gate, where he lived when he was not at his manor near Crediton.

John told him at length about the murdered silversmith from Totnes and the injured survivor lying in St James' Priory. Henry nodded sagely, but made no offer to intervene in the matter, even though technically he was the supreme overseer of law and order in the county.

'You can handle it, de Wolfe, I'm sure!' he boomed in his deep voice. 'Take whatever you need in the way of men. I know Ralph Morin is a good friend of yours, I'll tell him to go along with whatever you want.'

John nodded, well aware of the new sheriff's desire to hand over as much responsibility as he could, but he felt he had to point out a few home truths.

'These next few days will see Morin's men stretched pretty thinly. We'll be lucky to get away without trouble at the tournament – and keeping order in the town will be a job in itself.'

Henry waved his cup dismissively. 'No doubt you'll manage well enough. All my time will be taken up sorting out this bloody mess that de Revelle left behind.' He slapped his other hand on the pile of parchments on the table. 'God knows what schemes he was up to, it will takes months to get to the bottom of it – and I'm dependent on these damned clerks to tell me what it all means.'

For a moment John was tempted to offer him the use of Thomas de Peyne, whose reading, writing and arithmetical skills were superb. Then he thought that with all the extra work that de Furnellis was going to burden him with, he needed to keep all Thomas's help for himself.

The talk moved on to other things, foremost among them the arrangements for the next day's tournament. This was a topic dear to the sheriff's heart, as in his day he had been a keen tourney contestant himself and still followed news of the various big events across the country. Along with the portreeves, he was a prominent member of the council that had brought this contest to Exeter, and was keen to hear what John thought of the preparations at Bull Mead. They discussed this for some time, and John felt himself warming to the new incumbent of the seat opposite. Though he had known him slightly for years, he had never had much to do with Henry officially, but knew him to be a staunch ally of the King, which was good enough for John.

The wine finished, he rose and announced that he was going to seek Ralph Morin to talk about patrolling the city during the rest of the week. As he reached the door, de Furnellis had a last query.

'So what are you going to do about the slaying of this silversmith? It looks bad that a prominent merchant who hires one of our stalls in the fair should straightway get himself robbed and killed!'

De Wolfe shrugged. 'Little I can do until we get some

more information. I'm hoping this servant of his will recover enough to give us some description of his assailants. I'll keep you informed, never fear!'

Outside in the noisy hall, he moved up to the next door and went into the constable's domain, an office that had a more military stamp upon it. There were several tables with benches piled with equipment, and behind one Gabriel, the sergeant of the men-at-arms, was counting out a pile of pike-heads, to be sent down to the workshops in the outer ward to be fixed to their shafts. His craggy face creased even more into a smile of welcome as the coroner entered.

'I hear you are to umpire tomorrow, Sir John,' he said with evident pleasure. 'Any hope of you taking a turn yourself? That's a fine destrier you've got in Odin!'

John shook his head sadly. 'The last time I took lance and shield, I had my dear old stallion Bran killed under me – and got my own leg broken into the bargain.'

Gabriel scowled at the memory. 'But you were fighting an evil bastard with no sense of honour, Crowner. Tomorrow it would be a fair, friendly contest.'

De Wolfe smiled wryly. 'That'll be the day, when a joust is friendly, Gabriel! All those youngbloods might not want to kill me, but they damn well want to win – and that can be painful, even fatal!'

The door to the inner chamber opened and the burly figure of Ralph Morin emerged, followed by a soldier stumbling under the weight of an armful of wooden cudgels. The other room was supposed to be a bedchamber for the constable, but Morin used it for storing weapons, as, having a wife and two children, he lived in a large chamber on the upper floor.

'I'm breaking out some less lethal implements for my men,' he explained. 'We can hardly quell a few drunks with ball-maces or arrows!'

'That's what I came about, Ralph. As we expected,

our new man next door has passed on the responsibility for keeping order to us. Any problems?'

The massive constable pulled at one end of his forked blond beard, a mannerism he had, just as Thomas de Peyne always crossed himself and Gwyn scratched his crotch.

'All the troops will be on the streets for the rest of the week. I've only got two score to defend the whole of Devon, as the King has skimmed off the rest to take to France. But we'll manage well enough.'

For a time they talked about the disposition of the soldiers around the town and especially at the tourney field, where trouble was most likely to arise. They ended with the inevitable jars of ale brought in by one of the men-at-arms, before John made his way back to the gatehouse and climbed the twisting stone staircase in the thickness of the wall to reach his garret at the top. Here he found Gwyn sitting in his usual place, on the sill of the slit window that looked down over the city. He was aimlessly whittling a piece of stick with his dagger as he whistled tunelessly to himself.

'Where's that damned clerk?' demanded the coroner.

'Gone back to St James' Priory to see how that fellow is getting on.'

John nodded – he had forgotten that he had told Thomas to follow the progress of the assault victim.

'The little runt is starting to fret again over this priest business,' commented the Cornishman. The little that could be seen of his ruddy face behind the ginger hair and whiskers carried an unusually serious expression. 'He's been setting great store by this pardon from Winchester, but he's getting anxious now that he's heard nothing more for many weeks.'

De Wolfe shrugged and dropped down on to his bench behind the crude table that served as his desk.

'There's nothing I can do about it, Gwyn. This is entirely a Church matter, and you know how long winded they are about everything except money.'

Belatedly and reluctantly, the Church authorities had recognised Thomas's innocence and promised to reinstate him. So far, nothing more had been heard, and John was well aware that his own ecclesiastical enemies, who resented his faithful adherence to King Richard and his dogged opposition to those who favoured Prince John's scheming to seize the crown, were spitefully dragging their heels over Thomas to annoy him.

'I'll have another word with John de Alençon and John of Exeter,' he said, naming the Archdeacon of Exeter and the Treasurer, who were both King's men. 'But they know the score already, I doubt they can do anything more.'

Gwyn grunted and threw his stick out of the window. 'I know, Crowner, but I just thought I'd tell you. He's a melancholy little bastard at the best of times, and we don't want him chucking himself off the cathedral again.'

Some time before, the clerk had been so depressed over his situation that he had jumped from the roof of the nave, but had miraculously survived without serious injury.

Gwyn clumped away to seek a game of dice in the guardroom below and John reluctantly settled to practise his letters. For a long time he had been trying to learn to read and write, with some tuition from a vicar in the cathedral. Thomas, who would have been a far better teacher, had given up trying to help him, as de Wolfe was very sensitive about the process, which he felt was rather effeminate for an old warrior and former Crusader. His devotion to the task was sporadic, as he had no great incentive, and his progress was painfully slow. In truth, the process bored him and his attention

71

span was poor. After an hour, much of which he spent
gazing blankly at the sliver of sky visible through the
window, he abruptly pushed back his bench, grabbed
his cloak and clattered down the stairs to the open air.

The fair was now in full swing as de Wolfe pushed his
way down the central lane between the stalls. It was
crowded with people, jostling each other to get a better
look at the goods on offer and dodging the handcarts,
barrows and porters that were bringing new merchandise to the booths and carting away larger purchases
made by customers. There was a constant roar of sound,
compounded of the cries of vendors, shouted offers
from buyers, the clatter of hawker's rattles and the
excited buzz of chatter and gossip. Jugglers and acro-
bats performed between the stalls, sheets of cloth
spread before them to catch stray half-pennies.
Musicians, singly and in groups, performed on the
sackbut, shalmes and cornet, in the expectation of a
few half-pennies being thrown on to the threadbare
cloaks spread hopefully in front of them. Minstrels and
ballad singers, some good, some bad, added to the
cacophony, and as John neared the makeshift stage at
the centre of the fair a new collection of sounds assailed
his ears.

On the platform, a miracle play was being
performed, and he stopped for a few moments at the
edge of the crowd, his height allowing him to see over
their heads. This one was being enacted by clerics from
the cathedral and appeared to represent the temptation of Adam in the Garden of Eden. Several vicars
stood around the edges of the backdrop, on which was
painted a crude forest. They held flaming torches,
smoking with incense wafting out to the awe-struck
audience. A garish tree, made from wood and canvas,
stood in the centre, and the actors were posturing

around this in exaggerated poses. One was Adam, dressed in a tattered leopard skin, and another was dressed as the Devil, his face covered by a snake-like mask. Both were recognisable as secondaries, apprentice priests under the age of twenty-four, which was the minimum age for ordination. On the other side of the apple tree stood a young chorister in female dress, taking the part of Eve, as no women were allowed to appear in dramatic performances.

As John watched, the three actors went through the motions of the Genesis story, with the wicked serpent tempting Adam with a large red-painted wooden apple. They made no sound, apart from stomping around the hollow stage, but a loud, high-pitched commentary was delivered by a robed vicar, who stood at a lectern to one side, reading from a manuscript book, relating the tale as the players went through the motions. He spoke mainly in French, which many understood, but with some English thrown in, as the idea of these performances was to enlighten the common throng in their own language. De Wolfe thought it ridiculous that all church services, apart from sermons, were delivered in Latin, which was incomprehensible to the bulk of the congregation. The Bible, the Vulgate of St Jerome, was also in Latin, apart from a few fragmentary vernacular copies, so even if the faithful could read, they would not be able to understand a word if they only had English.

During the few minutes that he stood there, some of the audience began to drift away, for they had either seen it many times before or preferred the pageants put on by the guilds, which were usually more spectacular and often dealt with secular topics, rather than the well-worn biblical themes that the priests provided to drive home their messages of piety and morality. John himself soon tired of the show and walked on down through the lower part of the fairground. The silversmith's stall was deserted, all the stock taken away for safe-keeping by the two assistants. He knew that one had gone back to Totnes to tell Scrope's family of the tragedy and arrange for collection of the body as soon as the inquest was over. The other man was waiting in his lodgings until the coroner told him he was needed.

John again cut across to Magdalen Street and went on to Bull Mead, where there was now more activity than there had been that morning. All the erection work on the stand and the tents was finished and many more coloured pennants were flying bravely around the jousting arena. A number of knights and their squires were riding up and down the field, trying out the feel of the turf and practising the handling of their lances and shields, though today they wore no armour or helmets.

Behind the makeshift platforms for the more privileged spectators, several tilts had been set up in an area reserved for the contestants. These were crude mechanical targets for the combatants to try out their skills, normally used for training young men in the art of jousting.

John watched with a critical eye as several excited, sweating youths galloped their horses towards these devices. One consisted of a long cross-arm pivoted horizontally on a post. From one end hung a shield and on the other a sack full of sand. As the coroner watched with a sardonic grin on his face, he saw a young man charging his heavy horse at the tilt, yelling at the top of his voice, his lance lowered and his shield held before his chest. He rammed the target with his blunted point and ducked, but he miscalculated, and as the beam swung the sack came around violently and struck him on the back of his neck, knocking him clean out of his saddle.

There was raucous laughter from a group of his friends watching the debacle and as the youth picked himself up from the dried mud he screamed abuse at them and stalked across to punch the ringleader in the face. A scuffle began immediately, but broke up as two stewards and a couple of men-at-arms began yelling at them. De Wolfe knew that this was the sort of bad-tempered high spirits that could readily develop into a full-scale riot if not nipped in the bud, and he hoped that Ralph Morin would have enough men down here tomorrow to keep the peace.

He spent almost an hour on the field, watching the preparations and viewing the practice bouts with an experienced eye. The older knights were naturally more expert, many of them spending much of their time away from the battlefield going around the tournaments. Some had come from as far afield as France, the Low Countries and even Germany, all in search of winnings in the form of horses and armour. There would be no chance of ransom money in a small tourney like this, as there were no mock battles like those allowed near Salisbury and the other official tournament fields, but the professional jousters filled in between these events by visiting as many of the smaller events as they could manage.

A number of old soldiers were standing around the edge of the field, some of them aged and crippled in past battles. They were content to study these young men going through their paces, and watched with critical but dreamy eyes, seeing themselves long ago, when their joints were still supple and their eyesight keen. John stood for a while talking to them, realising that he too would soon approach their condition, a spectator with only memories and scars to remind him of his former prowess.

Then he shook his head angrily, telling himself that

there was plenty of strength left in his arm and iron in his soul, sufficient to show these callow youths a thing or two! He stalked off and, as if to confirm to himself his own virility, directed his steps purposefully towards the Bush Inn, where a pretty young woman waited to prove that senility and impotence were still well in the future.

Sir John de Wolfe spent a pleasant hour in Nesta's small room, a corner of the loft partitioned off from the rows of penny mattresses that were fully booked every night for the duration of the fair. They made relaxed, languorous love, the grim-faced coroner becoming a different man in the company of his amorous mistress. His lean, dark face softened and his eyes sparkled as he kissed and cuddled her – or '*cwtched*' her, as they said in Welsh, for the pair always spoke in the Celtic tongue that was her first language and the one that John had learned at his mother's knee, for she was also of Welsh stock. Her mother had been Cornish, but her father was Welsh, so half of John's blood was Celtic in origin. Even Gwyn spoke this 'language of heaven' with them, much to Thomas de Peyne's annoyance, for the western Welsh of Cornwall was almost identical with that of Wales, and quite similar to that of the Bretons across the Channel.

In the early evening they made their way down the ladder again, as Nesta claimed that such a busy night needed her attendance to make sure that her girls and Edwin were satisfying her customers' wants for food and drink. The taproom was crowded, the regulars being outnumbered by the many strangers who were attending the fair. The renowned food of the Bush was much in demand, and Nesta had hired an extra ale-maid and a kitchen skivvy for these hectic few days. The one-eyed potman had still managed to keep John's favourite bench and small table free beside the hearth, in which an autumn fire was now glowing from a circle of logs arranged like the spokes of a wheel.

The coroner sat there chatting to various acquaintances, as he contentedly downed a large pot of ale and later ate his way through a thick trencher covered in slices of roast pork and fried onions, with a pewter dish of boiled beans on the side. Life seemed tolerably good at the moment, with both his stomach and his loins satisfied. The only cloud on his horizon was the thought of his brother-in-law sitting at his own table in Martin's Lane, but he could hardly deny his own wife's right to entertain her only brother, as long as John was not forced to be present.

As dusk began to fall, Edwin went around the noisy, smoke-filled taproom and lit the tallow dips that sat in sconces around the walls. Candles were too expensive for most people, so small dishes of mutton fat with a floating wick were used to give a feeble light. Soon afterwards, a small figure entered and approached de Wolfe's table, diffidently sliding on to the stool opposite. Thomas de Peyne was not over-fond of taverns, his priestly upbringing leading him to consider them dens of iniquity. Even after a year in the coroner's service, he rarely entered one except when his duties demanded. This was one such occasion, as he had some news for his master.

'Crowner, I've been to the priory, as you commanded,' he announced in his rather squeaky voice. 'That man Terrus has recovered his senses – in fact, he's almost back to normal!'

John's black brows rose, as he had not been expecting the silversmith's servant to recover this quickly, if at all.

'Has he said anything useful?'

'The infirmarian allowed me into his cell for a few moments. Terrus told me that two men on horseback attacked them, and although he recollects nothing after being struck on the head, he now remembers something about them.'

John felt that Gwyn's long-windedness was rubbing off on his clerk, but held his impatience in check. 'And what was that?'

'He claims that they were not ruffianly outlaws – though they would hardly be on horses if they were. Though not gentlemen, he felt they were a better class of body servants – or maybe some manner of squires to lesser gentry. They wore plain but good tunics and breeches and their horses had decent harnesses.'

'Would he recognise them again, if he saw them?'

Thomas nodded emphatically. 'I asked him that question directly and he seemed in no doubt about one of them.'

De Wolfe glowered into his ale as he drank the last drop. It was a damned nuisance that the fair would finish in two days' time, for the chances were that these men had arrived in the area to attend it and would most likely be gone as soon as the fair ended.

'How soon will this fellow be up and about?' he demanded.

The clerk's peaky face brightened. 'Remarkably, by tomorrow, according to the monks who are caring for him. He has a constitution like an ox, they said, and is already off his pallet and demanding to be allowed to return home to Totnes. They will be glad to be rid of him, as he's eating too much and upsetting their quiet life in the priory.'

The coroner considered this for a moment. 'Then if I send Gwyn and a hired horse down there tomorrow, would they release him to us? I need him to identify the assailants, if he can.'

Thomas nodded. 'I'm sure they will, Crowner. Apart

from his being knocked senseless and dumped in the river, his other injuries are no threat to his life.'

Gwyn would have left the city for his hut in St Sidwells by now, to beat the closing of the gates at curfew, but John felt there would be plenty of time for him to give his orders first thing the next morning. Thomas made his escape from the alehouse to return to his free lodgings in one of the canon's houses in the close, where he had the use of a thin mattress in the servants' quarters. John sat on in the Bush for a long while, being content to have Nesta's company intermittently, between her bustling about between the patrons and haranguing her servants over the business of keeping her customers filled with food and ale.

Eventually, John judged that his odious brother-in-law must surely have left his house and, after a final discreet cuddle with Nesta at the back door, he left for home and the inevitable verbal skirmish with his wife.

On Wednesday, his duties at the tournament did not begin until noon, so he had ample time to dispatch Gwyn to St James' Priory. With him he sent a spare palfrey from Andrew's yard, the livery stable in Martin's Lane, with orders to bring Terrus back to Bull Mead.

De Wolfe then walked up to Rougemont to see whether any more deaths, rapes or other tragedies had been reported overnight to the guardroom, which was always manned. News of these events came in to the coroner from the city constables and from the manor-reeves of outlying villages. When the coroner's system had been introduced in September the previous year, there were supposed to have been three such officials appointed for the county, but only two could be found willing to undertake the unpaid work. Within a few weeks, the knight covering the north of Devon was killed when he fell from his horse, and it was only recently that a replacement had been found. John still had to cover a huge area in the southern half of the county, and there was no doubt that cases in the more distant villages often went unreported, as the distance involved in riding to Exeter was too great for many manor-bailiffs and reeves to contemplate.

This morning, the guardroom had nothing to offer, for which John was thankful. Sergeant Gabriel and most of the men-at-arms were already patrolling the fair and the city streets, so the castle was almost deserted. He found Thomas upstairs, busily writing out copies of inquest proceedings, executions, ordeals, amercements, attachments and other legal documents, which all had to be duplicated to present to the King's justices when they next came to Exeter. These judicial visits were very irregular, even though the judges were supposed to appear every quarter.

The Commissioners of Gaol Delivery managed to get around their circuit several times a year, to hear cases and clear the prisons of captives, either by hanging them, fining them or acquitting them. Much less often, the Eyre of Assize trundled along, with four senior members of the Curia Regis, to hear the most serious cases – and even more infrequently, the great General Eyre arrived. This looked into the more weighty matters of the administration of the county, a nightmare for the sheriff, especially the recently deposed one, who had had to cover up his embezzlement as best he could.

But today there were no legal problems for Sir John de Wolfe, and he retraced his steps back down Castle Hill and made his way through the crowded streets to the fairground. Business was in full swing, and though he was happy to see soldiers and stewards patrolling the lanes between the booths, there seemed to be no trouble, apart from an odd scuffle and the occasional drunk stumbling to upset a tableful of goods.

At one point everyone stood aside to gape and shout and clap as a colourful procession squeezed down the central lane. This was a guild pageant, put on by the craft organisations that controlled the many trades in the city. Several flat carts, covered in white and coloured cloth, were pulled by teams of apprentices to show off the tableaux displayed on these mobile stages. One was of a mock crusade, with half a dozen knights wielding wooden swords and axes upon twice their number of 'Saracens'. Again these were all apprentices, arrayed in garish costumes, accompanied by much yelling and screaming as the Christians vanquished the Moors.

Another cart had tumblers wheeling about alongside jugglers, a fire-eater and a sword-swallower. The last float was a sop to the ecclesiastical establishment, being a re-enactment of the John the Baptist story. While a parish priest shouted the story from a parchment, a tall bearded man in a white robe stood in a River Jordan made from a horse trough full of water, enthusiastically dousing a trio of the youngest apprentices with a pitcher normally used for ale. At the end of the wagon, another young man dressed in oriental female attire with a blond wig and padded bosoms portrayed Salome, holding aloft a tray on which was a realistically bloody severed head.

As John watched, the crowd cheered their appreciation and threw coins on to the carts, alms for the guilds to donate to the poorhouse near the West Gate. When the parade had passed, he followed the crowd of urchins that capered behind it until it reached the centre, where another miracle play was in progress, a competitor to the more popular guild spectacle.

As he walked past, John turned his head to look and saw that today they were performing 'The Wise and Foolish Virgins', again with a bevy of young choristers dressed as girls – in fact, several of the more comely ones were impossible to distinguish from females. As they tripped about the stage, over-dramatically posturing with their lamps and oil vessels, a vicar-choral chanted a commentary in verse, based on the Gospel parable.

But de Wolfe, who had seen them all before, loped on and made his way back to a form of entertainment that suited him better, on the turf of Bull Mead. The area was now crowded, compared to his visit yesterday, as the contests had been in progress for several hours. The stand was filled with the more exalted spectators, colourful in a variety of costumes, including quite a few women. They were by no means all dewy-eyed maidens come to wave a handkerchief at their champions, for a good half were the solid wives of burgesses, knights and several barons who had come to watch the bouts. Along the ropes marking off the battle area was a straggling line of lesser spectators, many from the city itself, together with supporters and gambling men from the Devon countryside and several other counties. As John arrived, a series of trumpet blasts from a herald marked the end of the morning's bouts and the field was cleared for workmen and boys to go out to shovel up piles of dung and to knock the worst of the hacked-up turf back into shape, after the pounding it had had from so many heavy hoofs.

John made his way to the recet, the contestants' area behind the stand, which was now crowded with men and horses. Both there and at the opposite end of the ground, where the circular tents of other competitors stood, he saw several men prostrate on the ground, some being tended by their squires, others lying groaning under horse blankets. At least they all seemed alive, he thought, as he saw no still bodies with a cloak thrown over their heads. He made his way to where a florid-faced man was talking to a pair of stewards, all

with red bands tied around their arms. Lord Guy
Ferrars broke off his conversation to greet the coroner.

'Good day, de Wolfe. You're early, but none the less
welcome.'

Ferrars, as the most influential baron in the district,
was overseeing the tournament, being convenor of
the committee that was organising it. A gruff, no-
nonsense man, with considerable wealth and estates
scattered all over England, he had the ear of many in
the King's Council and made a good ally, as well as a
bad enemy.

'I thought I'd get my eye in by watching a few bouts
before I start my duties,' John replied. 'Have there
been any problems so far?'

Ferrars shook his head, a pugnacious globe set on a
thick neck.

'Nothing of importance. A few cracked heads and a
couple of broken arms. These were the youngsters this
morning, with more spunk than sense! The serious
men will be on this afternoon, which is why we asked
you to keep an eye on things, being the most experienced fighter in Devon.'

This was a rare compliment, coming from the usually
taciturn and aggressive baron, and John could not
suppress a small glow of pride warming him from
within. They talked for a few moments about the
morning's events and the prospects for the later, more
serious contests, then walked over to a tent where some
food and ale were laid out for the stewards and judges.
As he would miss his dinner at home, John laid into a
few capon's legs, mutton pasties, hard-boiled eggs, fresh
bread and cheese, washed down with an ale markedly
inferior to Nesta's brew at the Bush.

'Who's likely to win the most loot today, d'you think?'
he asked Guy Ferrars, as they chewed and drank.

'A dozen good men in the running, I'd say,' replied

the other. 'There's a French fellow here, Reginald de Charterai. It seems he's a professional, going around all the tournaments both here and in France.' He wiped his bristly moustache with his fingers. 'Damned odd, when you think of it! Our King and thousands of our soldiers are fighting the bloody French year in, year out – yet one of their knights comes over here to win our money. Could be a damned spy for all we know, by Christ!'

John shrugged. 'Our men do exactly the same – they have far more tourneys in France than we do here and plenty of Englishmen take part.'

Ferrars grunted as he grabbed a couple more chicken thighs.

'I suppose so. War seems to make little difference to trade or learning. My sister's son has just gone to Paris to study some useless subject called philosophy, instead of staying home to hunt and learn how to use a lance properly!'

John brought him back to the subject of potential winners on the field.

'This Frenchman is tipped to do well, then?'

Guy waved a hand at some other men standing near by, who were rather furtively exchanging bags that clinked with coin.

'Plenty of money being wagered on him, I hear. It's not only the contestants who make or lose in this game, as you well know.' He tapped the side of his fleshy nose with a forefinger. 'The bloody priests pretend to abhor betting, but they're damned hypocrites, for I know for a fact that several canons not half a mile from here have got quite a few marks riding on the winners today.'

De Wolfe grinned, as he knew as well as Ferrars that though wagering was officially forbidden, half the people on the field today would be gambling between themselves, either for a penny or a few pounds. Many a time he had done the same himself, though today his sense of honour prevented him having a flutter, as he was one of the judges.

'Any others favoured for a win?' he asked.

The baron scratched the iron-grey stubble on his cheek as he considered.

'There's Thomas de Cirencestre, he's usually good for a few overthrows, though maybe he's getting on in years now. And Robert de Northcote from Lyme, he did well at Wilton a few months back. Of course, we've got the gang from Peverel as usual. The old man got himself killed earlier this year. He was a cunning old devil, God knows – but his sons are hungry fighters. I've no doubt there's a few wagers on Hugo and his brother Ralph today.'

John knew the Peverels by sight and recalled that they were not the most popular lords of the Devon manors, but if they were doughty fighters, then their other faults were none of his business.

The bouts had temporarily ceased as most of the knights and their squires wanted to eat and drink before the second half of the day began. When John went out of the meal tent, he could see that many people were seated or sprawled on the grass, drinking from flasks and skins and munching on bread and meat produced from their saddlebags or bought from the several stalls set up well back from the boundary ropes by enterprising traders.

The respite was as much for their horses as for the men, as the heavy destriers were being cared for by squires, varlets and grooms at each end of the ground. They were being fed oats and hay and watered from wooden troughs filled by a succession of small boys with buckets brought from nearby wells. But in less than an hour, the trumpet sounded again, discordant blasts giving a five-minute warning. There was a groundswell of movement, as spectators climbed back into the stand or moved towards the boundary ropes, some already fingering purses in anticipation of the next wager.

John made his way to the centre point of the combat area, meeting the other umpire for the afternoon, Peter de Cunitone, a knight from a small manor near Ashburton, farther down the county on the edge of Dartmoor. He knew him slightly, having been at a siege with him in France ten years earlier, where he had been wounded in the leg. A much older man than John, he had lost most of his hair and had such a ruddy complexion that the coroner suspected that he was too fond of brandy wine for his own good. But today he seemed sober and alert, and after discussing the way they were going to handle the events, they retired to stand one on either side of the arena, at about the halfway mark. John was on the side nearest to the herald and trumpeter and he gave them a signal that they were ready for combat to start again.

A wailing blast produced a flurry of activity in the recet, and a moment later two horsemen cantered out of the gate alongside the viewing stand, to the accompaniment of shouts and a few jeers from the spectators, who now numbered several hundred. They rode up to John, one of the destriers nervously jumping about and tugging sideways as his rider swore and tried to pacify him. Each man had a squire who ran behind and stood anxiously inside the ropes – they were the only persons other than the judges permitted within the combat area and were allowed to assist their lords if they came to grief. The contestants confirmed their names to the coroner and he called these out to the herald, who was a clerk from one of the fulling mills, able to read and write. The man checked the names on his parchment register and nodded agreement, then in a resounding voice announced them to the crowd.

De Wolfe waved the two fighters away and they wheeled about and pranced to opposite ends of the ground, their long wooden lances held upright, a coloured pennant flying from near the tip. Both were young men, as far as could be seen under their basin-shaped iron helmets with the long nasal guards.

The two horsemen turned at the ends of the field and waited, stiffly erect in their deep wooden saddles. Their long mail hauberks glinted in the sun, thanks to their varlets' efforts with dry sand and scrubbing brush to remove the pernicious rust. John raised his hand again and the unmelodious trumpet sounded for the last time. As if joined by an invisible cord, the two jousters simultaneously lowered their lances to the horizontal, pulled their shields stiffly across their chests and dug their spurs into their stallions' sides.

Slowly at first, but with rapidly gathering momentum, the big beasts pounded down the field, to the rising shouts and cheers of the spectators.

As they closed, there was a crash as the lances struck the leather-covered wood of each opponent's shield. A fragment of one flew off as both men rocked in their saddles, but then they were past each other with both men still astride their horses. To the accompaniment of more yells and cheers, they turned to face each other, one man making a tight circle, the other going wider to keep up his speed for the return pass. Again they charged each other, and this time the faster knight triumphed. His blunted lance took the other's shield squarely at the central boss and the force tipped the rider backward over the cantle of his saddle. He managed to grab it with one hand to break his fall, and hanging on the reins for a few more seconds stopped him from crashing to the ground. As soon as he began to be dragged along the turf he let go and his horse thundered on alone, though its training had taught it to stop as soon as possible.

The other man pulled his own mount around and trotted back towards the defeated knight, wary as to what he would do next. The options were for the downed man to submit – or to pull out his sword and prepare to fight on foot. As John and Peter de Cunitone advanced to get a closer view, the matter was settled quickly. The fallen knight pushed himself up, but then rested on his knees in the dirt, his head bowed in surrender.

Gallantly, the victor slid from his horse and helped his opponent to his feet, as the crowd either cheered or groaned according to whether they had won or lost their wagers.

The defeated knight offered his sword to the winner, hilt first, as a token of submission, though later he would have to hand over his armour and horse as well. As they walked together back to the recet, the trumpet sounded again and the herald yelled out the names once more, as well as the identity of the victor. As they passed the stand, both men saluted the grandees there by bowing their heads and putting a fisted arm across their chest, before vanishing into a tent for a welcome jug of ale.

'At least they behaved with good grace,' said John to the other judge, as they met briefly in the middle of the field.

De Cunitone nodded his polished head. 'Let's hope the rest will do the same, but it's a bit much to expect.'

They went back to their positions and the process was repeated with the next pair of contestants. This time, neither was unhorsed, but on the third pass the lance of one splintered in the middle and he threw it down in disgust. Sliding from his saddle, he hauled out his broadsword, three feet of tempered iron, and waited for his adversary to do the same. They closed and, with blows that raised sparks, hammered away at each other for several minutes. The tips of the weapons were rounded and the edges of the blade were also supposed to be blunted – but as these swords were designed for hacking rather than thrusting, the state of the tips was not all that relevant. As de Wolfe came nearer, he suspected that both men had failed to blunt the sides of their blades, but this was such a common ploy that he was not going to put it to the test.

The contest was soon over, as the heavier man, holding a shield with a black raven upon it, sidestepped and caught the other a resounding blow on his right arm, which made his weapon spin away like a whirling stick. He clutched his arm and yelled, but the chain links saved him from a wound, though no doubt he would have a painful bruise for a week. In the next contest, one young man was knocked from his destrier by a lance strike in the centre of the chest. He was saved from serious injury by the oblong metal plate laced over his hauberk to protect the heart. Again he would have a massive bruise there, which would have been even worse but for the shock-absorber effect of the gambeson, a padded shirt of quilted linen stuffed with loose wool, that every knight wore under his chain mail.

The afternoon passed in a similar fashion, with a bout every fifteen minutes or so. The results were clear cut in most instances, though one pair of jousters, a Fleming and a Breton, were reduced to bad-tempered fisticuffs when both lost their swords in a scrimmage. The two adjudicators had to forcibly pull them apart and dismiss them from the ground without any result being awarded, to the boos and jeers of the watching crowd, whose wagers were rendered null and void.

As the sun began to slip down the sky, the last few bouts were announced. One was between Ralph Peverel, of Sampford Peverel near Tiverton, and an older knight from Warwickshire, who was a regular on the tourney circuit. Much to everyone's surprise, Ralph unhorsed the Midlander at the first pass, knocking him clean off his destrier to crash on to the hard ground. He was knocked unconscious and his squire, who ran on to the field, had to call for men from the recet to bring a long board to carry him back to the tents, while the betting men were muttering at this win by an outsider with such long odds.

The next joust, almost the last of the day, was the one the crowd had been waiting for all afternoon, ever since the ballot had chosen who was to fight with whom. This was a contest between Hugo Peverel, the elder brother of the previous contestant, and the Frenchman, Reginald de Charterai.

Both had an impressive track record of wins and much money was being staked on the outcome. Hugo was tipped as a likely successor to his late father William, who had been a steady winner over many years, until his untimely death at Wilton. De Charterai, though a foreigner, had appeared at so many tourneys in England that he was very well known and his prowess was common knowledge to all those who followed the contests.

The trumpet brayed and the two men trotted out from the recet, their huge horses tossing their heads in excited anticipation of a few moments' glory in front of an appreciative audience. Hugo Peverel went down to the far end and waited expectantly.

The herald, now getting hoarse after a day's yelling, gave their titles, and at the second blast the thunder of hoofs began over turf that was now decidedly the worse for wear after more than forty great stallions had hammered across it that day. The first clash of lance upon shield left both riders upright, as these experts were adept at angling their shields to deflect much of the force to the side.

The second pass was equally ineffective in unhorsing either Hugo or Reginald, and they galloped past each other quite intact. Hugo was the bigger man, broad within his byrnie of iron links, his scratched shield carrying a crude emblem of two white chevrons on a blue background.

De Charterai was taller and thinner, his spine as stiff as a fire-iron. He wore no mail hood or aventail, trusting to the code of honour to safeguard his head from attack. Black hair peeped from beneath the rim of his helmet, matching the colour of a thin, sloping moustache that adorned his rather sardonic face. The pair wheeled around for the third pass, lowered their lances and charged. This time the Frenchman was able to vanquish his opponent, as with a grinding crunch his lance-tip hit Hugo's shield at just the right spot to neutralise the attempted deflection and the impact pushed the Devon man sideways off his saddle.

The experienced fighter grabbed the saddle-edge and girth and let himself down lightly, hanging on to his shield, but losing his grip on the long lance. There was a roar from the onlookers as he fell to his knees, but he was up on his feet again long before de Charterai could slow his destrier and pull him around to canter back. It was obvious that Hugo was going to make a fight of it, with his reputation and his property at risk from the foreigner. The latter slowed to a halt, dismounted and laid his lance on the ground, as his squire ran out to take his horse's reins and lead him away. Hugo's riderless horse had ran on several hundred paces and was being retrieved by his own squire farther down the field.

Hugo faced the Frenchman and hauled out his sword, which made a metallic rasp as it slid from the scabbard hanging from the baldric slung around his shoulder. De Wolfe watched keenly as Reginald gave a slight bow and pulled out his own weapon. The two men advanced on each other warily, shields held up by the left forearms pushed through the straps on the back. Their heavy swords were sloped downward until they got within striking range. Then, as they circled each other, the points came up, and with a yell Hugo lunged forward and tried a straight thrust past the edge of Reginald's shield. The Frenchman parried it easily and in turn brought down a slashing blow, which sent chips of wood flying from the edge of Peverel's shield. Time and again they slashed and smote, but they were evenly matched and neither could get past the other's guard. The spectators yelled their approval at this bonus to their expected entertainment.

Striking at the head was forbidden by the commonly accepted rules of chivalry, so the ambition of each man was to make a strike either with his sword point against his opponent's chest or belly or a heavy slash against any of his limbs. These would count as a win, even though the chain mail of the padded hauberks would hopefully protect against any serious injury. The two judges hovered a few yards away, far enough not to get in the way of the fighters, but close enough to check for a vital strike.

Then an unusual thing happened.

Hugo Peverel, the more aggressive of the two, gave another furious shout and stepped forward to smash his blue shield against the green of de Charterai's. Tilting it away, he lunged with his blade, aiming for the heart, but the other knight swung sideways and, as Hugo's sword arm came within reach, slashed down upon it.

The blunted edge struck the back of the Devon man's hand just below the wrist, and although he was wearing chain-link mittens the impact of the heavy steel temporarily paralysed his fingers and his sword went spinning away. The foreigner gave his own excited yell of triumph and stood back, clearly the victor. Both de Wolfe and Peter de Cunitone threw up their hands as a signal for a win and there was a trumpet blast in response.

It seemed, however that Hugo de Peverel, now in a vile temper, had other ideas.

Instead of kneeling in submission, as convention required, he cast about for his sword, apparently intending to pick it up again. But it had fallen almost at the feet of his adversary and so, to John's indignant surprise, he bounded sideways and snatched up his lance, from where it had fallen when he was unhorsed. With a roar of defiance, Hugo hefted it near its centre, brought his powerful arm back and threw it straight at Reginald de Charterai's head. Astonished at this unheard-of behaviour, the Frenchman stood stock still for an instant, then his well-honed instinct for self-preservation snapped into action and he brought up his shield before his face. The blunted tourney lance struck it with a loud thump and fell to the ground, instead of hitting him between the eyes.

There was immediate chaos on and around the field.

The two judges came running, shouting cries of recrimination. Along the barrier ropes, there was a roar of outrage and yells, boos and hisses rent the air. Even those who had money on Hugo Peverel were disgusted at his blatant disregard of the usual conventions. De Wolfe strode up to the culprit, his face white with anger, closely followed by his fellow adjudicator.

'What in Christ's name d'you think you're doing?' he yelled.

'Have you gone bloody mad?' snapped de Cunitone, hands on hips as he glared at Hugo. Peverel, sweating, red in the face and seething with anger, was far from contrite. 'There's no rule against a man continuing to fight!' he hissed.

'Rule? You've been in more than enough jousts to know what's proper!'

De Wolfe's nose was almost touching Hugo's now and he was in a towering rage. 'You're a knight, damn it, you have a duty to show an example to the squires and younger men. I'm ashamed of you, Peverel!'

Half afraid that he might strike him in his temper, John stepped back and forced himself to signal to the herald forty paces away. The man took the hint, and as the trumpet sounded again he roared at the top of his voice that the bout had been won by Reginald de Charterai.

The man named had remained standing where he was, his face white with shock at this unheard-of breach of conduct by someone who should know better. He said not a word, but turned and walked off stiffly to where his bewildered squire was holding his horse's head. The victor walked his mount back to the enclosure, to the sustained cheers and shouts of congratulation from both the crowd along the ropes and the more aristocratic audience in the stand.

'You had better send your squire to treat with de Charterai over the forfeit of your armour and destrier,' snapped de Cunitone, the contempt obvious in his voice as he spat the words at Hugo Peverel. 'Better keep clear of him yourself, or you might get a punch in the face, which you richly deserve!'

With that, the second judge turned and marched

after the coroner, who was making his way back to speak to the herald. Left alone in the middle of the field, the lord of Sampford Peverel glowered at everything within sight, unwilling to admit even to himself that he had seriously transgressed the unwritten codes of chivalry.

ChAPTER FOUR

In which Crowner John intervenes in a fight

The last few jousts following the Peverel debacle were something of an anti-climax, and less than an hour later everyone was streaming away from Bull Mead, heading for either home or the alehouses. They had plenty to talk about, and the Bush Inn was one of the places where the gossip was most rife. At his table near the hearth, John de Wolfe was relating the story to Nesta and Gwyn, with Edwin the potman and a few regular patrons standing behind them, their ears flapping to hear the details from the horse's mouth, so to speak.

'I've always heard that Hugo was a nasty piece of work,' growled Gwyn, over the rim of his pottery jug of ale. 'Terrible temper, they say. He was suspected of beating some poor sod of a groom near to death last year, for some trifling fault.'

The coroner's officer had not long arrived back from St James' Priory, though John had expected him much earlier. It seemed that the silversmith's assistant had suffered a dizzy attack after rising from his sickbed and the monks had insisted on his resting for a few more hours before leaving on the hired horse.

'How well do you know this Hugo?' asked Nesta, sitting close to John, her arm linked comfortably with his.

'I know little about him, except to recognise him by sight. After today, I don't want to acknowledge him at all, unless I have to in the line of duty.'

'He was in Outremer with us, wasn't he?' asked Gwyn, vigorously scratching his unruly mop of red hair where the lice were irritating his scalp.

'I recall that he was there briefly, but never in our formation, thank God. I believe he arrived at Acre at the same time as the King, but on a different ship from us. I never saw him in the Holy Land, but we have to give him the credit of being a Crusader, I suppose.'

'I heard a rumour that he left within a couple of months and went back to Cyprus,' persisted Gwyn.

'The other fellow, the Frenchman, he was there as well,' piped up Edwin, who, as an old soldier, was keen on any gossip that had a military flavour. 'He was with Philip's army at Acre, so they say.'

Gwyn scowled into his pot. 'They soon went home with their tails between their legs,' he said with unusual spite. The Church and the French were the Cornishman's two pet hates. De Wolfe could understand his aversion to their French enemies, but he had never discovered the cause of his anethema to all things ecclesiastical.

'What happened after the joust?' asked Nesta. 'This Reginald could hardly have been happy about the outcome.'

'Well, he won twice over – unhorsing Peverel and then striking his sword from his grasp. It was a fair fight until Hugo lost his temper and threw a lance at him.'

'And at his bloody head, too, by your account,' growled Gwyn, disgusted at this breach of knightly etiquette.

'So they just walked off together?' persisted Nesta, always curious about people's behaviour.

'Hardly together, the Frenchman couldn't bring

himself even to look at Peverel. He stalked away, white around the gills, and left Hugo glowering around like a baited bull. I presume their squires had to get together to arrange the hand-over of the winnings.'

'De Charterai will get his armour, his sword and his horse and harness, the usual loot for a winner,' added Gwyn, with evident satisfaction.

The landlady shook her head in wonder at the strange things that the aristocracy got up to. She had never heard tell of such goings-on in Wales, though it was true that some of the princes and heads of household were starting to ape the Normans in many of their ways.

Eventually, the group exhausted the talk about the tournament and the fair, moving on to other matters. Nesta pressed John to take some food, but he excused himself on the grounds that he had to attend a feast that evening in the Guildhall, given by the tournament council in celebration of the day's jousting. All the participating knights would be there, as well as the organising officials and the adjudicators – John was intrigued and a little apprehensive as to whether Hugo Peverel and Reginald de Charterai would be present. Though he had seen little of Matilda these past few days, he knew full well that she would insist on attending, as any event where the great and the good of the county were present was a magnet to her ambitions of social advancement. The dismissal of her brother from the shrievalty had certainly dampened her aggressive social climbing, but he knew she would turn out for an event such as this.

The tavern was even busier than usual this evening and the big taproom was crammed to capacity, with drinkers standing shoulder to shoulder, jostling those sitting at the few tables and benches set on the rush-covered earth floor. With the fire going and a full house, the atmosphere could almost be cut like a cheese, redolent with wood smoke, spilt ale, sweat and unwashed bodies. When Nesta and the potman had been called away to settle some domestic crisis, John turned to Gwyn to talk business.

'You took this Terrus fellow to his lodging, you say?'

His officer nodded, wiping ale from his luxuriant moustache. 'He was a bit weak after his ride, though it was no great distance. I left him with the silversmith who stayed behind on your orders.'

'We'll see him in the morning. I'll have to hold this inquest later, as the body won't keep much longer, even though the weather's fairly cool. And the family will be up from Totnes, wanting to take it for burial.'

Gwyn nodded. 'I'll round up those men from the quay-side and a few others for a jury – though I can't see us getting very far towards any conclusion. The bastards that killed the merchant could be in the next county by now.'

De Wolfe swallowed the last of his ale and stood up. 'I'm hoping they may still be hanging about at this fair, so maybe we'll get lucky tomorrow. We need that Terrus fellow to be out and about with his eyes open, to see if he can spot them. Now I'm off home to get ready for this damned feast.'

He waved a goodbye to Nesta, who was standing across the room with arms akimbo, watching Edwin and one of her regular customers drag a vomiting drunk out through the back door to pitch him into the yard to sober up. John smiled at the thought of such a pretty, affectionate and passionate woman having such an indomitable strength of spirit after all the troubles she had suffered these past few years, and he turned his steps homeward with a glow of pride at having her still love him.

*　　*　　*

The Guildhall was a single large chamber with a high beamed ceiling, entered directly from High Street through an arched dorway. The new stone building had replaced a previous smaller wooden one, needed as Exeter developed its commerce and wealth, mainly due to the wool, cloth and tin industries that were rapidly making it a rich city. But there were many more merchants and crafts than these staple industries, and most had their own guilds to protect the interests of their owners and workers, the Guildhall providing a centre for these organisations. The burgesses elected a pair of portreeves to lead the city council – though there was now talk of having a 'mayor', as in London and a few other cities. These two worthies were already sitting in the centre of the high table as John de Wolfe escorted his wife into the hall. As he had anticipated, Matilda had swiftly raised herself from her depression over her brother's fall from grace. The prospect of an evening among the upper class of the county was too great an attraction for her to miss, especially as she had to put on a good face before her matronly friends from St Olave's, who were the wives of burgesses and some manor-lords who had houses in the city. For Matilda not to lose face and to ride out the gossip and sniggers about her brother, she had to continue to appear in public as before – apparently unconcerned and proud to be the wife of the coroner, the second-most important law officer in the county.

Tonight she had tormented her maid Lucille into dressing her with special care, wrestling her lacklustre hair into two coiled plaits, trapped above each ear in a crespine of gilded mesh. She wore a new kirtle of deep red velvet, held at the waist by a gilt cord, the tassels of which swept the floor, as did the tippets on the cuffs of her ridiculously wide sleeves. Her best mantle of black wool was secured at the left shoulder by a large circular buckle, but she made sure that she pulled the corner of the cloak free from the silver ring as soon they entered the hall, so that her friends could get a good view of her new gown.

By contrast – and to his wife's eternal annoyance – John was dressed as usual in a dull grey tunic under his worn wolfskin cloak. His only gesture to sartorial elegance was the fact that the tunic was brand new and he had had an extra shave before coming, though he was not due for one until the following Saturday. He was the despair of Matilda in many ways, but in her eyes one of his major faults was that he refused to wear even the more restrained fashions, let alone the bright variety of colours sported by many of his acquaintances. She accepted that he would never become a strutting peacock like many other men, especially Hugo de Relaga, but she suspected that John stuck to his funereal garb just to annoy her.

Tonight, as they entered the already crowded hall, they were met by one of the guild servants, and Matilda was overjoyed when he led them to the upper end of the hall. As one of the tournament judges, as well as being coroner, John was awarded a place at the top table, albeit towards one end. His wife was delighted to be able to sit on the slightly raised dais and look down at the three long tables set at right angles below, where all her church cronies were seated, mild envy and a little jealousy evident in their eyes.

The feast was the usual noisy, boisterous occasion with plenty of food and too much drink. As soon as one of the cathedral canons had said grace, there followed a couple of hours of frantic eating, with servants hurrying a continuous succession of courses from the large kitchen hut behind the hall. The hall was crowded and, when laden with dishes, trays and jugs, the servants had to push and shove with ill grace through the narrow spaces between the rows of tables. Their work was made more difficult by uncaring diners getting up and moving around to chat and drink with friends elsewhere in the hall. Many were slightly the worse for drink even before they arrived, and drunken squabbles were to be expected where a crowd of lusty men were gathered, many of them young and full of arrogance. Tonight's assembly was even more volatile, with almost all the knights from the tournament present, half of them flushed with success and winnings, the other half resentful at the loss of both their pride and their accoutrements.

Martha had John de Alençon on her left, the archdeacon being a considerate and intelligent companion, for all his priestly asceticism. Beyond him was Henry de Furnellis, the new sheriff, not a great purveyor of conversation, but an amiable enough fellow on social occasions.

De Wolfe, last but one on the table, had the warden of the guild of tanners on the end next to him, but thankfully he was too devoted to eating and drinking to spend time boring John about the problems of the leather industry. He owned the largest tannery in the city, so was not himself a worker, but he still gave off the distinctive odour of his profession, contributed to by the pits of dog droppings that were used to deflesh the cow hides.

As the meal progressed and the autumn evening faded towards twilight outside, candles and tapers were lit around the room. The level of noise increased steadily as the wine, ale and cider flowed from the casks and wineskins stacked behind the top table. Hugo de Relaga and Guy Ferrars made thankfully short speeches of welcome and commendation for all who had worked hard to make the fair and tournament a success. Wisely, they did this early in the meal, before things got too rowdy and when there was still a chance of some of their audience bothering to listen.

The early courses had been devoured and much of the debris cleared away, the capons, geese, swans, ducks, mutton, fish and part-eaten trenchers all having been reduced to scraps, which were taken out to the street, where a small crowd of beggars were waiting expectantly to scrabble for the leftovers, chasing away the mangy dogs that had the same idea in mind. Now the sweets and puddings were served, together with fruit – mainly apples, pears and some more exotic imports from France, such as figs and oranges. A trio of musicians attempted to entertain the diners, but though they persisted valiantly, they could hardly be heard over the hubbub, and those who could hear them took little notice. The festivities had reached the stage where a few men were staggering out to be sick in the central gutter of High Street, and several more had fallen down senseless with drink, little notice being taken of them by anyone, except their indignant wives.

John's tanner eventually went to sleep across the table, his head on his arms as he snored. The coroner, who had eaten well himself, had little to do except study the crowd below, as Matilda was deep in conversation with his friend the archdeacon, no doubt discussing Church matters, which fascinated his wife even more than the social hierarchy of Devonshire.

As his eyes roved around, he picked out many of the contestants from Bull Mead upon whom he had adjudicated that day. The Frenchman, Reginald de Charterai, was just below him, near the top of the central spur table, talking animatedly with a fat merchant who had a thriving trade in woollen cloth, exporting it to Flanders and Cologne. De Wolfe's observations had long ago confirmed that his brother-in-law, the former sheriff, was not present. Although Richard de Revelle had a thick skin, John thought it unlikely that he would show himself at public functions in Exeter for some time yet, until the immediate memory of his disgrace began to fade.

But as he looked around, he was surprised to see another face, someone who, unlike de Revelle, seemed sufficiently immune to recent scandal to present himself at the feast. At the farther end of the right-hand line of trestles, his back to the aisle where de Charterai sat, was Hugo Peverel, alongside a younger man whose strong facial resemblance suggested that he was one of his brothers, presumably the same one who had had the successful bout this afternoon, though then the helmet and chain mail around the face had made identification difficult. John remembered that the deceased William Peverel had four sons, but he could not recall their names. Like many of his neighbours along the table, Peverel was well advanced in his cups, but he seemed in no danger of either passing out, retching or sleeping. In fact, the reverse seemed true, as he was loudly declaiming about something and banging a fist on the table as he ranted, though over the general clamour in the hall, de Wolfe could hear nothing of what he was saying.

A few moments later, the observant coroner saw that the French knight had risen from his seat and was pushing his way between the rows of revellers to reach the front of the hall, presumably on his way to relieve himself either in the street or the yard behind. As he came level with Hugo's broad back, the coroner fancied that he deliberately turned his head away to avoid any chance of eye contact, but fate was against him. Just as he was passing, a man seated at his own row of tables decided to lurch to his feet, his shoulder jostling Reginald and making him stumble against Hugo Peverel. It was a trivial incident which in any other circumstances would have gone unnoticed, but it distracted Hugo from his harangue to his cronies and he glanced back truculently. When he saw who was standing there, he gave a roar of anger and leapt unsteadily to his feet, knocking over his stool with a crash.

'Haven't you already caused me enough trouble today, you bloody foreigner!' he yelled, giving de Charterai an open-handed shove in the chest which sent him staggering back in the confined space between the tables. In spite of the noise in the hall, there was an immediate hush around the two men, which rapidly spread like the ripples around a stone thrown into a pond.

The Frenchman stared stonily at his former opponent and made to pass on without responding, but the belligerent Hugo moved into the narrow aisle to prevent him.

'Lost your tongue, foreigner? Or are you too high and mighty to speak to the likes of me?' he rasped, in a voice that carried around the now expectant hall.

De Wolfe was already out of his own seat and squeezing down the congested space between the end table and the wall, heading for what he knew was going to be a trouble spot. As he did so, Reginald lifted a hand against Hugo's shoulder to push him out of the way.

'I seek no trouble with you, Peverel! Our business was completed on the tourney field today.'

For answer, the Devon man gave his enemy another push, this time so hard that de Charterai staggered back and fell across the very man whose unintended action had triggered the crisis. Hugo drew back his fist to punch the Frenchman while he was still off balance, but two of his companions, one of them his brother, were still sober enough to restrain him, though they failed to still his tongue.

'By God's bowels, it was far from completed!' he yelled thickly. 'If those yellow-bellied judges hadn't interfered, we could have finished it properly – and I'd have bloody well won and saved my horse and armour, damn you!'

By now de Wolfe had reached the far end of the table and was coming around into the aisle, joined by Peter de Cunitone, the other adjudicator, who was hurrying along with a pair of stewards. Guy Ferrars and several other members of the tournament council were struggling to push through from the top table, but John was nearest to the rapidly developing altercation.

De Charterai was doing his best to avoid inflaming the situation, and when he found his feet again, he took a pace backward, his long, aristocratic face white with suppressed anger.

'You are a disgrace to your knighthood, Peverel!' he hissed, his voice vibrant with emotion. 'What you did today was against all the chivalry of the tournament. You have dishonoured yourself – and well you know it!'

'Ah, shut your ugly mouth, you damned French spy!' roared Hugo, his heavy, reddened features stuck forward pugnaciously as he stood swaying slightly on his feet. 'You're a craven coward as well as being a lousy fighter. I knew you in Palestine – your lot buggered off home early with that chicken-hearted simpleton you call your king and left us to do the fighting without you!'

De Wolfe reached the pair and tried to thrust himself between them, but too late to stop Reginald, insulted beyond measure, from giving Hugo Peverel a resounding slap across the face. With another angry roar, the befuddled manor-lord scrabbled for the hilt of his sword. Confused to find it missing, for guests could not come fully armed to a banquet, he reached around his belt for his dagger, but the coroner was too quick for him. Seizing his wrist in an iron grip, he forced him down on to a bench, where his brother Ralph and another friend grabbed him by the shoulders to keep him still.

'Now behave yourself, Peverel!' snapped de Wolfe, in a voice that could bend iron. He turned to the haughty de Charterai, who was quivering with rage at the public insult that he had suffered, and softened his tone somewhat.

'I apologise for this, sir knight. But this fellow is far gone in his cups, so perhaps you could make some allowance for the intemperance of a drunken man's tongue? All here know you for an honourable man and a worthy fighter.'

Reginald inclined his head stiffly, mollified by the coroner's conciliatory words.

'Thank you, Sir John. I appreciate your concern. I think it would be best if I absented myself now, to avoid making a bad situation worse.' He gave Hugo a look that he might use on seeing a dog turd on his shoe. 'The man is certainly drunk now – but he was sober this afternoon. I will meet him again some time – and then I will kill him!'

With that, he pushed his way to the end of the hall, ignoring the more senior men who attempted to add their apologies. There was a breath-holding silence as a hundred pairs of eyes watched him flick a mantle across his shoulders and stride out of the Guildhall into the darkness.

With Matilda on his arm, John walked slowly back to his house in a sombre mood. A stickler for correct behaviour in the knightly class, it exasperated him to see the codes of conduct flouted so flagrantly by an oaf such as Hugo Peverel, who was brought up to know better. He was a manor-lord of the line of William the Conqueror, even if it had come from the wrong side of the blanket more than a century ago. Like most sons of a lord, other than the youngest, who were often pushed into the clergy, he would have been sent first as a page or a varlet to another knight, then climbed to the status of squire, before eventually getting his own spurs in his late teens. Even the many landless knights, awaiting an inheritance that might never materialise, as well as those who had to carve out a living by hiring their swords or joining a campaign where booty was to be accumulated, all had to abide by the codes of honour that regulated relations between them. Since the old Queen Eleanor had introduced the fashion for courtly behaviour from Aquitaine, with this modern nonsense about fighting for a lady's favours and writing poetry and singing love songs, John felt that the former strict rules of combat and the comradely codes of honour between fellow warriors were being watered down by this namby-pamby romantic chivalry, but maybe that was a sign of him getting too old to be a campaigner any longer.

Matilda tugged his arm to jerk him out of this silent reverie. 'That was a sorry spectacle this evening, John,' she said. Secretly, she was pleased that it was her husband who had so publicly broken up the developing quarrel. It had been witnessed by all the people who mattered in the city, and some of the kudos must rub off on her when she next met her matronly cronies at their devotions. For the moment, the fact that she had been on the top table next to the archdeacon and the sheriff, as well as having her husband demonstrating his authority to half the county, allowed her to temporarily forget her shame at her brother's disgrace – and John's part in bringing it about.

As they reached their home, she was almost benign as she prompted him to sit by the fire and have a cup of wine, while she summoned Lucille out of her kennel under the stairs and hauled her up to the solar to undress her and prepare her for bed.

John contemplated taking Brutus down to the Bush, but it was quite late now and he had consumed so much food and drink that for once the thought of his mattress overcame even the attractions of Nesta. He sat in one of the monk's chairs by his great hearth, the cowled top keeping the draughts away from his head. Mary came in with a small wineskin and a pewter cup, and as she poured for him he told her of the drama in the Guildhall that evening. They kept their voices low, as high on the wall to the side of the chimney there was a Judas slit that communicated with the solar, but close to the fireplace they were out of sight of Matilda's prying eyes. Mary was always avid for titbits of scandal, and this time she was even able to tell him something about the Peverel ménage.

'My cousin is a seamstress at Sampford Peverel,' she volunteered. 'She calls to see my mother a couple of times a year, when the steward's wife brings her to buy at the cloth fair.'

Mary's mother was also a seamstress, in Rack Lane – her father had been a passing soldier who stayed only for the conception. 'She says that it's an unhappy manor, especially since the last lord died in that tourney. The family always seem to be fighting among themselves, and this Hugo is hated by almost everyone, even by his wife and his stepmother!'

John knew that servants' gossip was often exaggerated but usually had a grain of truth in it somewhere. 'What's the problem there, did your cousin say?'

Mary shrugged. 'I wasn't all that interested at the time. I wish I had taken more notice now. It seems that the old man took a much younger wife a few years ago and they were far from happy. But the main trouble when he died was that the eldest son was barred from the inheritance and it went to the second son, which was Hugo.'

John's black eyebrows rose. It was a serious matter if the heir to a large manor like Sampford had to forfeit his birthright. 'Did she say what brought that about?' he asked.

'My cousin said the elder son had some disability of his body, though she didn't say what. I know the matter was hotly disputed and they went to law in London over it.'

Mary knew no more, but when she left with the empty jug, John remained in his chair, pondering over what she had said. To have such a boorish, overbearing man as Hugo Peverel as the lord of a manor torn by family squabbles sounded like a recipe for a very unhappy village.

Early the next morning, Gwyn called at the house in Martin's Lane, keeping a wary eye out for the coroner's wife, who disapproved of the hairy Cornishman almost as much as she despised Thomas, the unfrocked clerk who was a sexual pervert, as far as she was concerned. Gwyn was safe enough today, as she was still in bed after her over-indulgence at the feast the previous evening, but John was already dressed, fed and watered by the faithful Mary. He buckled a short sword on to his baldric, stepped out of the vestibule into the lane and stalked alongside his officer into the main thoroughfare of the city.

'These men are lodging in Curre Street, you say?'
'Yes, they're dossing in a cheap room behind a

brothel. I've arranged the inquest in the Shire Hall for the tenth hour. Gabriel is sending a couple of men down to the Watergate to fetch the corpse up on a barrow.'

'What about a jury?'

For all that he looked like a huge ginger Barbary ape, Gwyn of Polruan was an efficient organiser. 'All fixed, Crowner. The porters and stevedores from the wharf make up most of them, but I've got a few stall-holders from the fair as well, men who were near the silversmith's booth.'

This Thursday was the third and last day of the fair and the last chance John had of spotting the men who had killed August Scrope, if they were still around. They collected the two craftsmen from a squalid room in the narrow street that ran from High Street to-wards the north wall and marched them down to Southernhay, giving Terrus of Totnes strict orders to keep his eyes peeled as they went. He had recovered well, and the previous day's weakness seemed to have passed, though he still had livid bruising and crusted scratches on his face.

The fair was still in full swing, though a few stalls had closed up, their owners having either sold all their wares or started on a long journey home. There was no rival attraction on Bull Mead today so the crowds were thronging the booths as thickly as on the two previous days.

Terrus and his fellow craftsman, Alfred, walked behind the coroner and his officer as they slowly paraded up and down the lanes between the stalls, the survivor of the assault swinging his head from side to side as he peered at faces in the press of people. They completed two circuits without result, and John began to wonder whether they were wasting their time. Going back up the centre again, they came to the stage and stopped to watch a performance of Moses ascending the mountain to receive the Ten Commandments. The onlookers were mightily amused when the false-bearded prophet slipped and put his foot through the lath-and-plaster simulation of Mount Sinai, giving vent to some colourful unbiblical oaths that drew cries of outrage from the vicar, who was chanting the appropriate commentary from the Old Testament.

John grinned and Gwyn added his belly-laugh to the jeers of derision from the crowd, but suddenly the coroner felt an urgent tugging at his sleeve.

'That's one of the bastards, I'm sure,' hissed Terrus. He half hid behind de Wolfe as he covertly pointed across the front of the platform at the crowd clustered on the other side. 'That thick set fellow with the leather cape!'

John saw a heavily built man of about thirty with a narrow rim of mousy beard running around his face, which bore a surly expression, even though he was watching the hilarious fiasco on the stage. His clothing was plain but of fair quality, a short, tightly belted tunic under a black shoulder cape that had a dagged lower edge and a pointed hood hanging behind his thick neck. To the coroner, he looked like a retainer in a household, either a bailiff or a manor-reeve.

'Are you sure? No sign of the other one?'

Terrus scanned the crowd almost fearfully, painfully reminded of the beating he had already suffered, then shook his head. 'No, just that one. But I'm certain it's him, even his garments are the same.'

'Right, you stay here until we call you.' He nudged Gwyn and together they walked behind the crowd to reach the other side of the stage where the man stood. They moved into position, one on either side of him.

'We want a word with you, fellow.'

Surprised, the man turned around, his square face

creased into a scowl. He had short, bristly hair the same colour as his beard, and his small dark eyes were deeply set under heavy brows.

'And who the hell might you be?' he rasped, showing a set of uneven brown teeth.

'The King's coroner – and this is my officer. Come over here where we can talk.' John waved a hand at an empty booth a few yards away, where there was no one to overhear them.

The man's scowl deepened. 'I'm coming nowhere! State your business here.'

For reply, Gwyn grabbed his arm and twisted it up behind his back, shoving him across the lane to the place his master had indicated. Though the man was burly and tough looking, he was no match for the Cornishman's strength and, cursing and wriggling, he was propelled under the striped awning of the deserted booth.

The coroner regarded him coldy. 'You can talk here – or in the gaol in Rougemont, it's your choice.'

'Holy Mary, what's the world coming to that a man can't watch a mystery play without being set upon by law officers?' he seethed, but John noticed a shifty look in his eyes which might suggest a lurking anxiety. Gwyn loosened his grip, but watched for any signs of escape.

'What's your name and where are you from?' was de Wolfe's first demand.

'It's none of your bloody business, but I'm Robert Longus, an armourer.' There were many such men about the town this week – they came either as free-lances or as retainers to their knights, attending to the weapons and armour used in the tournament.

'Where are you from, armourer?' asked Gwyn gruffly.

'Again, it's not your concern, but I come from near Tiverton. What in hell is all this about?'

For reply, John beckoned to Terrus, and hesitantly

the man approached, but stopped a few feet away from them, out of range of Robert's fist.

'This man claims you were one of pair who attacked him and killed his partner near Topsham on Monday morning,' snapped the coroner. 'Do you deny it?'

The upshot of his reply, peppered with oaths as foul as any that the two hardened campaigners had heard in two decades of soldiering, was to the effect that it was pack of lies and that he had never been near Topsham in his life.

John turned to the silversmith, who was cringing like a rabbit before a ferret. 'What do you say to that, Terrus?' he demanded.

'It's him, I'm certain of it!' babbled the man. 'I'll remember his face for the rest of my life.' He dodged behind Gwyn's large bulk as Robert Longus made a sudden movement towards him, but the Cornishman held out a hand the size of a salted ham to hold him back.

'Calm down, fellow! Just pay attention to the coroner.'

'So where were you early on Monday?' demanded de Wolfe. Something about this man didn't ring true, for all his protestations.

'I was working for my master and minding my own damned business!' cried Robert furiously. 'Ask him yourself, if you don't believe me.'

'We'll do just that, Longus. Where can we find him?'

The armourer hesitated for a moment. 'He should be at his lodging, no doubt breaking his fast at this hour.' It was late for most people's morning meal, but that was no concern of de Wolfe.

'Where's he staying? We'll go there now and settle this once and for all.'

Robert grudgingly told them that it was in High Street, and they set off up to the East Gate, which was the nearest entrance into the city from where they were. With Terrus following reluctantly behind, keeping his distance, they marched off, John and Gwyn staying close behind the man, to see that he didn't give them the slip. Once through the gate, de Wolfe was somewhat surprised to see the armourer making for the left side of the street, where the New Inn was situated. This was the largest and most expensive of the hostelries in Exeter, where the judges and other visiting dignitaries stayed.

'Who is your master, anyway?' John called out to the fellow's back.

'There he is – you can ask him yourself!' retorted Robert, rudely. He pointed to two figures standing outside the door of the inn, wearing riding cloaks and seemingly waiting for an ostler to bring their horses around from the yard at the back.

'It's that bastard Peverel!' muttered Gwyn in surprise. 'Who's that with him?'

'His younger brother, by the looks of it,' replied de Wolfe bitterly. With so much to do today, the last thing he needed was another quarrel with Hugo. Robert Longus had put on a spurt and hurried ahead. By the time the coroner and his officer caught up with him, he had managed a few gabbled words to the Peverels. Hugo scowled when he saw John approaching.

'Are you intent on persecuting me, de Wolfe? You've caused me trouble enough these past two days!'

The coroner ignored his words. 'Does this man belong to your manor?'

'He does indeed! Robert Longus is my armourer – and a very good one at that. What concern is that of yours?'

His tone was as abrasive as he could make it, almost a snarl to denote his contempt of de Wolfe's meddling in his affairs.

'My concern is that he is accused of assault, robbery and possibly murder.'

Hugo glowered at the coroner, then turned to the younger man, who could only be his brother.

'Ralph, see how I am treated by these Exeter people! They lose no opportunity to persecute me with trumped-up charges, anything to discomfit me.'

His brother shrugged but made no reply, and John gained the feeling that little love was lost between the two men. Ralph was a younger version of Hugo, probably in his late twenties, thought John. He had the same set to his features, but a less aggressive expression.

'There's no persecution, Peverel,' snapped John. 'Until this moment, I had no idea that this man was in your employ. Just give me a straight answer. He says you can vouch for his whereabouts early on Monday morning, when I have been told he was some miles away, perpetrating robbery with violence.'

As Hugo glared back, an ostler appeared, leading two horses by their bridles. 'I've no time to bandy words with you, Coroner. But if it gets you out of my hair, then yes, of course Robert was with me on Monday morning. We were preparing my equipment for the tourney. So you can forget any malicious nonsense about him being elsewhere.'

He reached up for the pommel of his saddle and swung himself up on to the beast's back, his brother doing the same behind him.

'Now I'm going home and am glad to be shaking the dust of this miserable city from my feet. I've met with nothing but insolence and antagonism ever since I arrived.'

He snatched up the reins, but at a sign from John, Gwyn grabbed the bit-ring and pulled the horse's head down to stop it moving on.

'That's not good enough, Peverel!' snapped the

coroner. 'I am holding an inquest this morning into the death of a silversmith and I need the attendance of anyone who can offer any evidence on the matter.'

For a moment, it looked as if the inflamed Hugo was going to give Gwyn's hand a crack with the riding staff that he held in his hand, but he restrained himself.

'That's no concern of mine! I've never heard of this dead man and have not the slightest interest in your problems.'

'Then your armourer here must attend. He has been accused of being involved in the death and needs to defend himself,' snapped de Wolfe.

'Indeed he will not!' shouted the manor-lord. 'I need him at home. Robert, get back to your lodgings, fetch your horse and follow us. We'll wait for you at St Sidwells.'

With that, he wrenched his steed's head away from Gwyn's grasp and, touching its belly with his spurs, jerked it away from the inn, his brother following impassively behind. On foot, there was nothing John could do to detain them and, glowering with frustration, he watched them trot away towards the East Gate. Then he swung round to Robert Longus, who was sidling away in the opposite direction.

'Hey, you! Don't you dare try to make off or I'll have you in shackles in the castle gaol.'

Gwyn strode after him and seized him by the shoulder.

'You'll be up at the Shire Hall in two hours' time, understand?' continued John. 'If you're not there, I'll have you attached and arrested, even if I have to come to Sampford Peverel to do it myself!'

The Shire Hall was an austere stone box on the left side of the inner ward in Rougemont. A virtually empty shell, its architecture was similar to that of a barn, a

single large chamber with an earthen floor, entered by
a high arched doorway that could have admitted a hay-
cart. The rough roof beams supported a covering of
stone tiles, and the only furnishings on a low wooden
platform facing the entrance were a couple of trestle
tables, a few benches and some stools.

For all its unprepossessing appearance, it was an
important place, and one in frequent use, not only for
the fortnightly Shire Court, but for meetings of free-
holders to conduct county business and for the peri-
odic visits of the King's judges and Commissioners for
the Eyres and Gaol Delivery. Coroner's inquests were
often held there, as well as other functions to do with
the forest law, frankpledge and many other legal, political and administrative meetings.

Today, John had little expectation of making much
progress with his inquiry, but the formality had to be
gone through, so that the corpse could be released for
burial. When he went across to the hall from his
chamber, he found that Gwyn had marshalled the reluctant jurymen into a straggling line below the dais,
where Thomas was already sitting at a table with his
pen, ink and parchment at the ready. To one side of
the jury stood an elderly man and two youths, together
with a middle-aged woman, who was quietly weeping
into her hands. De Wolfe assumed that these were a
brother, two sons and the leman of the silversmith, who
Gwyn had said had travelled from Totnes to collect the
deceased. In spite of John's threats, there was no sign
of the armourer Robert Longus, and the coroner vowed
to make him pay dearly for his flaunting of the law.

When two men-at-arms had dragged in a handcart
on which the body lay shrouded under a sack, they
were ready to start, and John pulled a stool to the edge
of the platform and sat down while Gwyn bellowed out
the customary opening call.

'Oyez, oyez, all persons having anything to do before the King's coroner for the county touching the death of August Scrope, draw near and give your attendance.'

As the dozen men were already drawn as near as they wished to be to the now foul-smelling cadaver, this produced no response, and the coroner went straight into the proceedings. He briefly described the circumstances of the death, then called forward the 'first finders', the two men from the quay-side. Haltingly, they described how they found the body in the river, which caused the men of the family to mutter angrily and the mistress to snuffle more heart-rendingly.

Then Alfred, the second silversmith, stated that his master and Terrus had left Exeter early on Monday morning to deliver expensive silverware to a client in Topsham and had not returned as they had promised. Terrus himself then came forward and displayed his injuries and related how he and his master had been attacked by two mounted men. He failed to recall what had happened to August Scrope, as he himself had been knocked unconscious, his wits not returning until he found himself in St James' Priory.

'But do you recollect the faces of the men who assaulted you?' demanded de Wolfe, leaning forward on his stool. The craftsman nodded vigorously.

'That I do, Crowner – at least, one of them! He was the man I pointed out to you in the fair this morning.'

John straightened up and directed his voice at the family members, as well as the jury. 'He was a fellow from Sampford Peverel, who calls himself Robert Longus. I warned him to attend this inquest but he has defaulted, and I therefore attach him in the sum of five marks to attend either a resumed inquest or the next county court. If he fails to appear then, he will be arrested or, failing that, attached to appear before the King's justices or his commissioners when they next visit Exeter.'

'Can't you arrest the swine now, Crowner?' called out the elder man from Totnes, obviously in a state of angry agitation. John explained the problem.

'Regrettably, all we have by way of evidence is the accusation of Terrus that this Robert was one of the assailants. The man denies it, so it is one man's word against another – and the fellow's master, the lord of Sampford, backs up his denial by claiming that he was with him at the time.'

The brother and sons growled again among themselves, but the coroner tried to reassure them. 'When I can get this man before a court and put him on oath, then we will see what further we can do to get at the truth. I will talk to the new sheriff about ways of bringing that about, for it is his responsibility to detain the man.'

Some hope of that, John thought privately. It was clear that Henry de Furnellis was going to leave all the leg-work to others.

The rest of the inquest was rapidly concluded, as John directed the jurors to file past the body on the cart, so that they could view the corpse's injuries. They did so with alacrity, none of them lingering near the body, which was beginning to swell and discolour. At a sign from his master, Gwyn covered the dead man again with the hessian sheet and the soldiers trundled it outside to wait for the relatives to transfer it to the ox-cart that they had brought from Totnes.

'In view of the absence of good evidence, especially the defection of Robert Longus, I have to adjourn this inquest until further information comes before me,' said John to the assembled court – though under his breath he added, 'If that ever happens.' He glared at the sheepish jury, who were wondering what purpose had been served by taking them from their labours for an hour.

'A coroner has to determine who the deceased was, where, when and by what means he came to his death. The identity has clearly been established and though it is obvious that no presentment of Englishry can be made, I will not levy the murdrum fine, as the corpse was discovered in the river and thus no particular vill can bear the blame. It is obvious that August Scrope was murdered. The time was last Monday and the place was on the high road between Topsham and St James' Priory. The cause of death was grievous wounding, and although the cadaver was found in the river I have no proof that he finally drowned. There is no evidence yet as to who attacked him and threw him into the water, so I will not demand a verdict from you the jury until I resume this hearing, hopefully when better information is forthcoming.'

After this long speech, de Wolfe nodded curtly to the faces below the platform, then turned to see how Thomas was getting on with his transcript. Leaning over his humped shoulder, he scanned the parchment on which his clerk was speedily inscribing his neat Latin calligraphy. Though John could not read more than a few words, he liked to check the length of the script, to make sure that Thomas was getting down an adequate description of the proceedings. He need not have concerned himself, as the little man was most diligent and took a pride in both the appearance and the content of his rolls, copies of which would be sent to the King's justices at the next Eyre of Assize, and eventually end up in the archives at Winchester or London.

When the jurymen had shuffled away and the grieving relatives had gone for their cart, Gwyn came across the empty hall to join them, his ever hungry stomach causing him to suggest adjourning to their chamber for their usual bread, cheese and ale.

As they walked across the inner ward to the gate-house, Thomas ventured a comment. 'At least your fears of multiple slayings this week have not come to pass, Crowner,' he said. 'The tournament passed off without a death – and the fair ends tonight, so hopefully only this one killing can be blamed on it.'

'Don't tempt fate, Thomas,' growled de Wolfe. 'We'll have to wait until tomorrow morning before we can congratulate ourselves on getting off so lightly.'

'What about this silversmith, Crowner?' asked Gwyn. 'Do you really think this damned armourer is one of the men we seek? His lord has given him a good alibi.'

John stopped and turned to face his officer. 'Would you trust the word of such a man as Hugo Peverel, after the way he's behaved? No, as soon as we have a free day, we'll ride up to Sampford for a few words with them – taking Gabriel and a couple of his men if necessary!'

Fate was to decree that de Wolfe's visit would occur sooner than he expected.

CHAPTER FIVE

In which a manor-lord goes missing

On the second Monday of every month, Sampford Peverel held its manor leet, a court where a wide variety of issues were heard, from accusations of drunkenness, theft and assault, to disputes over ploughing boundaries in the strip fields. For centuries past under the Saxons, these leets were the main arbiters of disputes and dispensers of justice within the little kingdoms that made up the manorial system of medieval England. The lord was master in almost every sense. He owned his bondsmen – the villeins and cottars – and even the freemen had little real freedom, except the choice of starving if they chose not to heed the master's wishes.

Though the vast majority of issues before the manor court were domestic and relatively trivial, serious crimes could be prosecuted, and if he so wished the lord possessed the power of life and death by hanging.

Since the arrival of the Normans, however – and especially since the relentless reforms of old King Henry, known as 'The Lawgiver' – the more serious offences were progressively being swept into the royal courts, bypassing the manor and even the county courts. In fact, part of the new coroner's function was to divert as much legal business as he could to the

King's judges and commissioners, to the advantage of the Lionheart's ever eager purse. His very title came from the phrase *custos plactorum corona* – 'Keeper of the Pleas of the Crown'.

For several generations at Sampford, it had become traditional for the lord himself to preside over the court, unless he was absent on some campaign. In most manors, the task of running the monthly leet was usually left to the steward, the most senior of the lord's servants, but here, wherever possible, one of the Peverels sat in dictatorial judgement over his subjects. This morning, at the October leet, there was some consternation among the steward, bailiff and reeve, as an hour after the appointed time for the court to begin there was no sign of Hugo Peverel in the large barn that was used for a courthouse.

Most other places used the hall of the manor house for the proceedings, but Hugo's late grandmother had objected to the despoiling of her home by a crowd of uncouth, smelly villagers who trampled her clean rushes with their muddy feet, spitting and peeing against the walls. She persuaded her husband to build another barn for use as a court, though it found other useful functions such as a shelter for farm animals and as a village hall, a place where ales and dances could be held on saint's days.

Now there were three score villagers standing aimlessly outside the high doors of the thatched wooden building, waiting for something to happen. Every man over fourteen had to attend the court, unless some vital farming duty detained him, for the leet was the parliament of the manor and in theory decisions depended on a consensus of opinion among the villagers. The established customs of the manor traditionally overrode the whims of the lord, as in return for the endless work they performed for him, he was under an obligation to organise their lives and defend them against the feudal uncertainties of starvation, natural disaster and the predations of robbers and civil war. In practice, the will of a strong lord or baron prevailed over this primitive democracy, especially in manors that were ruled by such a tyrannical dynasty as the Peverels.

The bailiff, Walter Hog, came striding across the courtyard, scattering chickens, pigs and small children from his path as he made for the steward, who was leaning against the weathered oak of the door post.

'Still no sign of him, Roger! Sir Odo refuses to come, says it's none of his business any longer, but Ralph promises to attend when he's finished in the privy. He says you are to start the hearings to avoid any more delay.'

Roger Viel was a heavy-featured man with fleshy jowls and loose skin under his neck like a cockerel's wattles. A born pessimist, he gave the impression that life was a burden to be borne stoically until death released him into a better place. He sighed as he turned into the gloomy interior of the court. Though Ralph Peverel was not so hot tempered and arrogant as his elder brother, he tended to be sarcastic and to show off his cleverness when put into any position of authority.

Where the hell had Hugo got to?, wondered Roger sourly.

Followed by a shuffling, muttering crowd, he took his place on a heavy oak chair, the only furniture in the place apart from a trestle table and stool where the manor-clerk occasionally sat when some more important issue required a record to be taken down. Along with the parish priest, the clerk was the only literate person in the manor, but today there was no need for his services, as the issues were all ones that could be dealt with summarily. Leaving the steward to get on with the business of dispensing justice, the bailiff walked quickly back to the manor house, a square, two-storeyed stone building. This was farther up the slightly sloping bailey, a two-acre compound within a stockade that defended the lord's residence. Like Rougemont, it had not been besieged since the last civil war between King Stephen and Empress Matilda half a century earlier, but with the present unrest between the King and his brother John, and the growing threat of a French invasion, the Peverels saw to it that their stout fence and gateway were kept in good repair.

Walter Hog clattered up the wooden steps to the main door, set well above head height in the wall. These steps could be thrown down in the event of an attack and a stout iron grille dropped across the heavy oaken doors. There was no communication between the floors above and the undercroft below, so the house was virtually impregnable against anything short of a siege engine.

Today the problem was less military than diplomatic, thought Walter wryly. The Peverels were a quarrelsome lot, always ready to take offence, bickering among themselves and hurling abuse and even blows at anyone in the vicinity. The bailiff had been at Sampford for only two years and was wondering whether he had done the right thing in moving here from his previous post in Taunton, even though it paid a few pence a day more.

Inside the hall, he found Warin Fishacre, the manor-reeve, waiting for him. He was a thin, reedy man with a stoop and a hacking cough, who permanently wore an expression of irritation verging on anger. His mousy hair was pulled back tightly to a clump on the back of his neck, where it was tied with a piece of cord.

'Any sign of him out there?' Fishacre asked in a rough, throaty voice. The bailiff had no need to ask whether he was talking about Hugo Peverel.

'None at all – the bastard's vanished off the face of the earth,' answered Walter in a low voice, his eyes swiveling to the stairway that led to the upper floor where the family lived.

'Some hope of that!' snarled the reeve, though his eyes too scanned for any sign of someone who could overhear them.

'Roger Viel is starting the court now,' said Walter. 'I suppose I'd better wait for Ralph before going back there.'

The bailiff was a much younger man than the reeve, though well above him in status, as reeves were representatives of the bondsmen and thus unfree themselves. This was not necessarily reflected in their wealth, as there were pauper freemen and rich villeins, but Warin Fishacre was neither, just an average villager with a comely wife, a pretty daughter and two strong sons.

Walter Hog was a compact man of twenty-eight, with cropped fair hair and a round, pink face that bore an earnest expression. He was a conscientious worker and was determined to better himself, either by becoming a steward to some other lord or working for a rich merchant in Exeter or Southampton. But at the moment he had other problems on his mind, and one of them now appeared in the entrance to the staircase.

'Walter, did you tell them I'll be over directly?'

Ralph Peverel was the third son of the William who had died near Salisbury the previous spring. He was a younger version of both his father and his brother

Hugo, though rather slimmer and better looking, clean shaven with red-blond hair cut short on the neck and sides to leave a thick circular cap on his crown. He wore a thigh-length tunic of green woollen cloth, with hose pushed into ankle-length leather boots with pointed toes. A surcoat of brown linen swung open to reveal a wide leather belt that was dotted with silver studs and carried a long dagger in an oriental sheath.

'Yes, Sir Ralph, I told them you were on your way. Roger Viel has started already. Shall I come with you now?'

Ralph shook his head and moved towards the outside door.

'Better that you two carry on looking for my brother. Mary, mother of God, but he was drunk last night! He's probably sleeping it off in a hay-loft, on top of some wench!'

It was as well that the speaker was moving away from the two servants, as the expression on Fishacre's face was one of undiluted hate, though whether at Ralph's words or some private inner thought, the bailiff could not determine.

'So where are we going to look again?' demanded Walter, as Ralph vanished down the steps. 'We've had all the house servants and the lads from the stables scouring the place for hours, without seeing so much as a whisker of him.'

'I never want to see the sod again, other than lying dead from some very painful disease,' snarled Warin Fishacre. 'But I suppose we had better look as if we're doing something. The swine will no doubt turn up in his own good time.'

There were lighter steps on the staircase, which was built into the thickness of the wall, and a woman appeared, dressed in a flowing kirtle of white samite.

Her blonde hair was braided into two long plaits which hung down over her bosom, the tips confined in gilded metal tubes. A voluminous mantle of blue silk hung from her shoulders and fell almost to the ground, secured across her neck by a gilt cord. About twenty-five years of age, Beatrice Peverel was undoubtedly beautiful, her fair skin and large blue eyes complemented by full red lips.

The two men bobbed their heads and touched a finger to their temples in respect to the lady of the manor, waiting to be spoken to first.

'Have you found my husband yet, Walter?' she asked in a soft, melodious voice which conveyed more annoyance than concern for Hugo's disappearance.

'Not yet, my lady. All the servants are out and about, searching for him.'

His hand swept around the hall to emphasise the fact that the usually bustling chamber was deserted. Behind her, in the shadows of the stairwell, her maid-servant hovered uncertainly, not sure whether her mistress needed a chaperone when the two men with whom she was alone were only the familiar bailiff and reeve. Beatrice sighed, her fingers playing with several large gold rings that adorned her small hands.

'Very well, I suppose he'll appear eventually, as he usually does.'

'Yes, my lady. I don't think he can be far away – his horse is still in the stable,' said Walter reassuringly.

She smiled faintly and turned to climb the staircase, which led up to the solar where she and Avelina spent their days, as well as to four other rooms where various members of the family slept. The two men went to the farther end of the hall, which was a large square chamber lit only by a pair of slit embrasures in each wall. Here a corner was partitioned off by wooden

129

screens, behind which was the bottler's domain, containing kegs and crocks of ale, as well as skins and flasks of imported wine. Food brought from the kitchen hut behind the house was served up here and some remnants of the early morning meal were still lying around. In the main body of the hall, which had a hearth and chimney instead of a central fire-pit, tables and benches were provided for eating and drinking, which was what the bailiff and reeve now had in mind. As the place was deserted, they went behind the screens and helped themselves to some bread, cold bacon and cheese, then drew ale from a cask supported on wedges against the wall.

'I reckon I deserve this. I've been looking for that bloody Hugo for nigh on four hours!' muttered Fishacre, taking his food and jug to the nearest trestle. As they sat champing at the coarse bread and savouring the salt bacon, Walter Hog ruminated on what might have happened to their lord and master.

'I can't see that it's connected to that affair in Exeter last week, but he's been like a boar with a sore arse since he came home!'

Though Hugo Peverel had not mentioned a word of the shameful incident at the tournament, everyone in Sampford was well aware of what had happened – even if Hugo's squires had kept their mouths shut, there were the armourers, several varlets, carters and a couple of body servants who would have whispered the gossip as soon as they got back.

'You know what I think of the sod!' grunted Warin Fishacre. 'It's God's burden that I should be stuck as a bondsman under that evil swine! If it wasn't for my wife and children, I'd be tempted to make a run for it to Exeter.' If a villein could escape to a town and remain uncaptured there for at least a year and a day, he could gain his freedom.

Walter laid a warning hand on the reeve's arm. 'Hush, man, keep your opinions to yourself in here, for your family's sake, if not your own.'

'Family!' snarled the gaunt man cynically. 'That's where the trouble lies, as well you know, Walter Hog.'

He buried his face in the earthernware mug of ale and sucked as if it were Hugo's very blood that he was drinking. It was just as well that he stopped his ranting at that moment, for feet clattered on the steps outside and a new figure came into the hall. It was the armourer, Robert Longus, who was one of their lord's favourites and who would have been happy to take the reeve's rebellious words back to his master.

'Any news, Robert?' asked the bailiff, as the man came across to them.

'One of the pig boys, the simple one with the harelip, now says he saw the master late last night with one of the servant girls, though he doesn't know who it was. The daft bugger kept it to himself until he came back from the waste just now.'

The waste was the rough ground at the extreme edge of the manor lands beyond the pasture, where assarting was slowly driving back the forest edge to provide extra arable land. It was good enough only for grazing pigs and goats until it had been put under the plough.

'No surprise there, he's been through half the girls in the village,' growled Warin under his breath.

'Where did this lad see him?' asked Walter.

'Behind the churchyard, soon after dark last night. We've been over that area several times, without a sign of him.'

The armourer looked questioningly at the bailiff. 'Are you going to tell her ladyship? And Lady Avelina?'

Walter looked uncomfortable – this sounded like a direct challenge to his courage. Lady Avelina was

BERNARD KNIGHT

Hugo's stepmother, a formidable woman at the best of times, which this wasn't.

'Let's wait until we find him – then he can tell them himself, if he wants to!' he countered.

'Be no surprise to either of the ladies to hear that he's been riding the young serving girls again,' sneered Fishacre. He seemed about to enlarge on this theme, but under the table the bailiff gave him a surreptitious kick on the ankle.

They finished their ale and went out into the pale autumn sunshine. With most of the men attending the court, the bailey was quiet, though almost all the female servants were wandering about the village, looking into chicken sheds, pigsties and hay byres in case their lord was lying somewhere in a drunken sleep. It would not be the first time, but usually he sobered up during the night and found his way back to the manor house.

Walter Hog led the way to the entrance in the stockade, where a drawbridge over a deep ditch protected stout gates, now wide open. He had lived here for a couple of years, but still found new sights to stare at, being a Somerset man from the hills of eastern Exmoor. Now he gazed down the rutted lane through the village to where he could see the bell arch on the roof of the church. Sampford Peverel was built on a low ridge above a small valley, through which ran a stream. It was a crossing on this brook that gave the village its name, derived from the Saxon for 'sandy ford'. The small wooden church of St John the Baptist was on the eastern end of the ridge. Beyond it, the track went eastward to distant Taunton, joining the high road back to Exeter about a mile away.

The manor house was a few hundred paces up the slope from the church, and between them was an open space that acted as the village green. Here the weekly obligatory archery practice took place, urchins played tag and passing pedlars and chapmen displayed their wares to the good-wives of the hamlet. Cottages and huts straggled around the green and along the track that led westward towards Tiverton. They were a motley collection, some mere shacks with rotting timber walls, others more substantial, being made of cob plastered between wooden frames. All had low thatched roofs, some of clean new reeds, others green with growing grass and moss. These tofts had a patch of croft around them where vegetables grew, and a few chickens, geese and maybe a house cow helped to feed the families within.

One dwelling on the green was slightly larger than the others and had a bush hanging from a pole outside, marking it as an alehouse, though every household brewed ale for its own use. It was the only palatable drink available, given the quality of the water supply, which, apart from some wells, came mainly from the stream below the church. This was good enough to turn the wheel of the mill, but as the rubbish, offal and night-soil of most of the village were thrown into it, the brook was shunned as a source of drinking water, though the women were content to use the mill-pond to soak their washing and beat it clean on the stones along the bank.

'I'll go for one more look down there,' said the bailiff, pointing towards the church. 'You go again up to the top end of the village. We can do little more until the men have finished in the leet.'

Grumbling under his breath, Warin Fishacre loped off in the other direction, determined to call in at his own toft for a rest, rather than pound around the village yet again. The more earnest Walter, determined to do the job as best he could, set off towards the green, his head swivelling from side to side as he went, in case

133

Hugo Peverel suddenly staggered out of some shed or hay-loft. He nodded to the wives and girls he saw on the way, who were now only pretending to look diligently for their lord after several hours of futile searching.

Opposite the green, he passed one dwelling whose end wall had fallen down, as the clay, straw and dung plastered on to panels woven from hazel withies had dissolved from rain streaming down from the decayed thatch above. Sitting outside on a large stone was the only man in sight, an old fellow who had suffered a stroke the previous year and could now only drag himself along on one good leg, using a crutch made from a branch. He lived with his daughter, who eked out a living for them by growing and collecting herbs and plants to make medicine for the villagers.

'God be with you, Adam!' called the bailiff. 'You saw no sign of our lord Hugo last night, I suppose?'

The cripple had been inside until now, lying on the heap of dried ferns that served him as a bed, so none of the searchers had yet spoken to him. He raised the arm that was not paralysed and beckoned the bailiff to come closer. When he approached, the old man made some gargling noises from a mouth that was sagging at one side, spittle dribbling as he tried to make himself understood. Leaning over the tattered fence of sticks that kept a pair of goats from wandering, Walter managed to make out what Adam was telling him. It was that late the previous evening, he had come outside to empty his bladder for the night and had seen Hugo Peverel staggering down the lane, dragging a girl by the hand. Adam seemed to find this no surprise, having lived for sixty-eight years in Sampford and seen a succession of Peverels seducing the village maidens.

'Did you see where he went?' asked Walter, not really expecting any useful reply. Adam muttered something about moonlight and raised his good hand to point unsteadily across the road at some cottages and other rickety buildings along the opposite edge of the village green.

'Across there, towards the ox byres,' he spluttered.

Walter left him with a word of thanks and ambled across the track that was Sampford's main street. Between the widely spaced cottages there were a couple of large shelters where the plough teams of oxen were stabled in the winter, though at this time of year they were grazing out on the meadows, waiting for the men to start work after the manor leet.

The stables had already been searched, but to humour old Adam the bailiff decided to have another look. He walked up to the sheds, which were little more than sloping roofs of old thatch supported on poles, with hurdles of woven branches forming the walls.

As he went into the gap that served as the entrance of the first stable, his lethargy was brought to an abrupt end by a piercing scream from inside. A woman he recognised as the wife of the mole-catcher was standing at the other end, alongside a hurdle that held back a high stack of winter fodder for the oxen. She had an armful of loose hay, which she dropped as he ran forward, holding her hands to her mouth, her eyes wide with horror.

'God's teeth, Gertrude, what's the matter with you?' he shouted.

Tremulously, she pointed over the hurdle. 'I was taking a bit of hay for my conies – only a handful,' she gabbled defensively. Walter knew that she kept rabbits penned in her garden for food and stole a little hay to bed and feed them, as did many other cottars. He peered over the panel of twigs and his pulse began to race as he saw a booted foot and most of a leg sticking out from under the pile of fodder. Gertrude, a heavily built matron with a bad turn in her eye, came nervously up behind him to look over his shoulder.

'I lifted a bit of hay and there it was, sticking out from under the rick.'

She pointed a wavering finger at the tight yellow hose that covered the leg like a second skin. With an oath, Walter Hog dragged back a hurdle and bent over the limb, hurriedly pulling away handfuls of the sweet-smelling hay. More fell down from above as he burrowed at the pile, and with another curse he seized larger armfuls and tossed them aside to clear a space over the body. He needed to expose it only up to the waist before he knew it was his lord and master, as he recognised the good-quality hose and the finely embroidered hem of the green tunic that came to the knees.

'Run, woman, go and tell the reeve, the steward – anyone! Go to the leet if you see no one on the road ... tell them the lord is found, though I fear he's dead!'

Gertrude picked up the hem of her shabby kirtle and hurried off, forgetting to pick up her scavenged hay on the way. Left alone, the bailiff, sweating with excitement and a little apprehension, decided to drag the body out, as the more he threw the fodder aside, the more cascaded down from above, the stack being well over head height. Walter had realised immediately that the body was a corpse and not just a drunken man, as his first touch on the man's calf told him it was cold and stiff.

He cleared the other foot and pulled on them both, the body sliding back easily on a layer of hay on the earthen floor. It was face down, and as soon as it was free the bailiff saw that in the middle of the back the tunic was saturated with a wide dark red circle of blood, in the centre of which were several small tears.

Walter rocked back on his heels, shocked and bewildered – trying to take in the fact that his master had been stabbed to death.

CHAPTER SIX

In which Crowner John rides to Sampford Peverel

Any thought of the usual noonday dinner was abandoned in the confusion that followed. The manor court had been cancelled halfway through and no work was being done in the fields or village, apart from seeing to the livestock. Virtually all one hundred and fifty inhabitants were standing around in groups, gathered at their garden gates, outside the alehouse or in the road to discuss the event which had fallen like a thunderbolt out of the blue. Some were even in the church, praying, not so much for the soul of Hugo but for salvation for the village in yet another time of crisis.

It was not just a topic for wonder and gossip, but a cause of real concern about their future. They had already suffered one upheaval this year, when William Peverel had been killed at the tourney, followed by the dispute about his successor. Now it had happened again, and the villagers were wondering who would lead them into the coming winter. An uncaring or inefficient lord could mean life or death for some, if the economy of the manor was not well run. There was always a thin line between survival and starvation in a bad season such as this one, and though a good steward and bailiff were vital, the real responsibility lay with the manor-lord. Some were muttering quietly under their breath that they were not all that unhappy that the unpopular Hugo was no more, but would his successor be any improvement? Some wished Odo would take over, as he should have done by right of primogeniture, but most assumed that Ralph would now become lord, as Joel was surely too young.

But at midday all this was academic as far as the freemen and bondsmen out in the lanes were concerned. What mattered was what was being said in the hall of the manor house, where the whole family and the senior servants were assembling. The three surviving brothers were sitting on stools and benches around one of the bare tables, and another dozen men were standing around in front of them. The low buzz of conversation was stilled as feet were heard on the stone staircase, and the male Peverels came to their feet as the dowager and the new widow entered the hall, followed by their handmaidens, who were dabbing at their eyes, more from a cautious sense of duty than sorrow. The bereaved ladies themselves showed no sign of grief, but rather a fretful anger at the disruption to their comfortable routine.

Odo came forward and held out his hand to courteously escort the ladies towards the only three chairs that the hall possessed. Brusquely, Ralph pushed in front of him and, with a sweep of his hand, invited them to be seated. The action was not lost on those present, who saw this as the first arrow-shot in the next battle for supremacy.

The Peverel ladies, Avelina and Beatrice, sat down, and their maids fussed around, arranging the skirts of their mistresses' kirtles and adjusting the fur-edged pelisses over their shoulders, for the day was cool and the fire in the hall did little to assuage the draughts coming through the window slits.

'This is an unhappy day for us all – indeed, an unhappy year!' said Odo sonorously. He was attempting to retrieve the initiative as the men sat down again at the table, with the ladies at one end, their handmaidens standing behind them. Odo, at thirty-seven, was the eldest of the late William's sons, and alone among them was not a tournament addict, being more interested in estate management and getting the best from the manor lands. It had therefore been all the more galling – indeed, humiliating – for him to be deprived of the inheritance the previous April. He was a tall, gangling man, less thickset than his father and brothers, but with the same straight Peverel nose and russet hair. The thin lips of a rather weak mouth were always turned down at the ends in permanent disgruntlement.

Not to be outdone by Odo's pronouncement, Ralph imperiously beckoned the senior staff forward.

'Roger Viel – and you, Walter Hog – stand before us there!' He pointed to the other side of the table, then crooked a finger at the others, so that the stable marshal, the master-at-arms, the falconer, the hound-master, the armourer and the steward's clerk came to stand in a row facing their betters.

Avelina spoke up for the first time.

'Where has my stepson been taken?' she demanded. Forty-one years old, and handsome rather than beautiful like Beatrice, her dark hair and high cheek-bones gave her a somewhat Latin or Levantine appearance, though she was in fact pure-blooded Norman.

'His body has been taken to the church, my lady.'

Roger the steward answered in a suitably sepulchral voice, having arranged the removal himself. 'When the bailiff found the body of our lord, he called me and I thought it the most respectful place, rather than bringing him back to this hall, which of necessity would be in turmoil for some time.'

The steward never used two words where ten would suffice, thought Walter Hog, waspishly.

'Hugo has not been left alone, I trust?' asked Beatrice, her blue eyes looking larger than ever as she gazed around at the men seated at the table, pausing fleetingly on the fresh face of Joel, the youngest son.

'He is attended by Father Patrick, madam,' said Ralph, rather curtly. 'He has orders not to leave the bier on any account.'

Odo suddenly thumped the table with his fist, making a couple of pewter wine cups rattle.

'We must decide what is to be done! My brother lies foully murdered. His death must be avenged and his killer brought to justice!'

'*Our* justice, brother!' snapped Ralph, ever anxious to assert his anticipated authority. 'We need no interference from king's officers. This is a manorial matter and we have an obligation to keep it within the manor. There is no need to wash our grubby linen in public.'

The bailiff, growing increasingly uneasy, ventured an opinion.

'Sir Ralph, whatever we might think of the powers in London or Winchester, the Chief Justiciar proclaimed new rules last year. When a body is found, the first finder must knock up the four nearest households to raise the hue and cry to search for the miscreants!'

Ralph Peverel glared back at the bailiff. 'There's no problem then, is there? This mole-catcher's wife was the first finder, virtually in your own presence. And as for raising the hue and cry, the whole bloody village was roused, not just four households!'

There was a murmur of approval around the table, but Walter Hog remained stubborn, though he saw trouble approaching at high speed.

'Indeed, sir. But these new rules, which it is said Hubert Walter issued at the express wish of King Richard, demand that the first finder must immediately notify the bailiff, who must straightway report the death to the coroner. I've even heard that the body should not be moved from where it was found – strictly speaking, moving Sir Hugo to the church was illegal.'

'To hell with that!' rasped Ralph irritably. 'Do you seriously expect us to leave our noble brother face down in an ox byre? If it was some villein or serf slain by outlaws, then this new officialdom could be tolerated. But here we have the lord of the manor done to death – so we can dispense with all that nonsense!'

Bailiff Hog looked even more uncomfortable as he took a deep breath, swallowed and confessed.

'I took it as my duty to inform the coroner, sir. An hour ago I sent the reeve on a good horse to Exeter to summon Sir John de Wolfe.'

A sound-winded palfrey could cover the fifteen miles to the city in less than three hours, and not long after Crowner John had returned from his dinner and a short sleep to the chamber in the gatehouse, Warin Fishacre clattered up the drawbridge and dismounted outside the guardroom. Sergeant Gabriel interrupted his game of dice to take the reeve up the winding stairs and waited while the hunched figure told his story to the coroner. Gwyn and Thomas were in their usual places and listened with interest – since the debacle on Bull Mead the previous week, the name of Hugo Peverel was all too familiar.

'God's guts, this is the first manor-lord we've had slain since I became coroner,' muttered de Wolfe. 'You claim he was last seen in the company of a maid from the village? What has she to say about the matter?'

Fishacre shrugged his stooped shoulders. His thin backside was still sore from the urgent ride.

'We don't even know who she was yet, Crowner! I

left Sampford soon after the body was discovered, but probably they've found her by now.' He stopped to cough noisily into his hand before continuing. 'I expect she'll get the blame and be hanged for it, whether she killed him or not!' There was a bitter sarcasm in his voice that was not lost on John.

'Have you any idea who might have wanted to kill Hugo Peverel?' he demanded. 'It seems unlikely that a willing maid would want to stab him in the back while he was having his way with her!'

'Some of the maids have been far from willing, Crowner. Not that it made any difference to our lord, if he took a fancy to a girl.'

Again John sensed that the reeve had a deeper interest in the seduction of serving wenches than that of a mere observer.

'Other than young women, have you no idea who might be a mortal enemy?' he persisted, knowing that manor reeves often had the best insight into the intrigues of their village. Warin Fishacre's gaunt features twisted into a sardonic smile.

'It's not my place to gossip about my betters, sir. But many would say that it would be hard to find someone who wasn't his enemy!'

With that, de Wolfe had to be content and, rising, he took his cloak from a wooden peg hammered between the stones of the wall and threw it over his shoulders.

'I'll have to go back home and tell my wife that I may be away for the night, which will not please her. Get your horse fed and watered, reeve, and we'll meet at the East Gate in an hour.'

As he left them, Thomas groaned at the thought of a few hours on the back of his pony, but Gwyn looked pleased at the prospect of a ride out of the city, especially as this sounded like something out of the ordinary run

143

of cases. He slapped the solemn-looking reeve on the shoulder and guided him towards the doorway.

'Let's get your beast fixed up, then we can get some food and drink in the hall before we set off,' he boomed heartily.

Behind him, the clerk collected up his writing materials and stuffed them into his shapeless shoulder bag, wondering gloomily what violent events he would have to record on them in Sampford Peverel.

Eventually, the pangs of hunger among the occupants of the manor house in Sampford overcame any vestiges of grief and a generally subdued household sat down to a delayed meal of mutton stew with leeks, then boiled pork, beans and onions. Bread, cheese and boiled eggs filled up any remaining spaces in their stomachs, though appetites generally were less robust than usual, not from any overwhelming sorrow, but because of the upset and uncertainty that such an event inevitably brought in its wake.

The two ladies were present at the meal, with their maids dancing attendance, though they both picked fitfully at the food. Joel, the youngest of the Peverel brothers, sat next to the new widow and was noticeably solicitous towards her, gently coaxing her to eat, drawing scowls from Ralph and Odo for his trouble.

For her part, Beatrice was wanly preoccupied, though she gave Joel some encouraging murmurs of thanks and sly glances from under the long lashes of her lowered eyelids. The elder woman, Avelina, sat impassively, her thoughts seemingly far away as she ate delicately from the trencher on the table before her, using a small knife taken from the embroidered pouch on her belt.

When the wooden platters of fruit were brought, few

bothered to take an apple or pear, but the bottler was kept busy refilling pewter cups with wine and pottery mugs with ale and cider. This was the time when discussion began again, and Ralph led off, again intending to stake his claim to leadership.

'Damn that busybody of a bailiff!' he snarled. 'Why in God's name did he go rushing to send for the bloody coroner!'

Though in the best circles in these times it was considered indelicate to curse in the presence of ladies, chivalry was not held at a premium in Sampford and neither of the women of the family turned a hair at coarse language. In fact, Avelina had been known to easily outswear the kitchen staff when something annoyed her.

Odo, though privately of the same opinion as his brother, felt obliged to contradict him as a matter of principle, to deny Ralph's bid for primacy.

'Walter was right in law. We could be censured for not complying with the new rules. Not that they are all that new – it's over a year since the Justiciar promulgated them at the Kentish eyre.'

The eldest son of William Peverel had spent a couple of years at the cathedral school in Salisbury, and as well as learning to read and write with moderate skill had harboured a frustrated yearning to become a lawyer until his disability ruled him out, just as it had disbarred him from his inheritance. He now followed the activities of the King's council and the politics of the day more closely than any of his brothers, who were concerned only with hunting and jousting. But Ralph was contemptuous of Odo's respect for the law.

'That damned fellow de Wolfe is an interfering nuisance! It was he who made the most trouble last week, when poor Hugo had that problem at the tournament. Anyone else would have let the matter rest, but de Wolfe had to make such a song and dance about it!' he ranted. 'And then at the feast afterwards, again it was he who interfered in a gentleman's dispute between Hugo and that slimy bastard de Charterai.'

At the mention of the Frenchman, Avelina's head came up and she glared at her stepson.

'That's no way to speak of an honourable knight who is a guest in our country! He was the champion at that tournament and was a Crusader, so he deserves some respect.'

There were a few knowing glances exchanged around the table, including a few covert winks between the ladies' maids. It was common knowledge that Avelina, who had attended the tourney in Exeter along with Beatrice, had met de Charterai on the field at Bull Mead – though only her own handmaiden knew that she had given him one of her kerchiefs to tuck into his sleeve as a favour before he took the field with his lance.

Odo took the initiative again, his solemn face set stubbornly as he returned to the practicalities of the day.

'The coroner will come, whether we like it or not. If the bailiff had not sent for him, the news would still have reached him – the murder of one of the county's manor-lords is not something that goes unnoticed.'

Ralph banged his ale jar on the table and snapped his fingers at the old bottler to get him to refill it.

'He'll get short shrift as far as I'm concerned. If he comes pestering me or the ladies for gossip, I'll tell him to clear off our land! We managed perfectly well for centuries without this new-fangled nonsense of a coroner.'

Odo was determined to contradict his brother at every opportunity. 'That's not quite true, Ralph. There was a coroner way back in Saxon times. The office just fell into disuse in Ethelred's time and Hubert Walter has revived it.'

'I don't give a fig for your history lessons, Odo!' shouted the younger man crossly. 'You've often heard what our good neighbour has said about coroners – they are just another way of screwing more money out of the population. Amercements and fines and deodands and confiscations! The bastards are just bloody tax collectors under another name, according to Richard de Revelle.'

'And he should know, having been dismissed for being caught with his hand in the royal purse!' cut in Joel mischievously, but this merely served to inflame the volatile Ralph.

'Another vile injustice on the part of this God-forsaken John de Wolfe!' he snarled, glaring at his youngest brother, who in looks was a fresher-faced copy of himself. 'He's long had this hatred for de Revelle, even though he's married to his sister. He plotted his downfall out of sheer malice and what's happened? We've lost a good sheriff and had some old dodderer put in his place, who'll dance to de Wolfe's tune!'

Avelina looked at Ralph with cold disdain.

'All this ranting is getting us nowhere. If you've nothing more useful to suggest, we may as well leave it to this coroner to investigate.'

Ralph bridled at her rebuke; he had never liked his stepmother and resented her taking his dead mother's place.

'Indeed I do have something useful to suggest, madam!' he snapped. 'We have a good neighbour not four miles away who knows more of the law than this swine of a coroner. I think we should prevail upon him to come over and advise us in our hour of need.'

'You mean Richard de Revelle?' asked Odo, for once not disagreeing with his main rival. 'It's true that as

Devon's sheriff he was responsible for enforcing the law in the county, so he must know it backwards.'

'Backwards is probably right!' said Joel sarcastically. 'Don't forget that he was dismissed in disgrace for malpractice.'

Again Ralph slammed a fist angrily on the table, making the wine cups rattle. 'Watch your words, young man! He was a victim of a conspiracy, concocted by this de Wolfe, because of his leanings towards Prince John.'

'Which I hope none of us here shares,' observed Odo carefully. 'We are all staunch King's men. Let us not forget what happened in Nottingham and Tickhill last year!'

He was referring to the final rout of John's rebellion when the Lionheart returned home from his captivity in Germany, but again his sarcastic brother Joel felt obliged to cap his words.

'No need to go as far as Nottingham, brothers! Just remember that in our own county, down at Berry Castle, the traitor Henry de la Pomeroy had his surgeon cut open the veins of his wrists, rather than face the wrath of Coeur de Lion! We need to think carefully before climbing on to de Revelle's wagon.'

Avelina, whose social excursions obviously gave her more insight into the political scene than her stepsons, nodded her agreement.

'I hear that he still has ambitions which would be fulfilled if Prince John gained the upper hand,' she observed sagely. 'I wouldn't trust our neighbour very far. He was always badgering my William to sell him six carucates of that part of our manor which abutted on to his land – and for a trifling sum.'

Ralph jumped from the table to stride impatiently back and forth, cider slopping from his quart jug as he paced.

'This is foolishness! What in God's name has his politics to do with the former sheriff giving us some help over this tragedy? He knows about hunting miscreants and about the law that can be applied in the manor when they are caught. Let us send for him quickly, before this interfering knight arrives from Exeter.'

He omitted to mention that, being good friends with de Revelle, he also wanted this senior man's support in any contest with Odo over the succession to the manor, in exchange for selling him the land that Avelina had spoken of. Though no one was enthusiastic, there seemed no good reason why Richard's advice should not be sought. More by default, Ralph Peverel got his way and volunteered to go across to de Revelle's demesne immediately to explain the situation.

The sound of his gelding's hoofs had hardly died away when a figure hurried up the steps and, pulling off his woollen cap, advanced into the hall in a state of some excitement. It was the falconer, who, like the rest of the servants, had been out checking on who was missing. He approached the table where the family were gathered, looking apprehensively from one to the other, unsure as to which one was now the master, to whom he should deliver his news. Solving the dilemma by moving his head from side to side and speaking to no one in particular, he blurted out the news that Agnes, the fourteen-year-old daughter of one of the cottars, was missing.

'She was one of the skivvies in the wash house, sirs. A girl no better than she should be, if you get my meaning. Not seen these past few hours, since the poor master was found dead.'

With Ralph absent, there was no one to challenge Odo, and he now rose to his feet and glared fiercely at the falconer.

149

'Are you saying that she was the girl who was with Sir Hugo last night?' he demanded.

Joel also sprang to his feet and, red faced, confronted his eldest brother.

'Have you no tact, Odo? Think of poor Beatrice having to listen to this!'

Hugo's new widow blushed, but more from the younger brother's chivalrous words than any revulsion or shame at the mention of her late husband's well-known carnal pursuits.

'I think it would be best if I retired to my chamber,' she said tactfully, and, with much fussing of maids, both women rose and gracefully vanished up the staircase to the upper floor. Odo resumed his interrogation of the falconer, a grizzled man of forty with skin like the bark of an oak tree.

'Well, was this the doxy that he was covering in the ox byre?'

'So says another maid in the wash hut. Agnes had been with him before, when it seems he had given her a whole penny for her trouble.'

Roger Viel coughed delicately and spoke up.

'I know the girl, she has a face like a pudding, but the rest of her is shapely enough. I fail to see why she should harm our lord, especially when he was so generous to her just for lying on her back for him.'

Odo rasped his fingers over two days' growth of gingery stubble on his cheeks. 'Nevertheless, it is vital that we find her and see what she has to say. If there is no one else forthcoming as a suspect, then maybe she will have to serve as the culprit!'

He waved the falconer out, with orders to search the whole village until she was caught. There was nowhere else she could go, as to leave the manor meant eventual death from exposure or starvation. No other village would take her in, and a girl could not even flee into the nearby forests to become an outlaw.

There was just one place she could go, however, and even though the fugitive was an immature drab of a laundry girl, desperation drove her to take advantage of it.

Sir Richard de Revelle arrived at Sampford something over an hour later, hurrying back with Ralph Peverel to make sure of getting there ahead of his arch-enemy, the coroner.

His keenness to help his neighbours was in part due to the chance of confounding his brother-in-law, but also as a potential lever in securing the desirable parcel of land he wanted. It was a wide tongue of pasture and forest which projected into his manor boundary. If he could acquire it, this land would form a continuous stretch which, when ploughed into strip fields, would form a valuable addition to his estate. Previous offers had been adamantly rejected by both old William and Hugo Peverel, and he had been working on the more amenable Ralph for several months, hoping that he could persuade the family to part with the ground.

Richard marched into the hall as if he owned the whole manor, slapping his soft leather gloves against his thigh as he advanced to the far table, where once again the ladies and all the other brothers were seated. Ralph ushered him to a bench and beckoned imperiously to a servant to bring wine. De Revelle, with hand on heart, inclined his head courteously to the ladies and murmured platitudes of sympathy on the sad loss of Hugo. His foxy face was triangular, narrowing below his moustached mouth to a small pointed beard, an affectation unusual among the Norman aristocracy, who were usually clean shaven. Similarly, his fair wavy hair was slightly longer than the usual cropped top above shaven sides that most men affected. A dandified man, he wore a long tunic of fine green wool under his yellow riding cloak, with golden embroidery around the square neck and lower hem. A wide leather belt, carrying a dagger and pouch, was of oriental style, designed to give the impression that he had been to the Holy Land, though in fact he had never ventured beyond France.

'I have told Sir Richard the sparse facts surrounding my poor brother's vile death . . .' began Ralph, but he was immediately interrupted by Odo.

'Since you left here, there has been more news. The girl has been found – and lost again.'

'Satan's horns, what's that supposed to mean?'

'The wench that Hugo took to the ox byre was one of the wash-house drabs. But before she could be taken, she gained sanctuary in the church!'

Ralph, the most short-tempered of the whole family, stared at Odo for a moment, then laughed. 'Sanctuary! Don't be so bloody foolish, brother. Let's get her dragged out and given a good beating – then have her brought here for us to question.'

Beatrice smacked her small hand on the table in front of her.

'You can't do that! It's sacrilege and I expect it's illegal.'

Joel, who wished to support Beatrice in everything, agreed.

'Besides, if you want to thrash senseless every girl that Hugo ever laid, there'll be little laundry or cooking done in the village,' he added cynically, forgetting his previous concern for Beatrice's sensibilities.

Ralph ignored his facetious younger brother and addressed himself to Odo and de Revelle.

'This is nonsense! The girl is nothing but a cottar's daughter, the lowest of the low,' he snarled. 'Why the daft bitch wants to seek sanctuary is beyond me, unless of course she did kill Hugo! Send someone to get the damned wench out of that church, before I lose my temper!'

Refusing to acknowledge Ralph's assumption of supremacy, Odo turned to the former sheriff for advice. 'What do you think about this, Richard?' He deliberately used his Christian name to emphasise his own equality in rank with another manor-lord. De Revelle stroked his little beard, an affectation he had when giving the impression of deep thought.

'It's an offence, of course, the breaking of sanctuary,' he said in his rather high-pitched voice. 'There is a rigid scale of penalties set down by law. But it is the Church, rather than the Crown, that sets its face so strongly against it, especially after King Henry's blunder in sending those knights after Thomas Becket.'

'So what should we do?' persisted Odo. 'You are the legal authority here.'

De Revelle scowled. 'Until I am reinstated after the foul conspiracy that deprived me of my shrievalty, I have no authority – but therefore am free to give advice, man to man.'

'And that advice would be?' questioned Ralph, returning to the fray.

'This is your manor,' brayed Richard. 'The slut is your property, the church is yours and no doubt you pay the priest who serves it. So drag the wretched girl out without further delay!'

The reeve led the coroner's team into the village up the last stretch of track that came from the high road to Taunton along the Culm valley. De Wolfe had never been to Sampford Peverel before; to him it was just a name, one of the scores of manors that dotted the county. Many belonged to the bishop, others to abbeys or the Templars or directly to the King himself, but the remainder were held by knights and barons, either as freehold tenants-in-chief of the King or leased from a greater landowner. He knew that the Peverels had been here since the middle of the century, the family having originally come over soon after the Conquest – some said as bastard relations of William himself. There were Peverels in a number of areas, from the Derbyshire peaks to farther down in Devon. The reeve gave a running commentary on the fertility of the rolling slopes on which the village was sited, local pride evident in his voice as he extolled the abundant crops and beasts that could be grown and tended here in good years. It was his job to organise the tilling of the fields and the ordering of labour that kept the economy of the manor in good shape. He grimly added a caveat to the prosperity of Sampford, however, as the first dwellings and the church came in sight.

'A pity the goodness of the soil is not matched by the contentment of its people,' he growled obscurely. Then, perhaps realising that for an unfree villein he had said too much in the presence of another Norman knight, he quickly changed the subject. Pointing at the squat wooden building coming up on the right-hand side of the track, he said, 'Our last master, Sir William, was going to rebuild the church in stone, but the good Lord took him before he could begin.'

A low dry-stone wall surrounded the churchyard, in which a few old yew trees stood among the grassy grave mounds, several of which had rough wooden crosses at their head. The church was a small oblong with a bell arch sticking up at the west end of the thatched roof, tattered from the previous winter's storms. A porch just big enough to hold a coffin and four bearers was stuck on to the south wall, from which loud voices could be heard as they reined in at the churchyard gate.

'What the hell's going on?' grunted Gwyn, as first shouting and cursing from several different voices then a feminine scream could be heard.

'Strange language for the house of God!' agreed the coroner, throwing his leg over Odin's broad back to dismount.

'Disgraceful profanity, that's what it is!' squeaked Thomas de Peyne, crossing himself energetically as the yelling increased from inside the church.

As the four men pushed through the small gate, the reeve hurried ahead, fearful of what he might find in his village church. A new voice erupted from the porch, in broad accents that John and Gwyn easily recognised as Irish, from their time fighting in that island.

'This surely is sacrilege and a grave offence against God and the Holy Church! Be assured that the archdeacon and the bishop will hear of this!'

As a blasphemous reply came to the effect that if the speaker wanted to keep his comfortable living he had best keep his mouth shut, a struggling knot of people erupted from the porch, watched by the bemused group from Exeter. A bare-footed young girl in a patched dress was squirming like an eel in the grip of two men, one of whom John recognised as the armourer he wanted to question about the death of the silversmith. The other was dressed in green and the coroner correctly identified him as a hunt-master.

Hanging on to the back of the girl's thin smock was a fat man with a priest's cassock and a shaven tonsure, still bewailing the sacrilege of breaking sanctuary and threatening every penalty from excommunication to being struck by a thunderbolt. The coroner loped forward until his predatory features loomed closely over the two men dragging the girl.

'Let the child be, damn you! What's going on here?' he rasped.

Agnes stopped yelling and looked up in terrified awe at this black-clad apparition from outside the village. Was she to be executed on the spot by this man, who looked like a gigantic hooded crow? Before she could find her tongue, a chorus of voices burst out from around John.

'These accursed souls are dragging her from God's holy sanctuary!' squawked the fat Irishman, blue eyes watering in his round, red face.

'What the bloody hell are you about, lads?' demanded Warin Fishacre.

'Just doing what Sir Ralph ordered!' shouted the hound-master. 'Or was it Sir Odo? Anyway, we was told to get her out of here and bring her to the hall.'

'I didn't do nothing, honest!' screeched the wash-girl. 'I was scared when I heard what had happened, knew I'd get the bloody blame and they'd hang me!'

De Wolfe held up his hands, his wolfskin cloak falling back like the wings of some huge bat. 'Be quiet, all of you!' he roared, then stabbed a long finger at the priest. 'You, Father – tell me what this is all about.'

Before Patrick, the village priest, could open his mouth, there was a deep, authoritative voice from behind them.

'I presume you are Sir John de Wolfe. You are welcome to my manor, sir, though I regret that such a sad event brings you to us.'

John turned to see half a dozen men coming down from the churchyard gate. The speaker, a tall man with a mournful Peverel face, was almost jostled for first place on the narrow path by a younger man whom he recognised as the brother who had been with Hugo Peverel outside the New Inn in Exeter when he had challenged them over the suspect armourer. But what immediately caught his eye was the all-too-familiar figure behind Odo Peverel.

'Oh, Mary, mother of God!' he groaned under his breath, as he saw his brother-in-law, Richard de Revelle.

chapter seven

*In which Crowner John is frustrated
beyond measure*

The castle brooded at the top of Winchester's High
Street like a massive grey hen sitting on a nest of
buildings. A circular room in one of the towers was
used by the Chief Justiciar as his official chamber
when he was in the city, which shared with London
the functions of England's capital. Though Hubert
Walter was also Archbishop of Canterbury, his epis-
copal duties played second fiddle to the virtual
running of the country, as he was regent of England
in all but name. A soldier as much as a priest, he had
been left to bring back the English Crusaders from
the Holy Land after the King had left on his ill-fated
voyage home, but on reaching Sicily he heard that
Richard had been imprisoned in Austria and
Germany. Hubert hurried to visit him there, then
returned to England to help retrieve the situation,
mainly by devising schemes to raise money and to
keep the peace in a troubled country where Prince
John was fomenting rebellion.

As he sat behind his parchment-cluttered table, he
took a moment to stare absently through a window
slit at a patch of cold blue October sky and wonder
why he was so devoted to his king, Richard with the
lion's heart. He accepted that the man was selfish,
arrogant, greedy and often cruel, but he could also

be charming, recklessly generous and ridiculously forgiving, as he been towards his brother John after his failed rebellion. As a monarch, Richard's main concern was with France, and though he had been born in Oxford, England remained nothing more than a colony to him, from which he could extort taxes and men to support his campaigns in Palestine and France. Richard had never bothered to learn to speak English, his queen, Berengaria, had never set foot in the country, and after spending only four months of his reign in England it seemed certain that he would never return, leaving Hubert to administer the realm and raise the vast sums that were needed to pay off his ransom and finance his armies. The justiciar had been thinking a few moments ago of his old fellow campaigner, John de Wolfe, another example of the blind loyalty that the monarch seemed able to engender in the most unromantic of people. Black John was not over-endowed with either imagination or much of a sense of humour, but was brave to the point of foolhardiness and almost painfully trustworthy.

It was these qualities which had decided Hubert, with the full approval of the King, to set John up as coroner in Devon, where he could keep an eye on that scheming potential traitor Richard de Revelle and the band of incipient rebels clustered around Bishop Henry Marshal and some of the barons, such as the de la Pomeroys. The threat posed by Prince John seemed to have abated recently, but it was essential to keep a reliable pair of eyes and ears open down in the West to forestall any secret plots. The recent removal of de Revelle as sheriff made things easier, thought the justiciar – but he doubted that the man's political ambitions had evaporated, and he must still be watched.

A chancery clerk came in with a fresh bundle of manuscripts and laid them on a corner of the table.

'These have just come from Shrewsbury and Chester, your Grace,' he said in an oily voice. Sliding the strap of a leather pouch from his shoulder, he laid it before the archbishop with something akin to reverence.

'And this has arrived from Portsmouth, on the latest cog from Harfleur.'

After he had bowed himself out, a habit that always irritated the blunt-natured Hubert, the justiciar opened the pouch and took out a parchment roll from which dangled the heavy royal seal. Cutting the tapes and cords with a dagger that he had personally taken from the body of a slain Saracen, he settled back and read the latest missive from the court at Rouen. Some of it was in the King's own hand, for, unlike some of his royal forebears, Richard could wield a quill almost as well as a sword.

Hubert sat for some time reading the bulky dispatches, his brow furrowing from time to time as some particularly difficult problem was propounded. He was a lean, wiry man, and dressed in a plain grey tunic he looked quite unlike the usual over-fed, over-dressed prelate, the only concession to his religious status being a small silver cross hanging around his neck. Eventually, he got to the end of the roll and dropped it back on to the table, reaching instead for a jug of wine and a pewter cup.

Sipping the rich red blood of the Loire valley, he stared again through the embrasure, though his thoughts were far from the streak of sky visible through the slit. As he mulled over the contents of the missive from the King, his mind's eye travelled westwards to Wales, and then once again settled on the dark stubble and forbidding features of the ever faithful John de Wolfe.

*　　*　　*

The group of newcomers stood blocking the path to the churchyard gate, glowering at the coroner's trio, who had turned to face them.

'There's nothing in this for you, John. You were sent for in error, there was some misunderstanding on the part of the bailiff.'

De Revelle's voice was haughty and condescending, as if he were still the sheriff, dismissing some servant.

'And what misunderstanding can occur over the murder of a manor-lord, Richard? Can you mean that Hugo Peverel is still alive?'

John's tone was deceptively mild as he tried to keep the sarcasm out of his voice, but privately he was livid that this bloody man had turned up to haunt him, after he had thought he had got rid of him for ever.

They were still standing outside the church porch, the girl now having ceased wriggling in the grip of her captors, her eyes round with bemusement as she found herself the centre of attention of all these high-born men. Richard had pushed himself to the fore and stood between Ralph and Odo, as if he were the new lord of Sampford rather than one of the Peverels. Joel stepped up on to an old grave mound to stand on Odo's left while behind them the bailiff and steward waited anxiously to see the outcome of this confrontation. Outside the gate, a cluster of villagers were gathering, mouths agape as the events of this dramatic day continued to unfold.

Odo's measured words attempted to reduce the tension that was becoming as tight as a drawn bowstring.

'We did not intend to bother you with this matter, Sir John. It's a long ride from Exeter and this is a matter that our manor can deal with. You will appreciate that the circumstances of my brother's death are not those which we would want broadcast around the county.'

Ralph hurriedly forced his own opinion into the dialogue.

'I want no outside interference, Crowner, this is purely a family issue!'

His words were less gracious than those of his more mature elder brother and he substituted 'I' for 'we' in his relentless pursuit of the inheritance.

De Wolfe scowled at them both, resenting Ralph's rudeness.

'What you may want is of no consequence! It is the King's peace that rules us all, whether you like it or not. Unless any of you are minded to defy the laws of King Richard and his council?'

He turned his glare full on to de Revelle, and no one was in any doubt as to his insinuation about the former sheriff's political leanings.

'What are you doing here, may I ask?' he snapped. 'You no longer have any official authority.'

Richard's thick skin allowed him to continue as if he were still in charge and the coroner was the interloper.

'Though it's none of your business, John, I am here as a friend and neighbour at the express invitation of the Peverel family. They naturally thought that my experience of such crises might be of help to them.'

John had to bite his tongue to prevent himself from observing that his brother-in-law had not the slightest experience of dealing with sudden deaths, having been content when sheriff to let others do all the dirty work, while he remained in his chamber thinking up more ways of embezzling from the county taxes. Drowning his irritation with a deep breath, he turned to Odo, who, though he had never met him before, he already recognised as the most reasonable of the brothers.

'Sir, will you tell me what exactly has been happening here? I have had only the bare bones of the matter from your reeve.'

Forestalling Ralph, the elder Peverel explained how Hugo had gone missing the previous evening and had eventually been found hidden under the hay in the ox byre, with savage wounds in his back. With neither of the ladies present, he felt less inhibited in explaining the circumstances.

'My brother, like so many other active men, was fond of slaking his surplus virility on common drabs like this girl here.'

'A common and understandable habit, even to be found among senior law officers!' sneered de Revelle, unable to resist a jibe at John's affair with his Welsh tavern-keeper.

De Wolfe again resisted the temptation to observe that if they were talking about the lusts of senior law officers, he had twice caught de Revelle with Exeter whores. Instead he once more applied himself to Odo.

'Though I understand from your reeve that the proper procedure of the first finder raising the hue and cry throughout the village was carried out – and that your bailiff quite rightly lost no time in reporting the death to the coroner – you have already committed two breaches of the law!'

The three brothers stared at the coroner, puzzled that anyone should even consider challenging their absolute authority on their own manor.

'And what may they be?' demanded Ralph.

'First, it looks uncommonly as if you have violated the right of every person to seek sanctuary. In addition, the body should have been left where it was found until my arrival, which I am told has not been done here.'

There was a simultaneous gabble of protest from the Peverels, in which de Revelle joined in enthusiastically.

'Do you seriously expect us to leave the lord of the manor face down in his own ox byre?' raged Ralph.

'Really, Sir John, you are a Norman knight yourself!' snapped Odo. 'Would you allow your closest relative to stay more than five minutes in such a degrading situation, for villein and serfs to come gaping at?'

De Wolfe glowered at them. 'I did not make the law, sirs, but I have been appointed to see that they are enforced and that I shall do!' he said stubbornly.

'Then you are an even greater damned fool than I thought!' bleated Richard offensively. 'Laws are made for the underlings of this world, not those of us who control it. Why do we need waste time on this tragic matter, when it is so patently obvious that this slut is the culprit?'

John ignored him and turned to the girl and the two men still hanging on to her arms.

'Let her go, I doubt that she'll attack you,' he said sarcastically to the armourer and the hound-master. Then he addressed Agnes, his tone milder as he looked down at the maid, whose mood swung between fear and indignation. 'I see no point in you going back into the church, girl. There's no need for you to seek sanctuary at this point. I will see that matters are conducted properly.'

'They'll hang me for sure, sir,' she said sullenly. 'I'm only safe in there.'

The coroner nodded understandingly. 'You were illegally dragged from sanctuary, so I promise that if things go ill with you, you can return here. But for now, you must go home until I come to ask you some questions. D'you understand?'

She nodded, but she was still in the grip of her captors, who looked uncertainly from the coroner to the group barring his way to the gate.

'This is beyond your jurisdiction, Sir John!' boomed Odo. 'Have you the power to override our wishes?'

'John, you are insufferable!' brayed de Revelle. 'You

have no right to interfere in this way, trying to ride roughshod over ancient manor laws!'

Gwyn moved closer to his master as the four men took a step nearer John and his hand moved gently to the hilt of his sword, but the coroner thrust his dark head aggressively towards his brother-in-law.

'No right? I've every right, and if you deny it you'll answer to the King and his ministers!' he snarled. 'I was appointed to keep the pleas of the Crown and part of those duties is the investigation of deaths from foul play. Another of my tasks is the taking of confessions from sanctuary-seekers and administering the abjuration of the realm. Both seem very relevant here and neither are any part of manorial jurisdiction!'

'Dealing with breaches of the peace is sheriff's business,' bleated Richard.

'And you are no longer the sheriff!' retorted John. 'Not that you did much about keeping the peace when you were one! It so happens that the new sheriff has deputed me to combine his duties with the prosecution of my inquests – with which the justiciar concurs, I might add.'

This was a fairly loose interpretation of Henry de Furnellis's expressed desire not to become involved with casework, but it would suffice to justify John's free hand in investigations. He scowled at the three brothers in turn, defying them to contradict him, especially as he had deliberately laboured the fact that he was a direct agent of the King's chief minister.

'Now, to business! I need to examine the corpse of your unfortunate kinsman and also to see the place where his body was discovered, before you so recklessly moved it.'

He swung away, and the tension of the moment subsided sufficiently for Gwyn to relax his fingers from around his sword hilt. The coroner looked beyond the indignant group in front of him and beckoned to a couple of women who were among the dozen or so villagers gawping over the churchyard hedge.

'Take this girl back to her home. Tell the family to keep her there until I come to talk to her.'

Under the sheer force of de Wolfe's personality, the brothers reluctantly stood aside. Grim faced, they watched while Agnes was taken by a pair of good-wives out of the gate and up the road towards the squalid cottage where she lived. Then John strode down the few yards of path towards the porch, followed by Gwyn and Thomas. As he passed the two men who had dragged the girl from the church, he jabbed a forefinger into the chest of Robert Longus, the bearded armourer.

'I want words with you later on another matter! You are now under attachment for failing to attend my inquest in Exeter.'

Without waiting for a response, he vanished into the building with his two assistants, followed more slowly by the three brothers and Richard de Revelle. The rotund Irish priest had scurried ahead, and when John's eyes had adjusted to the dim light coming from a few shuttered slits in the wooden walls, he saw that Father Patrick was standing before a simple altar at the far end. The floor of beaten earth was empty of any furniture, but around the side walls were narrow benches for the old and infirm to rest during services, the rest of the congregation having to stand. There was no separate chancel, the church being a simple oblong, with a large wooden cross hanging on the east wall above the altar, between two of the window slits. The light from these fell on a wooden bier, a narrow table with carrying handles at each corner, on which lay a still shape under a linen sheet.

De Wolfe marched up to one side of this, Gwyn taking up a position opposite. Thomas stood at the foot, bending his knee and crossing himself jerkily, his eyes fixed reverently on the brass cross on the altar table. As the coroner nodded to his officer to pull off the shroud, Ralph Peverel strutted forward in protest.

'Is this necessary, Crowner? Why can you not let my brother rest in peace?'

'Murder is murder, sir! Have you no desire to discover who took his life and see justice done to his killer?'

'Of course. But the deed has been done – what use is it to defile the dead further by your examination?'

His elder brother now came and put a restraining hand on Ralph's arm.

'The coroner has his duty to perform and we must tolerate anything which leads to the discovery of the perpetrator of this foul crime,' he said in a conciliatory tone, strengthening John's impression that, although a miserable sort of fellow, he was the most reasonable member of this prickly family. He had already dismissed the junior brother Joel as an immature and feckless young man.

Gwyn pulled the sheet back from the corpse's face and folded it down to lie across the feet. Hugo was dressed in a short tunic of dull yellow that came to mid-thigh, under which were woollen hose ending in pointed leather shoes. He wore a belt with a small dagger sheathed at the left side and a small scrip purse on the other. Wisps of hay and straw adhered to his clothing and his dark red hair.

'Can you not close his eyes, for decency's sake?' snapped Ralph, determined to be as critical as possible.

John bent to look closely at the blue eyes, which stared upward at the inside of the roof, where small birds chirruped and fluttered among the woven hazel withies that supported the thatch. The fronts of the orbs were already becoming flattened and cloudy with death, but otherwise the eyes were normal.

'No bleedings into the whites, nothing at all,' he muttered to Gwyn, and with his fingers he drew down the lids. The rest of the face had the pallor of death, and when he pushed down on the point of the chin he felt that the jaw was locked solid.

'He's stone cold and as rigid as a plank,' he announced, half to himself.

'Been dead many hours, that's for sure.'

'We don't need a coroner to tell us that,' sneered Joel. 'He was found earlier this morning and has been missing since last night!'

De Wolfe ignored him and nodded again at his officer. Gwyn, a veteran of scores of similar procedures, began his ritual of exposing the rest of the body to his master. He undid the belt and pulled up the tunic and undershirt, revealing the separate legs of the hose, supported by laces tied to a thong around the waist. John turned to the brothers and their servants, who were clustered behind Thomas at the foot of the bier.

'There's no need for you all to be here, if it distresses you.'

His attempt at concern for their feelings fell on deaf ears, as they all stood their ground, scowling, defying anyone to try to dismiss them from their own church.

'He's all bloody underneath,' grunted Gwyn, as he tugged the back of the tunic upward to the shoulders. The surface of the bier was slick with blood, which began to drip to the floor as the body was moved.

'We'll have him over the other way,' ordered the coroner. The family had been offered their chance to leave and he was not inclined to skimp his examination on their account. Hugo Peverel was a large man and his corpse was heavy, but the muscular Gwyn turned it as if it were a mere side of bacon, and laid it on its face.

'Soaked in blood!' commented the Cornishman cheerfully, grinning at Thomas as the little clerk blanched. Even after more than a year in the coroner's service, he was still squeamish at the sight of gore.

The back of the tunic and shirt were dark red, almost black, in colour, and at the sides they were stiff where the blood had dried. 'There was nothing like that amount of blood visible when we saw him in the ox byre,' ventured Walter Hog, the bailiff.

'But I was told that he was found face down,' snapped de Wolfe. 'Is that right?'

'He was indeed, I'll never forget the sight,' answered Odo, tensely.

'Then you wouldn't expect him to bleed much, until he was turned on to his back,' retorted the coroner irritably. 'Most of this blood issued from him after death. That's why it was remiss of you to move him. I need to see bodies in their original state.'

'What difference can that make?' sneered Ralph. 'He was stabbed to death, even our village idiot could have told you that.'

John glared at him, thrusting his head forward like an angry crow.

'If you've nothing helpful to say, I suggest you keep your mouth shut, sir! If I could be sure that he had not bled much before his body was interfered with, it would tell me that he was stabbed where he lay, probably face down. And that he died quickly!'

'How can you say that, Crowner?' asked Odo, with a trace of genuine interest in his voice.

'The blood has stained his garment only above the waist. If he had been on his feet, even staggering about for a few moments, it would have trickled down over his buttocks and thighs.'

Gwyn nodded sagely. Both he and the coroner prided themselves on being self-taught experts on death and injury, after twenty years on various battlefields, as well as a year investigating sudden death in Devon.

De Wolfe turned his attention to the back of the body, revealed now that the clothing was pulled up almost to Hugo's neck. It was a smeared mass of blood, with gobs of shiny clot adhering here and there. He turned to the priest, who was standing wringing his hands at the transformation of his church into a mortuary.

'Father Patrick, have you a cloth and some water we could use?'

The rotund cleric hurried away to a small door on the north side of the building, which opened into a small lean-to shelter that served as a sacristy and store-room. Here, in addition to his second-best cassock and his service books, he had a broom made from a bundle of twigs, a wooden bucket and some cleaning rags for the altar cross.

'This is all I have, Crowner,' he said, offering a strip torn from an old surplice and some dirty water left in the bucket. Gwyn took them and carefully wiped away as much of the blood as he could from the skin between the dead man's shoulder blades. A ripple of suppressed horror went round the audience, which now also contained the reeve, the steward, the armourer and a couple of other manor officers. They saw a pattern of marks on the skin of their late lord's back which told of a violent attack.

'You'll need to make a note of these as soon as we've finished, Thomas,' commanded de Wolfe. He peered more closely, his big hooked nose coming within a foot of the bloody wounds.

'Six, no seven, stabs, both sides of the spine. All roughly in the same direction – the knife must have been held at about the same angle for them all.'

'Narrow blade, by the looks of it, Crowner. But not all the wounds are the same length.' Gwyn was unwilling to let his own expertise go unemployed.

'The length depends how far the knife was pushed in, if it was a tapered blade,' answered his master. 'But I agree, a smallish blade – the widest wound is well under an inch across.'

He clicked his fingers at his officer and pointed to Hugo's own dagger, resting in its sheath on the discarded belt. Gwyn pulled it out and showed it to his master.

'That certainly didn't cause these wounds,' he grunted. 'Double-edged and much too wide.'

Having eliminated the dagger, de Wolfe now explored the depth of the stabs, and without hesitation rammed his forefinger into the biggest wound and pushed until his knuckle was against the skin.

'Goes deeply inside his chest, between the ribs,' he announced, before withdrawing the finger with a sucking sound. He absently wiped the blood with the soiled rag as he worked out something in his mind.

'The blade was held diagonally across the back, roughly in line with the ribs, so no bone was broken as it slipped between them. The killer must have been to the side of the victim, either right or left, when he struck – or she struck,' he added.

'A woman? Or a girl? That's the very thing we are suggesting!' snapped Ralph, with an I-told-you-so sneer.

De Wolfe shrugged. 'It may be unlikely, but I rule nothing out at this stage. It was a small knife such as women carry – and the force needed to slip a blade between the ribs, rather than smash through them, would literally have been child's play, let alone a woman's.'

Again there was a murmur of smug agreement among the brothers, who were only too eager to pin the blame on the laundry maid. As the coroner continued his examination, he found nothing else on the rest of the corpse, which he found interesting in itself.

'Not so much as a scratch on the hands or arms, so he made no effort to defend himself. Often an attacked man will fend off the blade with his forearm – or even grasp it to deflect it from his vital organs. There is nothing of that nature here.'

'And as the gentleman was an experienced tournament fighter, he would not have been taken easily,' Gwyn reminded him.

'Then my brother was obviously taken unawares by some cowardly assassin!' snapped Joel.

'Face down in the hay, he might well have been sleeping,' said John. 'Especially soon after having taking his pleasure with a girl.'

'Why is the skin dark red in places, but white over the shoulder blades?' demanded Odo, who seemed to have an inquiring streak in his nature.

'He has been lying on his back now for many hours, so the blood has settled to the lowest point,' explained de Wolfe. 'But lying on this hard bier has squeezed it from the shoulders and buttocks. Another reason for not moving the corpse until I had a chance to see it.'

He turned his attention back to the sinister-looking cuts on the cadaver, and together with Gwyn poked and prodded at each gaping slit in the skin.

'D'you think that a few of the wounds show a blunter end?' he asked his officer.

Gwyn, pleased to be asked his opinion, nodded. 'This one – and this, almost certainly.' He pointed a grimy fingernail at the upper end of a couple of the injuries, where a slightly squared-off termination did not quite match the sharply pointed lower end. 'I reckon it was a single-edged blade, not a regular dagger with two cutting edges.'

The coroner nodded his agreement. 'A narrow knife, blunt along the back.'

Richard de Revelle was determined to be dismissive and obstructive.

'A great deduction, indeed!' he said sarcastically. 'There are probably forty such knives in this village alone. And for all we know, the killer might well be an outsider, creeping in here at night to thieve.'

De Wolfe straightened up and stood with his fists resting on his sword belt. He would have liked to have used them to punch his arrogant brother-in-law on the nose, but restrained himself and said mildly, 'It's early days yet. Every small fact adds up when we are seeking a murderer.'

He nodded at Gwyn, who began to replace the clothing and lay the corpse face up on the bier, before covering it again with the sheet.

'I trust you have finished with poor Hugo now, Crowner?' said Odo, in a sepulchral voice.

'I have no need to examine his body again, certainly. But I will need to display it to the jury when I hold my inquest, as the law demands.'

'But surely we can go ahead with the funeral!' exclaimed Ralph. 'It is not decent to leave him above ground a moment longer than is necessary.'

The coroner shook his head emphatically. 'I am sorry, but that is not possible until I have held my inquiry and recorded it for the King's justices when they next come to the county.'

'And when will this precious inquiry be held?' sneered de Revelle, determined to make things as diffi-cult as possible.

'I will first have to speak to everyone who might have some information – which I'm afraid includes every member of the family and your manor-servants. Then anyone else in the village who may know something about this tragedy. As today is already well advanced, that will take until tomorrow morning, but I have to return to Exeter then, as I already have another inquest set for the afternoon.'

'So when are you coming back here?' demanded Joel.

'The day after tomorrow – Wednesday. You may arrange your burial for later that day. The weather is cool for October, there will be little problem with the body. Matters may have been more difficult in high summer. He can rest with dignity here before the altar.'

The brothers and their neighbour, de Revelle, protested at the delay, but the coroner was implacable.

'Now I need to begin speaking to all those who might have some information for me,' said John brusquely. 'Starting with that girl Agnes.'

'It was very unwise of you to insist that she be released so easily from our arrest,' huffed Richard de Revelle. 'That may be the last we see of her!'

'And where could she go, might I ask?' countered John. 'She'd hardly be welcome in the next manor, or anywhere else around here – a runaway serf belonging to Sampford.' He turned his back on Richard and addressed Odo. 'I'll walk to where she lives now, if someone will show me where that is.'

'We'll accompany you, Crowner!' snapped Ralph. 'She is our serf, I need to interrogate her myself.'

Again John noted that the 'we' slipped into 'I' – and he also observed that Odo's scowl deepened at the lapse. There was little filial affection between these two, he thought.

'You are certainly entitled to speak to your subjects as much as you wish,' he said. 'But not when I am conducting my enquiries. I wish to speak to her alone – or at most, with her mother present.' The Peverels huffed and puffed, but de Wolfe was adamant.

'In that case, the bailiff can take you,' grunted Odo.

'We will return to the manor house to discuss the matter further with Sir Richard and our ladies.'

With ill grace, the brothers and their steward left the church and a few moments later Walter Hog led the coroner and his assistants up the dusty track towards the western end of the village. Beyond the green they passed the manor house on their left, its stockade seeming to dominate the rest of the dismal village with menace, emphasising the downtrodden status of the folk who laboured to keep the Peverels in relative comfort. The whole place seemed shabby to John, especially in comparison with his home manor of Stoke-in-Teignhead, where his brother William prided himself on ensuring a decent living for both his freemen and his bondsmen. Here many of the houses were little better than hovels, with mouldy grass-grown thatch and in some cases, disintegrating walls where the cob had eroded from the frames on which it had been plastered. As he walked up the rough track, he noticed that many of the fences around the crofts were broken and had been roughly mended with branches and sticks to keep the livestock from straying. There were a few decent houses, and the bailiff proudly pointed out one as his own and another as the dwelling of the reeve.

The dusty road sloped up towards the west, where it went on to Tiverton. On the left, behind the line of crofts and tofts, were strip fields running away at right angles until they reached the meadow and waste, which in turn gave way to the edge of the forest. On the other side of the road, the fields sloped down into the shallow valley that carried the mill-stream, beyond which was more waste ground until the trees began again. Above these, low hills filled the horizon, sloping up towards the distant edge of Exmoor, the green beginning to turn brown as the autumn advanced.

As the village began to peter out, the dwellings became smaller and even more dismal. These belonged to the cottars, inferior bondsmen who had no land allotment in the fields like the freemen and villeins, but eked out a living by working for the lord at the more menial tasks. They tended cattle and goats, did the fencing, milking, ditching and thatching and some of the ploughing and raking on the lord's demesne. Others were labourers for the farrier, smith or miller, or cleaned the stables and byres and spread the dung on the fields.

The bailiff stopped at the last shack, a mere few hundred paces from where the dense trees closed in at the edge of the village.

'This is where Agnes lives. It's a poor place, I'm afraid,' announced Walter, with a trace of embarrassment.

There was a ragged thorn hedge around the quarter-acre plot and John pushed aside an apology for a garden gate, which was a few branches tied with twine. In front of the hut was a garden where vegetables grew, though many had already been harvested and others, such as rows of beans, had died back at the end of the season. He could hear the bellow of a cow and the grunting of pigs behind the house and as he walked to the door he saw a female goat tied to a stake on a patch of coarse grass.

The building was of the usual cob under a tattered thatch, once whitewashed with lime, but patches of the surface plastering had fallen away to reveal the straw and clay underneath. The door was a sheet of thick boiled leather hanging from the lintel, and the bailiff pushed this aside and stuck his head in to shout.

'Aelfric! Gunna! Are you there? The coroner wants to talk to Agnes.'

A small lad, little more than a toddler, shot out of the doorway, pursued by a barking mongrel, and vanished around the side of the house. Then a large woman of Saxon blood appeared, probably not more than thirty years old, her face lined and worn with toil. She had a small baby in her arms and her soiled and patched dress was pulled aside to allow it to feed from her breast.

She looked with lacklustre eyes at the bailiff, then at John and the two men standing behind him.

'My man is working, but Agnes is here. Two neighbours brought her home.' Her voice was flat and apathetic. 'You'd best come in if you want to talk to her. God knows how we'll manage if she loses her work at the wash house.'

Walter Hog held the door-flap aside and de Wolfe went in, Gwyn and Thomas standing at the threshold where they could hear what was being said. John found himself in a long room that smelt strongly of cow manure; as at one end a wattle screen penned in two brown calves and a stinking billy-goat. At the other was a heap of dried ferns on a wooden shelf that served as the matrimonial bed, under which was more bracken to soften the sleeping place of three children. A fire-pit in the centre was only smouldering at present, so there was little smoke to choke the atmosphere. Along the back wall was another wide wooden shelf with pots and dishes which appeared to be mainly used for skimming milk and brewing ale. Around the fire-pit, over which was an iron trivet from which hung a small cauldron, a few more pots and dishes indicated the cooking facilities. A couple of milking stools were the only other furniture, but the object of his visit was sitting on the floor with her back to the wall. Agnes had a sullen, defiant look on her round face, but this cleared somewhat when she saw who the visitor was.

'Thank you for delivering me from those men, sir,'

she said, in an unexpected bout of gratitude. 'I have done nothing wrong, I swear it.'

'You went with that . . . that man again,' snapped her mother. 'Is that not wrong?'

Agnes jumped to her feet, her face flushed with anger. 'What choice did I have? He was our lord and master – and you were glad enough of the two pennies I brought home.'

The woman shrugged and pulled the baby from her breast and laid it on a grubby cloth spread on the bed. Agnes went to the infant and sat alongside it, gently stroking its sparse fair hair to soothe it to sleep, while her mother unselfconsciously rearranged her dress and tucked the ends of her head-cloth into her neck-line. 'You answer this lord truthfully, girl,' she said sternly.

John thought it time to interrupt this domestic tableau. 'I'm no lord, woman, but an officer of the King determined to see justice done.' He turned to the girl, who looked up at him with suspicious eyes.

'Agnes, if as you claim you have done no evil, you have nothing to fear. I will not allow the new lord of this manor, whoever he might turn out to be, to blame you unjustly. Do you understand?'

She looked at her mother, then back at the coroner and finally nodded.

'Were you in that ox byre last night?'

'Yes, that's where he took me the time before. It's always empty this time of year, the beasts are kept on the waste.'

'When did you go there?'

'I left the wash house after they brought the cloths from the hall. Every night, we have to wash the table linen that they use for supper. Lady Avelina won't eat from bare boards, so they say.'

This was about as accurate an indicator of the time

as anyone in a village would be able to offer, with not yet a single clock in the isles of Britain. Dusk and dawn were the only sure markers, unless one stood within sound of the bells of a cathedral or abbey, whose sand-glasses and graduated candles indicated the times for the daily services.

'Was it dark, then?'

'Getting dusk, sir. Near enough dark by the time he had finished with me.'

John had no interest in hearing the details. 'Had Sir Hugo been drinking, Agnes?'

She grimaced. 'All men are drunk at night, sir. I could smell wine, not ale, but he could walk well enough – and do me until I ached.'

Her mother tutted under her breath, but John felt that she was not particularly distressed about her daughter's activities.

'Did he take you by force, girl – or did you go willingly?'

Again the plump-faced girl looked covertly at her mother. 'I had little choice, sir. In turn, he has been through most of the girls in the laundry and the kitchen. One who refused got a thrashing from him and was turned out of her job – so her father thrashed her again for being a heavier burden on the family. Sir Hugo always gave us a penny or two afterwards, so we didn't mind all that much.'

She sniffed and wiped her running nose. 'After tournaments was the best. If he won, he was in a right good humour when he came home. He once gave a maid in the kitchen four whole pence on one of those nights!' she said with wistful wonderment.

De Wolfe felt that they were wandering from the point.

'Now, when he had finished with you, what happened? Was he quite well when you left him?'

According to Agnes, after he had had his way with her in the hay, Hugo had produced two pennies from his scrip and told her to go home.

'So you left him in the byre alone?'

'He was still lying in the hay, sir. He sounded sleepy. I remember he yawned as I took the money. It was almost dark in there, but I could hear him yawn.'

'When you left, did you see anyone about the place?'

'Not a soul. I came straight home, up the road past the manor gate, where there were people talking in the bailey. But it was almost night, so I couldn't see very well.'

'She did come in then, sir,' cut in the mother. 'I was at the gate talking to my neighbour when she came. There was just a streak of light left in the western sky.'

John scratched his bristly face as he considered the sparse information. It had the ring of truth about it and, apart from anything else, he failed to see why Agnes should have murdered someone who occasionally gave her twopence.

'Do you own a knife, girl?' he asked.

She shook her head, almost grinning at the daft question. 'I've got a wooden spoon my father carved for me. I do my eating with that.'

'Broth and pottage is about all we have – there's little need for knives for the kind of food we have,' said the mother bitterly.

De Wolfe was running out of ideas now, but looked at the clothes that Agnes was wearing – a shapeless kirtle of brown wool, darned and ragged at the hem, with a soiled linen apron over the front. Her hair was plaited into a pigtail down her back and she wore no head-rail. The apron appeared free of anything that could be bloodstains.

'Have you changed your clothing since last night?' he asked.

The girl gave a hollow laugh. 'Changed! What into, sir? This is all I have – and this was my sister's before she died of the yellow ague.'

As she sat stroking the head of her infant brother, John saw a tear glisten in her eye, but whether it was for her dead sister or her own miserable lot, he could not decide. With some throat-clearing noises to cover his feelings, he prepared to leave, but as he moved towards the door he fumbled in his belt-pouch and produced two pennies.

Giving them to the sad-featured woman, he mumbled at her as he passed.

'She doesn't need to earn this in the same way. Get her something better to wear.'

'Sir Richard has returned to his own manor, Crowner. We cannot presume too much upon his kindness, he has his own affairs to attend to.'

Something in Odo's voice caused a worm of unease to wriggle in John's mind, though he could not quite say why. He had been brought back to the manor house from Agnes's hovel by the bailiff and was now sitting at a table in the hall. He had a jug of ale and a platter of cold meats, cheese and bread before him. He would have to stay the night, as it was now too late for him get back to Exeter, and in spite of the obvious reluctance the Peverel family showed to his continued presence, the rigid rules of hospitality overrode any overt antagonism, though Ralph's attitude came perilously close. Gwyn and Thomas had been taken off to the kitchens behind the house to be fed, and John had been offered a mattress next to the hearth for the night.

'We regret we have no vacant chamber, Crowner,' continued Odo. 'But the ladies occupy one each upstairs, as I do, being unmarried. Ralph and his family have a separate dwelling at the back of the compound, which Joel also shares.'

John was indifferent to his own comfort, having spent half the nights of his adult life wrapped in his cloak in barns, hedges, forests or deserts across the known world. 'I need to speak to you all before I leave in the morning,' he said. 'May we begin now, and perhaps later you will see if the ladies will be so kind as to present themselves?'

Ralph scowled at him from the other side of the trestle, where the brothers and their steward were lined up. 'And are you intending to question each and every one of the villagers? There are well over a hundred serfs and freemen in Sampford, including the women.'

'They will be assembled at my inquest on Wednesday and can be questioned then,' replied de Wolfe patiently. 'Unless you consider that any particular person has knowledge that I should probe before I leave?'

There was silence at this and no suggestions were offered, so the coroner began questioning each of them in turn. For all the use it turned out to be, he might as well have saved his breath. Odo was courteous enough, but volunteered nothing, answering only direct questions.

'When did I last see Hugo? It was after our supper last night. Unlike many households, we take a substantial meal in the evening, rather than confine our main meal to the middle of the day. Afterwards, we went our various ways, I to my bed quite early. As I went, I saw Hugo leave the hall and that's the last I saw of him – alive.'

'Had he been drinking heavily?'

Odo smiled wryly. 'What is heavily, Crowner? Hugo was fond of ale, cider and wine, as most of us are. But he had no greater capacity than most men. Last night, he took no more, no less than usual.'

John could prise nothing more useful from the eldest brother and turned to Joel, thinking to leave the more recalcitrant Ralph until last. The younger man seemed to treat the serious matter of a murder investigation as a joke and grinned and rolled his eyes as he lolled on his bench while the coroner asked his questions.

'Have you anything to add to your brother's recollections?' he said sternly, privately wishing to give the jackanapes a clout around the ear to wipe the insolence from his face.

'Not a word, Crowner! Hugo was not one to be questioned about his private activities. As the youngest, I have suffered from his short temper since childhood. He allowed no liberties to be taken and many is the time that he gave me a buffet that knocked me on my arse!'

'That doesn't answer my question to you about last night,' snapped de Wolfe. 'What happened?'

Quite unperturbed by the rebuff, Joel replied that after the meal had been cleared away he had had several games of draughts with his sister-in-law Beatrice, then, as it grew dark, he went to his bed in the house at the back of the bailey. He saw Hugo leave the hall while he was playing, and that was the extent of his knowledge about the matter. He related all this with an airy nonchalance that made John want to shake him, but there was nothing of any use in his story.

When he turned to the remaining brother, sitting at the end of the table, he was met with stony hostility.

'Have you reconsidered your quite unreasonable decision to force us to wait two days before we can decently bury our poor brother?' barked Ralph. 'I consider it an insult to the memory of a fellow-knight and manor-lord and I will be reporting your malfeasance to the bishop!'

De Wolfe glared at him. 'The bishop? What in hell

has the bishop to do with anything?' he snarled. 'Report what you like, sir, but at least do it to the correct authority. The proper quarter is the Chief Justiciar or the King's justices when they next come to Devon. All you'll get is confirmation of the legal procedure, but you are very welcome to present your complaint!' He thumped his fist on the table in annoyance. 'Now, sir, answer my questions. Is your recollection of the events of last evening similar to that of your kinsmen here?'

Grudgingly, Ralph agreed that Hugo had left the room soon after the meal, at which, as usual, he had drunk liberally. He had not been seen again that night and in the morning a search was mounted for him when his wife reported that he had not returned to their chamber all night. John pondered for a moment.

'Before the ladies are called, I will dispose of a more delicate matter. I assume from what I have been told by others that it was not unusual for him to take a wench somewhere for his pleasure?'

Joel grinned. 'Don't we all do the same at some time, Crowner? I have heard that you yourself are not above slaking your natural desires occasionally!'

'Mind your tongue, young man,' snapped de Wolfe. 'I am only concerned with Hugo Peverel's activities.'

Odo broke in with a rather weary voice.

'Whatever the rest of us do – and I am not a married man – Hugo had a strong appetite for life, be it food, drink, tourneying or women! Yes, he often took one of the servant girls for his satisfaction. They were not forced into it, but were often eager for both the experience and for the silver pennies.'

'My brother was no rapist, if that is what you're insinuating,' sneered Ralph. 'Yet this wash-house slut must surely have killed him! Perhaps she robbed him for the extra coins she saw in his purse.'

John, exasperated by the endless obduracy of the man, shook his dark head emphatically. 'There were still coins in his scrip – and the girl possessed no knife at all. Furthermore, her only raiment was free from even a single spot of blood.'

'None of those proclaim her innocent, Crowner. Who knows how many pennies were in his purse before she pillaged it?'

John sighed – nothing he could say would shift this man's stubborn notions, some of which he suspected had been planted by Richard de Revelle.

'Very well, then tell me if there is anyone in the manor – or without it – who had such a grudge against Hugo that they might have wished him dead.'

Again there was silence, though each brother cast a somewhat furtive glance at the others. Finally Odo answered.

'Not in the manor, of course not! Hugo was the lord, everyone depended upon him for their very life. The dwelling over their head, the food they ate, their daily employment – all were at his behest. Why should anyone hate him?'

De Wolfe saw little logic in this reply, as the maxim 'The king is dead, long live the king' applied as much to manors as kingdoms. But he seized on one phrase. 'You said no one in the manor, Sir Odo. Does that imply that he may have had enemies outwith the village?'

Ralph broke in, jealous that his brother was hogging the discussion.

'Unlike me, Odo knows little of the tournament scene. Like our father before us, Hugo and I were devoted to that noble sport, where passions often run high. Competition and rivalry are rife, sometimes to the point of personal enmity.'

'We saw good evidence of that in Exeter last week,'

drawled Joel mischievously. 'If that Frenchman de Charterai had been in this vicinity last night, I would withdraw my accusations against this slut Agnes.'

John noticed that, although the Peverel family had been in England for well over a century, they still considered themselves to be Norman enough for a Frenchman to be a foreigner.

'There are a number of knights who have lost heavily to Hugo on the tourney field,' said Ralph. 'Some have lost sufficiently, both in pride and fortune, to wish him evil. But I doubt they would come creeping into Sampford at night to stab him in the back!'

There was nothing more to be learned from these autocratic brothers – John found that extracting information from them was like pulling teeth. Grudgingly, Odo agreed to have the ladies called down and a few moments later Avelina and Beatrice appeared, chaperoned by their shadowy tire-women. Of Ralph's wife there had been no sign, but the bailiff had told John earlier that she had been delivered of her third child only two weeks before and remained feverish and weak in the house behind the manor. The men rose and waited until the two ladies had been settled in their chairs, then took their places on the stools on either side, the brothers' body language displaying an aggressively protective attitude.

'Keep this short, Crowner,' growled Ralph, his handsome face set in a stony glare. 'Our ladies are distressed and fatigued by these unhappy events.'

In fact, they looked anything but distressed. Avelina sat upright, alert and almost combative, while the newly widowed Beatrice had donned her best blue silken kirtle and snowy wimple. She looked radiant as she glanced covertly at Joel, who was clearly entranced by her interest in him. John wondered how they had comported themselves when Hugo was alive, as surely this amorous relationship could not have blossomed in the last day. With an effort, he brought his mind back to the present.

'Mesdames, I will not detain you for long,' he said politely. Their full attention swung to him and both women felt a tug of interest as they surveyed this tall, muscular man with the face of a black hawk. They knew of his reputation as a Crusader, an adventurer and a ladies' man. Awareness of his relationship with the Welsh tavern-keeper was not confined to Exeter, and with women's expert eyes they saw that his otherwise saturnine features were relieved by a pair of lips that betrayed his potentially passionate nature. Though Beatrice was too enamoured of Joel, Avelina was almost the same age as the coroner and could not resist a moment of imagination centred on the possibility of an affair with this man she had heard referred to as Black John. She pulled herself together as she heard those same lips addressing her.

'Lady Avelina, can I trouble you to tell me anything you know of the sad demise of your stepson?'

Her story was in essence the same as the others' and equally unhelpful. Hugo had still been in the hall when she retired to the solar upstairs.

'Father Patrick accompanied me as usual, to say with me my evening prayers for the soul of my late husband, taken from me so cruelly earlier this year,' she said. 'Then I went to my chamber where Florence prepared me for bed.'

She tipped her head towards the tall, silent girl who stood beside her chair.

'And you know of no one who might have hated Hugo sufficiently to want him dead?'

A flush rose slowly in her elegant cheeks. 'I will make no bones about it, Coroner. He was not a popular man.

His villagers were afraid of his intemperate nature and his lusting after their younger womenfolk was deeply resented.'

There was a shuffling of feet among the brothers and Ralph opened his mouth to protest, then it snapped shut as he thought better of it. Considering this a good opportunity to try to prise more from this fractious family, John said, 'It has been suggested that Hugo may have made enemies among the tourneying fraternity – persons such as Reginald de Charterai were mentioned.'

At this, Avelina was transformed in an instant. From being a calm regal figure, she suddenly blazed into a furious temper. Her eyes widened and her face flushed as she half rose from her seat and slapped her hand imperiously on the edge of the table.

'Who dared make such a suggestion?' she demanded hotly. 'Sir Reginald is a man of honour and integrity. I was ashamed to hear of the way that Hugo insulted him in Exeter!'

John raised his hand placatingly as the Peverels scowled at their stepmother and muttered under their breath.

'I merely gave that as an example, madam. I apologise if it gave offence.'

The handsome dowager glared at him, her transient interest in him vanishing like frost in the sun. 'I am well acquainted with Reginald de Charterai and know him for a man of impeccable character.'

She swept her gaze around her stepsons and decided to shock them with some news. 'In fact, some time ago I invited him to visit this manor so that we might renew that acquaintance. He should arrive tomorrow, as he is lodging in Tiverton.'

The object of the meeting was forgotten as the three brothers jumped to their feet in angry consternation, all vying with each other to speak the loudest.

'For the sake of Christ, Avelina, what were you thinking of?' yelled Odo, his usual restraint thrown to the winds. 'Hugo's body is barely cold and you're inviting his worst enemy to his home!'

'He is coming to pay attendance on me, not Hugo,' she said icily. 'My invitation to him was sent long before that distasteful episode in Exeter – and even longer before his death.'

'Then thank God he is dead, though I be cursed for saying it!' bellowed Ralph. 'For if he had been alive, he would have beaten your new paramour to within an inch of his life!'

Now flushed with anger, Avelina pointed a quivering finger at the speaker.

'How dare you insult me so, damn you! To call him my paramour! Had I my husband still, he would have thrashed you for your impertinence, though you were his son!'

Joel, usually whimsical in his sneering, was moved to be deadly serious for once. 'Lady, you must be out of your mind! To associate with a man who was Hugo's sworn adversary is bad enough – but to actually invite him here is folly beyond my understanding.'

The older woman remained quite unbowed under the unanimous condemnation and John, an admirer of mature womanhood, was greatly impressed by her imperious disdain of this masculine disapproval.

'Until my husband died – or was killed,' she continued with a hint of ambiguity that was not lost on John, 'this was my home, and I still consider it to be such. I am quite entitled to invite here whom I please. I am a widow and there can be no impropriety in my choice of a friend, be it male or female!'

'I am the lord now, madam,' hissed Ralph. 'As such, I choose who comes here and who does not! This de Charterai is *persona non grata* in Sampford Peverel after the emnity between him and my brother.'

The formidable Avelina, now in a towering rage, began to vigorously contradict Ralph, but was drowned out by the booming voice of Odo, who directed his venom at Ralph, rather than his stepmother.

'Brother, you forget yourself! You have no right to take upon yourself the mantle of manor-lord. I am your senior now by two removes, Hugo having been your elder brother, yet still ranking below me.'

'You lost the inheritance by the ruling of the law, Odo!' shrieked Ralph. 'You cannot hope to retrieve it now.'

'Why not? The court found for Hugo against me, unjust though that decision was. They did not rule me out against a mere youth like you, so do not assume airs and graces that do not exist, either in equity or law!'

De Wolfe, though beginning to despair of getting any sense out of this discordant family, nevertheless allowed the dispute to flourish, as he felt that anger might lead to some incautious admissions. They were all shouting and declaiming in such confusion, however, that little sense could be made of anything. The steward stood at one end of the table, his mouth drooping in astonishment, and the lesser servants in the background were enjoying the sight of the family in such undignified disarray. It would give them ample fuel for gossip in the kitchens for weeks to come.

When it became apparent to de Wolfe that he was going to gain nothing useful from this spiteful cacophony, he beat his fists upon the table and yelled at the top of his voice.

'God's guts, will you all be silent! Ladies, I apologise for my necessary intrusion upon your domestic disputes, but I have to attend to the King's business.'

There was an immediate lull in the arguing, more

from surprise at a stranger shouting at them in their own hall than from any desire to obey him.

'Lady Beatrice, let me ask you what I need, then I'll leave you all to your personal affairs,' de Wolfe continued.

The younger woman was the only one who had not joined in the general hubbub, sitting placidly through it all. John suspected that her virtues lay in her undoubted beauty rather than her brains or depth of character.

'I regret having to pester you in your bereavement, but is your recollection of last evening similar to the other sparse testimony that I have heard?'

Beatrice raised her long-lashed eyes to meet his, and in spite of the circumstances he felt a frisson of desire as she smiled at him.

'You are most genteel, Sir John, but there is nothing I can add. I played draughts with Joel after the meal ended, then I went to my chamber, where my maid prepared me for bed. My husband did not return before I went to sleep – but that was not unusual,' she added rather petulantly.

'And as far as you recall, he did not return at any time during the night?'

She shook her head, a wisp of golden hair appearing from under her silken cover-chief. 'He was not there after I awoke some time after dawn. And my maid, who sleeps on a pallet outside my door, said that he had not returned at any time.'

The dark-haired girl, who stood behind her chair, nodded but said nothing. All their stories were so similar that John suspected that they had agreed on them beforehand, but he philosophically accepted that this may have been because they were true.

'And being in the closest confidence of all, Hugo

being your husband, have you any reason to suspect any person who might wish him evil?'

Beatrice glanced quickly around her brothers-in-law, then lowered her eyes.

'None at all, sir,' she replied in little more than a whisper.

'A complete waste of bloody time!' grumbled de Wolfe. 'The whole lot of them clammed up like limpets at low tide.'

It was late that night and the coroner was sitting with Gwyn and Thomas in the village alehouse near the green, only a stone's throw from the byre where Hugo had been found. Though the tavern was a miserable place, John found it preferable to the hostile atmosphere of the manor house.

When he had abandoned his attempt to squeeze more information from the Peverel family, he had sought out his assistants in the kitchens and walked them in the dusk around the village, to get a feel for the geography of the place. Then he had brought them to the hovel with the bare bush hanging from a bracket outside the door, and they stood in the only room, drinking an indifferent ale, which from the expression on their clerk's face was only slightly preferable to hemlock.

The taproom was but a shadow of the superior accommodation at the Bush at Exeter. A low room with crumbling cob walls between worm-eaten frames, it had damp, dirty rushes on the floor, which rustled ominously as various rodents burrowed through it for scraps of fallen food. Inside the once whitewashed stones that ringed the fire-pit in the centre, some logs smouldered on the ashes. There were a few three-legged stools scattered about but no tables, and the coroner's trio stood together by the only window-opening, where they used the rough sill to support their misshapen pottery mugs. Against the far wall, a slatternly ale-wife ladled her thin brew into the mugs from several ten-gallon crocks standing on the floor. A dozen men stood about drinking, ignoring the stools and staring suspiciously at the three strangers near the window.

'Did you learn anything from the kitchen maids?' John asked Gwyn, knowing of his roguish ways with servant girls.

His officer finished filtering ale through his luxuriant moustache before replying. 'It's an unhappy manor, that's for sure, but I heard nothing much of use. A little more digging will probably turn up more scandal, though whether it would have any bearing on this slaying is doubtful.'

He wiped his mouth with the back of his hand. 'That Hugo was unpopular with everyone, that's for sure, but they wouldn't tell me why.'

John took another mouthful of ale and winced at the taste, comparing it unfavourably with the fruits of Nesta's expertise. 'When I've finished this horse-piss, I'll find a pallet in a corner of the hall, as long as those damned brothers have cleared off. But I want you to stay here for a while, Gwyn. See what you can wheedle out of these villagers. Here's twopence to ply them with ale.'

As he fumbled in his scrip for some coins, he spoke to his clerk.

'And you, Thomas, you can do what you have done to good account several times before. Seek out that fat Irish priest and play your cleric's game with him. It will be more honest now that you must surely soon be on your way to reinstatement.'

Thomas de Peyne felt a glow of pleasure, both at the trust his master placed in him and the reminder that his time as an outcast from his beloved Church was coming to an end. The little clerk had a gift for wheedling information from parish priests, who usually accepted him as one of their own with his threadbare cassock, shaven head and wide command of Latin. They were more free with their confidences, especially when their tongues were loosened by drink, which was a common failing among those disillusioned priests dumped in some obscure parish with no hope of advancement.

As the coroner and Thomas prepared to leave the dismal inn, Gwyn gave a valedictory piece of news. 'There's something going on between Richard de Revelle and the Peverels. I saw them with their heads together as he was leaving and I'll wager they were plotting some mischief – though God knows what!'

CHAPTER EIGHT

In which Crowner John attends a burial

After Tuesday morning's hangings, at which John had to be present to record the event and seize any goods and chattels of the felons, he went home to his noontide dinner. Here he received the expected frosty reception from Matilda, which was her usual reaction to him having been away overnight. Once again he reflected on the unfairness of her attitude, when it was she who had so eagerly supported his appointment as coroner a year earlier. Yet now she resented his absences from home carrying out the very duties that she had been so keen for him to accept. He knew she suspected him of taking the opportunity offered by these excursions to drink and womanise, though he thought wryly that, given the quality of the ale at Sampford and his current devotion to Nesta, neither of these allegations could possibly be true.

As he sat silently chewing poached salmon and cabbage, he threw covert looks at his wife, wondering what was going on in her mind. He had noticed lately that in addition to her devotion to religious observance – she went at least twice a day to services at either the cathedral or St Olave's – Matilda was becoming increasingly obsessed with her Norman ancestry, tenuous though it was. The de Revelles had left St-Lô in the early years of the century and those now remaining in

Normandy were but distant cousins. Several years before, Matilda had spent a month visiting them and had come home with the firm conviction that she was a scion of a noble house, exiled among English barbarians. The fact that she, together with two previous generations of ancestors, had been born in Devon could not shake her belief in her exalted heredity. Even though John's late father was of pure Norman stock, she had despised him for taking a Cornish-Welsh wife, and she looked on her husband as something of a Celtic mongrel. Of late, when she deigned to hold a conversation with him, the subject reverted increasingly to her noble family across the Channel and how she yearned to see them and the fair orchards of Normandy once again. Secretly, John wished she would take ship for Caen and never return, but so far she seemed to have no plans to repeat her pilgrimage.

After the meal, they sat on either side of the hearth in the monk's chairs whose side-wings kept out some of the draughts. Mary brought them each a pewter cup of red wine poured from a small skin on a side table and left them to their silent vigil.

After a few minutes, John felt that he should make an effort to converse with his wife to bring her out of her latest sulk. Knowing of her snobbish fascination with the local aristocracy, he thought the current drama in Sampford Peverel might catch her attention, and he related the events of the past day. If there was one group of people that Matilda knew almost as well as the ecclesiastical establishment, it was the Devon gentry, among whom she was always prodding her husband to advance himself. Her small eyes lit up with interest as she scented a prime topic for gossip with which to regale her friends at church.

'You know the scandal there was at Sampford earlier

in the year?' she demanded. 'After Lord William was killed at Salisbury.'

John shook his head in false innocence, hoping that he might glean something useful from this fount of rumour that was his wife.

'Well, with four sons, the manor should naturally have gone to the eldest, which was Odo. But the second son Hugo disputed the claim and it became a great issue, which had to be settled by the King's justices and even by the chancery in Winchester.'

'So what was the problem?' asked John. He had heard the bones of the story elsewhere, but maybe Matilda had the meat.

'The second son, this Hugo, contested the succession on the grounds that his brother was not a fit person to rule the manor. He claimed that Odo suffered so badly from the "falling disease" that he would be unable to attend properly to the duties of a manor-lord.'

What little de Wolfe had seen of Odo gave no cause for thinking that the man was incapable in any way, but he waited for his wife to add some detail.

'It was claimed, so I've heard from Martha, the goldsmith's wife, that this Peverel had sudden convulsions and strange aberrations of behaviour. Several times, he had fallen from his horse and damaged himself.'

'How would this lady know of that?' demanded John.

'Her husband is Wilfred, the master of the goldsmiths' guild. It seems he was in Winchester when the case was being heard, as he happened to be in some civil dispute in the courts over the quality of a necklace.'

Trust Matilda to be connected to the grapevine when some tasty scandal was being aired, thought John cynically.

'And obviously Hugo won the day,' he observed.

Matilda sniffed contemptuously. 'Huh, it was to be expected! Like his father, Hugo was well known on the tournament circuit, rubbing shoulders with barons and powerful knights who either jousted themselves or took a great interest in the wagering. This Odo was a dull stay-at-home, never so much as lifting a lance. That was probably on account of his affliction, but still, he had no powerful friends like Hugo, so he lost the decision.'

'Well, now the battle begins again,' grunted John. 'For though this Ralph has assumed he is next in line, Odo seems willing to dispute his claim on the grounds that the chancery decision related to him and Hugo, not Ralph.'

Matilda shrugged dismissively. 'Then he'll lose again, for I hear this Ralph is also devoted to the tourney field, so will know the same influential men who swayed the decision for his brother last May.'

With some careful probing, John discovered that his wife knew nothing more of any use, and soon the effects of a large meal and the wine sent her upstairs with Lucille to seek the solace of her bed.

De Wolfe, free from any tasks that afternoon, decided to seek his mistress, both for the pleasure of her company and possibly as another source of information from her fund of tavern gossip. With Brutus as a feeble alibi, he walked through the bustling city down to Idle Lane, where he had told his two assistants to meet him. He had ridden on ahead of his officer and clerk when they had left Sampford Peverel early that morning, as he had to hear two appealers before the hangings. These were persons who were accusing others of offences against them, one a theft of money, the other a wounding. The plaintiffs had to decide how they were going to seek justice – either by battle, by ordeal or through the courts. John's task was to try to sweep their dispute into the royal courts, which would benefit the exchequer as well as offer a more sensible solution than the old superstitious and barbaric practices. Having had no time the previous night to discover whether Gwyn and Thomas had learned anything useful in Sampford, he was keen to hear what they had to say.

When he entered the main room of the inn, he found his men sitting at his favourite table. Inevitably Gwyn was eating, demolishing a meat pasty supplied by Nesta. Brutus, who adored the dog-loving Cornishman, made straight for him and sat under the table, waiting for the titbits from the pie that he knew would come his way. John sat himself down on one of the benches alongside the scrawny clerk and waited for Edwin to limp across with a quart pot of ale. Gwyn had cider and Thomas a cup of watered wine, given in pity by Nesta, as she knew how much he disliked ale, even her superior brew.

'The mistress will be with you directly, Cap'n!' croaked the ancient potman, rolling the white of his blind eye horribly at the coroner. 'She's stirring the mash in the brew shed.'

While Gwyn finished chewing and then picking bits of mutton, onion and pastry from his whiskers, John asked his clerk whether he had heard any more from his uncle concerning his readmission to holy orders. Thomas was the nephew of the Archdeacon of Exeter, best placed to hear news of an ecclesiastical nature.

'Nothing at all for weeks, master,' replied Thomas dolefully, his weak face displaying his chronic concern that his long-awaited reinstatement might never materialise. 'I fear they have conveniently forgotten me in Winchester.'

'How do they reinstall you as a priest, Thomas?' asked Gwyn, after a massive belch. 'Do you have to be dipped in holy water – or maybe they circumcise you!' He could never resist teasing the poor fellow.

'I don't need to be made a priest again,' snapped the clerk huffily. 'Ordination is for life, nothing can remove it, not even the Pope himself.'

'So what happens?' asked John, genuinely interested.

'As I told this great oaf, ordination is indelible. The grace, once bestowed, is *ex machina*, it cannot be repeated, nor can it be removed.'

'So what happened when you were thrown out?' persisted Gwyn.

'The Church's authority for me to exercise my ministry was revoked and any sacramental acts carried out by me would thereafter be void. Though still nominally a priest, I have been falsely condemned to ecclesiastical impotence!'

As the Cornishman cackled at this, John spoke more seriously.

'Then how will you be restored?'

'There is no great ceremony. The bishop, during a celebration of the Mass at which I am present, needs only to publicly read the Chancellor's document, which cleared my name. Then hopefully he will add a personal blessing and restore me to my lost functions.'

'And that's all that's required?' queried the coroner.

'The bishop would need an assurance that I could sustain myself by employment appropriate to the status of a priest and also have a designated place in a consecrated building to celebrate Mass.'

'How are you going to manage that?' asked John. 'Does it mean you will need to find a living in some church?'

Thomas shook his head. 'There is no need – I will remain your clerk for as long as you wish. And my uncle has promised to intercede with the cathedral chapter to grant me a share in the stipendary service at one of the altars in the cathedral.'

He had brightened up during this talk about his

beloved Church, but now relapsed into a doleful depression. 'But none of this matters, if Winchester has forgotten my very existence.'

He looked so miserable that John was moved to encourage him.

'I'll do what I can for you, Thomas, though I have no influence in matters concerning the Church. When I next see the archdeacon, I'll raise the issue yet again. Meanwhile, tell me if you learned anything from that disciple of St Patrick you were with last night.'

Just as Thomas was about to speak, Nesta bustled up, wiping her hands on a white cloth, which she dumped on the end of the table.

'There's a splendid mash bubbling away,' she said cheerfully. 'A few more days and it'll be the best I've ever brewed, though I say it myself. A new recipe, with some young nettle leaves added, ones I dried last spring.'

John moved up the bench for her to slide alongside him and he slipped an arm around her waist to give her a squeeze.

'Damn the ale, just let me have the ale-wife!' he said, with a gaiety that momentarily transformed the normally dour coroner into a roguish lover.

Gwyn looked fondly at him across the table, seeing de Wolfe for an instant as he had been twenty years before, when they would both dash off uncaring into battles and brothels alike. Now it was only in Nesta's company that he saw John relax, cast off the cares and concerns that his doggedly conscientious nature insisted on bearing.

When they had settled down again, the patient Thomas began his story.

'As you guessed, Crowner, Father Patrick is quite fond of his drink. When I called on him, he had already got through half a jar of mead. By the time I left, he had soaked up most of the other half, as I managed to avoid all but a few mouthfuls.'

'But did you learn anything of use?' demanded de Wolfe, beginning to feel that his officer's gift for endlessly spinning out a story was rubbing off on his clerk.

'Some useful gossip, I think. He confirmed that the family is at loggerheads most of the time, especially since William was killed. He seems to have been a very strong character and kept the rest firmly in their places. Without him, they are all fighting like cats in a barn.'

'His widow seems a tough old bird as well,' observed Gwyn.

John felt this was a poor description of a handsome woman in her prime, but he agreed that she had a formidable personality.

Thomas tapped the side of his long, thin nose. 'It seems she has a suspicion that her husband's death was not altogether accidental,' said the clerk, in a dramatic whisper.

'How could it not be?' objected Nesta. 'I recall the chatter about it in here at the time. He fell from his horse in full view of hundreds of people.'

'I hope that the priest wasn't breaking the confessional when he told me . . .' Thomas stopped to cross himself. 'But he claimed that Avelina has several times accused Hugo of somehow contriving the death, so that he could inherit the manor.'

'That seems nothing but a widow's bitterness to me,' said Nesta stubbornly. 'First, how could he do it – and why was it not detected by those at the tourney who went to William's aid? Also, it was this Odo, the eldest son, who was to be the heir, not Hugo.'

'Did you discover any more details concerning why Odo lost the inheritance?' demanded de Wolfe.

'It was solely on the grounds that he has this falling

sickness. Patrick said that he has had this affliction since he was a youth. It isn't getting any worse, but Hugo seized upon it as an excuse to have him disinherited.'

'What happens in this condition?' asked Nesta. 'Does it occur often?'

Thomas lifted his humped shoulder in a shrug. 'I didn't go into that, but the priest said it can come on at any time, especially if Odo gets excited or harassed. Usually he just falls senseless to the ground, but sometimes he has a slight fit, with spasms of his limbs.'

'Did any other scandal drip from this fat Irishman's lips?' asked Gwyn sarcastically.

'Only about Hugo's wife – or rather widow now.'

'Beatrice? She was certainly making cow's eyes at young Joel,' grunted John.

Nesta's interest was raised another notch, as any romance intrigued her greatly. 'Was she unfaithful to her husband with his brother?' she asked eagerly.

Again the clerk twitched his shoulders.

'Father Patrick didn't say so in as many words, but he was the confessor to the whole family and must have known the truth, which he conveyed with nudges and winks. She had no love for her husband, that was obvious.'

'It must have been shaming for her, to see him so brazenly seducing the village girls,' pouted Nesta, championing a woman she had never seen.

'Enough to stick a knife between his ribs seven times?' queried Gwyn.

'A woman scorned is as dangerous as a squadron of mounted knights!' exclaimed John, feelingly – though he did not explain how he came to know such a thing.

'She couldn't have done it,' objected Thomas. 'She

went to bed while Hugo was still alive and her maid slept outside her door all night.'

'Pah! A maid is ever loyal to her mistress, especially if some silver changes hands,' said de Wolfe. 'That means nothing, but I don't see how she could pass back through the hall to get outside.'

'No need for that, Crowner,' said Gwyn. 'Yesterday I had a good scout around the buildings and found a little postern door at the back that the servants use to bring food in from the kitchens. It not only opens into the hall behind those screens, but also leads to a passage where there is another stairway in the thickness of the wall, leading up to the chambers above.'

'So any of the family could have gone outside without those left in the hall seeing them,' muttered John, half to himself. He turned back to his clerk. 'Did you gather if this affair between Joel and Beatrice is at all serious, or just a young stallion wanting to ride a pretty mare?'

'I just don't know that, master. There was a limit to what I could squeeze out of the priest, half drunk though he was.'

The coroner finished his ale and Nesta waved at one of the maids to fetch a large jug across. When their pots were refilled, he turned to Gwyn.

'What about you? Did you get any tongues to wag in that dismal tavern?'

The big Cornishman pulled at the ends of his moustache before replying.

'A surly lot, but eventually we got talking, with the help of those pennies you gave me to lubricate their tongues. Seems the whole damned village hated the Peverels, especially Hugo. Not many tears shed at his passing, that's for sure.'

'What's the problem, then? They can't all have daughters for him to seduce.'

'He was a harsh man in every way, so it seems. His father was a tough fellow, but they preferred him to his son.' Gwyn dipped his face back into his ale-jar to gain strength for his narrative. 'He drove the bondsmen too hard and was unreasonable when there was any problem. Hugo imposed crushing penalties at his manor court and he was over-fond of hanging people, which caused much discontent.'

'There are many manors where that applies,' observed John. 'Were there any who had a special grudge against him, enough to want him dead?'

Gwyn nodded, his tangled red curls bobbing around his large head.

'The reeve for one, according to the village harness-maker. It seems that his daughter was married a month ago and Hugo insisted on spending the first part of the wedding night with her, claiming droit de seigneur!'

An outraged Nesta clucked her tongue and Thomas almost hopped up and down on his stool in indignation.

'Droit de seigneur!' he squeaked. 'There's no such thing in law, it's just an immoral folk tale cynically conjured up by unscrupulous barons and manor-lords!'

John knew that, although the feudal system allowed a lord to impose the 'merchet', a monetary charge, on any of his subjects for allowing a daughter to be wedded, the alleged right to sleep with the bride on the first night had no legal justification. Yet there was no doubt that some lords indulged in it, because there was no one to challenge them in the tyrannical system of closed manorial communities.

'Not only did the reeve, this Warin Fishacre, swear that he would avenge his daughter's degradation,' continued Gwyn, 'but the bridegroom, who almost abandoned the marriage after Hugo stole his bride's virginity, put it about the village that he would also get even with his master.'

Thomas was still outraged at the idea that droit de seigneur continued to be thought of by some as a legitimate perquisite of the gentry.

'It is a total fiction, invented by some whose purpose it suits,' he squawked indignantly. 'They claim it to be an ancient tradition, under its other name, the *jus prima noctis*, the "right of the first night".'

Gwyn reached out and ruffled the lank hair of the little clerk.

'Calm down, dwarf! It just means that Sampford is conveniently living in the past.'

'So we have at least another two candidates for wishing the death of this figure of hate,' ruminated the coroner. 'Did you dig up any other scandal in that miserable alehouse, Gwyn?'

'It was hard to find anyone who didn't hate the bastard,' growled the Cornishman. 'This gossipy harness-maker told me that another bondsman who was rubbing his hands in delight that day was the village thatcher. It seems that soon after Hugo came into the lordship, he had the thatcher's youngest son hanged for poaching an injured stag that he came across in the forest when he was cutting thatching pegs. The father and his two other sons were said to be waiting for a chance to settle that score with Hugo Peverel, though it may have been all bluster.'

Nesta leaned across and took a mouthful of ale from John's mug.

'You seem to have a wide choice of suspects for your murder, Sir Crowner. Is there anyone in Sampford Peverel who didn't wish to see this hateful fellow dead?'

John gave her a squeeze. 'There's another, not resident in that unhappy manor, who declared in my presence that he would kill Hugo when he next met him!'

Nesta's big eyes widened at this. 'And who is that?'

'Reginald de Charterai, the knight who defeated Hugo fairly at the tournament on Bull Mead last week. I told you all about that, remember?'

'Yes, but you didn't say the Frenchman threatened to slay him.'

'Well, he did, after that drunken confrontation in the Guildhall, though at the time I thought it was empty words spoken in anger. But what's even more interesting, he's been staying in Tiverton these past few days, within a few miles of Sampford Peverel.'

The other three stared at him in surprise – this was the first they had heard of this twist.

'What the hell's he doing there?' demanded Gwyn.

'It seems he's paying court to Avelina, the handsome widow – the elder of the two handsome Peverel widows now,' he added whimsically. 'The brothers almost had apoplexy when she told them that she had invited Reginald to visit her at the manor today.'

'I don't see that she could ever be a suspect in this,' said Nesta. 'Whatever happens to her stepsons, she can never retrieve her dead husband's estate for herself.'

'But if she suspected Hugo had a hand in her husband's demise,' squeaked Thomas, 'and her new lover de Charterai had reasons for hating him sufficient to threaten to kill him, then either one or the other – or both – might have encompassed his death for revenge.'

De Wolfe gave one of his throaty rumbles, like an old lion. It could mean anything but often was a signal that he doubted some assertion.

'I can't see an honourable knight like de Charterai repeatedly stabbing a former jousting opponent in the back – though even chivalrous men will do terrible things when goaded by a fair lady!' He gave Nesta a pinch on her bottom that made her jump.

'So what's to be done next, Crowner?' asked the practical Gwyn.

'Back to Sampford early tomorrow to hold this inquest and see Hugo laid in the ground. I doubt we'll learn anything new, unless some of the villagers decide to voice their grievances.'

'Little chance of that – they still have to live under their new lord after we've left,' grunted his officer. 'Who's it going to be? I wonder.'

John rasped his fingers over his stubble. 'It sounded to me as if Odo was going to reopen his fight to inherit, though Ralph seemed confident that the justices would find for him against Odo, just as they did for Hugo.'

'Will that take a long time to settle?' asked Nesta.

'They were quick enough last time. I think they took the case straight to Winchester and got some members of the curia to deal with the matter. It doesn't do for a large manor like Sampford to be left in limbo for long.'

'God knows when the justices will come to Exeter next,' said Gwyn. 'If the Peverels want another quick decision, they had better go chasing the Chief Justiciar or the Chancellor again.'

John stretched his long legs out under the table, feeling the warmth of Brutus's brown fur against his calves.

'That's their problem, I'm glad to say. Though if I find that it was one of the brothers who dispatched Hugo to get his inheritance, then there'll be yet another dispute over who gets that unhappy manor.'

The next morning was unexpectedly fine and the high road leading north-east out of the city was in as good a state as it ever would be, the mud dried yet not powdered into dust. Thomas and the coroner left by the East Gate as soon it was opened at dawn and met Gwyn at St Sidwells, the nearby village where he lived.

A couple of hours later they were trotting down the road into Sampford, this time from the Tiverton direction, and soon passed Agnes's mean cottage, which marked the start of the village. Apart from a few women and children around the dwellings and some old men tending their tofts and animals, there seemed few people about, though in the distance an ox team was ploughing one of the strip fields.

'I trust that bailiff has assembled a jury as I ordered,' muttered John. 'But these damned brothers seem to delight in being obstructive.'

'You said you'll hold the inquest in that barn they use for a manor court?' asked Gwyn.

'It seemed the best place, especially if there was to be rain. Knowing them, they'll not yet have brought the corpse from the church, so let's ride there first to see what's going on.'

They trotted along the track, which followed the ridge past the manor house and the green to the church at the far end. Outside the gate, they dismounted and Thomas held the horses while Gwyn and his master went into the churchyard. Halfway down the path to the porch Gwyn stopped and pointed to a spot a few yards to one side.

'That wasn't there on Monday. Have they had another death already?'

De Wolfe looked across and saw a mound of fresh red earth. His face darkened as suspicion flowed into his mind like a spring tide.

'The bastards wouldn't dare!' he hissed and, lengthening his stride, he hurried into the little church. Inside the door he stopped and looked down towards the altar. There was nothing there – no bier, no body.

'Perhaps they've taken it to the barn ready for the inquest,' growled Gwyn, peering over John's shoulder.

'I very much hope so, or there'll be big trouble!' rasped the coroner, but his hopes were short lived. The rotund figure of the priest emerged from the tiny sacristy, an anxious expression on his podgy features.

'Where's the corpse?' roared John, careless of the hallowed surroundings.

Father Patrick shuffled forward in his faded cassock, his hands held out in supplication.

'I told them it shouldn't be done, after what you ordered, Crowner,' he babbled in his thick Irish brogue. 'But they insisted and I have no power to resist my lords, sir. My very living is within their gift.'

De Wolfe advanced until he was towering over the unfortunate priest.

'You mean he's already buried? That grave outside?' he bellowed.

The vicar nodded, cowering back from this irate knight, who looked as if he might unsheathe his sword, church or no church.

'Yesterday, Crowner. You see, his corpse was beginning to turn colour and my masters, especially Sir Ralph and Sir Joel, said it wasn't seemly.'

'Seemly! The law is the law, whether it's seemly or not!' thundered John.

Father Patrick nodded vigorously. 'Of course, Crowner! But then our neighbour, Sir Richard de Revelle, came across and recommended that we have a quick burial. As he was the sheriff until recently, we all assumed he knew that the law allowed it under those circumstances.'

De Wolfe looked at Gwyn and exhaled noisily. 'Bloody de Revelle! I might have known it.'

Ignoring the disconsolate priest, he turned on his heel, strode out of the church and, with an angry glance at the pile of fresh soil, went to his horse and cantered back towards the manor house, Gwyn and Thomas following behind. On striding into the hall, he found the three brothers sitting around a table with Richard de Revelle, all drinking ale and picking from a platter of savoury pastries. Standing near by were the steward, the bailiff and the reeve, looking decidedly anxious as they saw the King's coroner bursting in like an avenging angel – or perhaps devil was nearer the mark. He marched up to the table and stood aggressively with his legs apart and his fists bunched at his waist.

'Right, which of you ordered the corpse to be buried?' he snapped, without any niceties of greeting.

'Good morning, brother-in-law!' said de Revelle, with sarcastic false civility.

'You keep out of this, de Revelle. I'll come back to you in a moment.' He glared at the three Peverels until one of them stood up. It was Ralph, and it seemed that on this occasion Odo was content to let his brother assume seniority.

'It was a family decision, Sir John. We were of the opinion that your demand to leave our relative unburied for so long was utterly unreasonable.'

'You will abide by the law, sir. I expressly forbade you to dispose of the cadaver until today.'

Ralph, though more than a decade younger than John, tried to look as if he were a master chiding a servant.

'Your opinion was considered and rejected. The weather has become unseasonably warm and it was an insult to our brother's memory to allow some petty rule to worsen the anguish already suffered by this family.'

Odo thought better of his passive role and joined the argument.

'You had already examined the body yourself, Sir John – so what can be gained by leaving it above ground for two more days?'

211

'Because the law demands that it be before the jury at the inquest!' retorted de Wolfe. 'They have to see the corpse and confirm the wounds and cause of death with their own eyes, otherwise the proceedings are invalid.'

'Damned nonsense,' drawled the former sheriff. 'We did without coroners until last year. This country is becoming plagued by bureaucracy since Hubert Walter started playing at being king.'

'Have a care, de Revelle!' responded John in a dangerously restrained voice. 'What you say comes near sedition, as the Chief Justiciar was expressly appointed by King Richard to protect his interests in England. Though we all know that sailing near the political wind is something with which you are all too familiar!'

The coroner knew that, whatever their other faults, there was no suspicion that the Peverels were anything but faithful to the Crown, and that they were not tainted by any support for the Count of Mortain. He had added this pointed comment deliberately, to warn the brothers against becoming too close to such an untrustworthy figure as Richard de Revelle.

'That body must come up again – and right away!' he snapped, returning to the main issue.

Everyone in the hall stared at him – even the serving men and maids lurking around the screens at the back were hanging on every word.

'You mean . . . desecrate our brother even further? Never, sir, this is something we will not countenance!' Ralph's voice was almost a shriek.

There was a babble of protest from the others, even the steward and the bailiff joining in, though Gwyn noticed that the reeve, Warin Fishacre, was silent. John stood stolidly until the noise settled, then he folded his arms and addressed them in a voice that invited no contradiction.

'This manor has deliberately flouted an instruction by the King's coroner and will be amerced in the sum of five marks, to be confirmed by the justices at the next eyre in Exeter. If you claim to be the current lord, Sir Ralph, then I hold you personally responsible, and am attaching you in a recognisance of another five marks to appear at that court to answer to the judges for your actions.'

Ralph stared at the coroner as if the latter had just descended from the moon. 'This is outrageous, sir! You cannot fine me and drag me to court like any common villein. I am a knight of the realm!'

'And so am I – but I abide by the law, which you do not!' snapped de Wolfe. 'Furthermore, I will be holding an inquest in two hours' time, to inquire where, when and by what means your brother came to his death against the King's peace. For that, I require his body to be produced and I now command you, in the name of the King, to open that fresh grave and have the body brought to the building you use for your manor court. I trust that my previous instruction has been carried out – to get the men of the village there to act as a jury.'

Gwyn was standing just inside the door of the hall, with Thomas peering rather fearfully from under his arm. The big man grinned as he saw the mixture of astonishment and outrage on the faces of the Peverel brothers and their steward. The bailiff managed a deadpan expression and the reeve suddenly found that he need to rub a hand over his mouth to conceal his feelings.

Joel, the fresh-faced young man who had yet to learn that authority was not something to be trifled with, struck a pose and spoke with an attempted hauteur that Gwyn felt made him sound ridiculous.

'And what if we ignore your totally unreasonable

demands, Coroner? May I remind you that we have friends in high places.'

John looked at the speaker as if he were some errant schoolboy before his pedagogue.

'Then your friends must include the Pope and the Almighty, for they are the only ones who are more powerful than King Richard and his justiciar!' he said sarcastically. 'If you obstruct me further, then I will have to go back to Exeter and return with men-at-arms in a *posse comitatus* dispatched by the sheriff ... the *real* sheriff!' he added, with a scathing look at his brother-in-law, who had so far remained silent.

The eldest brother decided that conciliation was the only possible course.

'Sir John, much as this situation distresses all of us, I see that you are determined and therefore we cannot hold out against you,' said Odo. 'All I ask is that we now get this painful matter over as quickly as possible and with the least ill feeling.' He looked agitated, and his big face was flushed with emotion as he turned to the bailiff to give his orders. 'Walter, send that man who acts as sexton to find others and retrieve the coffin at once. Reeve, get yourself about the village and tell every man to be at the courthouse by mid-morning.'

And then he collapsed to the floor unconscious, all his limbs twitching slightly for a moment until he lay deathly still.

No one seemed too concerned by Odo's spasms, though the smirk on Ralph's face suggested that this was another confirmation of his right to assume the lordship. The steward and two of the house servants picked up the eldest brother and laid him on one of the tables, the same two servants remaining alongside to ensure that he did not roll off when he recovered.

John, feeling slightly discomfited by the thought that

he may have been the instrument of Odo's fit, was concerned for his well-being.

'How long will he be like this?' he asked Walter Hog.

'Usually only a few minutes,' replied the bailiff in a low voice. 'He'll wake up and then he always rubs his face with both hands. Then he'll stride up and down the chamber like a sleepwalker, before sitting down. Then he'll slumber for an hour and wake up in his normal frame of mind. It's always the same, his behaviour is identical every time.'

Ralph came across from where he had been looking at his elder brother and told the bailiff to get about his business.

'Do what Sir Odo told you, Walter. We have to please the coroner, don't we!' he sneered.

Turning to de Wolfe, he jerked his head towards the still figure on the trestle. 'You want me to come to your court, Crowner? Then I'll probably get you to mine as a witness, if I need to contest my poor brother's claim to the manor. You've seen how he reacts to a crisis. Can such a man be allowed to direct the lives of more than seven score people? I think not!' With that, he turned on his heel with a flourish and made for the staircase to the upper floor.

'You certainly know how to make enemies, John,' said a voice behind him. Turning, he found Richard de Revelle smiling sardonically at him. In token acknowledgement of the bereavement in the manor, he had left off his usual bright garments and wore a long tunic of black linen, but with ornate silver threadwork around the neck, hem and sleeves. Over this was a full cloak of dark grey serge, not unlike John's usual attire, giving him a funereal appearance.

'You had a hand in advising them to bury this body, against my express orders,' de Wolfe snapped.

'When the orders are foolish, unreasonable and

unkind, then that is the right counsel to offer,' retorted the former sheriff.

'Always the glib answer, Richard. Why are you interfering in the affairs of this manor? There must be something in it for you, you never do anything for nothing.'

'I am a good neighbour, John! My land runs along the Peverel boundary to the north and west. It is only right that I try to help friends in their hour of need.'

'Huh! Who needs enemies when they can have friends like you, eh?'

Turning his back on his brother-in-law, de Wolfe marched to the door and, with a jerk of the head at his clerk and officer, made his way back to the church.

Determined that there would be no evasion or duplicity this time, John stood near the grave to make sure that his orders were carried out. With Gwyn and Thomas at his side, he watched while Walter Hog supervised his men as they reopened the pit. Again a group of onlookers was gathered along the dry-stone wall around the churchyard, mostly wives and old men too infirm to work in the fields.

Two villeins were waist deep in the hole, throwing the rich red soil out with flat wooden shovels tipped with iron strips. As the earth had only been put in place the previous day, it was soft and light, so the work went ahead quickly and a large pile was soon heaped along each side.

'The box is not far down, Crowner,' the bailiff reassured them. 'It's on top of his father's remains, put there not six months ago.'

'Not a very fancy memorial for two lords of the manor!' grunted Gwyn. 'I'd have thought they'd have done better than this.'

'Most gentry are buried within the church itself, near the altar,' commented Thomas, automatically making the sign of the cross.

'That's the very point,' answered Walter. 'The old man, William, was planning to rebuild the church in stone to ensure that his immortal soul got a clear passage into heaven. This old wooden place has been here since Saxon times. But the Lord beat him to it, I'm afraid – and he's done the same to Hugo, who also claimed he was going to carry out his father's plan.'

'Then presumably the family will now build a new church and put William and Hugo under its floor?' asked Thomas hopefully.

The bailiff looked around and lowered his voice. 'Maybe, but I hear that money is short. Both Hugo and his father lost heavily in the tournaments these past couple of years – that's why Hugo was so incensed when that Frenchie beat him last week. According to what the steward tells me, there'll not be much money left for church-building, unless Sir Ralph can do better with lance and sword than his brother.'

'But this is a large, fertile manor,' said de Wolfe. 'It should be rich with all that land under the plough and those many carucates of pasture for cattle and sheep.'

The bailiff shrugged. 'I do my best, Crowner. Sir Odo is keen on making the best of the land, but he never gets support from the others. They never restock enough, neither beast nor seed – and they've sold off too much to repay their debts. Bad management, that's what's ruining this manor.'

Walter Hog's recriminations were cut short by a call from one of the villeins who acted as sexton. He was tapping something solid with the end of his spade, as his companion began scraping earth sideways.

'We're down to the box, Bailiff. Do you want 'er taken out or shall we open 'er where she lies?' he called, in the thick local dialect.

Walter looked enquiringly at the coroner, who shook his head.

'The corpse will be needed only for an hour or two. If you can get the lid off easily, just take the body out and carry it on that bier up to the courthouse.'

The coffin was a plain box made in haste from elm planks, and the top gave way without trouble when strips of iron provided by the smith were levered into the joints. John and Gwyn leaned over the grave as it was removed and watched with interest as the diggers peeled back the linen wrappings that shrouded the cadaver. Hugo Peverel appeared much the same as when they had seen him on Monday, still dressed in the tunic in which he had died. When a kerchief was lifted from his face, it was seen to be somewhat swollen and reddened, but otherwise in fair condition.

'Damned liars, saying that he had to be buried because he was going off!' muttered Gwyn. 'There's days of use left in him yet!'

They left the bailiff to see that the corpse was removed and carried up to the barn for the inquest, while they sought some sustenance after their ride from Exeter. John could have returned to the hall, where no doubt his rank would have ensured that he would have been fed, albeit grudgingly, by the hostile family. But he chose to avoid them and, with his two assistants, made for the alehouse on the green. As they passed the open space, Gwyn jerked his head towards the manorial gallows, two high posts supporting a crossbar, which, together with a pillory, stood threateningly alongside the area where the village lads played at football and the men practised their archery. It was empty today, but a rope noose swayed ominously in the breeze.

'That's where the thatcher's son came to his end,' he said. 'I wonder if his father or brothers had enough guts to stick Hugo the other night?'

De Wolfe grunted and shrugged his shoulders. 'God

knows! It could equally have been that reeve or his son-in-law, inflamed at Peverel bedding the daughter on her wedding night.'

The tavern was empty, as all the men were either in the fields or being rounded up for jury service, and the three officials had the room to themselves. The ale-wife had a blackened pot hanging from a tripod over the fire-pit and from it she ladled a thin broth into wooden bowls. Silently, she set these on the window ledge for them, together with a fresh loaf torn into pieces. From a leather bucket of dirty water set by the ale casks, she produced some horn spoons and rubbed them dry with the hem of her grubby apron. The stew tasted better than it looked, and even the ale she offered seemed less sour than on Monday.

'If I come here too often, I might even get to like the bloody stuff!' grumbled Gwyn, as he tucked in. The more fastidious Thomas ignored the drink, but found that the long ride had given him an appetite, so that he ate his broth with something approaching relish.

They discussed the relative merits of each candidate for the killing, but came to no conclusions. It seemed that virtually anyone in the village could have stabbed Hugo in the back, as the opportunity to creep up on him asleep on a dark night was universal – and motives were thick on the ground. When they had exhausted the possibilities, none of which John felt was likely to be confirmed at the inquest, Gwyn brought up the matter of the silversmith, murdered the previous week.

'What are you going to do about this Robert Longus, the armourer who refused to come to your inquest in the city?'

'Rest assured, I've not forgotten him! Before we leave, I'll attach him by sureties to attend a resumed inquest next week. If he doesn't show up, then I'll get him summoned to the Shire Court. Four failures to appear there and he'll be outlawed.'

'What about the other man that was said to have been with him when they robbed and killed the silversmith?' asked Thomas. 'If the armourer is from this manor, then so perhaps is the other?'

De Wolfe stared through the window opening as he finished his ale, thinking about this other problem. 'Unfortunately, that man Terrus who survived the assault says he has no recollection of the face of the other attacker, so there would be no point in getting him all the way up here from Totnes to try to pick him out.'

'I'll keep a close eye on the bastard today, to see if he has any particular crony in the manor,' offered Gwyn.

'With the lately deceased Hugo giving him such a firm alibi, we've only got the word of Terrus against theirs,' said John regretfully. 'I wonder if Ralph Peverel will back up the story too?'

'He will, Crowner,' said Thomas gloomily. 'If only to spite you. These people stick together like glue.'

'Especially an armourer,' added Gwyn. 'There's a special bond between a tourney fighter and the fellow who tends to his weapons and accoutrements, for the knight's life may depend upon him.'

The Cornishman said this with genuine feeling, as he had long been in that position himself. As de Wolfe's virtual squire, as well as friend and companion for twenty years, he was more like John's brother than servant – though he never took advantage by over-familiarity.

Through the window opening, the coroner noticed an increasing drift of people from the lower end of the village, all making their way towards the manor-house stockade. As well as the men and boys needed for the jury, women and children trudged past, the latter intent on congregating outside the barn to eavesdrop on the proceedings. Eventually, John decided it was time to move and, giving the ale-wife a penny for their food and drink, led his team out into the rutted road and walked up to the manor.

The barn was large and bare, with one chair and some benches at one end for the lord, his steward and other manor officers. The freemen and villeins spread themselves around the walls in their accustomed places, as they were well used to attending the compulsory manor leets.

When the coroner walked in, he found the Peverel brothers, including Odo, already seated. Their steward and bailiff, together with the priest, stood behind them. Though strictly speaking they should all have been in the body of the court with the jurors, John decided not to make an issue of it, though he took exception to Ralph lounging in the one and only chair. He strode across and stood in front of the putative manor-lord.

'I rather think it is the coroner who presides at an inquest, sir,' he said, trying to keep the sarcasm from his voice.

Recognising that he was pushing his luck a little too far, Ralph eased himself from the chair and sardonically waved de Wolfe into it, then sat down on a nearby bench next to Roger Viel, the steward. At this point, de Wolfe was irritated to see the dapper figure of Richard de Revelle enter and sit next to Odo, who seemed quite recovered from his falling fit.

John motioned to Gwyn to boom out the opening call for the proceedings, just as the sexton and another man carried in the bier with the shrouded form of the deceased lord. They set it down before the coroner, between him and the three score men who formed the jury.

'There is no point in enquiring into presentment of Englishry,' began the coroner. 'Of course, Sir Hugo Peverel was of Norman lineage and, especially given that he was stabbed in the back, then the murdrum fine will undoubtedly be levied.'

There was a groan from the assembly, as it would be the villagers, both free and unfree, who would have to find the money, not the ruling family.

'However, I will not fix any penalty now, but in these unusual circumstances of a murdered manor-lord, leave it to the justices in Eyre to decide on the amount of such a fine.' An almost audible exhalation of relief went round the barn at what was at least a postponement of their collective punishment.

The inquest then took its usual course, with the first finder being called to relate how the body was discovered. This was the good-wife who came to steal hay for her rabbits, and from then on the chain of events was followed through the bailiff and the reeve up to the point where the coroner was summoned from Exeter.

After this, the nervous Agnes was called, prodded to the front of the barn by her mother. With frightened sideways glances at the covered corpse, she snivelled her way through her account of the evening, drawing black looks from the brothers and de Revelle as she haltingly admitted to being ravished by the lord of the manor, even if it was willingly and for profit.

'He were fit and well when I left him, sirs,' she finished. 'Looked sleepy and contented as he lay back in the hay, so I left 'un there and went 'ome.'

John then heard from the bailiff and the steward, who could add nothing except what they had done after the body was discovered. Warin Fishacre, the reeve, gave his evidence in a surly, monosyllabic way, mainly about his being dispatched to Exeter by the bailiff to fetch the coroner.

Finally, de Wolfe called the male members of the ruling family. Though he felt inclined to make them stand before him in the body of the court, like the other witnesses, he had sufficient Norman blood in his veins to defer to their status enough to take their evidence from where they sat. Even so, Richard de Revelle mischievously objected to their being questioned at all.

In his high, braying voice, he claimed that it was unseemly, possibly unlawful, for manor-lords to be interrogated in their own manor.

'They have a position to maintain, Coroner. There is a gulf between them and their tenants and bondsmen which needs to be kept – or all deference and discipline will be put in jeopardy!'

John glared at the former sheriff, knowing that Richard was doing everything he could to make life difficult for him.

'This is a king's court, de Revelle, not a manor leet! We are all subjects of the Crown and must abide by the laws laid down by the Curia Regis, which is the instrument of the King's will. Those who disregard it, flaunt their loyalty to the sovereign.'

Once again, he prodded the issue of fidelity which was de Revelle's weak spot. Turning to Odo, he spoke more gently. 'I trust you are feeling well enough to answer my questions, sir?'

Another muted whisper spread around the barn at this hint of a fresh attack of the malady that was known to afflict the eldest brother.

Odo inclined his head and said that he was now in perfect health once again. John led him through the impoverished tale that he had heard before, about the period after supper when Hugo had last been seen. The same story, almost in the same words, was wrung from the more reluctant Ralph and Joel. John had the impression that only the brevity and uselessness of their account allowed them to deign to offer it without more strenuous objections.

De Wolfe then turned to the many faces ranged before him around the court, faces of all shapes and ages, from twelve-year-old lads to a few bowed and crippled greybeards.

'Is there any among you who has other information for me that might throw light on this tragedy?'

There was a general shuffling of feet on the packed earth of the floor and many scanned the faces of their neighbours to see whether anyone was likely to step forward. But the moment passed without any volunteers, though John felt a tension in the air that suggested that more than one would have voiced some opinion, if their masters had not been sitting before them, glowering around to see whether anyone dared step out of line.

With a sigh, de Wolfe raised a finger to Gwyn, who went into action and marshalled the large jury to shuffle past the bier. The coroner rose and went to the corpse, pulling down the winding-sheet to expose the puffy face. A ripple of concern went around the men, and the women at the door jostled and craned their necks, trying to see what was on show. Though all were country folk, used to perished and wounded animals and the frequent deaths of their generally short-lived population, the sight of their own lord in a state of early mortification was certainly out of the ordinary.

Gwyn then turned the body over and pulled up the tunic to reveal the stab wounds, which were still oozing blood and lay in skin that was purplish owing to the corpse lying for a couple of days on its back.

'See these wounds? They are from a blade with one sharp edge,' snapped John. 'Not a large knife, nor yet a dagger.'

Gwyn herded the jury past the corpse like a sheepdog with a nervous flock, until all had had the chance of a close look at the fatal injuries. Then he placed the body in its proper position and covered it with the shroud.

John went back to his chair and closed the inquest, confirming his earlier fears that no further evidence would be forthcoming.

'You will consider what you have heard and decide on a verdict. You need to be assured of the identity of the deceased and where, when and by what means he came to his death. All those matters will be easy for you to determine – what we do not know is who brought him to that death.'

The foreman of the jury, the village miller, rapidly announced their verdict. John stood for a final word, looking to the side to make sure that Thomas was scribing everything as he sat at the end of one of the benches.

'Sir Hugo Peverel, a Norman and lord of the manor of Sampford Peverel in the county of Devon, died on or about the tenth day of October in the year of our Lord eleven hundred and ninety-five, in the said Sampford Peverel, from grievous knife wounds to the back of his chest. And the manner of death was murder by a person as yet unknown.'

He turned to the brothers sitting brooding behind him. 'That completes the legal formalities. Your kinsman's body may now be returned to the church.'

There was a general exodus behind the bier, which was already being carried out through the tall doors. As he passed de Wolfe, Ralph gave him a look sufficiently sour to curdle milk, which was entirely lost on the coroner.

'I trust you are satisfied, Sir John,' he snarled. 'You have humiliated us, upset our ladies beyond measure and added further indignity to the body of our brother.'

'But I have upheld the laws of England, without which there would be disorder and anarchy,' retorted John, blandly.

Ralph and Joel marched away, noses in the air, but Richard de Revelle also stopped for a harsh word with his sister's husband.

'Your time is coming, John!' he sneered. 'I will be sheriff again, you mark my words. Perhaps not under this king, but under another, more worthy man. And when I am in power again, I will not rest until I have seen you humiliated, as you have done to these fine people here today.'

Before de Wolfe could think of an appropriate retort, de Revelle had stalked off, trailing the Peverels as they made their way to the churchyard.

John saw the steward and bailiff rounding up the villagers and soon most of the inhabitants were moving down past the green to the little church of St John the Baptist. A voice at his elbow told him that there was to be another short burial service, before the body was put back into its box in the ground. The voice belonged to the reeve, who had a strange expression on his face, part anxiety, part determination.

'I hope to God that this is the last we see of Hugo Peverel,' he muttered, half to himself, as he walked close beside the coroner. De Wolfe took the chance to sound him out a little further, as they moved with the tail-end of the crowd towards the church.

'I heard that the deceased caused some distress to your family?' he asked quietly.

'That's putting it very lightly, Crowner. My poor wife cried for days, to say nothing of my sweet daughter Maud. It affected not only our family, but that of Nicholas the smith, father of my son-in-law – who almost failed to remain my son-in-law, after what that bastard Hugo did to his bride.'

John looked behind him, to make sure that only Gwyn and Thomas were within earshot.

'It was totally illegal, Reeve, you know that? There is no such thing as droit de seigneur in the eyes of the law.'

Fishacre gave a bitter laugh. 'The eyes of the law are tightly closed in this manor, sir! What could we do? We are not only bondsmen, but cottars, the lowest of the low. These Peverels have the power of life and death over us, either by the gallows or by starvation if we do not bend to their will.'

'But lords have obligations, not least to keep to the traditions of the manor, as voiced in the manor courts,' reasoned John.

This only brought forth another sardonic response from Warin Fishacre. 'Tradition and the law count for nothing when there is no one to enforce them, sir. Matters may be different near Exeter, but here we never see a law officer from one year to the next. And the last sheriff, he was so thick with the Peverels that they could have hanged the lot of us without him turning a hair.'

De Wolfe had no answer to that, but wryly thought that the new sheriff was also unlikely ever to show his face here, as long as he had a coroner to do his work for him.

By the time they reached the church, the body had been taken inside, now wrapped in a new linen shroud. The men of the manor had all filed into the small building and the women and children congregated outside, either in the churchyard or along the wall that separated it from the roadway. He saw that the armourer, Robert Longus, and another rough-looking man were standing at the door to check that every

227

man, including all youths above the age of twelve, was attending to do respectful homage to their late lord. As John walked down from the lych-gate, he murmured to the reeve.

'Did they do this yesterday, when the illegal burial took place?'

Warin Fishacre shook his head. 'It was a rushed affair, Crowner. I think the old sheriff, de Revelle, talked them into it in a hurry. Only the brothers and the senior manor officers were present. They are trying to make up for it today, though they had said they would have a big memorial service in the future, when the new church is built – if that ever comes to pass!'

As de Wolfe was well aware that he was in bad odour with the Peverel family, he stood unobtrusively at the back of the crowded church, which was crammed full with the men of the manor, most looking sour and resentful. As was customary, none of the women of the family was present, but from his viewpoint he could see that the brothers, Richard de Revelle, the steward, bailiff, falconer, houndmaster and other more senior members of the household were grouped behind the bier, on the other side of which Father Patrick was again mumbling the words of the burial service.

Gwyn stuck close beside his master at the back, but Thomas, never one to miss the opportunity to attend any devotional event, wormed his way through the packed congregation until he was almost at the front.

As the muttered words of the priest droned on, lightened by the splashing of holy water on the corpse, John studied the atmosphere in the church. Though admittedly a funeral service was not an occasion for high spirits, he sensed a sullen mood among the massed villagers. He felt that they were there only because they had been ordered to attend, rather than from any feeling of respect or obligation to their late master. He decided that the reason that the thuggish armourer and his mate were outside the porch was to ensure that there were no absentees, and he would not have been surprised to learn that Longus had sent men to scour the village for skulking backsliders.

The Irish-accented Latin of the parish priest came to an end and a general shuffling at the front heralded the end of the proceedings. John beckoned to Gwyn and they left the church ahead of the rest and went to stand against the inside of the churchyard wall, a few yards from the open grave which still held the empty coffin. Behind them, the women and children gaped and whispered over the wall as the procession emerged from the porch. The men had squeezed themselves aside to allow the bier to be brought out first, preceded by Father Patrick, who slowly marched ahead along the grassy path between old grave mounds, holding aloft the cross from the altar as he quavered incomprehensible chants.

The corpse, swathed in its white bindings, was carried on the bier by two of the bailiff's assistants, and behind them came the Peverel men, de Revelle and then the manor officials. John managed to conceal a grin as he saw that immediately after them came Thomas de Peyne, who had insinuated himself into the procession and with his faded black tunic and persistent tonsure looked like an additional priest as he crossed himself and mouthed the Latin texts far more faithfully than the Irishman up ahead.

At the graveside, the sexton and another helper got down into the pit and took the corpse, which was handed down by the pall-bearers, as the family and their retainers stood at the head of the grave. Once the body was back in the planked box, they hammered home the nails of the lid and clambered out again. Now the men of the manor, directed by the armourer and his henchman, filed slowly past the open pit. Obviously acting on prior orders, each stooped to take a handful of soil from the heap alongside to throw down on to the coffin. Again the watching coroner had the firm impression that they did this sullenly and with bad grace, driven to the gesture only under the watchful eyes of the armourer and the family.

Each fistful of earth landed on the coffin with a dull 'thunk'. Some of the impacts seemed much louder than others, as if the thrower were expressing his feelings with unnecessary violence – though John's keen ears noticed that several times the opposite occurred, as if the reluctant mourner were merely miming the action. When the last of the villagers had paraded past, they began melting away, some making for the lich-gate, others to another gap in the wall behind the church, leaving behind only the Peverels and their attendants. Suddenly there was a roar of anger from Robert Longus, who had moved up to the grave and was peering in.

'Stop! All of you men, stop and come back here!' he yelled. The brothers, who were talking in low voices with de Revelle and their steward, were a few yards away and immediately hurried over to where the armourer was standing, gesticulating with a forefinger into the pit.

'Who did this? Own up, damn you!' he shouted generally to the rapidly thinning crowd in the churchyard. De Wolfe and his officer, sensing some new drama, also threaded their way between the grassy mounds to the new grave and joined the others as they peered down into the four-foot hole. Among the scattered red earth on the coffin lid, they saw a large pat of dried ox dung and a dead rat, swollen with putrefaction far more than the body inside the box.

'Get those abominations out of there!' screeched Ralph Peverel, grabbing the nearby sexton by the shoulder and almost pushing him down into the grave-pit.

As the man scrabbled to retrieve the offending objects, John realised why several of the farewell offerings had made so little noise, but he could not recall who was passing the grave at that moment – and he hoped that the others would also fail to identify the culprits.

The brothers fumed and ranted for a while and the bailiff, the steward and others tried to assist the armourer in chasing after the villagers, who were melting away like frost on a sunny morning. Naturally no one would admit to having thrown down these contemptuous offerings, and as the sexton and another villein shovelled the earth back into the hole the outrage gradually subsided.

The Peverels and Richard de Revelle also left, pointedly ignoring the coroner and offering him no refreshment in the manor hall before he departed for Exeter. John de Wolfe had one last task to perform, however, before he shook the mud of Sampford from his boots. Beckoning the bailiff away from the family group, he took him aside just within the lych-gate.

'Walter, I spoke to you on Monday about this armourer fellow, Longus. He deliberately refused to appear before my inquest in Exeter, so I am going to attach him in the sum of two marks to attend when I resume the inquiry into the death of a silversmith just before the fair.'

Walter Hog nodded; he was an intelligent man and knew that de Wolfe had the power to make trouble when necessary.

'I do not have a date for that inquest, but I shall send a message well beforehand. I trust that you will see to it that he understands the gravity of his situation and will give him leave to travel to the city. If he repeatedly fails to obey, then he may well be outlawed and nothing your manor-lord can do will prevent that, understand?'

'I will do my best, Crowner.' The bailiff looked around to make sure that the Peverels were well out of earshot. 'There may well be resistance from my masters, sir. Robert Longus is a favourite with Sir Ralph, because of their interests in the tourney, so he may try to protect him. But I will tell him the penalties if he fails – I can do no more than that.'

John clapped Walter on the shoulder. 'You do that, and I'll impress the same upon him before I leave. But tell me, is there any other fellow who is thick with this Longus? The matter I am investigating involved two men.'

Again the bailiff looked around uneasily. John had the impression that Walter, an outsider from Somerset who had not been long in this manor, was not all that happy with his position here and would be glad to move on when the opportunity arose. 'There is his assistant in the armoury, the man who was on the church door with him. By virtue of their common tasks with the weaponry, both in the forge and in the armoury, they spend much time together.'

John looked across to the corner of the churchyard, where Longus and the big, coarse-faced fellow were still haranguing a cottager about the offensive objects in the grave.

'His name is Alexander Crues – a man of little brains, but much muscle,' commented the bailiff disparagingly. 'They accompanied Lord William to every tournament and now do the same for Ralph.'

'What about Hugo Peverel?' asked de Wolfe, which caused Walter Hog to shrug before answering.

'Longus was Hugo's armourer and he depended on him greatly. They were more like master and squire, though of late they seemed to have become more distant with each other. I suspect that some animosity grew between them, and Longus seemed to cleave more to Ralph.'

John pondered this as he strode across towards the armourer, with Gwyn close behind. Thomas de Peyne had emerged from the church with Father Patrick and was looking uncertainly at his master, not wishing to get mixed up in any brawl, which seemed a possibility from the grim expression on the coroner's face as he advanced on Robert Longus.

'I want a word with you, fellow!' he snapped, looking from the man's truculent face to the rather piggish features of his clumsy-looking assistant. The armourer glared back at de Wolfe.

'If it's about my not coming to your damned inquest, then you can blame him!' he snarled, indicating the almost completed mound of earth which the sexton was hammering down with the flat of his shovel.

'What d'you mean?'

'Sir Hugo forbade me to stay behind in Exeter that day. He said he needed me at home here, to prepare for a tourney in Bristol the next week.'

Robert was a big man, but the coroner topped him by half a head and now he glared down at him. 'That's no excuse. It was you I summoned, not your master.'

'Then you try telling him that, Crowner! Though I'm a freeman, my bread and meat depend on the manor-lord, so I'm not going to cross him.'

'Very convenient, especially when the man is dead and can't confirm what you say,' retorted de Wolfe, but

BERNARD KNIGHT

the armourer seemed determined to argue to the bitter end.

'You heard what he said that day! He said I was with him all that Sunday and Monday and couldn't have been . . . been wherever you said I was, on the word of some half-crazed craftsman who was still out of his wits from a knock on the head. Sir Hugo said that as there could be no truth in the matter, there was no point my wasting his time by absenting myself at some useless inquest!'

'That's for me to judge, damn you!' snapped the irate coroner. 'So you'll appear at my court in Exeter when I send for you, within the next week or so. Understand?'

'I'll have to ask the new lord, Sir Ralph,' growled Longus reluctantly. 'If he says it's all right, then maybe I'll come, though he'll vouch for it being a wicked waste of time and travelling. And if it falls near a tourney day, then you can be sure he'll not let me go!'

It was all John could do not to grab the man and shake him till his few remaining teeth rattled. Gwyn was obviously of the same opinion.

'Shall I give him a few clouts to mend his manners?' he offered.

'You will attend or it will cost you two marks on the first failure, Longus! And then I'll attach you to the county court in the sum of five marks . . . and if you persist in absenting yourself, you'll find yourself an outlaw, not an armourer. It's not your job you'll have lost then, but maybe your head!'

For the first time, the man had no answer and stood sullenly scowling at de Wolfe, hate radiating from him like heat from an open fire.

The coroner jabbed a finger towards Alexander Crues, who stood open mouthed and loose lipped, listening to this heated exchange.

'This fellow, he is your assistant in the armouring?'

Robert jerked his head in reluctant reply.

'And was he in Exeter with you at the time of the fair and the tournament?'

'Where I go, he goes! We both attend on the lords when they are at the jousting.'

'And was he lurking near Topsham with you when you attacked and robbed that silversmith?' John had no scruples about bending the rules of legal procedure when he was not presiding in a court, but Longus failed to let slip anything incriminating.

'I was never at bloody Topsham, as well you know! Even if Sir Hugo can't speak for me, Sir Ralph will attest that I was with him all the time.'

De Wolfe prodded Alexander in the chest with a long finger. 'And I suppose you'll stick to the same story, eh?'

'I dunno what you're on about, sir,' he mumbled thickly. 'I was with Robert here all the time.' He said this with a mechanical certainty that sounded as if he had memorised it after numerous repetitions.

'Wasting our time here, Crowner,' murmured Gwyn.

John sighed his agreement. 'Right, Longus! When you are summoned to Exeter, you will bring this other fellow with you, understand? I'm attaching you both, so it will cost you a couple of marks apiece if you don't show up.'

With that, he turned on his heel and marched away, frustrated by his inability to make any impression on the two men, especially given that they were backed up by the support of Ralph Peverel. Unless he could obtain some further evidence from somewhere, even getting them to a new inquest would probably be a fruitless exercise. As they walked back to the manor stockade to get their horses for the journey home, he thought that the silversmith's death would remain as much a mystery as that of Hugo Peverel, unless someone came across with more information.

Within a few minutes, he was in the saddle and leading Gwyn and Thomas homeward, breathing a sigh of relief as he left the boundaries of that unhappy manor behind him and set off along the high road towards Exeter.

ChAPTER NINE

In which Crowner John has a French visitor

When he arrived back at Martin's Lane in the late afternoon, John found Mary waiting for him in the vestibule,
just inside the street door. She appeared worried,
unlike her usual placid self.

'You'd better get yourself into the hall, Sir
Crowner,' she advised, using the mildly sarcastic title
that she employed when she was either annoyed or
troubled.

The coroner shrugged off his cloak and slumped on
to the bench to pull off his dusty riding boots. He
looked up wearily at his cook-maid.

'What is it now? Is she in a temper because I've again
been away all day?'

The dark-haired woman shook her head. 'Better see
for yourself!'

She jerked a finger towards the inner door to the
main chamber of the house.

Pushing his feet into a pair of house shoes, he rather
apprehensively lifted the iron latch and peered
between the screens that stood just inside to keep out
some of the draughts. He had a view of part of the
large stone hearth and chimney-piece, in front of which
were the pair of cowled wooden chairs. At first he saw
nothing amiss, then he noticed that a hand hung over
one armrest, holding a pottery wine cup, tilted at a

dangerous angle. Below it he saw that the flagstones were stained red and, as he watched, the cup fell from the fingers and smashed on the floor.

He jerked his head back and glared at Mary. 'What the hell's been going on?' he demanded, as if it were his servant's fault.

'She's drunk, that's what!' retorted Mary sharply. 'Ever since I gave her dinner, she's been at the best wine. I doubt you've got much left.'

John pushed the door open wide and strode into the high, gloomy chamber, its timber walls hung with faded tapestries. As he crossed to the hearth, Matilda staggered to her feet, looking stupidly down at the mess on the flagstones. She seemed oblivious to his presence and clumsily tried to stoop down and pick up the fragments of the broken cup.

'Let that be!' he commanded. 'Mary will clean it up. You just sit down again before you fall.'

His voice was gruff, attempting to conceal the compassion he suddenly felt for this woman who was in such a bad way. He knew instinctively that the burden of her brother's shame and his own infidelity had finally broken down the stony façade of her grim personality. Though she had always been fond of eating to the point of gluttony, and was very partial to her wine, he had never before seen her so obviously drunk.

He took her arm and gently pushed her back down into her chair. She mumbled something incomprehensible, but did not resist him. The linen veil that covered her head was crumpled and in disarray, strands of mousy hair hanging from beneath it. Her face was red and puffy and her eyes watered as she stared up at him as if he were a complete stranger.

'John? Is it you, John?' she muttered.

'Yes, it's me, Matilda, the same old John! Are you unwell? Can I get anything for you? A cup of water?'

He felt the usual male helplessness in the face of female emotion or illness.

His wife shook her head slowly. 'What am I to do, John?'

Her speech was thick, as if her tongue had doubled in size. 'What am I to do? The shame and the misery.' These words were followed by a longer, rambling monologue which he could not follow, but it gave him time to desperately think of some response to what was becoming an unmanageable situation.

'Shall I call Lucille and get you to your bed? Maybe you will feel better lying down? Or shall I send for your cousin from Fore Street?'

Mary appeared behind him with a leather bucket and a rag to clean up the spilt wine, but he waved her away impatiently.

'Get Lucille,' he hissed, then turned back to Matilda, stooping over her chair like a big black heron.

'Tell me what ails you, Matilda. Is there anything I can do to comfort you?' He had not uttered words like this for more than a dozen years. Her hand grasped his wrist with surprising strength.

'I have no friends, John. No friends at all, not even you.'

'Of course you have, wife! There are all your companions at St Olave's and the cathedral. And you have three cousins and a brother.'

He could have bitten off his tongue as Richard de Revelle's name slipped out and she began sobbing – a strange sucking noise as her chest heaved and her eyes filled with moisture.

'Richard! Why do you hate each other so? Thank Jesus that our mother and father no longer live to see our shame!'

She fell to muttering again, then her head dropped to her chest and John wondered whether she had fallen into a drunken sleep. He looked around desperately, as he would rather face a thousand armed Saracens than a weeping woman, and was relieved to see Mary at the door, with Lucille close behind her. They advanced on Matilda and with difficulty raised the stocky woman from her chair. As they stumbled towards the vestibule with her, his wife seemed to awaken, mumbling again as her head lolled from side to side.

'Has she been like this before, when I have not been here?' John demanded of Mary's retreating back, as Lucille and he rarely spoke to each other.

'Not as bad as this, but recently she has been taking wine more than usual, both in the afternoon and the evening,' said the maid over her shoulder.

De Wolfe followed them through the side passageway to the yard like an anxious sheepdog following a flock. The steep open staircase up to the solar was a serious obstacle, as it was too narrow for the two maids to support Matilda on either side. John solved the problem by lifting her bodily into his arms and staggering up the steps with her, which said something for his physique, as his wife, though short, was solidly built. She snorted and muttered as they went, and at the top he left her with Mary and Lucille for them to get her undressed and on to the wide straw-filled palliasse that was their bed. Back down in the hall, John found his old hound Brutus looking puzzled at these unusual happenings, and stroked his grizzled head in reassurance.

'What's to become of us all, old fellow?' he muttered, picking up the shards of the broken cup and laying them in the hearth for Mary to deal with later. He went to the side table where the wine was kept and with some regret saw that all his good Poitou red had gone, the two pottery crocks being empty. Groping under the table, he found a small wineskin of an inferior vintage and, pulling out the wooden stopper, poured himself a liberal cupful. Brutus came and laid a dribbling mouth on his knee as John sank into the chair that Matilda had been using.

He slumped there for some time, turning over in his mind the events of that day and of those that had preceded it. A procession of scenes marched through his mind as the level in the wineskin dropped – the bizarre funeral at Sampford, with cow turds and a dead rat on the coffin, the arrogant indifference of the armourer, the strange Peverel family – and now the apparent breakdown of Matilda's normally iron resolve.

Eventually, Mary came in to report that his wife was now in a deep sleep, snoring fit to rattle the shutters, and that Lucille had gone off to Fore Street to fetch Matilda's cousin to sit with her. She was one of the poor relations of the family – not poor in the sense of lacking money, as her husband had a successful glove-making business, but as one who had married 'into trade', out of the de Revelles' social class. Matilda treated her in a patronising fashion, but seemed moderately fond of her.

'Shall I make a meal for you this evening?' demanded Mary. John could tell that, though she was one of his staunchest allies, the cook-maid was laying some of the blame for his wife's condition on him.

'No, I'll take myself down to the Bush – or I'll be out of favour with yet another woman!' he grunted.

After Mary had flounced out with a disparaging shrug of her shoulders, the coroner sat for a while longer until he had finished his cup of wine, then snapped his fingers at Brutus and made for the street. The cathedral Close was cool in the autumn evening and there were only a few children playing among the graves and a solitary beggar sitting on the steps of the great west front. John strode through the lanes, oblivious to the murmured greetings and forelock-pullings of passers-by, until he reached Idle Lane and the new front door of the Bush, set in a clean white-washed wall, repainted after the recent fire.

A smiling Nesta hurried over and took his arm to steer him to his table by the hearth. She at once noticed his doleful expression and soon he was telling her of his visit to Sampford Peverel and the strange state in which he found his wife when he returned.

'It's not just me, *cariad*,' he said in the Welsh they habitually used together. 'She's had years to get used to my misdeeds. I've done nothing particularly terrible lately.'

His mistress shook her head pityingly at the lack of insight of men.

'You were the instrument for disgracing her beloved brother – not that you could have done anything else,' she pointed out. 'He was the main culprit, even in her eyes, but that doesn't alter the fact that she feels that in the end it was you who pushed him over the edge.'

Like Mary, though Nesta was inordinately fond of this dour, dark man, she had an inexhaustible well of sympathy for anyone in trouble, including wronged wives.

'Lately, she's been talking a great deal about her family in Normandy,' he said. 'Not that they're close to her, nor do they probably want her bothering them again. But maybe she ought to go across the Channel some time, to get it out of her system.'

Nesta nodded her agreement. 'I know how she feels, John. It's three years since I left Gwent to come here with Meredydd and I've not seen my mother or my brothers and sisters since. Only two messages have come by carters to at least tell me they are still alive.'

She sounded wistful, not only when she spoke of her family, but also of her dead husband. If the Welsh archer had not been an old campaign friend of John's, he might have felt a twinge of jealousy.

'Maybe you too should make a journey home before long, Nesta,' he suggested. 'Though what would I do, with both the women in my life deserting me!'

The landlady poked him hard in the ribs with her elbow. 'I know damn well what you'd be doing the moment the dust had settled on the high road behind us!' she snapped, only half in jest. 'Where would you go first, man? To Dawlish or to the stews in Waterbeer Street?'

He grinned sheepishly, as Nesta knew all about his other former mistress, the blonde Hilda from Dawlish. In fact, she had once met her, and they had got along famously, having more things in common than just John de Wolfe.

He stayed at the tavern for a couple of hours, drinking the good ale supplied regularly by the old potman and eating an excellent supper of mutton stew followed by grilled herrings. Nesta, looking even more attractive than usual in a new yellow kirtle under her white linen apron, was hoping that her lover would stay either all night or at least for a few hours in her little room in the loft, but she soon sensed that the upsetting episode with Matilda had taken the edge off his usual keenness to get her into bed. Silently regretful, she settled down to be a sympathetic audience as he poured out his thoughts on the problems still plaguing him.

'I've made not a jot of headway on this slain silversmith,' he complained. 'This Terrus fellow claims that the armourer from Sampford was one of the villains, but it's only his word against that of the suspect, which was backed up by his lords, both dead and alive. Both Hugo and Ralph claimed that this Robert Longus was with them all the time and could never have been near Topsham when the man was robbed and killed.'

'So why are you insisting that this Longus must come to court in Exeter or risk being outlawed?' asked the practical Nesta.

'Just because the bastard refused to come,' snapped John. 'I'll teach him to flaunt the King's law officer.'

The Welsh ale-wife wrinkled her nose in doubt. 'I see no reason why this armourer's masters should lie for him. What would be in it for them?'

'Gwyn suggested that he was robbing on their behalf. It seems the Peverels are short of money, having lost heavily in the last year in wagering on the tournaments. But I think that's too far-fetched an idea.'

Nesta absently tucked a lock of copper-coloured hair back under her linen helmet.

'So who killed this Hugo? I fancy the French knight myself, for according to you he promised that he would.'

De Wolfe slid a hand on to her thigh under the table and for a moment her hopes of getting him up the loft ladder were rekindled.

'De Charterai? I don't think he meant it that seriously, it was said in the heat of the moment. And he's too chivalrous a fellow to stab a man in the back.'

'I'd believe anything of a man who has been insulted that badly,' countered Nesta. 'You measure everyone by your own standards of honour, John.'

'There are plenty of other possible killers, sweetheart. Gwyn and Thomas did their usual spying in the manor and came up with a number of folk who hated Hugo. And from what I saw myself, he had few friends there. In fact, he seemed a figure of hate to everyone.'

Always a lover of scandal and intrigue, Nesta rested her round chin on her hand and gazed at the bristly face alongside her. 'Tell me about them again!' she commanded.

'Well, this manor-reeve, Warin Fishacre, undoubtedly

hated Hugo's guts. I suspect that it was he who slung that ox turd into the grave. Either him or his son-in-law, as they both felt murderous towards their lord for deflowering their girl on her wedding night.'

'Damned disgraceful!' muttered Nesta, though the sentiment sounded much stronger in Welsh.

'Then there was Godwin the village thatcher, who'd had one of his sons hanged by Hugo not long ago. I put him down for throwing that dead rat.'

'And the family?' she persisted.

'I wouldn't put the dowager out of the running. It seems she suspects that Hugo had something to do with his father's death at the mêlée in Wilton. And poor sweet Beatrice must have had a bellyful of shame over her husband's flagrant ravishing of the village girls – as well as perhaps wanting to be free to take up with young Joel.'

'What about this Joel, is he a contender too?'

John took his hand off her leg to lift his quart pot to his lips. 'He was making sheep's eyes at the new widow all the time I was there. Whether he would kill just to get his way with her, I couldn't guess.'

'Do you suspect the other two brothers as well?'

'I suspect everyone in that bloody place!' growled de Wolfe. 'Ralph seems to have the best chance of becoming the manor-lord, so he had a good motive for getting rid of his elder brother. And poor Odo, the one with the fits, may have thought he would have another chance at being recognised as the heir if Hugo was out of the way.'

They sat talking about the problem for a while, with Nesta having to get up every now and then to sort out some problem or other, ranging from sudden scuffles between patrons who had had too much to drink to a panic in the kitchen shed when a pan of beef dripping caught fire.

It was well after dusk when John's conscience began pricking him strongly enough to drive him home to see whether his wife had recovered from her drunken stupor. He would dearly have liked to stay with Nesta, but they both knew that this was not the night for that, with his guilt pressing down on him. Dragging Brutus away from the meaty bone that old Edwin had thrown under the table for him, John gave his mistress a chaste kiss and wearily made his way back through the darkened streets to Martin's Lane.

Henry de Furnellis was a totally different character to his snobbish, supercilious predecessor. Whereas Richard de Revelle always closeted himself in his chamber with a guard on the door, remote from the common herd outside, Henry was often to be found in the main hall of the keep, sitting at a table with a mug of ale or a bowl of stew, chatting to whoever he could find to gossip with him. An old soldier, he was fond of companionship and liked nothing better than to swap tales of old campaigns with the castle constable, Ralph Morin, or Gabriel, the sergeant-at-arms.

To have John de Wolfe there as well was an added bonus, and the following morning the four of them sat talking, with clerks and stewards hovering impatiently in the background with their parchments and endless queries about administrative problems. De Furnellis ignored them as he listened to the end of John's description of the situation in Sampford Peverel.

'I knew the father, William Peverel,' he declared. 'A good fighter in his time, but a bad-tempered bastard if he was crossed. He hated losing at anything, especially at the tournament.'

'Did you know the sons?' asked Ralph Morin.

The older man shook his grey head. 'Only by sight at a few tourneys. This Hugo had a reputation as a rash fighter – he often won, but he took too many risks, they say, too desperate to win every time. Didn't know any of the others, but I heard about the dispute when the eldest son was barred from his inheritance.'

'So what's to be done, Sheriff?' asked de Wolfe. 'We've now got two unsolved murders to deal with – and if this silversmith's worker is right, then there's a link between them in Sampford.'

'Get this armourer to Exeter and put him down below!' suggested Gabriel, the most bloodthirsty of the group. 'I'll wager that an hour with Stigand's branding-irons in the undercroft would loosen up his tongue.' The sheriff, though not keen to put himself to too much effort, was more concerned with the slaying of one of the county's manor-lords.

'The King's ministers will be huffing and puffing over this,' he said glumly. 'The Peverels were not powerful barons, but they were known well enough by their tour-neying reputation. No doubt I'll have to answer a string of questions when I next take county farm to Winchester.'

'I wonder why de Revelle is poking his nose into their affairs,' mused the constable. 'Knowing him, it can't just be neighbourly concern.'

'There was some talk of his wanting to buy some of the Peverel land to add to his own,' answered de Wolfe. 'He seems to be buttering up Ralph Peverel and supporting his claim to the lordship, which I suspect Odo is going to challenge again.'

'Wouldn't trust that swine de Revelle any farther than I could throw my horse,' grunted Henry. 'He's up to something to his own advantage, you can be sure of that.'

Ralph Morin stroked his forked beard ruminatively. 'I heard a rumour that our unlamented former sheriff was going to involve himself in the tournament circuit. Maybe that's why he's so thick with the Peverels, as they've always been keen on that business.'

De Wolfe snorted in derision. 'Richard on the jousting field! My dear wife would perform better with a horse and lance than her damned brother!'

'I doubt he intends to put on his armour and buckle on a sword,' replied the constable. 'Knowing his love affair with money, I suspect he intends to play the field from the safety of the spectators' stands, wagering on the mad devils who go out to risk their gizzards on the end of a lance!'

Sheriff Henry cackled into his ale, as Richard de Revelle's lack of prowess with arms and his dislike of personal danger were well known in the county.

'Now that he can't cream off any of the taxes into his purse, he must be forced to look elsewhere for some loot,' he observed cynically.

John grinned with the others, though in fairness to his brother-in-law he had to acknowledge that Richard was an astute businessman, leaving aside his dubious history of corruption and embezzlement. He had several manors, one near Tiverton and another at Revelstoke near Plymouth, and made a good income from the management of these. In fact, he regularly topped up Matilda's treasure chest, which stood in the solar, from earnings on the inheritance that their parents had left her some years earlier. Still, the hint that Richard was snooping around the tournament establishment was interesting and might well explain why he was cultivating the Peverels.

Soon they all left for the courthouse, where an extra session was being held that morning for several stray cases that had missed the last county court. John was involved in a couple of matters, one concerning an irate fishmonger from near the West Gate, who was bringing an appeal against a porter for serious assault.

The fishman had caught the other fellow enjoying his wife's favours in the salting shed behind his house. According to the wronged husband, far from being abashed and contrite, the porter had given the fishmonger a severe thrashing. Now he was wishing to 'appeal' the man, leading to a physical combat between them, which, given the difference in physique between the two men, the husband was foolish to contemplate. The coroner, whose duty it was to listen to the story and make a record, managed to persuade the man to take the matter to the next visitation of the King's justices, where at least he was unlikely to lose his life to the burly porter. Other matters concerned the outlawing of two men accused of theft who had failed to appear after being warned for the last four Shire Courts. John had to confirm that their writs of attachment had been properly made and that the men had not answered to their sureties. This caused anguish among their relatives, who had put up the bail money to try to ensure their appearance and would now forfeit it to the King's treasury. The issue reminded John again that he needed to get Robert Longus down from Sampford for his resumed inquest.

His business done, he left the new sheriff and the others to deal with matters that did not concern him and went back at the ninth hour with Thomas and Gwyn to his chamber in the gatehouse for their second breakfast of bread, cheese and cider. Thomas was looking miserable again, as he had still heard nothing more from Winchester.

Gwyn was his usual cheerful self, looking like a disreputable giant in his leather jerkin and faded serge breeches with cross-gartering up the calves. The wind that moaned through the window opening ruffled his wild red hair as he stared down the steep track that led from the drawbridge to the gate in the stockade around the outer ward.

'Here's a familiar figure, Crowner,' he said eventually. 'I wonder if he's here to call upon you.'

De Wolfe looked up from one of his Latin reading lessons, irritated by his officer's characteristically obtuse remark. 'Who is it, for God's sake?'

For answer, Gwyn bent towards the doorway and put a hand behind his ear in an exaggerated posture of listening. 'Soon find out, Crowner!'

Sure enough, a moment later there were voices mounting the twisting stairwell and one of the men-at-arms on duty in the guardroom below pushed aside the hessian curtain.

'Gentleman to see you, sir!' he announced, standing aside to admit a tall, thin figure dressed in a green riding cloak, the hood hanging down his back. It was Reginald de Charterai, his face looking pinched from a long ride in a cold wind. John climbed to his feet and Thomas hurriedly left his stool, the only other place to sit.

'Sir Reginald, this is unexpected, but you are welcome! Forgive the miserable quarters the previous sheriff grudgingly allotted me, but please sit down.'

Reginald pulled the corner of his cloak from the silver ring that secured it to his right shoulder and shrugged it off, before sitting on the stool. Gwyn hoisted himself from his window ledge and poured the visitor a pot of rough cider, then winked at Thomas before scooping up the clerk and the soldier and diplomatically vanishing down the stairs.

The French knight took a sip of his drink and tried not to wince, then set his mug down on the trestle table and looked sternly at the coroner.

'Forgive my intrusion, but I felt that you were the best person with whom to discuss certain matters.'

Though his Norman French was John's own language, the inflexions betrayed his Continental origins, as he came from the Champagne country east of Paris and technically was an enemy, a subject of the French king, Philip Augustus.

Reginald's long face was finely featured and his whole appearance spoke of an aristocratic, rather cold personality. He stared gravely at the coroner as he sat stiffly erect on his stool.

'I rode from Tiverton to Bridport yesterday, intending to take ship to Barfleur,' he began. Bridport was in the next county, about twenty miles away in Dorset, and had considerable sea traffic with Barfleur, near Cherbourg on the Normandy coast. It was infamous for being the port from where many years ago the tragic White Ship had sailed, the sinking of which led to the death of the first King Henry's son and so to the long civil war between Stephen and the Empress Matilda. John failed to see what this had to do with him and waited patiently for de Charterai to elaborate.

'Owing to contrary winds, no vessel had arrived and I was recommended to try Topsham.'

John nodded and tried to look as if he understood where this was leading.

'I am attending a tournament in Fougères and will not return from Normandy for some weeks, for a grand mêlée at the battleground near Salisbury. I thought that as this Topsham is very near Exeter, I would call upon you and unburden some concerns that I have borne for a considerable time.'

John began to wonder whether the French nobleman had been taking lessons in long-windedness from Gwyn of Polruan.

'Are these concerns a matter for a coroner?' he asked politely.

Reginald inclined his head. 'They may well be – and

that is why I seek your advice, as I consider you to be another man of honour, a rare thing these days.'

John cleared his throat to cover his embarrassment at an unexpected compliment, as de Charterai continued.

'You may know that I have a considerable respect – indeed affection – for Avelina, the widow of the late William, lord of Sampford Peverel. Both something that she has imparted to me and also knowledge which I myself possess make me most concerned about the manner of her husband's death.'

At last he was getting to the point of his visit, thought John, who sat up at this hint of a suspicious death.

'Tell me what doubts you have, sir,' he prompted.

'I was there at the tourney field in Wilton last spring when Sir William died – in fact, I was the opponent he struck just before he died. He unhorsed me, but fell from his mount himself a moment later and was killed. In some ways, I might be looked upon as a factor in his death, for the force of his lance's impact upon my shield broke his saddle girth and he fell to the ground.'

De Wolfe's dark eyes held the other's blue orbs in a direct stare.

'So why do you have concerns? Your conscience must surely be clear at being a factor in his death. That is what tourneys are all about – striking at each other!'

De Charterai shook his head emphatically.

'No, no, there was much else to consider! William Peverel fell from his horse just as I did – a common occurrence in jousts, as you well know from your own experience. We all learn to accept it, unless we are unlucky enough to break our necks. But he was killed by being trampled by another horse – one ridden by his son, Hugo Peverel.'

The coroner nodded. 'I had heard something to that effect. But surely you are not claiming that this was deliberate . . . how could Hugo foresee that his father would fall in front of him?'

Reginald rapped the edge of the table with his long fingers, the first time he had been anything other than impassive.

'Because he may have foreseen it, Sir John! As soon as I saw my opponent beneath the hoofs of another destrier, I picked myself up and ran forward to offer assistance, as did several others. I grabbed the reins of his stallion, which was prancing about and threatening to run wild. It was then I saw that the saddle was almost off its back, as the girth under its belly was hanging free.'

De Wolfe wondered where this was leading. 'This is also common knowledge,' he said doubtfully. 'Though rare, a broken girth is well known to occur from time to time.'

The French knight shook his head. 'This one was not broken. As I held the horse once it had steadied, I looked at the leather strap where it hung loose, instead of passing around the stem of the buckle. The treble rows of stitching that secured it had all almost been cut through, so that its strength was but a fraction of what was required.'

John's black eyebrows lifted. 'That is a serious accusation! How could you be sure?'

'I spend my life with horses and their harness, Crowner. I know that no stitching could be so sharply snipped in such a regular fashion as that, from wear and tear. It had been deliberately tampered with.'

De Wolfe pondered for a moment. 'Did you draw the attention of anyone to this?'

Reginald shook his head. 'All was confusion at that time. Peverel's squire came running to take the horse, as well as some grooms and officials from the tourney. I left the beast with them and went to see if I could aid the fallen man, but it was obvious that he was dying, as his chest and skull had been crushed by the hoofs of his son's horse.'

He sighed, as if once again replaying the drama in his mind.

'When I went back to the recet to take a closer look at the damaged harness, it had vanished, though the stallion was there in charge of some of the Peverel retainers. I had no proof nor even any further chance of confirming what I had seen.'

'You said you have some other evidence which gave you concern?' prompted the coroner.

'Lady Avelina, she had firm ideas as to what had happened,' continued de Charterai. 'Though, like me, she has no proof, she is convinced that Hugo plotted his father's death. The sabotaged girth and the fact that Hugo conveniently managed to run his fallen father down with his own horse seem strong evidence that this was no accident.'

'But why should Hugo Peverel wish to commit the awful sin of patricide?' demanded John.

'He was in dire need of money, having lost a great deal at the tournaments the previous year, both in forfeiture of horse and arms and injudicious wagers on other fighters. Avelina and I are convinced that he wished to displace his father from the lordship and claim the manor for himself, as a means to clearing his substantial debts.'

'But his elder brother was next in succession, so how could he have gained?' objected de Wolfe.

The lean Frenchman fixed him with a sardonic stare.

'You well know what happened next! Hugo took his brother to law and had him displaced on the grounds of incapacity, due to his falling sickness. This must have been planned in advance – his stepmother is utterly convinced that her husband was murdered by his son.'

254

De Wolfe grunted. 'Well, he has paid for his sins now – stabbed in the back!'

'But by whom?' demanded de Charterai. 'Has recent history repeated itself? Who is now contesting the lordship of the Peverel estates?'

John nodded slowly. 'That had occurred to me, sir. But there are a number of candidates for the dispatch of Hugo, apart from his brother Ralph.'

'And what do you intend to do about it, Crowner?' demanded Reginald. 'Both father and son slain and no one brought to account.'

De Wolfe slowly shook his head. 'As to the father, I have no jurisdiction whatsoever. This occurred in Wiltshire and is the business of its sheriff and coroner. Did you not think to report it to them at the time?'

Reginald de Charterai's austere features took on an almost contemptuous look. 'What, with no proof? The harness vanished immediately – a suspicious thing in itself. And I would remind you that I am a Frenchman, not overly loved by many on this side of the Channel, especially as my relationship with the Peverels was not too cordial at previous tournaments. Then that disgraceful affair here in Exeter would make any accusation of mine appear spiteful mischief-making. It was only when I recognised you as a man of integrity that I decided to speak out privately to you.'

John digested this oblique compliment and made a somewhat grudging attempt at satisfying de Charterai.

'I am not acquainted with either the sheriff or the coroner in Salisbury, but as soon as the opportunity arises I will raise the matter with them – though without any proof, I fail to see what can be done at this late stage.'

He rubbed a hand over his dark stubble as an aid to thought.

'However, the death of Hugo is very much my

responsibility – at least, our sheriff here has made it so, in addition to my duties as coroner. I can assure you that the issues are very much in my mind. I am arranging to interrogate further witnesses from both Sampford Peverel and elsewhere.'

The French knight jerked his head in acknowledgement and suddenly stood up.

'I have taken enough of your time. Thank you for listening to me. I shall be lodging at the New Inn here in Exeter for a day or so, until I get word that a vessel is sailing from Topsham. If there is any news, please let me know – otherwise, I will call upon you again when I return from Normandy in a few weeks' time.'

De Wolfe rose and saw him to his horse, which was tethered outside the guardroom, where Gwyn, Thomas and Gabriel were keeping out of the way. They looked curiously at the stiff-gaited Frenchman as he mounted and rode away. Gwyn, never one for the niceties of speech, spat on the ground.

'Miserable sod, that one! He'd likely crack his bloody face if he tried to smile.'

For once, John found no reason to disagree with his officer.

CHAPTER TEN

*In which Crowner John receives a
royal commission*

It was proving to be a busy day for Devonshire's coroner, measured by the number of visitors and interruptions. After Reginald de Charterai had left, John went back to his chamber and began struggling again with his reading lessons. Every time he felt he was making some progress, some crisis seemed to drive it all from his mind and he had to start afresh. He could now write his name tolerably well and recognise several dozen words in Latin, mainly those dealing with the legal matters that arose repeatedly in the Shire Court and in Thomas's inquest rolls. His progress was painfully slow, however, and he accepted that at his age he could never become really proficient.

For the moment, John was alone at the top of the gatehouse tower, with only the whistle of the breeze through the pointed window openings for company. Gwyn had gone to the soldiers' quarters in search of a drink and a game of dice, while Thomas had taken himself to the cathedral scriptorium, with the excuse that he must scrounge some more ink from the canon, who ground the best gall and soot pigment in the city. In reality, he wanted to let his feet tread the hallowed stones and boards of an ecclesiastical building, which was the nearest place to heaven that the little clerk could find on earth.

An hour passed and John began to fidget over his parchments, wishing that the noon bell of the cathedral would ring to release him and allow him to go home for his dinner, even though this meant facing Matilda in her present strange mood following her drunken episode. Just as his wandering attention settled on speculation as to what Mary might have cooked for the day's main meal, footsteps again sounded on the staircase outside. This time, there was no soldier to announce the visitor, as the face that poked through the sacking screen was that of a servant from the close. It was a pimply boy who worked as the bottler's assistant in the house of Canon John de Alençon, and he brought a message to the effect that his master the archdeacon would be obliged if the coroner could call upon him at his earliest convenience.

'Give him my compliments and tell him I will be with him very shortly!' commanded John, and as the boy scuttled away down the steps he rose to roll up his parchments with a sigh of relief and take his grey cape from a peg on the wall.

Outside, the October day had turned colder and grey clouds and wind warned of a grim autumn. The wet summer of that year had already provided a very poor harvest, and if winter turned out to be a hard one he feared that starvation would claim many before the next spring.

He walked briskly down Castle Hill to High Street and turned into Martin's Lane. He passed his own front door but refrained from going in, for fear that domestic problems would detain him from meeting his good friend the archdeacon. It was unusual for de Alençon, to send for him, and even the lure of Mary's cooking failed to divert him.

When he arrived at the tall house in Canon's Row,

the continuation of Martin's Lane past the north side of the cathedral, a servant showed him straight into the spartan room that the canon used as his study. A table carrying several books, two stools and a large plain cross on the wall were the only furnishings that the austere priest allowed, a marked contrast to the lavish luxury enjoyed by many senior members of the cathedral establishment. But John de Alençon's face was anything but austere today, for he advanced on the coroner with a beatific smile and sat him on one side of the table while he took the other stool. Almost immediately, his bottler, a skinny old man with a bulbous nose, entered with two glass goblets and a glazed pottery jar whose seal told de Wolfe that it was the very best quality Anjou wine.

'Why the celebration, John?' he asked his namesake. 'Is it your birthday or have they at last made you a bishop?'

'Neither, my friend, but I have some good news,' replied the archdeacon, his blue eyes twinkling in his thin face. 'Your clerk – my nephew – has at last been granted readmission to the clergy! I had a message from the chapter clerk of Winchester today, announcing that Thomas de Peyne is to present himself there in seven weeks' time!'

The stolid coroner was incapable of tears, but he felt an unaccustomed prickling in his eyes for a moment as he thought of the joy that this would bring to his woebegone clerk. It was through de Alençon's intervention that the near-starving Thomas had been taken on by de Wolfe as his clerk, and they both held considerable affection for the little man, whose intellect and devotion more than compensated for his poor body and unprepossessing appearance.

'Does he know of this yet?' John asked, as they raised their goblets in celebration of this long-awaited event.

'It's little more than an hour since I had the message,' replied the archdeacon. 'I've no idea where he might be, which is partly why I sent for you, to discover his whereabouts.'

The matter was soon resolved, as the boy with the pimples was sent off at a trot to the cathedral archives above the chapter house, where the coroner rightly suspected he would be found, in his quest for ink.

Within a few minutes, Thomas appeared, rather apprehensive at the summons, especially when he found his master with his uncle, both of them wearing spuriously grim expressions.

'Oh God!' he gasped, the words being a genuine supplication rather than an oath. 'Please don't tell me that they have changed their minds!'

As he seemed on the point of fainting, the two Johns hurriedly dropped their charade and broke into smiles as they told Thomas the good news. Then he almost fainted again, falling to his knees and bursting into tears, rocking back and forth on the floor, crossing himself and blubbing prayers of thanks between his sobs. His uncle, more used to pastoral emotions than the discomfited coroner, laid a gentle hand on his head. De Wolfe took a spare wine cup from the table and filled it.

'Here, boy, take this and join us!' he said, holding it out. 'I know you dislike ale and cider, but drink this with us in celebration. You're unlikely to have the chance of tasting this quality again!'

Thomas staggered to his feet and gradually his tears subsided as his elfin face became wreathed in smiles. The archdeacon told him of the need to be in Winchester some weeks hence and they discussed the practicalities of the journey and the need for someone to accompany him on the lonely and dangerous roads.

'I'll send Gwyn with you, to make sure you get there

in one piece,' promised de Wolfe. 'How I'll manage without either my clerk or my officer, I don't know, but we'll worry about that when the time comes.'

Thomas's euphoria suddenly evaporated, as a look of desperate concern appeared on his face.

'I'll not leave you, master! Even when I am taken back into the bosom of Mother Church, I will remain your clerk until you have no further need of me.'

John fidgeted with his wine cup. 'Don't concern yourself with that now, Thomas,' he muttered gruffly. 'You enjoy this moment and the prospect of what your heart has desired for so long.'

After a few more minutes of discussion about this great event, Thomas became agitated again and pleaded to be excused.

'I need to spend the rest of the day on my knees before the high altar, giving thanks to God for my deliverance.' He made his escape as soon as he could and the two older men watched him go with benign smiles on their faces.

'Thank God for that, and I have never meant it so sincerely,' commented the archdeacon. 'I think my poor nephew would eventually have pined away and died, had this never come about.'

'Even I will go down on my knees beside my bed tonight and offer up my thanks for it,' grunted de Wolfe. 'But before that, we must have a celebration at the Bush this evening and try to get the little fellow drunk for the first time in his life!'

There was much of the day left before any such celebration could take place. First John had to get back to his house to make muttered excuses for his late appearance at dinner. Matilda looked very rough; her eyes were red rimmed and her face even more sallow than usual. For once she had no caustic comment to make on his tardiness at coming to table and sat silently with downcast eyes, chewing without enthusiasm the salt fish followed by boiled mutton that Mary had prepared. Afterwards the cook-maid brought them apples, which were now in season and, though small, were smooth and round, unlike the wrinkled fruit that they would get in the winter.

John made a few attempts at conversation, including the news that Thomas was to be readmitted to the Church. He had hoped that his wife's partiality to things ecclesiastical would allow her to be pleased at the return of a priest to the fold, but her dislike of Thomas prevented her from showing any interest, and he relapsed into silence again.

When Mary came into the hall to collect the remains of the trenchers and the platters, she dropped a wooden tray on the flagstones with a loud clatter. Matilda winced and screwed up her eyes as if a dagger had been plunged into her ear, and John realised that she was still suffering badly from the effects of her drinking the night before. She was still managing to swallow a respectable quantity of the less expensive wine that remained after her excesses, however, and they sat in uncompanionable silence while they emptied their cups. John once again tried to strike up some conversation to ease the strain between them, and this time he had more success when he tapped the snobbish, rather than the religious, vein in his wife's nature. He told her of the unexpected visit of Sir Reginald de Charterai that morning, and her eyes, though still bleary, showed a spark of interest at the mention of an aristocrat from across the Channel.

'He is very well known, John, as well as a charming and handsome man,' she grunted. 'You would do well to cultivate his friendship.'

Surprised, John enquired how she came to know him.

'I saw him at the feast where he had that altercation with that evil Peverel fellow,' she replied. 'And I have seen him once or twice at tournaments in past years – usually when I went with my brother, as you were absent for most of my life!'

Even in her present low state, she could not resist jabbing her husband with her barbed tongue.

'It seems that he is enamoured of Lady Avelina, the widow of William Peverel,' he informed her, somewhat spitefully, as he suspected that Matilda was harbouring a distant admiration for the august Reginald, a man who seemed the type to appeal to ladies of a certain age. This news appeared to double her interest and she was almost animated as she enquired about the Frenchman's visits to Sampford Peverel. John could almost hear the gossip mill grinding away outside St Olave's church next Sunday.

'It seems odd that he is paying court to the wife of a man at whose violent death he was present and who now, months later, he alleges was murdered!' observed John. 'One might even wonder if he is raising a smoke-screen to divert suspicion from himself.'

He himself did not for a moment believe this, but cussedly prodded Matilda's obvious partiality for the Frenchman. His wife immediately rose to the bait.

'What nonsense you do come out with, John! Sometimes I despair of your common sense. Sir Reginald is a knight of impeccable character – and why should he now raise the issue of foul play if he himself was involved?' She glared scornfully at her husband and downed the last of her wine. 'Look elsewhere for your culprit and be glad that this man's sense of honour brought him to you with information that might prove useful.'

De Wolfe sighed, chastened by his wife's fondness for de Charterai. She would deem him innocent even if he were found clutching a bloody knife. Even worse, she was almost certainly right.

The third interruption of the day came in mid-afternoon, when de Wolfe was in the sheriff's chamber, checking the names of those who were to be hanged the next day. Henry de Furnellis had inherited his sheriff's clerk from Richard de Revelle, a wizened, miserable cleric in minor orders, by the name of Elias Pulein. Though he was probably not yet forty, he looked and acted like a man twenty years older. No one could ever recall seeing him smile, and his attitude was one of martyred resignation at having to serve a succession of high-born idiots. His one saving grace was an ability to read and write almost as well as Thomas de Peyne, and a pedantic attention to detail and routine that kept the somewhat haphazard adminstration of justice in Devonshire in some sort of order.

Now he stood at the sheriff's elbow with a sheaf of parchments, comparing one list with another.

'Edwin of Cullompton died of a fever in the South Gate gaol last week and Robert de Combe had his throat cut by another prisoner, so we can cross them off our list.' He spoke in a tired, dispassionate voice, as if he were cancelling invitations to a guild dinner, rather than an appointment with the gallows-tree.

'So how many are there left?' asked John irritably.

'Five, including one woman . . . the girl who poisoned her husband for beating her.'

John had to attend the hangings on Magdalen Street, the high road to the east outside the city walls, to see that the executions were correctly recorded for presen-tion to the King's justices when they eventually came to hold the General Eyre. This was the major inquiry into the adminstration of the county and might not occur for several years, but all legal events had to be catalogued for their perusal. In addition to the more frequent Eyres of Assize, there were the courts of 'Gaol Delivery', held by commissioners who could be either judges or senior officials from Winchester or London, and who came to clear the congested gaols of prisoners awaiting trial. These gaols were not places of punishment after conviction, as no such penalty existed – they merely held those awaiting trial until they were acquitted, fined or hanged. In actual fact, a significant proportion of those on remand never reached the courts, as they either died, were murdered or escaped, the latter through widespread bribery of the gaolers or the connivance of the local inhabitants in small towns and villages, where the cost of guarding and feeding miscreants for long periods was unwelcome.

After agreeing on the names of the felons to be dispatched on the morrow, Elias Pulein began a litany of cases to be dealt with at the next Shire Court, due the following week. This was mainly the responsibility of Henry de Furnellis, though he seemed content to nod sagely at intervals and let his clerk make all the arrangements. Some of the cases needed some input from the coroner, such as declarations of outlawry, depositions about appeals and the confessions of 'approvers' trying to save their necks by incriminating their accomplices.

The dry voice of the chief clerk droned on and John fancied that he could see the sheriff's eyelids drooping as he slumped behind his table. Indeed, the coroner himself felt drowsy from the combination of a heavy dinner and Elias's boring monologue. Abruptly, they were delivered from this wearisome catalogue by a rapping on the heavy door and the appearance of Sergeant Gabriel's helmeted head.

'Sorry to disturb you, sirs, but what looks like an important visitor has just turned up at the gatehouse, wearing the royal livery. Got two armed escorts and says he comes from London on the King's business.'

John uncoiled himself from the corner of the table where he had been perched and Henry managed to shake himself fully awake and get to his feet.

'Who is it, Sergeant? Where is he now?' asked the sheriff, looking slightly confused.

De Wolfe stalked to the door ahead of him and hurried out into the main hall of the keep. As he made for the door at the top of the wooden staircase, two tall men-at-arms on either side of a shorter, youthful figure appeared in the arch. All wore round iron helmets and leather cuirasses, over which were tabards bearing the three golden lions on a red ground – the royal arms of Richard Coeur-de-Lion. Judging by their dusty and mud-spattered appearance, they had ridden long and hard.

The man in the middle – hardly more than a youth, though he had a knightly bearing – advanced with a smile and offered his right arm in a forearm grasp of greeting.

'I know that you are Sir John de Wolfe. I saw you last year with the King at that short but bloody fight at Nottingham after his release!'

He introduced himself as William de Mora and said he was acting as a herald for Hubert Walter, the Chief Justiciar and Archbishop of Canterbury. By this time, Henry de Furnellis had arrived, puffing, and introduced himself to the newcomer as the sheriff, immediately pressing the herald to eat, drink and rest.

'First I must deliver my message, sirs, which my Lord Hubert emphasises comes from the King himself. Then I will gladly avail myself of your hospitality, though we must set off with your reply tonight, as apparently the matter is of some urgency.'

Henry dispatched Gabriel with the two escorts to see

that they were fed and to make sure that their horses were looked after, then led the way back into his chamber off the hall. Elias Pulein was still standing there, looking aggrieved that such a trivial matter as a messenger from King Richard should interrupt his routine.

The young knight was a fresh-faced fellow, obviously from the family of one of the major barons, who had been placed on the fringe of the royal court as a good launching point for his career. Henry fussed over him, divesting him of his riding cloak and getting him seated with a cup of wine pressed into his hand.

'Now, William de Mora, what urgent business can the King have with me? Has he decided to sack me already?'

The herald smiled and shook his head deprecatingly – John thought that the lad's easy manner would take him far in the corridors of power.

'I fear my business is not with you, Sheriff, though I may say that your name is spoken of with great respect at court.'

Henry de Furnellis looked uncertain as to whether he was being praised or snubbed, but relief at not having new orders to bother him won the day.

'No, I have a message for the coroner,' went on de Mora. 'Dictated from the lips of the Justiciar himself.'

He slewed around on his seat to unlace a pouch at the side of his belt and drew out a parchment package, heavily sealed with tape and red wax. Handing it to de Wolfe, he repeated his plea for an early reply.

John stared at the square of vellum, folded over at either side to make an envelope. The main seal, carrying a mounted rider and a cross, was recognisable as the personal emblem of Hubert Walter.

'Please open it at once, Sir John,' requested the young knight, who could only have earned his spurs very recently. The coroner turned the package over, then back again, before pulling the tapes to crack the brittle wax from the seams of the parchment.

It was a single sheet, carrying a few lines of elegant script and a further seal at the bottom. He stared at the manuscript, but although he recognised his own name at the top and a few scattered words, the Latin was beyond his simple capabilities, and he cursed under his breath as he remembered that Thomas was on his knees in the cathedral, instead of being at his side to translate.

He looked across at the sheriff, who shrugged helplessly, but at once Elias Pulein came to the rescue and held out his hand for the letter. To be fair to the man, he managed to suppress the supercilious sniff that he could have made to express his disdain for the barbarians he had to work with.

'Shall I read it out, Crowner?' he asked with a deadpan expression.

John nodded curtly, wondering whether the courtly herald could read and, write and if so, what he thought of these clod-hoppers in Devon.

The sheriff's clerk quickly scanned the message from top to bottom.

'It's in Latin, but I'll give you sense of it in our usual tongue.'

He converted the words into Norman French rather than Middle English, as he felt it more fitting for a royal message.

'Archbishop Walter sends you his warmest greetings and says he thinks often of the times you were together in campaigning and battle . . . and so on.' The clerk seemed to gloss over these pleasantries as if they were a waste of his effort.

'Then he says that Our Sovereign Lord King Richard himself sends his personal greetings to you through the Justiciar, remembering your faithful service to him in the past, both in Outremer and on the fateful journey home.'

A note of respect crept into Elias's voice as he related this part.

'The King now wishes your further aid, in that he commands you to be at Chepstow Castle in the Welsh marches by the sixteenth day of this month, to escort an embassy to meet the Lord Rhys, Prince of South Wales. William, Marshal of England, will lead the deputation and will be supported by the Archdeacon of Brecon, Gerald de Barri.'

Elias looked up, clearly awe-struck by these great names.

'There is no reason given for the embassy, but the Justiciar says that you are an ideal escort and guide, as you are familiar with Wales, speak its language and are known to both the marshal and to Gerald de Barri.'

John thought whimsically that he could have added a further qualification – that of having a Welsh mistress!

The clerk gave a last look at the bottom of the manuscript. 'It ends with the felicitations of Archbishop Walter and his confidence that you will carry out this royal commission in your usual faithful and efficient manner.'

There was a silence as the now respectful Elias handed the manuscript back to the coroner.

Henry de Furnellis, his bushy eyebrows climbing high on his lined forehead, grinned at de Wolfe. 'You should have been sheriff in place of me, John, with all these friends in high places!'

There was no rancour or sarcasm in his voice, and John thought that he probably meant what he said. Before he could reply, the herald broke in with an easy but firm voice. 'I am to return with a reply as soon as possible, Sir John. Though I take it that you are in no mind other than to obey the King's wishes?'

De Wolfe had not a second's hesitation. Though the notice was short and a prolonged absence would make things difficult, to him his monarch's wish was an absolute command.

'Of course, I will be at Chepstow next week! Have you any idea how long this enterprise may take? I have many arrangements to make.'

William de Mora turned up his hands. 'I cannot be definite, but I gathered from the Justiciar that this was to be a single visit to the Welsh prince and a quick return, as I understand that William Marshal needs to be back in Normandy without delay.'

This was all John could glean about the journey, and after the sheriff had fussily shepherded the young knight away for food, drink and rest, the coroner went in a slightly dazed mood back to his house and sat by his fireside with a quart of ale to think through this sudden turn of events.

Thomas de Peyne did not get drunk that evening, but enough wine was forced on him to bring a flush to his sallow cheeks and to keep a smile on his usually melancholy features. When Nesta heard the good news, she immediately chivvied her maids into making extra pastries and a huge cauldron of mutton broth; a dozen capons were set turning on spits in the cook shed.

By the seventh hour that evening, the Bush was full of well-wishers, some of whom Thomas hardly knew. A few of the cathedral clergy came along, vicars, secondaries and some choristers, though the only senior member was his uncle, John de Alençon. Apart from Brother Rufus, the jolly fat monk who was the castle chaplain, the rest of the crowd were laymen, ranging from Henry de Furnellis to Ralph Morin, Gabriel, the two town constables and of course Gwyn and the coroner. One unexpected visitor was John's business partner, Hugh de Relaga, who turned up in an outrageous new surcoat of green velvet over a blue brocade tunic, with a floppy feathered hat to match. He had in tow a young man of about seventeen years, whom he introduced as his nephew, Eustace de Relaga.

The festivities carried on for much of the evening, though people came and went, after clapping the frail Thomas on the back and roaring out their congratulations and good wishes for the future. As dusk fell, many made their way home before curfew, though in these times of peace it was barely enforced – especially tonight, when both the enforcers, the constables Osric and Theobald, were themselves in the Bush.

Eventually, the remaining celebrants gravitated to a couple of tables near the hearth, the coroner's team being augmented only by Nesta, the sheriff, Ralph Morin, Gabriel and Hugh de Relaga and his silent relative. With some platters of savoury pastries and ample drink being replenished by old Edwin, the conversation moved on at last from Thomas's forthcoming restoration, which had been discussed up hill and down dale all evening. Henry de Furnellis, who had sunk an inordinate amount of ale, boisterously took the subject in a new direction.

'Your clerk's going to Winchester, John, but what about your own journey to Wales – and in such exalted company?'

All eyes swivelled to look at the coroner, who had said nothing to anyone yet about his royal summons. Not even to Matilda, who had been out at her cousin's house for supper, which gave him the opportunity to get to the Bush early.

'Wales? Are you going to Wales, John?' demanded Nesta, for whom the word conjured up nostalgic visions. There was a chorus of queries from around the tables and de Wolfe held up his hand for quiet.

'I only heard this afternoon,' he explained gruffly. 'I suppose it's really a state secret, but I trust no one here is going to rush off to tell Philip of France.'

'Tell him what, Crowner?' grunted Gwyn.

'That you are coming with me to Chepstow Castle to meet William the Marshal and escort him down west to pay a call on the Lord Rhys.'

There was a squeak of horror from Thomas de Peyne. 'But I am due in Winchester next month, Crowner!' he said, aghast at the prospect of missing his bishop's benediction.

'Don't fret, my lad. I'll not need you on such a journey, especially as you would never keep up, slung side-saddle over that broken-winded pony of yours! In any case, Gwyn and I will be back long before you go off to Winchester.'

The clerk's fears assuaged, the coroner told the whole story as far as he knew it – that because of his ability to speak Welsh and his familiarity with the country, he had been chosen by the Chief Justiciar on behalf of the King to accompany an embassy to Prince Rhys ap Gruffydd, the powerful ruler of most of south and west Wales, universally know as the Lord Rhys. John produced the parchment from his pouch and it was handed around the gathering. Although few of them could read a word, it was studied as reverently as if the King had penned it with his own hand.

'I don't know why the marshal is going to see him, and it's none of my business,' he added sternly. 'My task is to help make sure that he gets there and back safely.'

'You went around Wales like this once before, John,' said the excited Nesta. 'Wasn't it to guard some bishop?'

'Back in '88, that was,' broke in Gwyn. 'I was with him when we paraded around the country with old

Archbishop Baldwin, drumming up volunteers for the Holy Land – and ended up taking the cross ourselves!'

De Wolfe nodded. 'That's why Hubert Walter picked me for this,' he said. 'It's the same sort of job, nothing glamorous about it, just a bodyguard who can speak the language and find my way through the Welsh woods and hills.'

Nesta, her eyes glistening with pride at her lover's achievements, refused to let him belittle the honour.

'John, the King himself picked you and sent you his personal greetings, so you said the parchment states. You are an important man!'

De Wolfe felt that perhaps some of Matilda's revelling in fame was rubbing off on his mistress, but he was in too good a mood to complain.

'Gwyn, we have to be in Chepstow by next Thursday, a three-day journey, if we cross the Severn by boat. So we must leave no later than Monday.'

The coroner's exciting news kept the conversation going through another platter of meat pasties and another gallon of ale. There was much discussion about the politics of the ceaseless conflict between the English Crown and the independent Welsh princedoms, but as most of the news from there was weeks or months old by the time it reached Devon, no one was quite sure what the present political situation might be. When a lull came in this discussion, Hugh de Relaga shifted his portly, multi-coloured figure from his stool and dropped himself down with a bump on the bench alongside John.

'Before you go rushing off on your royal excursions, John, there's something I want to raise with you.'

The coroner expected his friend and business partner to launch into a discussion about the price of wool or the cost of shipping it abroad, but instead he beckoned to the young man, who came over and stood expectantly behind his uncle.

'Eustace is my brother's youngest lad,' he began, patting the youth affectionately on the shoulder. 'Until a year ago, he was a pupil in the cathedral school at Gloucester, and since then has been staying with me while he attended the pedagogues in a college house in Smythen Street.'

John wondered where all this was leading. He knew that Hugh's brother was a successful tin merchant in Tavistock, one of the Stannary towns on the west side of Dartmoor. He also knew that a few small centres of higher learning had sprung up in Exeter, as they had done some years ago in Oxford. Here the sons of wealthier people paid to attend lectures on subjects such as philosophy, grammar, logic and rhetoric, given by educated clerics, usually monks, canons or other learned clerks. Exeter, though a long way behind Oxford, was rapidly gaining a reputation for such colleges, most of the teaching being held informally in houses in Smythen Street, strangely to the accompaniment of nearby smiths and metal-workers banging their anvils.

De Wolfe looked from his old friend's face to the placid one of Eustace de Relaga. 'No doubt you were a good student, lad. But how can an old soldier like me be of any service to someone bursting with brains and learning?'

Eustace spoke for the first time, his voice high and clear and completely free of any Devon accent. 'My parents, especially my mother, had set their hearts on my entering the priesthood, sir. My education has been directed towards that end, but I fear that I feel no vocation for it.'

Thomas de Peyne, who had been chatting to Nesta, pricked up his ears at this statement. For anyone to decline the opportunity of entering his beloved Church was to Thomas almost a blasphemy. As his bright little eyes fixed on the young man, Eustace glanced rather bashfully at his uncle, who took up the tale.

'My brother and his wife have now accepted that he will not train for holy orders, nor does he wish to follow his father into the tin trade. But they agree with his desire to enter the public service in some capacity and hopefully work his way up to some useful position of trust and authority – maybe, in the fullness of time, even into government service in London or Winchester.'

The coroner still failed to see what this had to do with him, and rather bluntly said as much to his friend. The tubby portreeve took no offence.

'Eustace speaks, reads and writes Latin, French and English and is conversant with all modern learning, thanks to an excellent education. What he lacks, quite naturally at his tender age, is practical experience and a knowledge of the everyday world. I and his parents would dearly like to attach him to you as a sort of apprentice in the coroner's service – a kind of assistant to Thomas here, who might welcome some help in his copying of documents and suchlike.'

John's black brows came together as he thought about this sudden proposition. Hugh may have taken this for rejection, as he hurriedly went on to reassure his friend.

'There would naturally be no salary required – indeed, I would be happy to reimburse any expenses that might be entailed. It would be but for a trial period, to see if you could put up with him! And now that Thomas is to become actively involved again in ecclesiastical affairs, perhaps with a parish or prebend of his own, you may in the future be seeking a new clerk.'

The coroner looked across at Thomas, who was listening intently to this exchange.

'What do you think of this notion, Thomas? Would you like an acolyte to sit at your feet and help you with your quills and inks?'

The little clerk, until then euphoric at the prospect of his return to his beloved Church, abruptly seemed more sober.

'If it is your wish, Crowner, I see no reason why he should not follow us to learn something of the clerk's trade,' he said rather stiffly. 'But I have assured you that I have no intention of leaving your service, even though I am returned to the priesthood. I owe you much, even my very life, and I would never abandon my duties until I was sure my services were no longer required.'

De Wolfe read this as a warning shot against any move to displace Thomas in the short or long term, and he suspected that Hugh and his nephew got the same message from the tone of Thomas's voice.

'What about you, Gwyn? What do you think of having an addition to our little team?'

The big Cornishman shrugged. 'It's all one to me, Crowner! If the young fellow can ride a horse and drink ale, he's welcome to tag along.'

John turned back to the portreeve and his nephew, whose fresh, almost girlish face was tense with anticipation.

'We'll give it a try, Hugh, for a few weeks at least. Eustace, you can join us at our visitations to all the legal incidents that concern us and attend the inquests and various courts in which we are involved. You will take your instructions from Thomas de Peyne here, and help him in any way in which he directs you. Is that agreed?'

The young man nodded enthusiastically and thanked the coroner in his too-perfect English. His uncle added his own effusive thanks and ordered a flask of Nesta's most expensive wine as a final celebratory drink for everyone. After everyone had toasted Thomas's good news for the last time, the portreeve added another salute, this time to the addition of his nephew Eustace to the ranks of those who upheld the law in Devonshire.

As he downed the dregs in his cup, John glanced at Thomas's face and hoped to God that he had done the right thing by the little clerk.

As he strode home alone though the darkened lanes, John's thoughts slid away from the relatively minor problem of Thomas and Eustace and returned to the more portentous news of the day, his trip to Wales. There was much to be done in the time before he departed, especially another effort to resolve the death of the silversmith and the mystery at Sampford Peverel, which he was convinced were connected. As he tramped past the first street light, a guttering pitch-brand stuck above the Beargate leading into the cathedral close, he wondered how the coroner's business would survive without him for at least two weeks, which was an optimistic estimate of the time it would take to get into the hinterland of Wales and back again. His counterpart in North Devon, who had been appointed a few months back, could cover for some of the major cases in the centre of the county, but he could not be expected to ride down to the south coast, except in exceptional circumstances. John shrugged in the darkness – Hubert Walter could not have his loaf and eat it. If he wanted John in Wales, then he would have to accept that his new coroner system would be over-stretched for a time. It was already almost impossible for only two officers to cover every death in the huge county, and he knew that many cases went by default. The original Article of Assize from the King's justices in Kent, a year last September, had decreed that three coroners were to be elected in each county. That was all very well, but where were they to be found? Few active men had the time or inclination to take on a demanding and often distasteful job for no recompense at all.

Two weeks away from home! At least he would have a respite from Matilda's gloom and despondency, which were as bad as her usual carping and nagging.

As he reached the narrow entrance into Martin's Lane from the Close, where there was another flickering torch stuck in an iron ring above the arch, de Wolfe suddenly stopped dead. He had been struck by the glimmerings of an idea. If he was going away, so was Reginald de Charterai. And he was going to Normandy ... and Matilda was always pining for another visit to her relatives! His mind raced ahead, like a horse suddenly released from a stall. If she went away, why could Nesta not go with him to Wales, at least as far as Gwent, where she too had her family?

He slammed a fist into his palm, suddenly exultant at these interlocking ideas, which had tumbled down upon him like an avalanche.

Jauntily, he strode into the darkened lane and made for his front door.

chapter eleven

In which Crowner John visits a prince

A small group of people stood on a rough quay a few yards long, set in the bank of a small inlet, where a stream came down to the vast mud banks of the Severn estuary. It was a grey, overcast day, and across the wide river the distant hills of Wales were partly hidden by rain.

'Always bloody pouring down over there,' muttered Gwyn. 'Never been in the damn country but it was pissing down.'

The patriotic Nesta gave him a playful kick on the ankle at this slur against her native land, but she was in high spirits at being able to see it only a couple of miles away, even if it was through a rain cloud.

They were waiting for a boat to pick them up and take them across to Chepstow. This was a Saxon name, the Welsh calling it Cas-gwent – and the Normans knew it as Striguil, from which the lordship took its name. The small ferry was already in sight, now that the tide was fast coming in across the huge expanse of muddy rock that was exposed for half the day.

John de Wolfe was a few yards away, with Sergeant Gabriel and the two men-at-arms that the sheriff had insisted on sending as an extra escort as far as Chepstow. They were negotiating the passage money with the owner of the ferry, a villainous-looking

Fleming who John strongly suspected of having a side-line as a channel pirate.

The group had made good progress from Exeter, as Nesta was an excellent rider, having spent much of her youth on the bare back of a Welsh cob. After one night's stay at the castle in Taunton, claimed by John as an emissary of the King, and another at an inn at Wedmore near the Mendips, they had reached the tiny hamlet of Aust on the southern shore of the Severn the previous evening. From here, small craft plied the dangerous tidal streams of the river, ferrying both goods and passengers. Some went across to Beachley on the peninsula east of the mouth of the Wye, others west to the Norman strongholds at Newport or Cardiff. The destination that the coroner was bargaining for was Chepstow Castle itself, a couple of miles up the River Wye, almost directly opposite where they were now standing, shivering in the cold breeze of a murky dawn.

Gwyn, brought up on the cliffs of Cornwall, was fascinated by the speed at which the tide flowed in and covered the miles of mud and stones. Squeezed by the funnel shape of the estuary, the mass of the Western Ocean seethed in as fast as a man could walk. A Polruan fisherman in his youth, Gwyn looked with interest at the tiny boat that was coming towards them, with a ragged sail and four men at long oars keeping it straight in the turbulent water.

They were leaving their horses in Aust, in the care of the two soldiers until they returned, as new mounts would be found for them in Chepstow. John had left Odin in the farrier's stables in Exeter, for a large and ponderous warhorse was hardly suitable for long, fast journeys. Instead, he had hired a strong mare for the ride to Aust.

Nesta, enveloped in a Welsh plaid blanket as a cloak,

stood close against Gwyn for shelter from the wind, which was constant and penetrating along this dead flat shore, only a couple of feet above the high-water mark. Away to their right, the ground rose into a cliff of banded red rock at a bottleneck in the estuary, but here there was no place for a boat to land. The miserable village of Aust owed its existence to the ferry, though all it consisted of was a few huts and two dismal inns for travellers waiting for tide and weather.

The landlady of the Bush still only half believed that she was here, going home for more than a week to her beloved family. When John had turned up at the Bush the day after Thomas's celebration, to say that she was going with him to Gwent, she had supposed it was some ill-considered joke. Yet he was adamant, and all her feeble protests about having no one to run the inn had been overruled by him in a peremptory fashion. He explained that he was sending Matilda to France and that such a chance would never come again – so her capitulation was not difficult to achieve. After a day or two of frenzied preparation, she left the Bush in the confident hands of Edwin and her two maids and, spurning the offer of a side saddle, borrowed a pair of boy's breeches and rode off astride the horse that John had hired for her.

Now, as the small boat clawed the last few yards into the muddy creek below them, she looked again at the river and the land beyond and thought of the last time she had seen them. Then, she had been coming with her husband Meredydd to start a new life in Devon. Even that had been at least partly due to John de Wolfe, as he had extolled the opportunities of Exeter to his archer comrade and had even helped find a vacant tavern for them, when both men gave up campaigning. Now Meredydd was long dead and John had taken his place – but Nesta still loved them both.

Her reverie was ended by the arrival of the little craft, small enough to fit into the taproom of the Bush. Minutes later, they were adrift on the choppy waters, aiming diagonally upstream to take advantage of the last of the flood tide to get into the centre of the estuary. Nesta felt that they would end up in Gloucester, but as soon as the short period of slack water arrived, the ship-master – a leather-faced man without a single tooth in his head – dropped the tattered sail and hauled the steering oar about, and the men started to row directly across the stream, until the ebb tide began carrying them back down, close to the other bank.

'We'll not be long now, *cariad*,' said John comfortingly. He was afraid that his mistress would be sea sick, as Gabriel was looking decidedly green in the face from the slight pitching and rolling of the flat-bottomed craft. But Nesta was enjoying every moment and hugged his arm as they sat close together on the planks that served as seats in the stern of the boat.

John watched as they approached a little island set near the mouth of the Wye, the river that came down here to join the Severn, after its long journey from the mountains of central Wales. Now that they had the Wye to contend with, the four oarsmen began to earn their wages, and though the master hoisted the sail again to catch the southerly wind, most of their progress was due to muscle power.

As they crawled past the flat banks towards Chepstow, a mile upriver, John had time to think over the events of the past few days. Though not a vain man, he felt that it had been a stroke of genius for him to think of moving the characters in his life around, like pieces on a chessboard. After that night at the Bush, when he had had his first tentative thoughts of taking Nesta with him to Wales, he had spent a day in a flurry of diplomatic manoeuvring. Although Matilda had readily jumped at the idea of visiting her family, he had to track down de Charterai and beseech him to chaperone his wife to Normandy.

After two days of hectic preparation, he accompanied Matilda to Topsham, she riding side-saddle on a palfrey and Lucille walking behind. A sumpter horse was piled with her luggage for at least a month's stay with her distant cousins near St-Lô, which was convenient for Reginald de Charterai, as it was on the route from Barfleur to Fougères. What her relatives would say when she turned up on their doorstep, John preferred not to think about. And for the return journey, she would have to find some escort to the port herself, as Reginald was returning to England within a few weeks, to fight again at Salisbury.

With a sigh of contentment, John sat in the boat with his arm around Nesta and thanked God most sincerely that all these machinations were now behind him. The fact that Matilda might eventually find out that he had been with his mistress while she was away was a possibility – but that was well into the future, as they would be back in Exeter long before his wife returned home.

On the smoother waters of the Wye, Gabriel's nausea abated and he gazed about him with interest. After a mile or two the banks began rising steeply, and as the ferry rounded a bend the little town came into view, clinging to the slope above the river where a rocky gorge began to appear. Above the town, which had a wooden stockade around it, was the castle, one of the first stone fortresses built after the Conquest. A massive oblong tower stood on the top of the ridge, a deep ditch between it and the town. On the other side, an almost sheer cliff dropped into the river, making the stone and timber walls of a bailey necessary only on the south and west sides.

'William the Marshal fell in for a nice little place when

he married,' commented Gwyn, staring up at the castle as they headed for a landing stage below the town. The elder brother of the Bishop of Exeter had been given Isabel de Clare as wife by Richard the Lionheart, soon after he came to the throne in 1189. Isabel was the heir to vast estates, so at a stroke the marshal became Lord of Striguil and Pembroke.

Sentries placed at lookout points along the river had reported their imminent arrival at the castle, and by the time they reached the quay-side several soldiers and a groom had brought horses down to meet them.

After they landed, Nesta and John had to part, as the coroner thought it unwise to arrive at the castle with his mistress in tow.

'You know what you have to do, Gwyn?' he demanded.

The blue eyes of the amiable Cornishman twinkled in amusement.

'Don't you fret, Crowner!' he said reassuringly. 'I'll look after her like she was my own baby. I'll deliver her to her mother's door inside a couple of hours and be back here with you before you know it.'

Nesta came from near Trelech, a small village a few miles north of Chepstow on the hilly ground towards Monmouth. It was well within the Marcher lordship of Striguil, but, as in other parts of South Wales, the less fertile areas were left by the Norman rulers to the Welsh, as long as they paid some taxes and caused no trouble. John had long ago learned that her father was dead, but her mother, two brothers and a sister lived there as free tenants virtually outside the Norman feudal system. They survived mainly by herding sheep, though a couple of acres of ground around their dwelling provided enough to live on in the way of vegetables, milk, pigs and poultry.

Nesta climbed up behind Gwyn on the back of his

borrowed mare and rather tearfully said goodbye to John, who promised to come to Trelech to collect her. 'Our embassy to the west should not take more than about eight days, so as soon as I am freed from my duty, I'll come with Gwyn to collect you and meet your family.'

John watched her ride off sedately with his officer, taking the road westward around the town until they struck off into the wooded countryside. He had little fear for their safety, as both spoke Welsh and Nesta was now almost on her home ground – to say nothing of Gwyn's brawny arms, his broadsword and ball-mace. When they were out of sight, he turned back to where Gabriel was patiently waiting.

'Right, Sergeant! Let's climb this damned hill to the castle and see what's in store for us.'

CHAPTER TWELVE

In which Crowner John returns to
Sampford Peverel

Being back in Exeter again was something of an anti-climax for de Wolfe, but there was so much pending business that he had little time for soul-searching – an activity he rarely indulged in at any time.

With Matilda still away the house was peaceful, and he hoped it would be at least a few more weeks before she landed again at Topsham. Soon he would ride down there and ask his shipowner friends when they expected their various vessels to return from the Contentin part of Normandy, which was the most likely region of embarkation from St-Lô. It even crossed his mind to go down to Dawlish to see Thorgils the Boatman, who ferried to Normandy most of the wool exports from his partnership with Hugh de Relaga.

He soon thought better of that, however, as his conscience was telling him that it was only an excuse to see Thorgil's wife Hilda, who intermittently had been John's mistress for many years. Now that his love for Nesta had deepened so much, even the temptation to visit the lovely blonde had to be ruthlessly suppressed.

Meanwhile, he basked in the quiet of the house, with only Mary and Brutus for company. On the first morning, his coroner colleague from the north of the county called by, as he had personal business in the city – like John, he was a retired knight who had ploughed his campaign winnings into a commercial venture, though he dealt in leather rather than wool. He reported a few cases that he had dealt with for de Wolfe and his clerk sent Thomas a copy of his rolls with details for presentation to the King's justices when they eventually arrived for an eyre.

After he left, John called upon Henry de Furnellis and had the inevitable cup of wine with him, while he related his doings in Wales.

'It was something of an anti-climax,' he confessed. 'William the Marshal was a pleasant enough riding companion and the archdeacon was as garrulous and amusing as ever. But the journey was nothing but hard riding for a few days, with not a vestige of trouble to liven it up.'

'I thought there were plenty of wild Welshmen in those parts, eager to ambush any Norman within bow-shot!' said the sheriff.

'The Lord Rhys had sent one of his many sons with a dozen men to escort us, once we left our settled lands in the south. Gwyn was sorely disappointed at not having any excuse for a fight.'

'What success did the mission have?' Henry liked to keep abreast of what was going on in the complex politics of Winchester, London and Rouen. The coroner took a mouthful of wine before answering.

'I honestly don't know. William Marshal kept everything very close to his chest, but Gerald de Barri looked very glum after a whole day closeted with Rhys ap Gruffydd.'

'The King and the Justiciar will have to get up very early in the morning to outwit the Lord Rhys,' Henry observed sagely. 'He was a thorn in old King Henry's side, until they came to an agreement. As soon as

Henry died, he went rampaging through South Wales and the Lionheart did very little to stop him.'

John nodded, and privately he doubted whether William the Marshal's expedition would achieve much in the way of curbing the territorial ambitions of the old Welsh prince. More likely, his unruly sons would eventually be his downfall, not English troops.

'What about this mess at Sampford Peverel?' demanded the sheriff, his big nose getting more ruddy as he poured a third cup of wine for them both.

John shrugged. 'I've not had time yet to see if there's anything new from there, but at least there are no reports in the guardroom of any more mayhem from that manor.'

The lower chamber in the gatehouse was where messages were left for the coroner by reeves and bailiffs from out of the city. There had been a few reports of deaths, but nothing from Sampford. Gwyn was out now, seeking more information about the new incidents, but until he returned later in the day, there was nothing John could do about them. When he went back to his garret above the portcullis chamber, he found Thomas sitting at the trestle table, copying yet more rolls to provide duplicates for the courts. Looking over his shoulder was Eustace de Relaga, who had begun his trial apprenticeship that morning and was following the quill with breathless attention, as if Thomas were penning Holy Writ. His pink cheeks, still with only adolescent down upon them, looked as if they had been freshly scrubbed and his fair hair curled over his neck and forehead like a girl's. Though not nearly as flamboyant in dress as his uncle Hugh, he wore a bright blue tunic under a surcoat of green serge and shoes with fashionably curled, pointed toes. The contrast between his attire and the threadbare black cassock of John's clerk was heightened by their expressions. The young man was eager and enthusiastic, but Thomas de Peyne looked annoyed, his thin lips clamped together as if to prevent him saying something out of place, as the youth prattled on about almost every word that the clerk was putting on the parchment.

As soon as Eustace saw the coroner, he bobbed his head deferentially and retreated backward across the room, as if in awe of this tall, dark man who hovered over his clerk.

'Learning the trade already, Eustace?' asked John, trying be jovial. He was never at ease with children and young people – to him they seemed a different breed of mankind.

The portreeve's nephew began babbling his thanks and protestations of unfailing dedication to his work, which seemed to deepen the grim look on Thomas's features. When the flow had stopped, the clerk asked his master whether he could have a private word, and John sent Eustace off to the hall with a recommendation that he get something to eat and drink.

'This is his first day, Crowner, but already he's driving me mad!' blurted out Thomas, as soon as Eustace's footsteps had vanished down the stairs. 'He wants to know every little thing – and he tries to correct my Latin and my penmanship!'

De Wolfe groaned under his breath. He had seen this coming the moment Hugh de Relaga introduced the idea in the Bush, on the night of Thomas's celebration.

'He's young and keen, Thomas, you must make allowances for his age.'

'If he'd just sit and watch, it would be fine,' retorted the clerk. 'But he feels obliged to comment about everything. He gives me an inquisition about the why and when and how of every detail of our work. I'll never get my tasks finished at this rate!'

289

John suspected that there was more to this pleading than mere irritation and he sought to reassure Thomas.

'He's not here to displace you, you know. He's just a big child, wanting to learn so that he can make his way in the world. Don't think for a moment that the portreeve and I have some dark scheme up our sleeves to get rid of you.'

Somewhat mollified, the clerk fiddled with his goose quill as he stared at the table.

'I'll not leave you, Crowner. I said that in the Bush and I meant it. I wish to be taken back into the Church more than anything in the world, but ordained clerics can perform many tasks, other than becoming some stagnant parish priest or an obscure prebendary in some distant vill.'

John patted Thomas's humped shoulder awkwardly.

'I know, lad, and I appreciate it. Let's see what happens after you've been to Winchester. Maybe your uncle can find you some appointment which will still let you assist me, for I don't know how I would manage without you.'

Thomas glowed inside at this rare praise from his austere master and sighed his acceptance of the irritating Eustace.

'I'll just have to put up with him, sir. Perhaps he will quieten down after the first flush of enthusiasm passes off.'

'Get him to copy some of these rolls, why don't you?' suggested John, waving a hand at the yellowed tubes of parchment on the table. 'We need duplicates for the commissioners, who are due next month. Give Eustace some of the drudgery – it may cool him down and will give you a chance to see what sort of job he makes of it.'

Rather than be present when Eustace returned for

a rapprochement with Thomas, the coroner stomped back down the stairs and walked back to Martin's Lane for an early dinner. The bells of the cathedral and the many city churches had not yet pealed out for noon, but he was hungry and knew that Mary would soon have something ready to eat whatever time he appeared. He thought of going down to the Bush for a meal, but decided that Nesta would be in a flurry today, picking up the threads of her business after a fortnight's absence.

He sat in solitary state in the cavernous hall, birds twittering high in the rafters above him. The fire was lit, but Mary had put only a few logs across the iron dogs, as the weather was still dry and had turned mild, the autumn trying to make up for the atrocious weather of the spring and summer. John poured himself a drink and reflected that his stock of wine had recovered since Matilda had been away. She must have been going at the drink in quite a heavy fashion these past few months, since the trouble with her brother. This brought his thoughts around to Richard de Revelle and he tried to make out what interest his brother-in-law might have in the Peverel family. He knew that he wanted part of their land, but was this sufficient cause for his interference there?

From there, his mind came around to the mystery at Sampford itself, and he felt annoyed at the impasse that had developed. The silversmith Terrus was adamant that Robert Longus was one of the assailants, yet the armourer denied it and had his assistant and Ralph Peverel to back it up. Even the dead Hugo had told de Wolfe to his face that Longus had been with him all that day. This posthumous evidence, coupled with that of Ralph and the other armourer, made it impossible in law to sustain the evidence of Terrus.

And what of Hugo's death? If Robert Longus was the murderer of one man, could he not also be responsible for the slaying of the other? But what possible motive could there be for killing a master of whom it appeared he was a favourite?

As Mary bustled in with a wooden tray bearing an iron pot of rabbit stew and a thick bread trencher with a wide cutlet of boiled salmon resting across it, he determined to get himself back to Sampford as soon as possible and shake a few trees to see whether anything fell out of them.

Later that day, Gwyn returned and dragged him off to view several bodies at the places where they had met their deaths. One was that of a young boy who had fallen into a mill-stream at Ide, just outside the city. Mills were dangerous places and deaths, especially of children, were common, either from drowning in the mill-race or being dragged under the turning wheels. Others, including the millers and their men, sometimes became caught in the crude but powerful cog wheels that drove the stones, and John had seen horrific injuries that had been inflicted before the machinery could be stopped by the slow process of diverting the sluices.

The other corpse was that of a thief who had fallen from the top of the city wall, after being chased by half a dozen irate householders who had surprised him rifling a dwelling in Bartholomew Street. It was close to the twenty-foot wall that ran right round the city, and the robber had climbed up, hoping to outpace the pursuers, who were still down below. As he sped along the battlements towards the towers of the North Gate, a gate porter suddenly appeared in front of him and, losing his balance, the fugitive crashed over on to the stony footings in Northernhay and stove in the side of his head. He was still alive when the hue and cry reached him, but expired soon afterwards.

There was nothing sinister about either case, but John had to take account of them and hold inquests, partly to see whether there was anything to be gained for the King by way of 'deodands', the seizure of any object that had caused death. As he could hardly impound a section of the mill-stream or the city wall, he knew there was nothing to be gained unless he could find some breach of procedure on the part of those involved. This seemed unlikely here, but the formalities had to be gone through, and Thomas – or now, perhaps, Eustace – would have to record the tragedies on the coroner's rolls.

John told Gwyn to get the bodies moved up to Rougemont, where they used a lean-to cart shed in the inner ward as a mortuary.

'I'll hold inquests on them tomorrow morning,' he told Gwyn. 'Then we'll get ourselves away to Sampford to see what's going on there.'

As they walked back from Northernhay, the coroner told his officer about the potential friction between Thomas and their new apprentice clerk. 'I've tried to pour some oil on the troubled waters, but de Peyne's feathers have been ruffled by this lad,' explained John. 'He's afraid that he'll be eased out of his job if Eustace becomes too proficient.

Gwyn gave a deep belly-laugh. 'He can be a prickly little devil when he chooses! But the prospect of going up to Winchester, to be anointed or whatever they do to him, will soon clear his mind of anything else.'

As it was now early evening, Gwyn left his master at the corner of Martin's Lane to go on to his home in St Sidwells. He often spent the night in the city, gambling and drinking with his cronies, but after almost two weeks away, his rudimentary conscience drove him back to his small hut in the village outside the East Gate where his wife and two boys, to say nothing of his dog, were missing his company.

De Wolfe called at his house to tell Mary not to prepare any supper that evening and went straight down to the Bush, where he intended to eat, drink and spend the night with Nesta.

At the inn, they sat recalling the events of their trip to Wales, with Nesta still basking in the memories of a whole week with her kin, especially her mother. The visit had reassured her that all was well with them and that being in Exeter was not like being at the end of the world.

'You are the kindest of men, John, to have taken me back there,' she said, hugging his arm as they sat at his table, picking over the last remnants of a grilled pheasant that lay on a pewter plate between them. 'I want us to go on like this for ever – I know you can never marry me, but seeing you almost every day – and sometimes at night – is almost as good.'

He too felt contented, albeit temporarily until his wife came home. Richard de Revelle no longer plagued him in Exeter and the new sheriff was an amiable if lazy man who caused him no trouble. Even Thomas had cheered up markedly since the date of his restitution became known – the spat with Eustace was but a mere irritation that John hoped would be forgotten by the next day. So there was little to worry the coroner, except for his unsolved cases, primarily the murders of August Scrope and Hugo Peverel. Even these faded into limbo at the prospect of climbing up the wide ladder at the back of the taproom, to Nesta's small cubicle – but much later, as he sank into a contented slumber in her arms, his last thoughts were that he must ride for Sampford the next day.

Odo and Ralph Peverel were no longer on speaking terms.

In the intervening weeks since Hugo's death, the elder brother had firmly announced his decision to assume the lordship himself as senior member of the family – and Ralph had equally forcefully disputed the claim and had ridden to Dorchester to consult an advocate to present his case to the justices at the next eyre, which was due to come to that town before it was likely to visit Exeter. He took Richard de Revelle with him – in fact, the former sheriff had insisted on accompanying him, as additional support. Until the matter was resolved, the two brothers refused to sit at table with each other and never spoke, other than through Joel or one of the senior servants, Walter Hog or Roger Viel.

Avelina upbraided both of them for behaving like children, though her sympathies tilted in favour of Odo, who had not had another fit or fall since the time of Hugo's burial, which strengthened his own position as master of the manor.

This antagonism between the two elder brothers made it easier for Joel to pursue the comely Beatrice, which he now did openly, courting the young widow like some love-stricken swain. When Hugo was alive, they had had to content themselves with making cow's eyes at each other and an occasional furtive kiss or fumble when her husband was away at a tournament, but now they felt free to flirt at will. Ralph and Odo were too concerned with their own feud to bother with him, but Avelina covertly disapproved of the younger woman's behaviour so soon after her bereavement, even though everyone knew that the marriage had been a sham, with only lust on Hugo's side and martyred forbearance on hers.

'The old lady wants to condemn her,' confided the steward to Walter Hog one day, when they were alone in the empty courthouse. 'But she's in a cleft stick, for she's planning to marry that Frenchman, even though Lord William's only been dead for half a year.'

'What's in it for him?' asked the bailiff curiously. 'I know she's a fairly handsome woman, but there are plenty of young beauties who would climb into bed with such a well-known tournament champion, if that's what he was after.'

Roger Viel, who knew most about the finances and deeds of the manor, shook his head. 'She's worth quite a lot, that woman. She is the daughter of a wealthy baron from Somerset, who settled a large annuity on her when she married. Then her husband William willed her a third share of all the profits of this manor for the rest of her life – and said nothing about it being forfeit if she remarried. Odo and especially Ralph were as mad as hell when they found out, for it eats into their own pockets at a time when they are not too well off themselves.'

This conversation had taken place a few days before the coroner came back to Sampford, a day when another visitor prompted the exchange between the bailiff and the steward. Riding up the track from the south came an erect figure on a black stallion, followed by a young Breton squire on a brown mare, leading a sumpter horse that carried, among other baggage, a mailed hauberk carefully wrapped in canvas, draped across the panniers. The lead rider wore a blue tunic under a black surcoat, with a hooded leather riding cape tied across the back of his saddle. Reginald de Charterai was dressed in his best, for he was coming to call upon his lady.

Only Odo saw his arrival at the hall and he pointedly walked away in the opposite direction, whilst a servant escorted the Frenchman to the upper floor. Suitably chaperoned by her maid, Reginald spent the next few hours in Avelina's quarters. Neither appeared for supper, food being taken up to the dowager's chamber, and Ralph and Joel sat at table in the hall with Beatrice and her handmaiden. When the women had retired, they set about savagely abusing the French intruder, but they could do nothing about his unwelcome visit. With the lordship in limbo until the court in Dorchester made a decision, all they could do was fume and bluster, as Odo refused to intervene – and with Avelina's legal rights in the manor equal to theirs, they were unable to forbid her to associate with her foreign suitor.

De Charterai spent the night in a spare chamber and was gone the next morning, but it was whispered by the maids that he was staying at an inn in Tiverton until he was ready to ride on to the next tournament at Wilton. Later that day, Avelina and her maid rode out in that direction, and the next morning Joel was deprived of Beatrice's company, as she went with her stepmother-in-law to Tiverton, leaving a disgruntled trio of brothers to contemplate the possible break-up of the family.

Life in the unhappy manor had to go on much as before, however, as there was little alternative to a feudal routine that had been largely unchanged for centuries, even though Saxon *eorls* had been replaced by even harsher Norman lords. The freemen and villeins tilled the same soil and herded the same animals. The cottars thatched their roofs and shoed the beasts and the miller ground their flour. In the churchyard, Hugo quietly rotted away with the others and Patrick the priest mumbled his Latin prayers and covertly swigged his wine.

In the yard behind the manor house, Robert Longus hammered new links into Ralph's coat of mail, repairing it ready for the next tournament, and his assistant Alexander ground and stropped the edges of various swords and daggers until they were sharp enough to be used for shaving. Agnes was back in the laundry hut, pounding clothes, towels and bedding in tubs of hot water with a dolly-stick and throwing them over racks outside to dry. She missed her occasional penny from the lord, but made do with the odd ha'penny from a quick tumble behind a barn with some of the wealthier villeins.

Into this scene of uneasy normality, John de Wolfe intruded once more on the Tuesday after his return from Wales. The coroner's team was augmented this time by Eustace de Relaga, trotting behind on a smart palfrey provided by his uncle, again contrasting sharply with the moth-eaten old nag ridden by Thomas de Peyne. They dismounted in front of the manor house to be confronted by Ralph Peverel, who stood at the top of the steps and seemed reluctant to move aside.

'What do you want now, Crowner?' he snapped rudely. 'I thought we'd seen the last of you.'

John climbed the few wooden steps and stood close to Ralph, looking down at him from his few extra inches in height.

'I am on the King's business, as always. Have you any disagreement with that?'

It was an infallible door-opener, as any denial could be construed as disloyalty, if not treason. The middle brother grudgingly stood aside, but not without further protest.

'Why do you persist in persecuting our family? Don't you think we've suffered enough?'

'Your brother Hugo was murdered and his slayer is

still at large. And I have strong reasons for thinking that another man here is a killer.'

'You mouth the same nonsense every time, Crowner! If the murderer of my kinsman is to be found, then we are the ones to find him – not you outsiders. And as for your delusion that Robert Longus was involved with the death of this fairground merchant, I tell you once again, he was within my sight all the time you claim him to be robbing and killing this fellow.'

John was tired of the repetitive bandying of words with this truculent man and pushed past him into the hall, beckoning Gwyn and the other pair to follow.

'I hear that this lordship is once more in dispute. Until the King's justices decide otherwise, I will assume that Sir Odo is the senior figure in this manor. Tell me where he can be found, please.'

Ralph scowled. 'Odo was disqualified months ago by your precious justices, Crowner. Thus by default I am the rightful lord of Sampford Peverel and you will deal with me!'

John slowly shook his head. 'Not so, sir. The courts gave preference to Hugo over Odo, not over you! They may come to a different judgment this time – and until then, I will accept the eldest as the inheritor.'

Ralph went red in the face. 'Then find him yourself, damn you!' he snarled, and walked out of the hall and clattered down the steps.

'Nice fellow, that!' quipped Gwyn, grinning after his retreating figure. 'His language is not fit for the ears of innocent young virgins like you, Eustace!'

The Cornishman had decided to treat the new apprentice with light-hearted baiting, not out of any malice, but to reassure Thomas that he was the old and trusted favourite.

De Wolfe had advanced into the hall and was glad to see the bailiff coming out from behind the serving screens at the far end.

Walter Hog greeted the coroner civilly and invited them all to sit at table and partake of food and drink, calling for a servant to attend to them.

He sat with them after Eustace had been introduced and brought them up to date on the few happenings that were relevant. The main one was the arrival of Reginald de Charterai and his open courtship of Lady Avelina.

'You say he is now staying in Tiverton? I must call upon him to get news of Matilda's safe delivery to Normandy.'

'I doubt you'll need to go that far, Crowner. He's more than likely to escort the ladies back this afternoon. Beatrice has been acting as a chaperone recently – she seems to relish getting out of this place as much as possible, though usually it's with young Joel.'

When they were refreshed and had made sure that their horses were being fed and watered, John explained the reason for his visit. By now the steward, Roger Viel, had joined them, but there was no sign of any of the Peverels.

'I wanted to know if anything had transpired over the killing of Sir Hugo – and also to question Robert Longus and his assistant, about the murder near Exeter. They will have to come to the city soon when I resume the inquest. I had no time to hold it before I journeyed to Wales.'

Roger Viel shrugged. 'There's nothing new about our dead lord and master. Somehow it seems that it never happened. No one even mentions his name if they can help it – especially his widow, who seems happier than she ever was.'

'That's because she's having this great romance with

young Joel,' commented the bailiff, with uncharacteristic sarcasm.

'There was that business about the grave again,' added the steward, as an afterthought. John looked at him quizzically, but it was Walter who answered.

'You remember the scandal about the shit and the dead rat in the grave ... we all know who did that, but no one owned up to it. Well, a few days after the burial, Father Patrick went out early in the morning and found two dead crows, some stinking offal and pig's guts from the village midden draped across the grave mound.'

'He wasn't a popular man,' added Roger, superfluously.

'Do you think there was any connection between whoever desecrated the grave and the killer?' asked de Wolfe.

The bailiff and the steward looked at each other, then grimaced in doubt.

'Who can tell? I'm damned sure the rat and the turd came from either Warin Fishacre, Godwin Thatcher or Nicholas Smith,' answered Walter.

'They had serious scores to settle with Hugo for raping Maud Fishacre and unjustly hanging Godwin's son,' added the steward. 'But it doesn't prove that any of them killed him.'

There was the sound of hoofs cantering into the bailey outside and Gwyn wandered over to the door to look out. He groaned and looked back towards de Wolfe.

'You're going to like this, Crowner! Your brother-in-law has just arrived. He's talking to brother Ralph outside and doesn't look pleased at what he's hearing!'

A moment later, the dapper figure of the former sheriff stormed into the hall, his face like thunder. He was closely followed by Ralph, and the pair advanced upon de Wolfe. Gwyn stood stolidly alongside his master, but Thomas and Eustace slunk back a few paces.

'Can't you leave these people in peace, de Wolfe!' snarled Richard. 'Everywhere you go, you stir up trouble. For Christ's sake, mind your own business. Go back to Exeter where you can play at being God with that lazy oaf Furnellis, who that mad justiciar appointed in my place!'

'That mad justiciar? I must remember to give him your opinion of him when I next see the archbishop,' said John mildly. 'He is the prime agent representing the King in this country, so are you saying our sovereign is also out of his mind?'

De Revelle opened his mouth, then closed it again, defeated by John's frequent ploy of dangling the threat of sedition over him whenever he spoke out of turn.

Ralph pushed forward and glowered at the coroner.

'What do you want here? I had hoped that after this blessed respite when you stayed away, you would have forgotten us.'

'The Chief Justiciar sent me to Wales at the King's personal command – together with William Marshal, Earl of Striguil and Pembroke,' he retorted, deliberately dropping in the great names to emphasise that they should not attempt to push him aside like some petty local officer.

There was a pause while they digested this, then Ralph continued in a somewhat less belligerent tone.

'We have no more to tell you, Crowner. There has been nothing new forthcoming about my brother's death since you were last here.'

'That damned whore from the laundry is the culprit, I'm sure of it!' snapped Richard de Revelle. 'The time has come to try her at the manor court and get her hanged out of the way, the dangerous bitch.'

De Wolfe glared at him. 'That's utter nonsense, and you know it! She had neither the weapon nor the motive to repeatedly stab the victim.'

He jerked his head at Gwyn to follow him towards the door.

'I came to question your armourer and his assistant again. They will be required in Exeter the day after tomorrow for a resumed inquest on the murdered silversmith. You will make sure that they are there an hour before noon at the courthouse in the castle. This man Longus failed to appear last time, but if he flaunts this attachment that I have placed upon him, you'll soon be looking for a new armourer!'

With his team trailing after him he marched out, ignoring his brother-in-law completely. Out in the bailey, he stopped and rubbed his stubble thoughtfully.

'Before we go looking for Longus and his crony, I may as well have a word with the girl Agnes. I suppose she'll be around the back of the house in one of those huts.'

Gwyn was most familiar with the domestic arrangements, as at every place they visited he made a point of rapidly getting on good terms with the domestic servants, especially the cooks.

'The wash house is next to the main kitchen,' he declared, striding around the side of the manor house. They found Agnes, together with another girl who worked at laundering and mending the Peverels' linen, dumping a batch of washing into a large wooden tub. A ten-gallon cauldron hanging on a tripod over a fire-pit supplied hot water, and Agnes was rhythmically prodding the soaked fabric with a club-like stick. The other girl, little more than a child, was throwing in a handful of crude soap, made from goat's tallow boiled with beech ash.

When Agnes saw the men approaching, she dropped her dolly and came hesitantly towards them, wiping her reddened, crinkled fingers on her ragged kirtle. The big, dark man had been kind to her before, saving her from those bastards Longus and Crues, when they were dragging her from the church, so she felt no fear of him.

'We just wanted to make sure that you were well, Agnes,' said John reassuringly. 'No one has tried to harm you, have they?'

The girl shook her head, the untidy plait of hair swinging as she did so.

'Thank you, sir, but I have been left alone. Though I fear that if you stop coming here, one day they will seize me again, because they need someone to blame.' She looked at him with eyes that held more than a spark of intelligence, belying her rather bovine face. John thought that for a young girl who had almost certainly never set foot outside this village in her whole life, she was far from being a simpleton.

'You remember nothing more of that night when Sir Hugo died?' he asked, with little hope of any useful reply.

Agnes's podgy face creased in a frown. 'I can't actually recall any more than I told you before, but . . .'

She left the sentence hanging in the air and de Wolfe seized upon it.

'But what, girl?' he rasped, then was afraid that he had spoken too sharply and might have frightened her words away.

'That night, sir – and when you gave me questions – I was upset. Now I seem to remember hearing voices when I was leaving the ox byre, but I cannot be sure and I don't know who they might have been.'

'You said "voices"? You mean there were more than one?'

The girl look abashed, rubbing her bare toes in a half-circle in the dirt of the yard and twisting her fingers together in nervous concern.

'I'm just not sure about any of it, sir! It's sort of come to me slowly as I've thought about that terrible night. I seem to half remember hearing someone – maybe it was one, maybe two. Or maybe none at all!'

She began to cry and Gwyn, the softest heart among them, went to kneel by her and put a huge arm around her shoulders. 'Don't fret, good girl! You just stop worrying about it, it may come back to you later.'

He threw a warning look at de Wolfe, but the coroner could not resist one last question.

'And you have no idea whose voices they may have been?' he asked, in what he imagined was his most gentle voice.

Agnes sniffed and gulped, then shook her head. Gwyn wiped away her tears with a finger the size of a chicken thigh and, as they left her in peace, he slipped half a penny into her hand.

'Interesting, but of little use, even if what she says was true,' muttered John, as they left the wash house. 'Maybe more than one assailant – and we presume men, not women.'

'Never saw this stabbing as a woman's crime, Crowner,' growled Gwyn.

'Two women had a motive – and everyone in the damned village had the opportunity,' retorted de Wolfe. 'Avelina thinks Hugo killed her husband – and Beatrice was tired of living with a philandering adulterer, when she was sweet on brother Joel.'

They were walking towards another, larger open-fronted shed, set right at the back of the compound against the stockade. This was the forge and armoury, where they expected to confront Robert Longus.

He was there, as well as his assistant, the heavy oaf Alexander Crues. Both were wearing stained and scorched leather aprons over their tunics and breeches, to protect them from the sparks and hot metal that spat from the anvil on which they were hammering at some small glowing objects. Behind them in the forge, an older man was tending a furnace and a small boy was pumping away at a bellows to keep the charcoal incandescent.

Longus scowled when he saw the coroner and his three attendants. So far, poor Agnes seemed the only person in Sampford Peverel who was not unhappy to see them. The conversation took its expected course, with Longus denying any knowledge of anything and truculently refusing to come to Exeter on Thursday, on the grounds that he had absolutely nothing to say about anything at any inquest.

'You'll come and like it!' barked the coroner. 'Why were you not there the last time?'

'I told you before, because my master, Sir Hugo, said that I was not to go. It was a waste of time, he said, and he needed me here to do my work. And he was damned right, too!'

'Well, as I told *you* last time, if you're not there on Thursday, the sheriff will send a posse to fetch you back to the gaol in Rougemont! And if you feel like vanishing to avoid them, I'll outlaw you, which is as good as you being dead. Understood?'

He glared at Robert Longus, then switched his pugnacious expression to the inarticulate assistant, who was standing stupidly with his mouth open.

'And all that goes for you, too!'

They strode away, leaving the armourer to blaspheme under his breath at their retreating figures. He pulled off his apron and heavy gloves and threw them on to the ground.

'I'm off to see Ralph about this. If we've got to go to Exeter, then I want him with us.'

Eustace was enthralled by what he saw as the drama of the day's visit, and though he continued to plague Thomas with whispered questions, the clerk had become less irritated by the earnest young man. In truth, Thomas began to relish his superior knowledge as the teacher in him came to the fore. He began to enjoy explaining the intricacies of legal procedures and the difficulties of this case, where no hard evidence was forthcoming from anywhere.

'What are they doing now?' murmured Eustace, as they followed John and Gwyn from the forge back out into the village.

'Going to see two other suspects again,' said the clerk. 'It often happens that, deep inside, the conscience of a guilty person gives them the desire to confess. If you keep at them, sooner or later they may break down.'

Thomas delivered this with the air of an expert, though in fact he had only once witnessed the coroner pull this off. Eustace was suitably impressed, however, and looked at the clerk with added respect. They all went out of the manor bailey and up to the reeve's dwelling, where they found Warin Fishacre outside in his half-acre croft, hammering in a stake to tether the house cow on to a fresh circle of grass. His son-in-law Absolon, whose father was Nicholas the smith, was holding the stake, while Warin struck it with a heavy wooden mallet. He stopped as de Wolfe led his men through the lopsided gate and they both waited uneasily for them to approach. They were some distance from the thatched house, where a young woman sat outside on a stool, feathering and gutting a pair of fowls.

'What brings you here again, Crowner?' asked the reeve, suspiciously.

John went straight to the heart of the matter, his frustration over this case making him feel that there was nothing to lose.

'Did you or your son-in-law kill Hugo Peverel?' he asked bluntly. 'You both had good cause, as I understand it.'

Fishacre looked quickly across to the house and decided that his daughter was out of earshot. 'Good cause indeed, Crowner! I would gladly have hanged for his death – but God saw fit to bring it about by other means.'

'And I thought of killing the bastard, but I was too much of a coward,' said Absolon, a large young man with an open face and shoulders like an ox from working in his father's smithy. 'No, Crowner, we didn't send him to hell, where he surely is. But I will admit to you that I threw that cow turd on to his coffin, for I suspect that you'll not tell our masters in the manor house.' He looked with sad eyes towards his young wife. 'Though it's early days, she already suspects she's with child. And the devil of it is that we'll not know if it's mine or his.'

'Unless the child is born with red hair,' muttered Warin, looking up at his son-in-law's black locks. 'But it won't be the first Peverel bastard in the manor. There are a few here already, living in squalor while their fathers enjoy the fruits of our labour, living in style in their big house.'

His voice dripped with bitterness, and de Wolfe glimpsed again the enmity and hate that seemed to pervade this village. He kept at them for a few more moments, trying to shake their stubborn denials, but his heart was not in it. John felt instinctively that much as the Fishacres had yearned for Hugo's death, they had no hand in it – and in truth, looking at this riven family, he would have had little stomach for trying to prove it, even if they had.

The Exeter men moved on up the track to the thatcher's hut, which was smaller than the reeve's dwelling, just a single room of wattle and daub. At least it had a good roof, as Godwin could ply his own trade upon it, using reeds and straw left over from other buildings.

The thatcher's family were having their dinner when John arrived. He motioned to the others to stay at the gate, while he went to the open doorway and put his head inside. The hut had virtually no furniture apart from a few stools grouped around the clay rim of the central fire-pit. Hazel-withy hurdles divided off two corners where straw and ferns under sacking covers provided beds for Godwin, his wife and surviving son, a youth of about eighteen. The far end of the long room had a more substantial wooden partition, beyond which could be heard – and smelt – a cow and a suckling calf. In a small wooden cage on the floor, a slinky ferret scrabbled at the bars, desperate to escape. No doubt the owners would claim it was to catch rats, but John knew that a more likely purpose was illegal coney-hunting.

Godwin, a burly man of about fifty, had flaxen hair turning grey at the temples. One side of his face was stained a livid red from a birthmark that extended from his eyebrow to his jaw. He sat on one of the stools, eating porridge from a wooden bowl with a horn spoon. His wife, a wan, sickly creature, was standing over the fire, ladling the thick gruel from a pot into a bowl held by her son, who crouched on the other stool. There was no table, but a shelf on one wall seemed to function as the woman's kitchen, as it carried a few earthenware cups and some homemade wooden platters.

When they saw the coroner's shadow in the doorway, the thatcher and his son climbed to their feet and stared at him, while the wife backed away to the wall, a hand to her mouth in consternation.

'You're back, sir?' said Godwin, more as a question than a statement. 'We thought the law had given up on Sir Hugo's death.'

John raised his hand, palm forward in a placatory gesture. 'Sit down and finish your dinner. I'll not keep you long. I've not been able to return lately, as I had to go out of the county these past couple of weeks.'

'What brings you now, sir?' asked the youth, a younger copy of his father in his Saxon colour and features, though he had been spared the disfiguring birthmark. He had bits of straw in his hair, which showed that he was following his father's trade.

'We've not forgotten the crime that was committed here,' said de Wolfe. 'These matters take time, but the law never gives up trying to administer justice.' He managed to say this with more conviction than he actually believed, given the calibre of many law officers, such as the corrupt de Revelle or the lazy de Furnellis.

Godwin waved an arm at his wife, who was cowering against her cooking shelf. 'Gunilda, bring that other stool for the coroner. Sir, will you have a cup of ale? That's all I can give you, unless you would like some of this poor fare.' He pulled his spoon out of the porridge, which made a sucking noise, so glutinous was the texture.

John hastily declined both the offer of a seat or refreshment.

'I have to ask this, Godwin Thatcher – of you and of your son here. It is common knowledge in the village that you had cause to hate your last lord, Hugo Peverel. Is that not so?'

Gunilda gave a muffled sob and buried her face in

her arms. Her husband looked stolidly at the coroner.
'Why should we deny it? He was a cruel and vile man.
He took my eldest son and killed him on his damned
gallows-tree, before our very eyes.'

The son suddenly kicked his stool across the room
in a fit of anger.

'And for what? Killing an already wounded hind, so
that we could have something decent to eat for once.
This is not part of the royal forest with their harsh
laws, he could easily have overlooked it.'

John nodded, for he knew that poaching was a way
of life in the villages, especially for the poorest people.
The only real offence was getting caught.

'That's as may be, but did you kill him in revenge?
You had motive enough and everyone in the manor
had the opportunity.'

The wife burst out crying and fled to the other end
of the hut, where she vanished behind the screen to
cower down with the cattle.

'Would I admit it now, if I had, Crowner?' said
Godwin calmly. 'I tell you, if I had known that I could
have got away with such a deed, I would have killed
the bastard. But I am a coward and have a sick wife
and a son to look after. I could not afford to let my
neck be stretched like my poor Edwin.'

'And your other son here? Did he avenge his
brother's death?'

The younger man shook his head slowly. 'It never
came into my mind, sir. Perhaps it should have, but it
seems beyond the comprehension of simple cottars
like us to even think of killing one of our lords. We
don't dare even to speak out of turn before them, let
alone murder them.'

As with Warin Fishacre, the coroner felt that these
folk were telling the truth – and if they were not, there
seemed no prospect of them admitting anything. He

tried badgering them a little more, but was met with the expected stolid denials.

As he turned to leave, he had one last question.

'And the putrid rat?' he asked, with a lift of his black eyebrows.

The shadow of a smile passed over Godwin's face.

'It must have fallen from my pouch when I bent over the grave, Crowner!'

CHAPTER THIRTEEN

In which Crowner John examines a strap

In spite of the bailiff's forecast, Reginald de Charterai did not appear at Sampford by the time that John de Wolfe was ready to leave. As he wished to ask him for news of Matilda, he decided to return to Exeter by way of Tiverton, the distance being about the same as going down the Culm valley via Cullompton.

With Gwyn alongside him and the clerk and his eager pupil behind, he trotted through the early autumn afternoon along the rutted but thankfully dry track. When the village was left behind, they passed through wooded land for a mile, where some trees had already turned yellow or russet.

'Maybe we're on Richard de Revelle's land now,' observed Gwyn. 'Perhaps he'll arrest us for trespassing!'

John was in no mood for jokes where his brother-in-law was concerned. 'It's the King's highway, though no doubt he'd like to seize it for himself and put it to the plough,' he rasped. A ready sense of humour was not one of de Wolfe's attributes and the mischievous Gwyn often teased him, though John was usually unaware of it.

'Where are we going to find this French fellow?' he asked.

The coroner nudged Odin with his knees to speed

him up a little – he disliked using his spurs except in urgent situations.

'He's lodging there, so if there's a half-decent inn, that should be where we'll find him.'

'Be discreet, then, if he's with two comely ladies!' said the irrepressible Cornishman. 'Best knock on the chamber door first!'

That managed to raise a grin on John's face, though the prim little Thomas tutted under his breath as he caught the gist of it from behind.

But de Wolfe was wrong about finding them in Tiverton, for as they rounded the next bend between the trees, they saw a small cavalcade approaching. At a walking pace, de Charterai was on his black charger between two palfreys carrying Avelina and Beatrice sitting side-saddle, both enveloped in hooded riding cloaks that left only their faces and gloved hands visible. Behind came two grooms on ponies, carrying cudgels and maces. The ladies' maids had been left at home, as the pair of widows acted as each other's chaperone.

The two groups met and remained mounted, but when introductions had been made, they rearranged themselves in an almost hierarchical fashion. John stopped alongside Reginald, Gwyn gravitated to the escorting grooms and Thomas and Eustace went to pay their respects to the ladies. Eustace seemed to make a hit with Beatrice, with his smart clothes, charming manners and cultured speech, and even Thomas became quite articulate with Avelina, who was of a religious disposition and soon learned about the clerk's imminent readmission to the Church. This left de Wolfe free to talk to the French knight about his wife's journey to Normandy.

'Everything went well, I'm happy to report,' said Reginald in his correct, formal way. 'Your charming wife survived the voyage with only a touch of *mal de mer*, though her poor maid seemed to wish herself dead before we reached Barfleur.'

John wondered how Reginald had come to regard Matilda as charming, but he decided that there was no accounting for taste.

'And she reached her family without incident?' he asked.

'I delivered her to their threshold myself. They seemed surprised to see her arrive.'

That must be the understatement of the year, thought John, but he thanked de Charterai solemnly for his kindness and chivalry, before the Frenchman edged his horse away from the rest of the group a little and leant forward in his saddle to speak more confidentially.

'Have you made any more progress over the death of either of the Peverels?' he asked in a low voice. 'Avelina is more convinced than ever that her husband was murdered.'

John explained that he had had no opportunity to communicate with the Wiltshire sheriff or coroner, as he had been away – but he felt that after this lapse of time and with the absence of any physical evidence there was little that could be done. As for Hugo's death, there seemed to be a conspiracy of silence in Sampford, as far as the family was concerned.

'Tell me,' he added. 'Does Lady Avelina know of any reason why the former sheriff, Richard de Revelle, seems to so earnestly cultivate the friendship of the remaining brothers? You will be aware that his reputation is not without flaws.'

This was another understatement, but de Charterai nodded understandingly.

'Your wife regaled me with some of the facts on the

journey. I feel sorry for her, especially as your legitimate role in the matter could not have helped. But as
to his presence in Sampford, Avelina can think of no
reason but de Revelle's desire to get hold of that
parcel of land that he so covets.'

He looked over his shoulder at his mature lady love,
then continued. 'But do not think that he is wooing
all three Peverels! Ralph seems his main target, as
Odo, like his father before him, wishes to keep the
manor intact. And like most of us, de Revelle appears
to think that Joel is an empty-headed wastrel. It is
Ralph that he wants to succeed to the lordship, as
then he will have the power to grant him these
disputed acres.'

After some more polite conversation and John's
promise to keep Reginald informed of any develop-
ments, the two parties disentangled their mounts and
continued on their way. After a few hundred yards,
Gwyn looked over his shoulder at the retreating figure
of the stately Frenchman, then raised his bushy
eyebrows at his master.

'He's a deep one, that! I still wouldn't put it past
him to pay back the insults that Hugo Peverel laid on
him, both in the tourney field and in that banquet.
So don't cross him off your list yet, Crowner!'

Just as the coroner was wrong about finding Reginald
in Tiverton, so he was wrong about next seeing Robert
Longus in Exeter for the inquest.

On the second morning after his visit to Sampford,
the bells had barely finished ringing for terce, sext
and nones at about the ninth hour, when there was
a repetition of the familiar pattern of a lone horseman
clattering up to the gatehouse with an urgent message
for the coroner.

This time it was not the reeve but an ostler sent by

the bailiff, to distance the latter a little from the displeasure of the Peverels for meddling in their manorial independence.

'The girl Agnes, sir, she was found dead in the mill-stream this morning. Walter Hog thinks you should be told about it straight away,' the man announced in his strong rural accent.

John de Wolfe rarely felt much emotion about his deceased customers, but this unexpected news saddened and angered him. He assumed straight away that this would be no accident, and he thought of the placid but intelligent girl who, after nothing but fifteen years of unremitting toil, poverty and abuse, had ended up dead in a brook. Within the hour, they were on their way back to Sampford, with Thomas and Eustace trying to keep up with Gwyn and the coroner as they went at a brisk trot along the shortest route to the troubled manor. By dinner time, they had reached the village and saw the bailiff and a few of his men waiting for them at the edge of the green, opposite the church. There was no sign of the Peverels and de Wolfe was in no hurry to have them ranting their protests at him.

'Is the poor maid still where she was found?' he demanded, as he slid from Odin's back.

'We had to pull her from the water to make sure of who she was, but the body is lying on the bank,' explained Walter Hog, motioning two of the men to take the horses away for hay and water. Leading the way, he took the coroner's party across the track and down a steep lane at the side of the churchyard, which led down into the little valley below.

'So she didn't go in at the mill?' snapped John, knowing from his previous visits that this was farther upstream.

'No, this is the run-off from the wheel, quite a way

down. Shallow it is here, except when there's heavy rain.'

Below a small wooden bridge at the bottom, the brook was only a few feet wide and could easily be waded, but the bailiff took them under some trees and walked along the muddy bank for fifty paces to where a wide, deeper pool was formed where some rocks and a fallen tree had partly dammed the stream. On the edge, under a willow turning brown, was a still body, lying face up on the weeds. Standing near by was Agnes's mother, red eyed and being comforted by a shabbily dressed man who he assumed was her father. John muttered some platitudes of sympathy, which were none the less sincere for their gruffness, then crouched over the pathetic remains of the young woman. She wore a better kirtle than the ragged one he had seen her in before, so her mother must have made use of the two pence that he had given her for the purpose. It was mud-stained on the front and the upper half was soaking wet.

'She was found by a woman picking watercress, soon after dawn,' explained Walter. 'The poor girl was face down in the trout pool, her hair all streaming out in the current. Most of her body was on the bank – I can't understand how she could drown like that.'

John looked up at Gwyn, who nodded back.

'This was no drowning, Bailiff! Look at her neck!'

The victim's face was tinted violet and seemed slightly swollen, even allowing for her normal chubbiness. Around her neck, just above her Adam's apple, was a band of pinkish skin about half an inch wide. Below it, her neck was pale by contrast with the livid colour above.

'She's not been drowned, man – she's been strangled! By a ligature pulled tight around her throat.'

The mother burst into tears and her husband

awkwardly pulled her to his chest and patted her back. Thomas, full of compassion as usual, knelt by the corpse, crossed himself a few times, then went to the woman and began murmuring consoling words to her and her husband.

'We can't examine her here, especially with them looking on,' muttered de Wolfe to Gwyn.

'The church is nearest, let's get her there,' suggested the Cornishman.

With scant ceremony, apart from John taking off his cloak to cover her, Agnes was carried in Gwyn's great arms like a baby, back up the hill and into the church, where Father Patrick appeared from the sacristy, flushed in the face and smelling of brandy wine.

Walter Hog and another man lowered the bier from where it was suspended from the rafters by ropes and laid the girl's body upon it, this time near the back of the chancel away from the altar.

'We'll only look at the head and neck for now,' grunted John, with a delicacy that belied the appearance of these large, gruff men. 'Walter, you can get some village woman later – perhaps the one who acts as midwife – to check the rest of the body, to make sure she's not been roughly violated.'

Thomas had finished his pastoral efforts with the mother and came in with Eustace on his heels, to peer around John as he made a more thorough examination of the dead girl. As Gwyn lifted her head, he looked at the back of the neck, where the red band continued around the nape, crossing over in the centre. At the front and sides, it was sharply demarcated on the skin, with a line of tiny red spots along the upper edge.

'Plenty of blood in the skin and eyes,' observed Gwyn, pointing at the outer eyelids, which were peppered with a fine red rash, and at the whites of the eyes, which were visible under the half-closed lids. Here there were angry bright red haemorrhages, and in the skin of the face, especially around the jaw-line, were dotted bleeding points under the congested skin.

'Even some crusted blood in the nose and one of the ears,' piped up Eustace, who was avidly taking in the dramatic scene. Thomas, whose interest in the signs of violent death was non-existent compared to the others', drifted off and went to talk to the rather unsteady parish priest, who stood uncertainly in the middle of the beaten-earth floor of the nave.

'Do you know anything of this, Father?' he asked.

The Irishman shook his head slowly and spoke as if his tongue were too large for his mouth. 'Only that she was found in the stream early today. Her mother, God give her peace, told me that she did not come home last night, but I am afraid that that was nothing new for Agnes, if she found a man with a penny to spare.'

He seemed fuddled and could offer nothing else useful, so reluctantly Thomas went back to where Eustace was avidly following the coroner's pronouncements. With the bailiff and his assistant also looking on, Gwyn and John were closely studying the mark around the neck.

'A narrow belt or strap,' declared Gwyn. 'Not a cord or a rope, as there's no twisted pattern and the edges are too regular.'

De Wolfe grunted, which could signal agreement or dissent. Then his long forefinger pointed to three places on the mark, one under the angle of the jaw on the left side, another under the point of the chin and the third beneath the right ear.

'These look too squared off to be mere chance,' he

snapped. 'There's something on the strap at those points.'

'What help is that, sir?' ventured Eustace de Relaga.

'If we can find a strap with something fixed to it exactly at those points, then it might well be the instrument of the poor child's death.'

Privately, Gwyn thought this a slim chance, but he kept his opinion to himself. There was nothing else to find and Thomas persuaded the tipsy priest to find an old cassock in the sacristy to cover up the corpse, to allow John to reclaim his wolfskin.

'Best bring the mother in here to keep vigil over her daughter for a time,' suggested de Wolfe. For some reason, the killing of the poor wash-house skivvy had pulled at his heart more than the usual run of pathetic deaths that he dealt with week in, week out.

He marched out of the church, leaving Thomas to say some prayers over the body, in default of any help from Father Patrick.

'Have your masters in the hall been told of this?' he asked Walter Hog.

'Indeed they have, Crowner. Sir Odo seemed quite concerned, but Ralph just shrugged and said she had probably tried to steal an extra penny off a customer and got herself choked for her impertinence. As for Joel, he just sniggered at Ralph's explanation and told Roger Viel that he'd better look for another laundry maid if he wanted clean cloths on the table tonight.'

John's opinion of the two younger brothers fell even more, but their callous indifference was none of his business. Discovering who killed Agnes certainly was, and he strode towards the manor-house compound with grim determination. As they marched through the wide gate in the stockade around the bailey, Gwyn wanted to know how they were going to set about things.

'We've had little success with anything else so far in this damned place,' he said critically. 'No doubt everyone will again claim to have been deaf and blind this last day or so, with nothing at all to tell us.'

As he stamped up the steps to the hall doorway, John half turned to his officer.

'We've got two suspects who may already have killings to their discredit. Robert Longus and his stupid crony Alexander are high on our list of suspects for August Scrope, so let's start with them as candidates for the girl.'

'I'd like to add bloody Ralph to that list, for he's a nasty enough bastard to have got rid of his brother to gain the lordship,' boomed Gwyn, careless as to whether anyone heard him inside the hall. The only one in sight, however, was the steward, Roger Viel, sitting at a table with a roll of accounts before him. Apart from the priest and Odo Peverel, he was probably the only inhabitant of Sampford who was able to read and write, a necessity for the administrator of a large manor.

He rose to meet them, anxiety written over his lined face as yet another death brought the King's coroner to the village. After greeting them and calling to a servant behind the far screens to bring food and drink, he invited them to sit at his table, where they were joined by the bailiff, Thomas and Eustace. There was still no sign of any of the masters and mistresses of the house – the steward said that Joel had gone off riding with Lady Beatrice and Avelina was in Tiverton visiting Sir Reginald.

'I've no notion where Sir Odo and Ralph might be. They are probably somewhere about the bailey,' he concluded, but almost as he spoke Ralph Peverel stalked into the hall, slapping his thigh with a pair of leather gloves. Judging by his boots and cloak, he had been riding, and when Robert Longus appeared behind him, carrying a battered shield and a sword, it seemed obvious that Ralph had been training for the coming tournaments at Bristol and Wilton. On a previous visit, John had noticed an area just outside the stockade where the grass was churned into a welter of hoof marks and where two rotating tilts were set up for lance practice.

He strode arrogantly across to the table and stood with his fists on his hips, glaring at John de Wolfe.

'By Christ's wounds, Crowner, are you pestering us again? I'll have to start charging you rent if you spend much more time here!'

His attempt at sarcastic levity was lost on the dour coroner.

'You know damned well why I'm here, Peverel! Another murder in Sampford and I suppose you know nothing about it and care even less!'

Ralph flushed with anger.

'You have no call to speak like that to the lord of a manor – especially before my servants!'

'In my eyes, you are not the lord of this manor until the justices declare it to be so,' retorted de Wolfe. 'Now then, have you anything to tell me about the strangling of this poor girl?'

Ralph walked to the next table and threw himself into one of the three chairs that the hall boasted.

'What should I know about the throttling of some wash-house drab? You know her reputation. Undoubtedly some disgruntled customer from the village took exception to something she did – or didn't do!'

He said this with such uncaring nonchalance that John felt like shaking him until his teeth rattled.

'You do not find it a coincidence that this is the same girl that your brother lay with on the night that he was slain?' he said sarcastically.

Ralph seemed to have an answer for everything.

'Why should it be? We do not have so many whores in this village that the same one should not be at risk with men who wish to slake their passions.'

'Could it not be that someone, like yourself, who declared that the girl was the killer of your brother, took the law into their own hands?'

'The law should be in our own hands, Crowner! This is a manor with all the rights of manorial custom. We told you at the outset that we did not want your interference from Exeter, but could settle this ourselves.'

John glared at the younger man, whose arrogance and insolence seemed to increase by the day.

'Are you confessing to having taken the law into your own hands? Did you kill this girl, Peverel?'

'Don't be so damned foolish, de Wolfe! D'you think I'd soil my hands on the dirty offspring of a serf? And if I had, would I be daft enough to admit it to you?'

The coroner turned around slowly and looked back down the hall towards the door, where Robert Longus was still standing, the weapons trailing from his hands. He glared back defiantly, his hard face devoid of any expression within the rim of beard that encircled it.

'I want to search the dwelling of your armourer – and his assistant, Alexander Crues.' John spoke over his shoulder to Ralph, who immediately jumped up and stalked over to the coroner.

'What in hell's name for?' he shouted. 'Have you not intruded enough into our affairs? This is too much, I forbid you to interfere any further!'

De Wolfe glowered back at the angry man. Gwyn saw that his patience with Ralph Peverel was wearing thin and his fingers wandered unconsciously towards his sword hilt, in case this developing feud got out of hand.

'Are you defying me, sir? Remember that no one is above the King's law, not even manor-lords!'

'I have friends in high places, Crowner, you will hear more of this! Why on earth should you wish to ransack this man's quarters, other than from spite and prejudice?'

'Longus has been accused by a respectable silver-craftsman of being a robber and a murderer,' retorted John. 'Only your word now stands in contradiction, since your brother is dead.'

The escalating battle of words was interrupted by the sudden appearance of Odo, who came through the door that led upstairs. As he had been said to be outside in the bailey, John realised that he must have entered through the postern door from the kitchens. In his temper, Ralph seemed to forget that he was not supposed to be speaking to his elder brother and burst out with his complaints about the coroner.

'He wants to search the place, brother! This is becoming intolerable!'

Odo turned a calmer face towards John, though it was still disapproving of this outside interference.

'I fail to see how that can throw any light on the murder of this poor girl,' he said critically. 'But as the innocent have nothing to hide, I see no objection to pandering to his whims.'

With this backhanded agreement, Odo went to the far end of the room and poured himself some ale from a large crock, taking no further interest in the argument. Ralph simmered with anger as he watched de Wolfe walk back to Robert Longus to question him.

'We meet sooner than I thought! Can you account for where you were throughout last night?'

'I was in the inn until two hours or so after sunset, then in my bed until dawn. I'm not married, so I've no wife to vouch for me!'

This was delivered with thinly veiled insolence, in the expectation that Ralph would support him in everything he said.

'And that big lump who assists you? Where was he?'

Robert shrugged indifferently. 'I'm not his keeper, Crowner. He was in the inn as well, but he left before me. God knows where he went – maybe to his bed, maybe to roll a wench – for, like me, he has no wife living.'

Tired of this verbal fencing, John jerked his head at Gwyn and the two clerks.

'Come on, I want to see where these men live.'

Grabbing Robert's arm in a grip like that of a lobster's claw, he pushed him towards the door. The armourer resisted, but Gwyn came round to the other side and he had no option but to stumble along with them, dropping the sword and shield on the floor. As they propelled him to the door, he screwed his head around to make a last appeal to his master, but Ralph had stalked away to the screens and was shouting for someone to bring him wine.

Out in the bailey, the coroner and his officer relaxed their grip on the armourer, who angrily shook himself free.

'Keep your bloody hands off me! I don't know what you expect to find, but for God's sake let's get it over with, then I can get back to some work. The Bristol tourney is only a few days away!'

He led them around the back of the manor house and past the kitchens and laundry hut to the forge and stables. Back to back with the forge, under the same shingled roof, were a couple of small rooms, and Robert Longus led them to the first door, where a heavy leather flap served to keep out the weather.

'I live in here and Crues has the smaller one next

door,' he explained in a surly voice. 'So help yourself, and be damned to you!'

He stood back indifferently while John pushed past the flap, followed by Gwyn and Eustace. Thomas decided that a mean, odorous room was no concern of his and stayed outside.

In the dim light from a small shuttered window, John saw a lodging that was as barren as a monk's cell. A straw-filled palliasse lay along one wall; the only other furniture was a rough table with a three-legged stool below it. Some metal-working tools, a pitcher of ale and two clay cups stood upon it. From pegs and hooks on the wooden frames of the cob walls, lengths of chain mail, two helmets and various oddments of armour hung under a coating of dust.

'The horses are housed better in the stables than this fellow in here,' grunted Gwyn. Eustace was looking around in astonishment. His first days in the coroner's service were opening his eyes to the way most people lived – a world away from the comparative luxury of his rich parents' home.

'Nothing for us here,' murmured John. 'Not that I expected much.'

They pushed out into the daylight, where Longus was waiting, a sardonic look on his face.

'Satisfied, Crowner? I said you were wasting your time – and mine.'

De Wolfe scowled at him. 'Do all armourers live in such hovels?'

'This is only my working home. I am a journeyman with a decent house in Southampton where I live during the winter. The rest of the time I hire myself out to whoever pays the best.'

Insolently, he turned on his heel and walked away towards the manor house.

The coroner looked at the other half of the lean-to

building that abutted on to the forge. 'We may as well look in there, now we're here.'

He pushed into a similarly squalid room, which also contained just a mattress and a table, though it was littered with oddments, scattered on the earthen floor and hanging from the walls. Most of it was chain and scrap metal, plus a few broken shields, but John's eye was caught by some belts and straps thrown over a wooden bar nailed across one corner. There were baldrics, one still carrying an empty sword sheath, and other strips of leather which looked like broken pieces of harness.

'Gwyn, seize that stuff and bring it out into the light,' he commanded.

Ten minutes later, they were again bending over the bier in the little church of St John the Baptist. Agnes's parents had gone, the mother having been so overcome with grief that her husband had helped her home to sit sobbing in their empty dwelling, now bereft of both her daughters.

John was staring again at the mark on the neck, now slightly more prominent as the blood in the adjacent skin had started to drain away since the corpse had been lying on its back. At his direction, Gwyn was going through the bundle of belts and traces, picking out those that were of about the correct width. He selected four and stretched them out one by one in front of de Wolfe, laying them across the chest of the dead girl, where four pairs of eyes stared at them intently. There was silence for a moment, then the exuberant Eustace could contain himself no longer.

'That one, Sir John! What about that one?' He pointed with a quivering finger at a worn leather strap about three feet long, which was torn through irregularly at each end and had some short side-straps hanging off it.

'I see it, lad,' said John as patiently as he could, for he had already recognised it as a possible match. Picking it up in both hands, he stretched it out and moved it back and forth lengthwise across the mark on Agnes's neck.

'There!' grunted Gwyn, unnecessarily, as the places where three of the side-straps were stitched to the main one came exactly over the squared marks on the skin.

'Could that be mere chance?' piped up Doubting Thomas.

De Wolfe lowered the strap and curved it around the front of the neck, adjusting it until the marks coincided to within a hair's breadth.

'I don't think so. It's not as if the branches were spaced regularly ... there's different distances between them, yet they still match.'

'Good enough for me, by God!' murmured Gwyn. 'Certainly good enough to ask this Alexander a few pointed questions!'

'A pity some skin couldn't have rubbed off on to it – that would clinch it,' observed their still-critical clerk. Then Eustace chipped in once more, for his keen young eyes were better than those of the older men and Thomas's slight squint.

'There's a spot on the back of the strap – look there!' He used a piece of straw from the floor to point out a darker mark on the mottled brown of the old leather. It was half the size of a grain of wheat, but had a glazed shine to it that suggested it was recent. John picked at it with a dirty fingernail and carefully slid it off on to the back of his other hand.

Then he licked his forefinger and rubbed it across

the loosened fleck. Immediately, a tiny crimson streak smeared across the skin below his knuckles.

'Blood, by damn! Must have come from her nose or ear,' he exclaimed triumphantly. Having now destroyed this piece of evidence, the coroner earnestly instructed Thomas to write an exact record on his rolls at the earliest opportunity, naming those present who could vouch for the presence of the blood spot and of the congruence of the strap with the strangulation mark.

'Right, let's go and do the sheriff's work for him!' announced de Wolfe, straightening up and carefully rolling the strap into the pouch on his belt. 'This Alexander Crues has some explaining to do.'

The assistant armourer's explanations consisted entirely of denials, his slow mind producing nothing but a dull repetition of the fact that he knew nothing of any girl's death, he hadn't done it and he had no recollection of any strap hanging in his room.

The coroner's team had found him sleeping in a corner at the back of the empty forge, in a warm spot near the banked-down furnace. Gwyn interrupted his snores by kicking him with the toe of his boot, but Crues was little more articulate when awake than he was when asleep. Frustrated at the man's stupidity, John hauled out the strap and waved it in his face.

'You used this, damn you – you throttled the poor girl with it! Come on, admit it, we know this was the thing that killed her!'

For the first time, a flicker of fear appeared in Alexander's bovine features, but he continued to shake his head and mutter denials. Gwyn grabbed him by the throat and shook him as a stimulus to his memory. Crues was not as big as the Cornishman, but he was a strong fellow, accustomed to wielding a forge hammer, and he used his strength to pull free of Gwyn and give him a heavy punch in the chest. He found it was like hitting a stone wall – the only effect was to make the officer roar with anger. He seized the armourer by the wrist and twisted his arm up behind his back, at the same time grabbing a handful of his unkempt hair and dragging back his head.

'Confess, damn you, or I'll break your bloody neck!' roared Gwyn, who was very averse to young girls being throttled. There was a large wooden trough near by, filled with dirty water to cool red-hot metal from the anvil. Without a moment's hesitation, Gwyn forced Crues to his knees, then rammed his head under the surface. Struggling violently, the man was helpless in Gwyn's iron grip, though the filthy water splashed over the floor as he thrashed about in an effort to get free.

'You did it, didn't you, you bastard?' yelled Gwyn as he hoisted Alexander's head back by the hair. Amidst the spluttering and retching there was a vehement denial, so Gwyn shoved his head back into the trough and banged his face on the hard bottom for good measure.

John looked on impassively, not bothered by some coercion if it produced results. It was part of his official duties to attend hangings, blindings, mutilation of hands and genitals and the torture of the Ordeal and occasionally the *peine forte et dure*, so Gwyn's method of persuasion was mild in comparison. Eustace looked on with a mixture of horror and fascination, his previous experiences in his sheltered life having been rapidly expanded by the things he had seen in the past few days. Thomas, though more used to the brutal reality of law enforcement, looked away as he crossed himself and murmured prayers for the victim, as he fully expected Gwyn to drown Alexander Crues.

331

Gwyn repeated his dunking and shouting twice more, until de Wolfe came to the same conclusion as Thomas.

'Try not to kill the swine,' he advised his officer. 'He may have some valuable information for us.'

Gwyn hauled Alexander out of the trough and dropped him heavily on to the ground. He lay still, and Thomas thought that perhaps he was already dead. Then he gave a great retch and vomited water, food and mucus, and began to push himself up on his hands, coughing and spluttering to rid himself of the rest of the foul water in his windpipe.

Gwyn grabbed his hair again and bent his head back. 'Ready for another bath, you murdering bastard? Or are you going to tell us the truth?'

Befuddled and half drowned, Crues momentarily forgot that escaping another submersion in the trough by confessing would inevitably lead to a hanging. But as he croaked and gagged his admission, he tried to shift the blame.

'Not me . . . 'twas Robert!' he gasped. 'He made me help, I swear!'

Gwyn released him and he crawled painfully up on to all fours, then slumped over with his back against the trough, still coughing and spitting out water.

De Wolfe stood over him menacingly, dangling the strap before him.

'You used this for the deed, you evil lout! Did you each pull one end, eh?' he snarled. 'I think you're a liar, Longus had nothing to do with it.'

Alexander shook his head, his sodden hair hanging lankly around his face. 'I tell you it was him. I want to turn approver, Crowner.'

'Time for that later, maybe,' snapped John. 'You'll first have to prove Robert Longus was involved at all. But I think you ravished this Agnes, then killed her either in perverted passion or because she mocked your lack of prowess.'

De Wolfe was deliberately inventing this scenario, as there had been no opportunity yet for a village wise-woman to examine Agnes for any signs of intimate violence. Alexander, now miserably cowed, rocked his head like a dying bull in a baiting-pit.

'It wasn't like that at all. I never laid a finger on her. May God above strike me dead if I lie.'

'He probably will, on the gallows in Magdalen Street,' retorted John. 'But if you claim you didn't ravish her, why should she be throttled?'

Crues leaned forward and retched again, spitting water on to the floor.

Gwyn grabbed his hair again and shook his head until his teeth rattled.

'Answer the coroner!' he roared, wishing to keep up the pressure and stop the man relapsing into a sullen silence.

'Because we were afraid that she had recognised our voices when that damned Hugo was killed. There was gossip in the village that said she might have recovered her memory of that night, so Robert said she had to go, for our safety's sake.'

De Wolfe's phlegmatic nature rarely allowed him to be thunderstruck, but here was a bolt from the blue. In getting this dull-witted oaf to confess to being involved in one killing, they had seemingly stumbled upon another.

'Hugo? You killed Hugo?' he barked.

'I killed nobody, Crowner! I was just there when it happened,' wailed Crues.

'Are you saying that Robert Longus killed his master? Why, for God's sake?' demanded John.

Alexander slumped sideways and beat his fist upon the hard earthen floor of the forge. 'I don't know, I just don't know, sir! Robert was thick with all the Peverels, William, Hugo and now Ralph. I don't know what schemes he had with them, but he told me one night that it was too dangerous for him to let Hugo live and that I must help to get rid of him.'

John was becoming bewildered by the pace of these revelations, and he was to be further astounded by Alexander's next admission.

'I think he was afeared that Hugo would withdraw his promise of protection over the robbing and killing of that silversmith – but there was something else as well, I'm sure. He never told me anything, except ordering me to do this, do that!'

This long speech brought on another fit of spluttering and spitting, giving the coroner time to digest the fact that now three of his homicides seemed to be on the point of being solved. But Alexander Crues, slow-witted as he was, seemed to have decided that he had made enough admissions and that the best thing to do when one is in a hole is to stop digging. All further questions were answered by a denial of any more knowledge about anything, and even Gwyn's threats to push his head back into the trough failed to make him concede anything useful. He slid farther over to lay on his side, and apart from intermittent coughing and spitting seemed uncaring about his fate.

John turned to Thomas and Eustace, who had been listening open mouthed to these dramatic revelations.

'You are witnesses to what has been said, so mark the words well. And you, Thomas, will get them on parchment as soon as you can, in case our blackbird here refuses to sing any more.'

Gwyn looked down at the inert, wheezing figure at his feet.

'What's to be done with him, Crowner?'

'He'll have to come back to Exeter with us, roped on to a horse. Tie his wrists and feet for now, to stop him wandering off, while we find this Robert again.'

CHAPTER FOURTEEN

In which Crowner John throws down his glove

When de Wolfe went back to the hall, he found that all three Peverel brothers were there and, to his dismay, they were accompanied by Richard de Revelle, in riding cloak, boots and gloves. The last thing John wanted was any interference from his brother-in-law at such a sensitive time.

The former sheriff was seated at a table with Ralph Peverel and the armourer, their heads together in earnest discussion. Odo was standing near the fire-pit, talking to his steward and the bailiff, while Joel was sitting under a window slit with Beatrice, a chess-board between them. The game they were playing seemed to consist more of pressing their knees together under the small table than moving the pieces on the board. There was no sign of Lady Avelina, and John wondered whether Reginald de Charterai was still in the neighbourhood.

Conversation ceased abruptly as the coroner walked in ahead of his pair of clerks, Gwyn having stayed in the bailey to guard their prisoner.

'I hear you continue to intrude upon our privacy, de Wolfe!' sneered Ralph. 'When I next go to London, I shall have something to say to certain barons concerning your behaviour.'

'Well, tell them that I have today arrested one of

your armourers – and soon I may well take the other one, unless he can provide me with a very convincing explanation.'

There was a series of scraping noises as the three men at the table skidded back their stools to stand up and face the coroner.

'What mischief are you up to now, John?' brayed de Revelle, his little beard jutting out like the prow of a ship.

'Arresting who?' shouted Ralph. 'My armourer is here beside me!'

A grave-faced Odo came across to listen, and even Joel turned his head to watch with a sardonic smile. The steward and the bailiff looked on uneasily.

'I am taking that man Crues back to Exeter, roped to a horse. He has confessed to being involved in the murder of the girl Agnes and I have sure proof of that.'

John could have sworn that a look of relief flitted over Ralph's face, but it was Odo who responded first.

'Alexander Crues? That's hard to credit. He's a stupid clod, but I would not take him for a murderous rapist.'

'He claims he was a reluctant accomplice – he says the prime culprit is Robert Longus there!'

John jabbed a finger towards the armourer, who had moved close to Ralph, as if seeking shelter.

'Crowner, I fear for your sanity!' rasped the middle brother. 'What gibberish are you trying to peddle to us now?'

De Wolfe ignored him and carried on. 'Not only that, but he implicates Longus in the murder of your brother Hugo, as well as the silversmith Scrope, down near Topsham.'

'Alexander is an idiot, he doesn't know what he's saying!' yelled Robert, stepping out from behind Ralph and gesticulating wildly at the coroner. 'His brain has been addled since childhood, all he's good for is beating metal with a hammer and cleaning chain mail.'

De Wolfe ignored him and addressed himself to Odo, who was looking as worried as if he expected the sky to fall upon them at any moment.

'Sir, I look to you as the lord of this manor. In view of the accusations of Crues, who has already confessed, I must take this man Longus back to Exeter.'

'Why, for Christ's sake?' exploded Ralph. 'The babblings of that fool Alexander are no grounds for this! I even doubt his confession is worth a dog's turd. Did you beat it out of him?'

John avoided an answer to this, but again directed himself to Odo.

'The death of your brother, a well-known manor-lord, is no ordinary murder. There will be questions asked by the highest in the land, especially the King's Curia and his Justiciar. To have someone accused of such a crime makes it vital that he be properly questioned – and that is the business of the sheriff, the ultimate keeper of the peace in this county.'

He said the last words with a pointed look at his brother-in-law, the former sheriff, who had made little effort in that direction.

'I've done nothing, this is a nonsense!' shouted Robert Longus. 'I know nothing about any silversmith. Both Lord Hugo and you, Sir Ralph, vouched for me at the time.'

Ralph advanced on the coroner, until his angry face was within inches of John's long nose.

'You're not having him, understand!' he snarled. 'There's no evidence against him, apart from the blatherings of a dull oaf, from whom you probably tortured this false confession. And I need my armourer here, to make ready for the next tournament in Bristol, to say nothing of the grand mêlée due soon at Wilton.'

His voice rose to a crescendo. 'You're just not having him, understand!'

'To hell with your tourneying, man!' blazed de Wolfe. 'A matter of three murders cannot be compared in importance with your prancing about a jousting field.'

'You exceed your powers, John,' brayed Richard de Revelle. 'You are just the coroner, appointed by some whim of Hubert Walter to dabble in the recording of cases. Arresting felons is the sheriff's business, not yours.'

'Then it was a pity that you were so reluctant to do your duty when you were sheriff, Richard,' retorted John. 'I have been deputed by Henry de Furnellis to act for him whenever it seems necessary.'

'I do not think that is sufficient warrant for you to come into this manor and remove my servants in this way, Sir John,' said Odo gravely. He did not use the hectoring tones of either Ralph or de Revelle, but he had a certain heavy authority that was impressive.

'I warn you against obstructing my investigations into three deaths, one of which was your own brother's,' snapped de Wolfe.

'Get out of here, Coroner!' spat Ralph Peverel. 'You are a vindictive and spiteful nuisance, using your alleged powers to misuse this family, against whom you seem to have taken a dislike. Just clear off, we'll not allow you to take either Crues or Longus.'

Ralph, Odo and de Revelle crowded around de Wolfe in a way that was openly threatening, and even the languid Joel left his lady-love and came across. The steward and the bailiff stood back uncertainly, but the armourer, heartened by the show of defiance being put up by his masters, pressed closely behind them.

Thomas and Eustace retreated rapidly to the door and the clerk beckoned urgently to Gwyn, who was holding the reins of the horse to whose saddle Crues's wrists were tied. When the coroner's officer hurried into the hall, he was just in time to see the climax of the confrontation between de Wolfe and Ralph Peverel.

'You will all suffer greatly when this comes to the ears of the Justiciar and then the King himself!' warned John, white lipped with anger.

Ralph, emboldened by the solidarity shown by his brothers and de Revelle, gave John a hard shove on the shoulder with the heel of his hand.

'You are unwelcome here, Crowner!' he yelled. 'Just get on your horse and go home. You broken-down old Crusaders should stay by your firesides, dreaming of times past, not be given useless sinecures as a reward for long service!'

This insult was bad enough, but now the impetuous Ralph went too far.

'Get out and stay out!' he shouted, with another push at John's chest. 'I'll wager that all you ever did in your much-vaunted campaigning was to line your own purse with loot and keep safely out of the heat of battle!'

This was too much for both Gwyn and John de Wolfe.

The Cornishman roared and strode across towards the group, intending to grab Ralph by the throat and throw him across the room, but his master was too quick for him. First he punched Ralph hard on the nose, causing blood to spurt from his nostrils. Then he turned and snatched a riding glove from his foppish brother-in-law's hand. With it, he slapped Ralph violently across the face.

'I hear this is the new French method of challenge!' he snapped, throwing Richard's glove on to the floor at Ralph's feet. 'Now I'm off to Exeter to fetch the sheriff and his men-at-arms. When I return by noon tomorrow, I expect to meet you in the bailey with sword and mace. Then we'll see how I fare in the heat of battle!'

*   *   *

There was consternation in the Bush that evening, when Nesta discovered what had happened in Sampford. Tearfully, she pleaded with John to give up this mad idea of a duel with Ralph Peverel, but the obstinate coroner would not listen, even to his mistress's heartfelt supplications.

'It's a matter of honour, *cariad*. He called me a coward – me, who's been at the siege of Acre, the battle of Arsulf and many others, to say nothing of years in Ireland and France! That bastard's not been farther than a few skirmishes in the Vexin!'

Nesta was uncaring about their military histories. 'He'll kill you, John! He's years younger than you, faster and fitter – call off this nonsense, no one will think the worse of you.'

But nothing would shift the obdurate coroner. He had been insulted and he was going to have satisfaction for it, even if cost him life or limb.

Gwyn tried to reassure Nesta that her lover would be the victor, though privately he was equally concerned that his master, now forty-one years old, might not be a match for a man not only fifteen years his junior but who regularly trained for the jousting field.

Later, as they walked back towards Martin's Lane, he tried to tactfully talk de Wolfe out of the contest, but without success. Once John had made up his mind, especially over a slur on his bravery, there was no way he would ever back down.

Earlier that evening, on their return from Sampford, John had gone to see Henry de Furnellis to tell him all that had taken place there. They had left Alexander Crues behind after the confrontation, John reckoning that if they were coming back in force for Robert Longus, they might as well collect his assistant at the same time. The only danger was that both would vanish overnight, but the arrogant confidence

341

of the Peverels suggested that they would brazen out the situation.

The sheriff readily agreed to return with John the next day and take a posse of soldiers with him, but when he heard of the challenge, he too was concerned for his friend's safety. Like the others', his tactful pleas fell on deaf ears, but as an old campaigner himself Henry accepted that Ralph's insult could not be overlooked by any honourable man.

Thomas de Peyne was beside himself with worry, as he revered the coroner as the man who had taken him in and saved him when his life seemed at an end. He spent half the night on his knees before the altar of St Radegund in the cathedral, praying that the life of John de Wolfe would be spared on the morrow.

In his almost empty house, John sat late by his fire, drinking ale and wondering whether this might be his last night on earth. He was not too concerned – he had experienced too many similar eves of battle to unnerve himself with worry. He remembered the last time he had challenged a man, almost a year earlier – but that had been on horseback with lance and shield. John had ended up with a dead stallion and a broken leg, but at least he had survived, which was more than his opponent had.

Saying nothing of the matter to Mary, as he could not face another tearful woman trying to persuade him to swallow his pride, he went to bed and slept soundly until dawn.

The cavalcade that rode up the track to Sampford the next morning was far more impressive than the usual coroner's team. It was a true posse, as the sheriff himself led the group alongside the coroner – the *posse comitatus* had been introduced fourteen years earlier by old King Henry in his 'Assize of Arms' and authorised the sheriff to call out any able-bodied men of the county to seize suspected criminals or to defend the realm.

Behind Devon's two most senior law officers came Ralph Morin, the constable of Exeter, and Gwyn of Polruan. Leading a dozen men-at-arms in boiled leather jerkins and round helmets was Sergeant Gabriel. Today both Thomas de Peyne and Eustace de Relaga had been left at home to write up their rolls, in case there was serious trouble. Thomas was beside himself with anxiety, especially as he would not know the outcome of the contest until the posse returned to Exeter.

The village seemed ominously quiet as the column rode along the ridge track from Tiverton to reach the manorial compound. There were people about, all staring silently at the mounted men as they passed. Godwin Thatcher looked down from a ladder against the roof of a cottage and Nicholas the smith stopped pumping his bellows as they went by. Agnes's mother sat by her door, her cheeks still wet at the thought of her daughter still lying unburied in the church.

When the sheriff and the coroner turned into the gate of the bailey, they found the whole staff of the manor turned out in front of the house. Grooms, ostlers, cooks, brew-maids, stable lads and houndsmen were standing sullenly in a large half-circle, with the more senior servants in front of them. It seemed that the steward, bailiff, huntmaster and parish priest, together with all the more lowly servants, had been ordered to witness the humiliation of the county coroner by one of their lords. The armourer and his assistant were also present, standing at the end of the inner line.

As the posse dismounted, figures appeared at the top of the steps leading to the hall. Odo and Ralph stopped dead on the platform to gaze down at the new arrivals. They were disconcerted to see such a show of force, having expected only the sheriff and a guard or two. Once again, John fumed to see the familiar figure of Richard de Revelle coming down behind the brothers. As the trio came down the staircase, two ladies took their place at the top, snug in fur-lined pelisses against a chill breeze. The ever gallant Joel accompanied Beatrice and Avelina, their maids standing behind them, eager to watch what they hoped would be a bloody combat.

Henry de Furnellis marched forward to meet the Peverels and to establish his dominance of the occasion. John often thought of him as an easygoing, lazy individual, but Henry could be an imposing person when he wished. Though getting on in years, he was still active enough, and his tall, muscular figure reflected his long experience as a warrior.

'I am here as the King's representative in this county,' he began in his deep voice. 'You have refused to cooperate with the coroner here and I therefore command you to obey my requests, on pain of the serious consequences for defying officers of the Crown.'

He moved to be face to face with Odo, who looked more troubled than ever at this turn of events. John hoped that it would not trigger another of his falling fits, as he fervently wished Odo to win his legal wrangle with Ralph over the succession to the manor.

'Sir Odo, it pains me to know that you sided with less sensible men in refusing to allow the coroner to take two of your servants into custody,' said de Furnellis in a sonorous voice. 'I thought as the new manor-lord you would be more aware of your legal responsibilities.'

The eldest brother looked abashed, but before he could respond Ralph virtually pushed him aside to glare at the sheriff.

'Sir, there is other business to attend to before these time-wasting falsehoods about a couple of our servants. There is a matter of honour to be settled, as you well know. Let us get on with it!'

The sheriff looked at him sourly, as if bemoaning the fact that this new generation had none of the manners of the old.

'That will be attended to forthwith,' he replied. 'But whatever the outcome, be assured that those two men who are under suspicion will be taken back to Exeter with us. If anyone tries to prevent us, you will regret it, both now and in due course, before the King's justices.'

With this threat, he walked back to where de Wolfe was standing with Gwyn and Ralph Morin. A couple of soldiers had taken their horses back to the gate, where the rest of the men-at-arms were waiting on their own mounts, in case of trouble.

'Right, John, let's get you ready,' said Henry with a sigh. Gwyn was acting as John's squire, as he had done for many years, and now led up a packhorse that the last soldier in the line had dragged on a head-rope from the city. Slung over its back was his hauberk and a calf-length suit of chain mail, now slightly rusty, together with the padded gambeson that went underneath. They had once belonged to Simon de Wolfe, John's father, who had been killed in the Irish wars years before. Gwyn and Ralph Morin helped hoist the mail over John's head and settle it into place before lacing the hood to its neckline and placing the round helmet on his head.

'Short sword and a mace, that's what we agreed,' muttered Gwyn, getting more worried as the moments passed. There was no need for a baldric to support a scabbard, as John's riding sword was pressed directly into his hand. This was much shorter than a more massive battle sword, but was still three feet of heavy steel. The short handle of a ball mace was thrust through his belt, carrying a chain ending in a spiked sphere of iron. Morin unlashed John's shield from the side of the sumpter horse and slid the inner loops over his left forearm. The device on the battered wood was that of a white wolf's head on a black field, and the dents and chips on the surface told of many previous fights.

By now a considerable number of villagers had sidled in through the gates and were standing opposite the occupants of the hall, forming a straggling circle around the sparse muddy grass of the manor forecourt. Ralph had vanished into the hall while John was putting on his armour and now reappeared with his brothers, Richard de Revelle and the armourer behind him. His shield carried the Peverel emblem of two white chevrons on a field of azure, but otherwise he was attired in identical fashion.

Gwyn patted his master and old friend on the back and sent him to walk a few paces forward, his anxiety increasing as he noticed the slight limp that John had tried to hide since breaking his left shin bone at the beginning of the year. The two combatants advanced to face each other some ten paces apart, and the murmur of voices from the onlookers died as the tension rose. An uncaring crow croaked from the roof of the manor, making the sudden silence all the more ominous.

Henry de Furnellis, as sheriff and the most experienced knight present, took it upon himself to act as marshal and loped forward to stand between the two men. They looked at him as he spoke, both sinister in their metal garments, their profiles distorted by the ugly nose guards of the helmets.

'Sir John de Wolfe, and you Sir Ralph Peverel, are you willing to settle your differences or are you firmly set upon this combat?' boomed the sheriff.

'This man impugned my courage and my honour,' growled de Wolfe. 'I cannot let that go unchallenged!'

'And I intend killing this fellow who has persecuted my family,' shouted Ralph. 'I'm going to cut off his member and ram it down his damned throat!' he added unnecessarily. A rumble of discontent ran around the crowd at this blatant lack of chivalry, which reminded Gwyn of brother Hugo's gross lapse of conduct in his bout with de Charterai.

Henry de Furnellis stepped back reluctantly.

'So be it, if you are determined upon this foolishness! But I will see to it that you fight fair. I have a dozen men here to ensure it!'

He moved back almost to the ring of spectators, to stand alongside Gwyn. They noticed that Joel Peverel and Richard de Revelle took up similar positions on the other side.

There was no formal trumpet blast or herald's cry at this contest. The two men began circling and spiralling in towards each other until they were within sword's reach. A sudden clash of steel and thump of metal on wood signalled the first contact, and from then on it was a solemn, potentially lethal dance of advance, strike and retreat. The two men were equally matched, de Wolfe being more experienced in real battle and cunning in the use of his shield in defence. Ralph was younger, faster and more aggressive, but even his frequent practice in mêlées and jousts had not made him the equal of John in the tricks and techniques of swordsmanship.

Back and forth they moved, rotating within a small space on the dusty ground, neither giving way to the other as their swords resounded off the ill-used wood of their long shields. The swords were made for slashing, not stabbing – but these were real weapons, not the blunted ones used in tournaments, and their points were still dangerous.

The silence was gradually broken by yells of excitement and encouragement from the spectators, though it was not clear who was shouting for whom. The clash of weapons became almost rhythmical, and although probably no more than five minutes had elapsed, it seemed like half a day to Gwyn as he watched his master fighting for his life. The weight of the chain mail, the shield and the sword meant that even the most Herculean fighter could not continue for long, as the physical exertion involved was too much for any man to sustain unless he was on the back of a horse.

The two men backed off for a moment, each panting to get his breath back, as they slowly circled again. Gwyn was beginning to feel more optimistic when they clashed again, as John managed to get in a heavy blow to Ralph's left shoulder which made his opponent howl. If this had been a tourney, it would have counted as a point against him, but this was a fight to the finish. After a few more advances and retreats, Ralph struck the side of John's helmet, making a dent and evening up the score, but of more concern to Gwyn was the fact that his master's limp was becoming more pronounced and he was slowing down. The break in his leg from being trapped under his dying horse had healed well and the coroner had made light of it in recent months, denying that anything was wrong, but Gwyn knew that he still had twinges of pain in it, especially after a long ride or sudden exertion. Now it was becoming obvious that he was tiring and the leg was dragging. Ralph began dancing around him more quickly, in a deadly ballet whose outcome now seemed all too predictable.

'Christ help him!' muttered the Cornishman desperately. Though he despised most churchmen and their institutions, he believed in God, as did everyone else, except a few deranged heretics, and now his tongue sought to find long-neglected prayers. But God seemed deaf that day, and a moment later a rapid blow from the younger man struck John's wrist and sent his sword spinning away across the dirt. Stumbling back, the coroner dragged out his mace as his remaining weapon and, with his shield held in front of him, stood like a bear chained to a post, waiting for the next attack of the dogs. Ralph came in again and was repulsed by a smashing blow from the spinning chain, the heavy ball gouging splinters from the edge of his shield.

'Go on, follow it up!' bellowed Gwyn, now in almost tearful anxiety. There were similar shouts from around the edge of the arena as the two combatants went at it hammer and tongs, the spiked ball whirling a defensive pattern around the coroner as Peverel tried to swing his sword edge down on his opponent. Gwyn's heart lurched with hope as the chain wrapped itself around Ralph's sword, but the iron blade slid out of its grasp and was free again. Now both men were tiring, but de Wolfe was in worse shape and was now limping badly. The end came suddenly as the next sally by Ralph drove John back, and just as he was counter-attacking by swinging his vicious ball around the edge of his shield, his leg gave way completely and he fell sprawling on the ground, virtually at his enemy's feet. He still had the mace in his hand, but his left arm was trapped in the thongs of his shield, on to which he had fallen. With an almost contemptuous movement, Ralph kicked the mace away and pushed the coroner back to the ground with the point of his sword. Gwyn closed his eyes, hardly able to believe that his revered companion of twenty years was about to die in the dirt of a Devon bailey, after all the perils they had shared around half the world. Complete silence had descended on the manor compound, as everyone watched the dramatic tableau with bated breath, expecting the fatal *coup de grâce* at any second.

Then there was a hoarse cry from where the family and servants were standing, incongruously delivered in a broad Irish accent.

'For the love of God and in the name of Jesus and the Holy Virgin, have mercy, Ralph Peverel!'

Father Patrick, his face flushed from both emotion and his early morning drinking, stumbled out towards the vanquished and the victor, waving the cross from his altar unsteadily above his head.

'Gain God's indulgence by showing compassion and mercy! Think of your immortal soul and gain credit in heaven!'

Ralph, who now had the point of his sword at John de Wolfe's throat, looked up at the flabby priest, irritated by his interference.

'Keep out of this, you drunken old fool!' he snarled.

But the cleric, whether from bravery or befuddlement, continued to totter across the arena, to wave his cross almost under Ralph's nose.

'You have won the fight and made your point – what good can it do you to kill a king's officer and bring great trouble upon you and your family? Will that bring you success in your lawsuit? To say nothing of incurring God's displeasure.'

Ralph stared at the dishevelled priest, then down at the man on the ground, now clutching his leg and groaning with the pain of cramped and knotted muscles. With an abrupt change of mood, he gave de Wolfe a heavy kick in the ribs, then turned and walked away without a word. A ragged cheer went up from some of the crowd, but whether this was to applaud Ralph's success or in thanks for the coroner's survival, it was impossible to tell. As Gwyn, Morin and de

Furnellis hurried to help John to his feet, the spectacle broke up as quickly as it had formed. At this abrupt anti-climax, the villagers melted away, the servants went about their business and the family vanished into the manor house.

'It was your leg that let you down, Crowner,' said Gwyn solicitously, his voice quavering with suppressed relief as they helped John hobble across to the stairs to the hall and sit on the lowest step.

De Wolfe shook his head wearily, slumped forward with his arms on his knees. 'No, Gwyn, not just my leg. I was an old fool for thinking that I could overcome a younger man on foot. Given a horse, things might have been different.'

The sheriff consoled him as he pulled off John's helmet and began unlacing his mailed hood. 'You did well, old friend! But you should leave it another year before you try it again, to let your leg heal properly.'

John gave a cynical laugh. 'In another year, I will be fit only to sit by my fireside with a shawl around my shoulders. I should be grateful to Ralph Peverel, not only for sparing my life, but for showing me that my fighting days are over.'

He felt humiliated, old and useless, and all the reassurances of his friends around him did little to lift his mood. After a few minutes, the pain in his leg subsided enough for him to stand up, allowing Gwyn and the others to help him off with his hauberk.

'What do you want to do, John?' asked de Furnellis. 'You should rest that leg for a time and should have some food and drink.'

'I'll not go into that damned hall again and face the smirks of those people,' he growled, a little spirit returning. 'Let's get over to that poxy alehouse, at least we can have lousy fare without them crowing over me.'

He sat down again while Gwyn and Ralph Morin

motioned a soldier to bring over the packhorse to carry his armour. Gwyn examined his leg but could see nothing amiss, though the muscles on the back of his calf were exquisitely tender.

'A day's rest and it will be sound again,' he said consolingly. 'No doubt Nesta will have some salves that will help.'

'If I challenge anyone again, it'll be from the back of Odin!' promised de Wolfe. 'I'll not trust being on my own two feet again!'

Already his confidence was returning, even though a few minutes earlier he had fully been expecting to feel the point of Ralph's sword puncturing his throat. When the hauberk was tied across the pony's back, the castle constable advised him to hold on to it for support as they set out for the tavern on the village green, but after only one step a voice above him brought him to a halt.

'How are the mighty fallen, John!' sneered his brother-in-law from the top of the steps. 'Perhaps my sister would have had a twinge of regret if Ralph had spitted you on his sword, but few others would mourn your passing, apart from your alehouse mistress!'

Mortified at Richard's advantage over him, John could find no words in reply, but Henry de Furnellis angrily stepped into the breach.

'Your spite does you no credit, de Revelle, but you never were an honourable man,' he flared. 'So watch your tongue, for the eyes of Winchester are still upon you and you can ill afford to take liberties. You owe your own life to de Wolfe, remember? But for his inter-cession, you would long ago have swung by the neck.'

Richard made a rude noise in reply, but retreated back into the hall under the baleful glare of all those below.

'Get the crowner to that tavern,' commanded the

sheriff, who today seemed to have found new energy and initiative in place of his usual amiable torpor. 'I have business inside this hall, so we'll have those men-at-arms over here in case there's trouble.' He motioned to Ralph Morin to fetch Gabriel and his troops across from the other side of the bailey, while Gwyn slowly led the sumpter horse away, with the defeated coroner clutching at its baggage.

Though his leg was still sore, de Wolfe was able to limp up to Rougemont the next day to attend to the urgent matter of the two armourers. He had got back from Sampford the previous afternoon without trouble, as once on a horse with the weight off his leg he felt perfectly fit. It was his self-esteem which had suffered most injury, the humiliation of being first defeated and then spared by Ralph Peverel almost too much to bear. In fact, he almost wished that Father Patrick had not intervened, as a quick death may have been preferable to this nagging shame that now plagued him. And yet a worm of defiance was already beginning to writhe inside his head, which demanded retribution for the insult he had suffered.

Nesta had been overcome with relief when he showed up at the Bush the previous evening – and the fact that he had been ignominiously defeated seemed of little consequence to her, as long as he was safe. Gwyn wisely did not give her the details of how close John had been to death at the end of Ralph's sword and left her to fuss over applying her ointments and salves to John's leg, under a winding of linen bandage.

Thomas and Eustace were also enormously relieved to have him home in one piece, and the news that the sheriff had dragged back the two suspects was welcome news to them.

Henry de Furnellis, still surprising people with his

new-found energy, was waiting for John in his chamber, the inevitable jug of wine ready on his table.

'Try to forget yesterday's trouble,' he advised solicitously. 'You acquitted yourself well, so put it behind you now. We have to get to the bottom of these killings and need to squeeze as much as we can from these two villains.'

After John had limped off to the alehouse the day before, the sheriff had virtually invaded the manor house with his posse and, ignoring all the violent protestations of the Peverel brothers and Richard de Revelle, had hauled out the two armourers and put them on a couple of spare horses that they had wisely brought with them. Hands tied and surrounded by Gabriel and his soldiers, they were brought back to Exeter and thrust into the squalid cells beneath the keep of Rougemont, delivered into the tender care of Stigand, the repulsive gaoler who ruled the undercroft.

'This Robert Longus was screaming his innocence all the way back,' said Henry. 'But the big, stupid fellow seemed cowed and silent. It was just as well that Longus was bound to his horse or I think he'd have killed Crues for implicating him.'

When the constable arrived at the sheriff's chamber, they all went out into the inner ward and down some steps into the undercroft, which was the basement of the keep, partly below ground level. A dark and dismal cavern, its vaulted roof was damp and black with mould. A rusty iron grille set in a stone wall, behind which were a few prison cells, divided the space in half. The rest was partly storehouse and partly torture chamber, as well as being the gaoler's living quarters – a grubby mattress sat in one of the rat-infested alcoves.

Already assembled on the rubbish-strewn floor were Thomas and Eustace, the latter looking apprehensive about what awful scenes he might have to witness. Also present was Brother Rufus, the portly and usually jovial monk who was the garrison chaplain, as well as Sergeant Gabriel and three of the men-at-arms who had been part of the expedition to Sampford.

'Bring them out here, Stigand,' ordered Ralph Morin, pointing to the gate in the iron grille. The grossly obese Saxon waddled across with his ring of keys and, with Gabriel and a soldier as escort, went in and returned with the two armourers in wrist shackles, Longus struggling and blaspheming all the way. As Henry de Furnellis had described, the large, drooping figure of Alexander Crues seemed quite apathetic, staring despondently at the ground. He was the one they questioned first, John leading off, as soon as one of the escort gave Longus a buffet across the head to silence his loud protestations.

'Crues, tell us again what you admitted to me yesterday about these deaths.'

Dully, the man came out again with his allegation that he had simply stood by while Robert Longus strangled the girl Agnes with a piece of old harness strap. This provoked more bellows of denial from the armourer, and Morin had him taken back to the cells to give them some peace while they dealt with his assistant, though his shouts could still be heard, echoing from beyond the grille.

The essence of Alexander's tale was taken down by Thomas, who sat on a sack of horse feed and rested his parchments and ink on an empty wine cask. It was to the effect that in the last few days a tale had begun circulating about the village that Agnes had begun to recollect hearing voices when she left Lord Hugo on the night he was killed. Afraid that she might eventually remember whose voices they were, Robert had decided that she must be silenced. He got Crues to offer her a penny for her favours that night, and when they met by arrangement at the trout pool, the armourer was hiding in the trees. When she lay down for Crues, Longus leapt out and strangled her, pushing her head into the water in the hope of passing it off as an accident by drowning.

'But why be concerned at whose voices she might have heard?' asked the sheriff. The answer was obvious, but he wanted it down on Thomas's rolls.

'Because the voices were ours,' muttered Alexander. 'It was Robert Longus who stabbed Lord Hugo to death. We found him sleeping in the ox byre – Robert made me come along to help him in case he struggled!'

'But why should you help him?' demanded the coroner.

Crues shrugged hopelessly. 'Because I always do what he wants. He's my master – and he gave me money.'

Henry de Furnellis looked confused. 'Why should he want to murder Hugo Peverel? He was his personal armourer, I thought they were on good terms.'

'I don't understand what was going on, sir. I think Hugo wanted Robert to do something he didn't wish to do – and something about taking away our protection.'

He suddenly dropped to his knees on the stony floor and wailed into his tied hands. 'He dragged me into his schemes against my will, I don't know what he was up to! I don't want to hang, I want to turn appealer against him.'

Slumped against the ground, the massive shoulders began to heave as he sobbed his heart out, but the coroner had not yet finished with him.

Motioning to the guards to pull Crues back to his feet, he continued.

'What was this "thing" that Longus did not want to do for Hugo?'

Alexander's agonised face stared back blearily through his tears.

'I don't know, sir. I think he mentioned Lady Avelina once, but I'm not very quick at catching on to people's meanings.'

Further questions from the sheriff and constable took them little farther, and with a grunt of annoyance de Wolfe waved to the soldiers to drag the man to one side. He went across to Thomas and, with Eustace peering around him, looked at the newly scribed parchment lying on the barrel.

'The man's a brainless oaf, but did you get that down, such as it was?' he demanded. Thomas nodded, but Eustace broke in with an intelligent question that made the official clerk scowl.

'If Longus killed the girl, Crowner, why was the strap found in Alexander's lodging?'

De Wolfe barked the query at Crues, and the man raised his head and gave a slow shrug. 'That's where it came from, so that's where I put it back.'

'Damned fool!' growled Gwyn. 'He's too stupid even to commit a murder properly.'

Now Robert Longus was brought out again, and he was a different proposition altogether – a moderately intelligent, certainly a cunning, journeyman. He again wrestled his way from the cells in the grip of Gabriel and a man-at-arms. Although he had been in the cells only for one night, he was dishevelled and dirty, his jerkin and breeches stained and scattered with bits of stinking straw. After a few more slaps and punches had quietened him down, the sheriff took up the interrogation.

'Your accomplice has turned appealer and we know the broad outlines of your crimes, so there's no point in these continual pleas of innocence,' he said brusquely. 'We now want the details to record and place before the King's justices.'

But cajole and threaten as much as they would, all they got from the armourer was a litany of oaths, abuse and denials, mostly to the effect that Alexander Crues was a warped mental defective who, for personal reasons, was producing a vindictive tissue of lies against him.

After five minutes of this, everyone was becoming restive, especially as Henry was having difficulty in finding a break in Robert's tirade to get in his own questions.

'That's enough!' yelled de Wolfe eventually. Not the most patient of men, especially on a day like this when his spirits were low, he appealed to de Furnellis.

'Sheriff, this man seems immune to reasonable questioning. Has the time not come for more persuasive methods to arrive at the truth?'

Henry nodded, having seen the slight wink that John gave him as he spoke.

'I agree, Coroner. Do you think the *peine forte et dure* would be appropriate?' He was referring to a form of persuasive torture in which heavy weights were progressively piled on the victim's chest until he could no longer breathe.

'Either that, or perhaps the Ordeal might also be appropriate, as it is intended to determine guilt or innocence. We now have two priests here, though only one is necessary to validate the process.' He pointed at both Brother Rufus and Thomas de Peyne, which greatly pleased the little clerk, in spite of the doleful circumstances. Robert Longus fell very quiet at this exchange, looking from coroner to sheriff and back again, to gauge how serious they were.

'You cannot torture me, I'm a freeman and a craftsman!' he cried. 'It's illegal, you cannot do this!'

'Who's to say that we can't?' retorted the sheriff

calmly. 'We are the law in this county and can pros-
ecute it in any way we think fit!'

He turned to the gaoler, who was standing by expectantly, his piggy eyes gleaming in the poor light from
a few guttering torches on the walls.

'Stigand, have you made the preparations I ordered?'

The lard-faced Saxon, almost bald and wearing a
filthy apron stained with blood, grinned to show his
few blackened teeth.

'The water is on the boil, sir. And I have irons heating
in the brazier, in case you prefer them!'

'Right, bring him over to the wall,' commanded de
Furnellis.

Longus began screaming as he was dragged across
the floor towards a large iron vat that was supported
on stones over a wood fire in a shallow pit. It was full
almost to the brim with murky water that was bubbling
under the scum on top. Near by was a latticed iron
brazier filled with glowing charcoal, into which were
stuck several branding irons.

'Robert Longus, this is your last chance to confess,'
snapped de Wolfe. 'You know the ritual of the Ordeal
– you will plunge your right arm into this vat and pick
out this stone.'

Stigand handed him a round stone the size of a large
apple and John nonchalantly tossed it into the boiling
water.

This part was an obvious bluff, as the Ordeal was not
intended as a means of extracting confessions, but was
an ancient test of guilt or innocence. If the scalded
arm healed without peeling or suppuration, the subject
was judged innocent; otherwise he was deemed guilty
and hanged. The Church was becoming uneasy about
this unchristian ritual, which smacked of magic, but
the Vatican had not yet actually banned it.

John wagged a finger at Stigand, and he drew one

of the irons from the fire and spat upon the cross-shaped end, the spittle hissing on the red-hot metal.

'The choice is yours, Longus. The cauldron or the brand!'

As the man was hustled nearer the fires, Thomas averted his eyes and Eustace ran back to the steps up to the doorway to watch, as if distance might lessen the awful spectacle. The rest of the onlookers, including Brother Rufus, stood impassively, waiting for a result.

A closer sight of the boiling scum and the glowing iron suddenly broke the armourer's will.

'No, stop! I'll tell you all!' he screamed.

As with Crues and the water trough two days earlier, the imminence of intolerable suffering overshadowed the more distant prospect of the gallows. Half an hour later, Thomas had it all inscribed on his roll and the two men from Sampford were back in their squalid cells to await the next visit of the Commissioners of Gaol Delivery and the certainty of a hanging.

Back in the sheriff's chamber, the same officials gathered to consider what they had learned in Stigand's parlour down below.

'It's extraordinary how all this links together,' enthused Brother Rufus, who was a jovial busybody and liked to be in on any intrigues that were going on. 'Three murders for different reasons, all by the same men.'

'Really only one man, in that that poor dolt Crues was just a blind tool of Robert Longus,' said Ralph Morin. 'Though he'll hang for it, just the same.'

'It's such a tortuous tale that I need to get this clear in my mind,' growled Henry de Furnellis. 'I gather that Hugo Peverel paid Longus to interfere with his father's saddle-girth and then kept close behind him at the

Wilton mêlée, so that he could trample him to death when he was unhorsed?'

'That's right, then they made sure that the harness vanished soon afterwards, not knowing that Reginald de Charterai had already noticed the damage to the stitching,' confirmed John.

The sheriff shook his head in sad amazement. 'Killing his father! That's a terrible crime. I'm glad the bastard got his reward at the end of a knife.'

'Which was also wielded by Robert Longus!' snorted John.

'I'm not clear why that had to happen,' said the constable, doubtfully.

'How was it connected with the death of that silversmith, miles away?'

'Not so fast!' complained the sheriff. 'Hugo killed his father to succeed to the manor, right? But what about Odo, the eldest brother – he was already there, as the sitting heir, so to speak?'

'Hugo must have worked all that out beforehand, trusting that he would win any legal contest on the grounds of Odo's falling sickness. It was a gamble, but it paid off.'

'And August Scrope, the silversmith?' asked Gwyn. 'I didn't follow all that Longus said about that – he was gabbling too fast.'

Thomas, scanning his parchment version of the confession, explained what had happened.

'Scrope was staying at the New Inn, as were the Peverels. It so happened that Longus came to the inn to get some instructions from Hugo about preparing his armour for the tournament. Longus stopped for some ale in the taproom and overheard the silversmith, his tongue loosened by ale, unwisely telling some drinking companion of his trip to Topsham the next morning with his valuable jewellery. The armourer decided to take Alexander Crues and rob the man, as a profitable sideline. It seems that they had occasionally indulged in armed robbery before this and found it easy pickings.'

'And the callous bastards also decided to kill him, to avoid being recognised,' growled Henry. 'It's fortunate that the silversmith's servant survived. They deserve to be hanged twice over.'

'So how did it come about that Hugo later gave him a false alibi when Terrus spotted Longus as one of the robbers?' asked Rufus.

John shrugged. 'Longus was very close to his master and was valuable to Hugo as his armourer, so he wouldn't want to lose him to the gallows.'

'And Longus already had a hold over him, knowing that he had deliberately run down his father,' added de Furnellis.

'He must have gabbled this out to Hugo when he ran ahead of me outside the New Inn that day, when I made him take me to his master,' said John thoughtfully. 'That's almost certainly another reason why Hugo decided to give Longus an alibi – just to spite me.'

'What do you mean by that?' asked Henry.

'Well, I was on the point of arresting his armourer, so it must have given Hugo great delight to frustrate me! He was paying me back for humiliating him over his behaviour with de Charterai, both on the tourney field and at that banquet.'

'So why then should this Robert later want to slay Hugo?' asked a puzzled Rufus. 'It seems that they were literally as thick as thieves.'

The coroner took up the story again.

'Longus claims that when Hugo discovered not only that his stepmother Avelina had been left a substantial life interest in the manor's income but was likely to go off with it with his arch-enemy Reginald de Charterai, he tried to get him to produce a fatal accident for her as well! But evil as he is, Longus baulked at killing such a high-born woman, partly because of the risk, but also because of her past kindness to him.'

'The business of her paying for an apothecary for him?' asked the sheriff.

'Yes, he says he was taken with a severe bloody flux last year and claims Avelina saved his life by getting a leech out from Tiverton to treat him.'

'So why kill Hugo?' persisted the sheriff.

'Because Hugo threatened to withdraw his alibi for the killing of the silversmith if he refused to arrange some lethal mishap for Avelina. Longus claims he wouldn't go along with that and the only way out, if he wanted to avoid the risk of Hugo betraying him, was to get rid of him. So he and Crues followed Hugo on one of his night-time adventures with a village girl and stabbed him as he lay sleeping in the ox byre.'

'And poor Agnes remembered hearing their voices?' said Rufus.

The coroner shrugged. 'She wasn't sure of that, poor girl. And she didn't know who they were, anyway. But once the rumour got around the village, Longus couldn't risk it and she had to go. Probably unnecessarily, as it happens.'

There was silence as they all reflected on this sad catalogue of violence. It was broken by Henry, who picked at his big nose and flicked the harvest on to the rushes.

'How do the other Peverel men come out of this? Have we got anything against them?'

John scowled ferociously. 'I certainly have! I owe that arrogant bastard Ralph something, but there's nothing that we can arrest him for!'

'Joel is just a selfish young fool and Odo seems in the clear,' observed the sheriff. 'I feel sorry for him, with that affliction that hinders him taking his rightful place as manor-lord.'

'And that swine Ralph will probably defeat his claim again, when it comes to court,' added de Wolfe, with feeling.

'Where does our late unlamented sheriff fit into the picture?' queried the castle constable. 'De Revelle soon made himself scarce when we burst in to arrest those two men.'

The coroner gave a sardonic laugh. 'There's only one thing, apart from whores, that interests Richard, and that's increasing his wealth. He desperately wanted that land which old William Peverel refused him, so he was buttering up the sons to get hold of it, as they seemed more amenable to the idea.'

'I wouldn't put it past him to have planted the idea of getting rid of the old man in Hugo's head,' grunted Henry. 'But we can never prove it.'

John rose from his bench and beckoned to his officer and clerks.

'There will be inquests to arrange, now that we know what happened,' he declared. 'At least the families of August Scrope and Agnes will have the satisfaction of knowing that justice has been done – or will be when the next visit of the judges is due, for those armourers will surely hang.'

'If they survive Stigand's hospitality,' said Ralph Morin. 'Lately, we've had a few dying down below of the yellow ague. I think it's from all those rats that infest those cells.'

Thomas shivered as he made for the door – he had spent a few days in that awful place some months ago when falsely accused of a series of murders and the memory lingered. The rest of the group filed out, with de Wolfe following them. Henry de Furnellis came to the door with him, and put a hand on his shoulder.

'Try to forget yesterday's episode, John! I know you feel shamed by what happened, but you must put it behind you. That Ralph is not worth your continued anger – I feel there is something evil about him, and no doubt God will repay him sooner or later.'

As de Wolfe departed, he thought to himself that perhaps he was not prepared to wait that long.

The official tournament ground between Salisbury and Wilton was once again busy, to the gratification of the treasury clerk who oversaw the collection of the entry fees. At the rates that the Curia Regis had set for the benefit of King Richard's exchequer, he would be taking many hundreds of marks back to Winchester at the end of the three-day event. As usual, this first day was for the grand mêlée, before the jousting began on the morrow.

Two hours after dawn, on a blustery day in early November, the Red and Blue teams assembled on their respective hillocks. As it was one of the main meetings of the year before winter set in, there were more hopeful contenders than usual, from all over England and the Continent. The number of spectators was also larger, both high-born and those commoners who came in the hope of enjoying blood and maiming, as well as those whose main interest was gambling on the winners.

A large open-fronted tent with a few rows of benches had been set up alongside the recet for the aristocracy and their ladies, offering shelter from occasional rain showers and the curious stares of the more lowly folk straggling along the boundary ropes. Two of these ladies were Avelina and Beatrice, chaperoned by their maids and by Joel Peverel, looking dandified in a fur-lined surcoat over a red-and-gold tunic. The women also wore heavy pelisses against the wind and ornately embroidered felt coifs tied firmly under their chins.

The heralds and umpires were ready at their stations in front of the recet and soon the trumpet blasts and stentorian cries announced the imminent start of hostilities. In the front row of almost three score mounted knights, in the Red army away to the north, was Ralph Peverel. He had fretted for days because he had been deprived of his usual armourer, Robert Longus, but had managed to hire another man from Dorchester who seemed adequate enough. His chain mail was bright, though this rain would soon tarnish it, his weapons were sharp and his shield had been repaired and repainted after that swine John de Wolfe had chopped a piece out of it.

While waiting for the final trumpet to sound, he looked along the line and saw some familiar faces from the tourney circuit, but there was no one he knew well. He despised his weakling brother Joel for being more interested in getting his leg over a woman than pursuing a man's sport, for he had no partners today, as he had when his father and Hugo were alive.

A quarter of a mile to the south, a similar mass of men and destriers were assembled, all displaying their blue markers. Towards the end of the third rank was a big grey stallion with hairy feet, carrying a tall man with a hooked nose and dark-stubbled cheeks. His right hand supported a twelve-foot lance and his left arm bore a black shield with a white wolf's head.

John gazed at the distant Reds. Though by no means an imaginative man, he wondered whether the instrument of his death was among them today. Would that man kill him this time, as he had almost done two weeks earlier? As the tension built all around him, with horses shuffling, snorting and pawing the ground, he thought back over the days in which the idea of settling once and for all his debt of honour with Ralph Peverel had fermented.

Both Gwyn and Henry de Furnellis had tried to dissuade him from his plan – and as for Nesta, she was beside herself with desperate anxiety at the prospect of him once again putting himself in peril of death. Stubborn and intractable, de Wolfe had shrugged off all their arguments, pointing out that, once on the back of Odin, his leg would be no problem and that he was otherwise as fit as any other man. Eventually Gwyn accepted the inevitable and devoted himself to preparing John's equipment and pestering Andrew the farrier to ensure that Odin was in perfect condition. They trained almost every day on Bull Mead, where the swinging practice tilts had been left in place after the last event, until even the Cornishman was satisfied that his master was as good a fighter as he had ever been.

Now here he was, with Gwyn anxiously pacing the boundary ropes as his squire, hoping fervently that he would not be needed to carry back John's bleeding and broken body. Thomas and Eustace had been left behind in Exeter, once more in a ferment of concern that a two-day journey lay between them and news of the outcome.

The long-awaited final trumpet blast wailed across the scrubby heathland and with a roar of excitement and the yelling of war-cries the massed horsemen lumbered off, picking up speed on the slight slope down into the shallow valley that ran down from the recet.

John lowered his lance to the horizontal and rested the shaft on the pommel of his saddle, so that it stuck out obliquely past Odin's left ear, which was now flattened back as the stallion joined in the surge of excitement that flowed over the Blue squadron.

As the two waves of warriors hurtled towards each other, John kept a sharp lookout for a blue shield emblazoned with white chevrons.

Ralph Peverel knew that he was here, as John had seen him earlier, staring from a distance at his wolf's-head emblem. The coroner had ensured, when he arrived to pay his fee, that he was not placed in the same army as Peverel, which would have wrecked his plans. Thankfully, he knew several of the marshals who were organising the event and a quiet word, without explanation, ensured that they were separated.

As the moment of collision approached, John's main concern was not to be diverted from his purpose by some other knight engaging him in a lengthy duel – or even worse, wounding or unhorsing him before he had the chance to confront Ralph. As soon as he spotted the blue-and-white shield, he dropped back and swerved to avoid an enthusiastic youngster who seemed intent on challenging him.

The thunder of hoofs diminished as the long charge degenerated into a swirling mass of horses and men, but de Wolfe managed to weave through them towards Ralph Peverel, who seemed to have the same objective. John fended off one half-hearted thrust from the lance of a knight on a white destrier, but they moved past him and he then found himself twenty paces in front of Peverel.

They were too near for a worthwhile charge, but both spurred their chargers forward and began hostilities with a simultaneous attack on each other's shields, which did nothing more than add a few additional scratches to the wood as the tips of the lances slid off. As they passed each other, Ralph yelled a taunt above the general hubbub around them. 'No drunken Irish priest to save you today, de Wolfe!'

Then he was gone, and the two riders hauled their huge horses around, like ships manoeuvring at sea. They were now fifty yards apart, and as soon as a pair of knights slashing madly at each other with swords had cleared out of their way, they pounded towards each other again. This time the impact was shattering, but their long experience allowed them to use their shields to divert the impacts without harm, though Ralph was rocked back painfully against the wooden crupper of his saddle.

Three times they circled and returned, each yelling abuse at the other as their determined horses thundered past, each on the other's left side.

At the third pass, a few inches of the tip of John's lance snapped off, but he was not concerned as he was not aiming to stab Ralph to death, only knock him out of his saddle. His leg was aching, but this was from the strain of steering Odin by the pressure of his knees, and he felt none of the crippling disability he had suffered during their combat on foot. In fact, he felt the familiar exhilaration that only potentially fatal combat can generate.

He deliberately ran out farther on this circuit, to increase his speed on the return, dodging several pairs of other fighters, their blue and red arm-flags streaming wildly as they battered each other. John felt that it would be this next run which would make or break their contest – if only he could unhorse Ralph, his honour would be restored and he could look every man in the eye again.

Gwyn, watching with anxious approval from the sidelines, also had the feeling that this next clash would be critical. He saw the two men wheel around a little apart from the main throng and poise themselves for the next charge. As loose turf scudded up from the massive hoofs of their destriers, they began moving towards each other, but suddenly a black horse bearing an erect figure suddenly burst out of the main mêlée and thundered past John. Already moving fast, the new stallion had double the speed of Odin by the time he reached Ralph Peverel, who just had time to pull his horse's head around and realign his lance to meet this unexpected challenge.

The impact was like a thunderbolt and the lance flattened Ralph's shield against his chest and hurled him clean over his horse's rump. As John cursed and swerved Odin to the side to avoid a collision, he saw Peverel fly through the air and land on his head. The crack as his neck snapped could be heard even over the tumult around them.

Three nights later there was a new face among those clustered around the coroner's table in the Bush. As well as his officer, his clerk and Eustace, Henry de Furnellis was there with Ralph Morin, but the stranger was Reginald de Charterai, his noble figure looking slightly out of place in an Exeter tavern.

'I have already expressed my sincere apologies to Sir John for interfering in his matter of honour,' he intoned gravely. 'But I had no idea that he was deliberately engaging that scoundrel.'

De Wolfe had arrived back in the city with Gwyn that afternoon, and now sat with his arm around Nesta, who had at last stopped weeping with relief that her lover had returned in one piece. Reginald had appeared at the castle while John was regaling the sheriff with the events in Salisbury. He was on his way to Brixham to take ship back to Normandy, but had broken his journey to explain the circumstances of Ralph Peverel's death. John had recommended the Bush as a good place to obtain accommodation for the night before he continued his journey, and now he was telling the story again, after an excellent supper provided by Nesta.

'Some time ago, I had informed the coroner here of certain allegations made by Lady Avelina – who incidentally is soon to follow me to France, as she has consented to become my wife.'

There were murmurs of congratulation from around the table, but they were short, as the audience was impatient to hear his story.

'Lady Avelina was convinced that Hugo Peverel had somehow brought about the death of her husband William,' interjected de Wolfe. 'And Sir Reginald here had the support of his own eyes, as he had seen how the saddle-girth of William's horse had been tampered with.'

The stately Frenchman nodded and took a sip of the Bush's best wine.

'Later, she told me of further scandalous happenings at Sampford. Coming down the stairs from her solar one day, she heard her name mentioned in the hall, in which only Hugo and Ralph Peverel were present. She stopped behind the arch leading into the hall and heard them discussing the provisions of her husband's will, which gave her a life interest in a third of the manor. They suggested that it would be very beneficial for them if that life interest was very short, and Hugo said he knew a way in which this might be brought about. Someone came into the hall then and she learned no more, but she was so anxious about the threat that she sent me a message and I came to give her support, for by then I had formed a strong affection for her.'

'So that swine Ralph had knowledge of Hugo's plan to get rid of the lady,' said Henry indignantly. 'I always said he was evil, John!'

'Thank God that Robert Longus refused – though he has other crimes enough to answer for,' observed Morin.

De Charterai traced circles on the boards of the table with his cup.

'When I heard of the arrest of the two armourers and then the results of their confessions, which are now common knowledge about the county, I realised that Avelina might still not be safe in Sampford, especially if Ralph won his case to become lord of that manor.'

He stared defiantly at the faces around the table.

'Originally, they desired to extinguish her life interest. That man might still have extinguished her life!' he said firmly. 'I could not take that risk, and that is why I have hurried ahead with the marriage to take her to a place of safety.'

'But what about Wilton?' asked the sheriff.

'I knew Ralph would be there, as he never misses a major tourney – he desperately needs the winnings. But I had no idea that Sir John would also be there, with almost the same purpose as my own.'

'I didn't go there to kill him,' grunted de Wolfe. 'I just needed to vanquish him, to even up the score for the sake of my self-respect.'

'Neither did I intend his death,' declared Reginald. 'Though it had passed through my mind more than once. I wished to injure either his body or his pride by soundly defeating him. Then, when he was under my heel or my sword, I would tell him that I knew of his plotting with Hugo and if he as much as looked askance at Avelina before she left, I would cut him into small pieces and feed him to the crows!'

He sighed and drained the rest of his wine. 'But as God willed it, the matter was settled more permanently, and I would be a liar if I said that I will lose any sleep over his demise.'

There was silence, eventually broken by Henry de Furnellis.

'So Brother Odo will become lord of Sampford Peverel after all, fits or no fits, for I can't see that foppish Joel running the manor.'

372

'Then I wish him well of it,' growled de Wolfe. 'That sad place needs all the help it can get.'

'Amen!' intoned Thomas, crossing himself, as he was thinking only of his blessed visit to Winchester in three weeks' time.

A week before his clerk's departure, Sir John de Wolfe rode alone to Topsham. Two days earlier, a messenger had come from a shipowner friend to say that their cog, the *St Peter and Paul*, was due in the estuary on Tuesday. A faster vessel had just arrived with the news, having passed the *Peter* at sea, both having come from Barfleur. There was no guarantee that Matilda would be on it, but as the season for crossing the wide end of the Channel was almost over, there would be few more chances of a passage before the winter gales set in.

John sat in a tavern all morning, having given a boy half a penny to go down the river bank for a mile and run back when he saw a ship approaching. His mood was mixed, as part of him was saddened by the end of his weeks of freedom, yet the house in Martin's Lane seemed even more bleak and empty without Matilda's dour presence, to which he had become accustomed, much as a penitent gets used to wearing a hair shirt.

In the early afternoon, the lad came back breathlessly to report a sighting, and an hour later, when the tide was high enough, John was on the quay-side scanning the deck of the heavily laden vessel as she tied up to the sound of the sailors' hymn of thanks to the Virgin for a safe voyage.

He soon saw Matilda's squat figure, bundled up in a huge cloak, haranguing Lucille and a seaman over her baggage. When the landing-plank was pushed out to the wharf, he went forward to meet her, his heart suddenly heavy when he saw her downturned mouth and surly expression.

There was no embrace or kiss as they met. She looked around her and glared up at the grey sky, from which a fine rain was beginning to fall.

'What a miserable country, after the fair fields of France!' were the first words she spoke. Then she fixed her husband with her gimlet eyes.

'And what have you been up to, John, while I've been away?'

The coroner sighed as he bent to pick up one of her bundles.

'Nothing much, Matilda. Nothing much at all!'